12505 NW CORNELL RD
PORTLAND, OR 97229
(503) 644-0043

WITHDRAWN
CEDAR MILL LIBRARY

The Accidental Further Adventures of the Hundred-Year-Old Man

ALSO BY JONAS JONASSON

Hitman Anders and the Meaning of It All

The Girl Who Saved the King of Sweden

*The 100-Year-Old Man Who Climbed Out
the Window and Disappeared*

The Accidental Further Adventures of the Hundred-Year-Old Man

A Novel

Jonas Jonasson

Translated from the Swedish by Rachel Willson-Broyles

An Imprint of HarperCollinsPublishers

Published in 2018 by 4th Estate, an imprint of HarperCollins UK.

This book is a work of fiction. References to real people, events, establishments, organizations, or locales are intended only to provide a sense of authenticity, and are used fictitiously. All other characters, and all incidents and dialogue, are drawn from the author's imagination and are not to be construed as real.

THE ACCIDENTAL FURTHER ADVENTURES OF THE HUNDRED-YEAR-OLD MAN. Copyright © 2018 by Jonas Jonasson. Translation copyright © Rachel Willson-Broyles 2018. All rights reserved. Printed in the United States of America. No part of this book may be used or reproduced in any manner whatsoever without written permission except in the case of brief quotations embodied in critical articles and reviews. For information address HarperCollins Publishers, 195 Broadway, New York, NY 10007.

HarperCollins books may be purchased for educational, business, or sales promotional use. For information please e-mail the Special Markets Department at SPsales@harpercollins.com.

FIRST HARPERLUXE EDITION

ISBN: 978-0-06-284584-9

HarperLuxe™ is a trademark of HarperCollins Publishers.

Library of Congress Cataloging-in-Publication Data is available upon request.

19 20 21 22 23   ID/LSC   10 9 8 7 6 5 4 3 2 1

The Accidental Further Adventures of the Hundred-Year-Old Man

Foreword

Right, there's one more thing. I cannot stress enough that this is a *novel* about recent and present events. A novel. Or make-believe, as my grandfather used to say. He preferred telling stories himself, rather than letting others do it. No one was better at make-believe than Grandpa. Any attempts to fact-check his tales were met with the response "Those who only say what is true, they're not worth listening to."

In creating the plot of this piece of make-believe, I draw upon a number of public figures, and of folks in their immediate vicinity. Several of the characters in this book go by their real names, but I want to make sure you never forget that I have, in the spirit of my dear grandfather, made up what these potentates say and do in the novel. What they say and do in reality, however, is something neither I nor my grandfather can take responsibility for.

Since these leaders sometimes look down on, rather than up to, ordinary folks, it's reasonable to poke a little fun at them. But that doesn't make them less than human, every one, and as such they deserve a moderate amount of respect. To all these potentates, I would like to say: On behalf of my grandfather, I am sorry (let's blame him, shall we?). And: Deal with it. It could have been worse. As well as: What if it is?

Indonesia

A life of luxury on an island in paradise ought to be satisfactory to just about anyone. But Allan Karlsson had never been just anyone, and his hundred-and-first year of life wasn't the time to start.

It was, for a certain amount of time, gratifying to sit in a lounger under an umbrella and be served drinks of various colors at whim. Especially when one's best and only friend, the inveterate petty thief Julius Jonsson, was right next to one.

But soon old Julius and the much older Allan grew tired of doing nothing but frittering away the millions from the suitcase they'd happened to bring with them from Sweden.

Not that there was anything wrong with frittering. It just got so monotonous. Julius tried renting a fully staffed 150-foot yacht so he and Allan could sit on the foredeck with fishing rods in hand. It would have been a pleasant break if only they enjoyed fishing. Or, for that matter, eating fish. Instead, their yacht excursions involved doing the same thing on deck as they'd already learned to do on the shore. Namely, nothing at all.

Allan, for his part, made sure to fly Harry Belafonte in from the United States to sing three songs on Julius's birthday—speaking of too much money and not enough to do. Harry stayed for dinner even though he wasn't paid extra for it. Altogether, this constituted an entire evening of pattern-breaking.

By way of explanation for his selection of Belafonte over anyone else, Allan pointed out that Julius had a soft spot for this newer, youthful sort of music. Julius appreciated the gesture and didn't mention that the artist in question hadn't been young since the end of the Second World War. Compared to Allan, he was, of course, a child.

Although the superstar's visit to Bali provided no more than a speck of color in their otherwise dull gray existence, it would prove to affect Allan and Julius for a long time to come. Not because of what Belafonte sang, or anything like that, but because of what he brought along and devoted his attention to during breakfast prior to his journey home. It was a tool of some sort. A flat black object with a half-eaten apple on one side, and on the other a screen that lit up when you touched it. Harry touched and touched. And grunted now and again. Then tittered. Only to grunt once more. Allan had never been the nosy sort, but there were limits.

"Perhaps it's none of my business to pry into the young Mr. Belafonte's private matters, but if I may be so bold as to inquire what you're doing there. . . . Is something happening in that . . . well, in *that*?"

Harry Belafonte realized that Allan had never seen a tablet before and was delighted to demonstrate. The tablet could show what was going on in the world, and what had already gone on, and it verged on showing what was about to happen. Depending on where you touched, up came pictures and videos of all imaginable sorts. And some unimaginable ones. If you touched other buttons, out came music. Still others, and the tablet began to speak. Apparently it was a "she," Siri.

After breakfast and the demonstration, Belafonte took his little suitcase, his black tablet, and himself, and headed to the airport for his trip home. Allan, Julius, and the hotel manager waved adieu. The artist's taxi had no more made it out of sight before Allan turned to the manager and asked him to procure a tablet of the same sort Harry Belafonte had been using. Its diverse contents had amused the hundred-year-old and that was more than could be said about most things.

The manager had just returned from a hospitality conference in Jakarta, where he had learned that the main duty of hotel staff was not to deliver but to over-deliver. Add to this that Messrs. Karlsson and Jonsson were two of the best guests in the history of Balinese tourism, and it was no wonder that, by the very next day, the manager had a tablet ready for Karlsson. And a cellular phone to boot. As a bonus.

Allan didn't want to seem ungrateful, so he didn't mention that he had no use for the phone since every-one he could imagine dialing had been dead for at least fifty years. Except Julius, of course. Who had nothing to answer with. Although that particular point could be remedied.

"Here you are," Allan said to his friend. "It's really a gift from the manager to me, but I have no one to call but you, and until this moment you didn't have any way to answer."

Julius thanked him for his kindness. And chose not to point out that Allan still couldn't call him, but for the opposite reason.

"Just don't lose it," Allan said. "It looks expensive. It was better before, when phones were stuck to the wall with a cord so you knew what they were up to."

The black tablet became Allan's most treasured possession. What was more, it was free to use since the hotel manager had instructed the staff at the computer store in Denpasar to set up the tablet and phone with all the bells and whistles. This included, among other things, linking the SIM cards to the hotel, which found its total telephone costs doubled, although no one understood why.

Once the hundred-year-old man learned how the remarkable contraption worked, he no sooner woke for the day than he turned it on to see what had happened overnight. It was the minor delightful news items from all the corners of the world that amused him most. Like the one about how a hundred doctors and nurses in Naples took turns signing each other in and out so no one had to work but everyone still got paid. Or the one about Romania, how so many government officials had had to be locked up for corruption that the country's prisons were full. And how those officials who had yet to be arrested had a solution to the problem: legalize corruption so they would avoid the need to build more prisons.

Allan and Julius developed a new morning routine. The old one had involved Allan launching into every breakfast with complaints about his friend's loud snoring, which he could hear through the wall. The new one involved the same, but with the addition of Allan's reports about what he'd found out on his tablet since last time. At first Julius enjoyed the brief news updates, not least because they took the focus off his snoring. He was immediately delighted by the Romanian notion of making the illegal legal. Just think how much easier it would be as a petty thief in such a society.

But Allan quickly disabused him of that thought, because if petty thievery were to become legal then the concept would cease to exist. Julius, who had been on the verge of suggesting that he and Allan leave Bali and move to Bucharest, immediately deflated. The joy in being a small-time thief was, of course, mainly derived from tricking someone out of something, preferably someone who deserved it or at least wouldn't suffer too much from it. If swindling could no longer be considered a swindle, what was the point?

Allan consoled him with the information that the Romanians had turned out to a man to protest against the politicians' and officials' plans. The average Romanian was not as philosophically inclined as those in power. He or she reasoned that those who stole should be locked up, no matter their title or position, and whether or not there was anywhere to lock them up.

Breakfast times at the hotel in Bali ended up revolving ever more often around where in the world Julius and Allan should go now that life had become so humdrum in their current location. When the leading news story on the morning in question told him that it was twenty degrees warmer than usual at the North Pole, Allan wondered if that might be an option.

Julius stuffed fried noodles into his mouth, finished chewing, then said he didn't think the North Pole was the right place for him and Allan. Especially not if the ice was about to melt. Julius caught a cold whenever his feet got wet. And there were polar bears, and all Julius knew about polar bears was that they seemed to get out of the wrong side of bed every morning from birth onward. At least the snakes on Bali were shy.

Allan said that perhaps it was no wonder a polar bear might lose its temper given that the ground was melting beneath its feet. If things were about to go down the tubes, that bear probably ought to stroll to solid ground while it still had time. Canada, in that case, because the United States had a new president again—had Allan already mentioned this to Julius? And, by golly, this new guy wouldn't allow just anyone over the border.

Yes, Julius had heard of Trump. That was his name. The polar bear may have been white, but it was a foreigner first and foremost. So it shouldn't get its hopes up.

The news on Allan's black tablet had the curious habit of being both big and small. Mostly big, unpleasantly enough. Allan sought out the small and charming but got the rest of it in the bargain. It was impossible to see the molehills for the mountains.

During his first hundred years of life, Allan had never reflected upon the bigger picture. Now his new toy was telling him that the world was in a dreadful state. And reminding him of why he had, once upon a time, rightly chosen to turn his back on it and think only of himself.

He recalled his early years as an errand boy at the gunpowder factory in Flen. There, half the workers had devoted their free time to longing for a red revolution, while the other half was horrified at the threat from China and Japan. Their understanding of the Yellow Peril was nurtured by novels and booklets that depicted a scenario in which the white world was devoured by the yellow one.

Allan did not care about such nuances, and he continued along the same path after the Second World War when brownshirts made brown the ugliest color of them all. He noticed this as little then as he did the next time people converged around an ideological expression. This time it was more a longing *for* something than away from it. Peace on earth was in, and so were floral VW buses and, frequently, hash. Everyone loved everyone else, except Allan, who didn't love anyone or anything. Except his cat. Not that he was bitter: he just *was*.

The flowery era of life lasted until Margaret Thatcher and Ronald Reagan took over in their respective realms. They thought it was more practical to love oneself and one's own successes. But if you insisted on disliking someone it should be the Russians. Essentially there were no other threats, and when Reagan killed Soviet Communism simply by *talking about* sending missiles from space, it was peace and joy for all, except the half of humanity who had no daily food and the several thousand British miners who no longer had a mine to go to. The new view was that there was no reason to care about your neighbor; it was enough to tolerate him or her. And people did, until the winds of change blew once more.

A bit unexpectedly, perhaps, the brownshirt ideology made a comeback. Not by way of Germany this time, at least not first and foremost. Or even second and middlemost. But in a number of other countries it was in. The United States wasn't first among them, but it soon became the most noticeable, thanks to its recently elected president. It was impossible to say how much he really believed in it: that seemed to change from day to day. But the old adage about doing something yourself if you want it done right wouldn't suffice: it was time to point out external threats to the white Western lives we all deserved to live.

Allan, of course, wanted to consider his black tablet a tool of pure entertainment, but he had a hard time shielding himself against the broader contexts he was beginning to perceive. He thought about putting the tablet down. Leaving it be for a whole day. And another. Only to admit reluctantly that it was too late. The man who had, more than anyone else, not bothered to care about the state of things had started to care about the state of things.

"I'll be damned," he mumbled to himself.

"What's that?" Julius wondered.

"It was nothing. Except what I just said."

"Damned?"

"Yes."

Indonesia

O nce Allan had come to terms with his newfound relative interest in the rest of humanity, his black tablet helped him regain lost ground. It greeted him with the news of a Norwegian who had his own lake, where he fed the roach and bream pellets full of carotene. When the pike in the lake ate the recently fed fish their flesh turned pink, whereupon the Norwegian caught them, filleted them and sold them as salmon. He minimized his risks by exporting the frauds solely to Namibia, where, naturally, there lived a retired health inspector from Oslo. The inspector sounded the alarm, the Norwegian was locked up, and the price of salmon in southwestern Africa went back to normal.

And so on. The black tablet helped Allan enjoy life again, even as Julius continued to live in frustration. It had been *months* since he'd managed a single dishonorable undertaking. In his last few years as a criminal at home in Sweden, he had devoted himself to a mild form of that Norwegian pike-salmon business. He'd imported vegetables from distant lands, had them repackaged, and sold them as Swedish. There was a lot of money to be made there. The cool northern climate in combination with a sun that never set meant that tomatoes and cucumbers matured slowly and developed world-class flavor. Or, as the nineteenth-century poet Carl Jonas Love Almqvist put it, "Only Sweden has Swedish gooseberries."

Gooseberries in particular were not of interest to Julius; besides, there was little market for them. But the same was not true of green asparagus. When spring became early summer, people would pay four or five times as much for a bunch of asparagus, as long as it was Swedish.

Julius Jonsson's Swedish asparagus, at that point, was shipped all the way from Peru. For a long time business was good. But then one of Jonsson's middlemen grew too eager and began to sell Gotland asparagus on Hötorget in Stockholm at least five weeks before it was even to be found on Gotland. This led to rumors of fraud, and the Swedish foodstuffs authorities began to stir. Suddenly there were spot checks when and where there shouldn't have been. In short order Julius lost three whole Peruvian lots, all seized and destroyed in the name of the law. Moreover, his middlemen—unlike Julius—were locked up. Such is a middleman's lot.

But even if the long arm of the law couldn't reach all the way to the brains behind it, Julius had lost interest. He was tired of Sweden being orderly beyond all reason. Who'd ever died of eating Peruvian asparagus?

No, honorable petty thieves might as well not bother anymore. So Julius had chosen to retire. He made some moonshine, poached a moose here and there, borrowed the neighbor's electricity without permission—and that was about it. Until a hundred-year-old man unexpectedly knocked on his door. The old man said his name was Allan, and with him he had a stolen suitcase they opened after a pleasant dinner and accompanying vodka. It had turned out to be full of millions.

So one thing had led to another, and another to the third. Julius and Allan had shaken off all the stubborn individuals who wanted their money back and ended up in Bali, where they were doing away with it at a steady pace.

Allan saw that Julius was hanging his head. He tried to inspire his bored friend by reading aloud from his black tablet about various types of immorality from all the corners of the world. Romania, Italy, and Norway were already settled. President Zuma of South Africa managed to take up a whole breakfast when it turned out he'd built a private swimming pool and a theater with taxpayers' money. A Swedish dance-band queen received well-deserved attention after calling seven dresses and eighteen pairs of shoes a "business trip" on her tax return.

But the head-hanging didn't stop. Julius needed something to do before he became depressed for real.

Allan, who hadn't let himself be concerned about anything at all for a hundred years, could not feel at peace, given his friend's lost spark. Surely there must be something Julius could engage himself in.

That was as far as he got in his musings before chance stepped in. It happened one evening after Allan had crawled into bed, while Julius felt he still had sorrows in his soul to deaden. He sat down in the hotel bar and ordered a glass of local arak. It was made of rice and sugarcane, tasted like rum, and was so strong it made the eyes water. Julius had learned that one glass would blur one's troubles and a second would chase them away. Just to be safe, he tended to have a third glass, too, before bedtime.

The evening's first was empty and the other well on its way when Julius's senses expanded enough for him to notice that he wasn't alone in the bar. Three chairs away sat a middle-aged Asian man, also with arak in hand.

"Cheers," Julius said, raising his glass.

The man smiled in response, whereupon both turned bottoms up and grimaced.

"Now things are starting to look up," said the man, whose eyes were as full of tears as Julius's.

"First or second?" Julius asked.

"Second," said the man.

"Same here."

Julius and the man moved closer and each decided to have a third glass of the same.

They chatted for a while before the man chose to introduce himself. "Simran Aryabhat Chakrabarty Gopaldas," he said. "It's a pleasure!"

Julius looked at the man who had just said his name. And had enough arak in his body to say what he was thinking. "Surely no one could have a name like that."

Yes, one could. Especially if one was of Indian origin. Simran Whoever. had ended up in Indonesia after an unfortunate incident with the daughter of a far-too-unsympathetic man.

Julius nodded. Dads of daughters could be more unsympathetic than most. But was that any reason to possess a name that took an entire morning to say?

The man, who was named what he was named, turned out to have a pragmatic attitude toward the significance of his own identity. Or perhaps he just had a sense of humor. "What do you think I should be called instead?"

Julius liked the exiled Indian. But if they were going to become friends, all those names in a row just wouldn't do. He had to seize this opportunity. "Gustav Svensson," he said. "That's a proper name, rolls off the tongue, easy to remember."

The man said he'd never had trouble remembering Simran Aryabhat Chakrabarty Gopaldas either, but he agreed that Gustav Svensson sounded pleasant. "Swedish, isn't it?" he asked.

Yes. Julius nodded again. Couldn't get much more Swedish than that.

And there and then, his new business idea began to take root.

Julius Jonsson and Simran Something truly hit it off as the third glass of arak took hold. Before the night was over they had decided to meet again. Same place, same time, the next night. In addition, Julius had decided that the man with the impossible name would henceforth be called Gustav Svensson. Simran Aryabhat Chakrabarty Gopaldas thought that was just as well. The name he'd had so far hadn't brought him an overabundance of luck.

The old men went on in the same vein for several nights in a row. The Indian grew used to his new alias. He liked it.

He'd checked into the hotel under his previous name on the day the two had met, and he continued to stay there while he and Julius laid plans for their future partnership. When the hotel manager informed him, at increasing volume, that he wanted payment for the Indian guest's stay, Gustav told Julius that he intended to depart from the place permanently. Without paying. And without announcing his intentions. The management would never understand, after all, that Gustav couldn't be held responsible for Simran's bill.

But Julius understood. When was Gustav planning to depart?

"Preferably in the next fifteen minutes."

Julius understood this too. But he didn't want to lose his new friend, so he sent the man off with the phone Allan had given him. "Here's something so you can be reached. I'll call you from my room. Now go. Take the way through the kitchen. That's what I would do."

Gustav followed Julius's advice and was gone. Later that evening, the hotel manager appeared after wandering around for at least an hour in pursuit of the now-vanished Indian guest.

Julius and Allan observed the sunset from the shore, each in a comfortable chair and with an accompanying drink. The manager apologized for the intrusion. But he had a question. "Mr. Jonsson, is there any chance you have seen our guest Simran Aryabhat Chakrabarty Gopaldas? I've noticed the two of you spending some time together here at our establishment in recent days."

"Simran who?" said Julius.

Thenceforth, Gustav Svensson and Julius Jonsson had to meet somewhere other than the hotel when the time came to talk business. The manager couldn't exactly lay the blame for his vanished guest at Jonsson's feet, but that didn't stop him aiming a slightly raised level of suspicion at the Swedish gentlemen. In their case, there was considerably more money at stake. Thus far they had always paid up, but currently the bill was larger than usual and it seemed advisable to proceed with caution.

Jonsson and Svensson's meetings were instead held in a filthy bar in central Denpasar. Gustav turned out to be almost as much a petty thief as Julius. Back home in

India, he had spent many years living large by renting cars, switching their engines, and returning them. It often took the rental agency several months to discover that the vehicle in question had become seven years older, and by then it was impossible to say which of several hundred renters was the guilty party. Unless it was someone on the staff.

In those days, fancy cars had become part of Gustav's daily life. As a result he noticed that the nicer the car, the greater the potential to attract a beautiful girl. This equation got him into trouble more than once. To such an extent, most recently, that he had found it best to leave the automotive industry, the girl, and all of India behind, since the girl had become pregnant. Her father had turned out to be both a Member of Parliament and a military man, and when Gustav, for strategic reasons, had asked for the girl's hand in marriage, the father responded by threatening to send the seventh infantry after him.

"What a grumpy bastard," Julius said. "Couldn't he think of what was best for his daughter?"

Gustav agreed. A complicating factor was that the father had just noticed that his six-cylinder BMW had become a four-cylinder while he was on a business trip to Singapore.

"And he blamed you?"

"Yes. With no evidence."

"Were you innocent?"

"That's beside the point."

In conclusion, Gustav said it felt right that Simran Aryabhat Chakrabarty Gopaldas was no more.

"But it's too bad he didn't have time to settle up with the hotel. Cheers to you, my friend."

Some time after their initial, cheerful meeting at the bar, Julius Jonsson and his new partner Gustav Svensson, with the help of a substantial amount of the money that remained in the suitcase, took over an asparagus farm in the mountains. Julius held the reins, Gustav was the site manager, and a great number of impoverished Balinese people bent their backs in the fields.

With the help of previous contacts in Sweden, Julius and his new partner now exported "Gustav Svensson's locally grown asparagus" in lovely bunches tied with blue-and-yellow ribbon. Nowhere did Julius or the man who had, until recently, been named something else claim that the asparagus was Swedish. The only thing Swedish about it was the price, and the name of the Indian grower. Unlike the Peru project, this wasn't as illegal as Julius would have preferred, but you couldn't have it all. Furthermore, he and Gustav succeeded in establishing a supplementary, and shadier, line of business. Swedish asparagus had such a good international reputation that Gustav's Balinese variety could be shipped to Sweden, transferred into different boxes, and exported to a series of luxury hotels around the world. In Bali, for example. High-profile hotels there had their international reputations to consider, and it was worth every single extra rupiah it cost to avoid serving guests the bland, locally grown variety.

Allan was glad his friend Julius was back to his old self. And with that, life surely would have been a gas once more for both Julius and his hundred-year-old friend with the black tablet, except the money in the suitcase that never ran dry was starting to run dry. The income from the crop fields in the mountains was respectable, but life at the luxury hotel where the friends resided was anything but free. Even the imported Swedish asparagus in the restaurant cost half a fortune.

Julius had wanted to broach the topic of their finances with Allan for some time. He just hadn't got round to it. At breakfast that morning, however, the time had come. Allan had brought his black tablet along as usual, and the day's news was a story about the love between siblings. The North Korean leader Kim Jong-un had just had his brother poisoned to death at an airport in Malaysia. Allan said he wasn't overly surprised: he'd had his own dealings with Kim Jong-un's father. And grandfather.

"Both father and grandfather did in fact intend to take my life," he recalled. "Now both of them are dead, but here I sit. Such is life."

Julius had grown used to Allan popping up with such reflections on the past and was no longer surprised by them. He had probably heard that particular story before, but he didn't quite recall. "You met the North Korean leader's father? And grandfather? How old *are* you?"

"A hundred, almost a hundred and one," said Allan. "In case that somehow escaped you. Their names were Kim Jong-il and Kim Il-sung. The one was only a child, but he was very angry."

Julius resisted the urge to inquire further. Instead he guided the conversation toward the topic he'd been planning to discuss from the start.

The problem was, as Julius had hinted earlier, that the suitcase of money was increasingly transforming into a suitcase without money. And it had been two and a half months since they'd last settled their debts with the hotel. Julius didn't want to think about what the bill would say.

"Then don't," Allan suggested, taking a bite of his mildly seasoned *nasi goreng*.

More urgent was the issue with the boat-renter, who had been in touch to say that he had throttled their line of credit and intended to do the same to Messrs. Karlsson and Jonsson unless their debt was settled within the week.

"The boat-renter?" Allan said. "Did we rent a boat?"

"The luxury yacht."

"Oh, right. So that counts as a boat, does it?"

Then Julius confessed that he'd been planning to surprise Allan on his hundred-and-first birthday, but their financial situation was such that the celebration couldn't be up to Harry Belafonte standards.

"Well, we met him once before," Allan said. "And my birthday parties and I have never quite seen eye to eye, so don't worry about that."

But Julius did. He wanted Allan to know he had appreciated the Belafonte gesture. It had been above and beyond. Julius was no spring chicken himself, and at no time in history had anyone done anything as nice for him as Allan had.

"Though I wasn't the one singing," Allan said.

Julius went on to say that there would absolutely be a party: he'd already ordered a cake from the one bakery he'd been able to find that would make it on credit. Thereafter awaited a hot-air balloon ride over the beautiful green island, along with the balloon pilot and two bottles of champagne.

Allan thought a hot-air balloon ride sounded pleasant. But perhaps they could skip the cake, given that their finances were strained. Even the 101 candles might cost a fortune.

The state of the friends' joint capital didn't hinge on 101 birthday candles, according to Julius. He had dug through the suitcase the night before and made a rough estimate of how much was left. Then he made another based on what he expected the hotel thought they owed. When it came to the yacht, he didn't need to make an estimate, since the lessor had been kind enough to tell him the exact amount.

"I'm afraid we're at least a hundred thousand dollars in the red," said Julius.

"Is that with or without the candles?" Allan asked.

Indonesia

The hundred-year-old man had always had a calming effect on those around him, except during isolated moments in history in which he had riled people beyond all rhyme and reason. Like the time he'd met Stalin in 1948. That had led to five years in a gulag. And a few years after that, it had turned out the North Koreans weren't great fans of his either.

Oh, well, that was all in the past. Now, he had got Julius to agree that they would *first* celebrate his hundred-and-first birthday according to the plan (since Julius so desperately wanted to) and *then* they would sit down and deal with their finances. Everything would work out. With a little luck, perhaps a new suitcase full of money would turn up.

Julius didn't believe it would, although one never

knew what might happen in Allan's company. Despite their suboptimal financial situation, he had gone along with Allan's suggestion that there be four bottles of champagne in the hot-air balloon rather than two. There might be a lull in the air up there, and in that case they would need some way to amuse themselves.

"Perhaps a few sandwiches as well," Julius mused.

"But why?" said Allan.

The hotel manager was keeping a close eye on the old man and his even older friend, these days. Their unpaid bills had surpassed a hundred and fifty thousand dollars. That was only a small part of what the manager had made from the spendthrift Scandinavians in the past year, but at the same time it was far too much to let it go unpaid. He had taken certain steps and measures. A few days ago, or nights ago, he had put a man on discreet watch outside the gentlemen's luxury bungalow, just in case they should get it into their heads to climb through one of the paneless windows and vanish.

But there was a certain amount of gratitude involved in the manager's relationship with Messrs. Jonsson and Karlsson. The former had, in a fairly believable manner, suggested that more money would be on its way before the week's end. And, after all, this wasn't the first time Jonsson had clung to his money just a little too long. Maybe the whole issue was simply down to him loving his cash. And who didn't?

All in all, the manager thought it prudent and strategically smart to lie low, and to join in celebrating the older man's birthday on the beach, with cake and a few carefully selected words.

In addition to the birthday boy, Julius, and the hotel manager, the hired balloon pilot was present for the party. Gustav Svensson would have liked to attend, but he had the good sense not to.

The balloon was inflated and ready. Only a classic anchor around a palm tree kept it from taking off on its own. The heat in the balloon was regulated by the pilot's nine-year-old son, who was deeply distressed as he would much rather have been next to the cake a few yards away.

Allan stared at the 101 unnecessary candles. Imagine the waste of money. And time! It took Julius several minutes to get them all lit, with the help of the hotel manager's gold lighter (which ended up in Julius's pocket).

At least the cake tasted good. And champagne was champagne, even if it wasn't grog. It seemed to Allan that things could have been worse.

And, all of a sudden, they were. For the hotel manager was tapping his glass with the aim of giving a speech. "My dear Mr. Karlsson," he said.

Allan interrupted him. "That was well said, Mr. Manager. Truly charming. But surely we can't all stand around here until my next birthday. Isn't it high time we took off in the balloon?"

The hotel manager became flustered and Julius gave the nod to the balloon pilot, who immediately put down his piece of cake. After all, his primary purpose for being there was to work.

"Roger that! I'll go and make the call to the weather service at the airport. Just want to be sure that the winds haven't changed. Back in a minute."

The danger of a speech had been averted. Now it was time for boarding. It was easy to step into the basket, even for a 101-year-old. There was a set of six portable stairs outside and a slightly smaller variant with three steps inside.

"Hello there, little man," Allan said, ruffling the hair of the nine-year-old assistant.

The nine-year-old responded with a shy "Good day." He knew his place and was good at his job. The anchor was no longer necessary, not with the added weight of the foreigners.

Julius asked the boy for a demonstration and learned that the heat and, as a result, the balloon's altitude, was adjusted by way of the red lever at the top of the gas line. When it was time to take off, all you had to do was turn it to the right. And back to the left when you wanted to come in for a landing.

"First right, then left," said Julius.

"Exactly, sir," said the boy.

And now three things happened simultaneously, within the span of a few seconds.

One: Allan noticed the nine-year-old's longing glances at the cake and suggested that the lad run over quick and help himself. Plates and cutlery were both on the table. The boy needed no coaxing. He hopped out of the basket almost before Allan had finished speaking.

Two: Julius tested the red lever, turning it both left and right, and twisted it so hard it came off in his hand.

Three: the balloon pilot exited the hotel looking unhappy, and said that the ride would have to wait for the wind was about to become northerly. The balloon was in a poor position for such a wind.

At this, three more things happened, also rather simultaneously.

One: the balloon pilot caught sight of his nine-year-old son with his nose in the cake and scolded the poor boy for leaving his post.

Two: Julius swore at the red lever that had come off

just like that. Now hot air was streaming into the balloon, which . . .

Three: . . . began to lift off the ground.

"Stop! What are you doing?" cried the balloon pilot.

"It's not me, it's this damned lever," called Julius.

The balloon was at an altitude of ten feet. Then thirteen. Then sixteen.

"There we go!" said Allan. "Now this is a party."

The Indian Ocean

It took quite some time for Karlsson, Jonsson, and the balloon to float far enough across the open sea that they could no longer hear the screaming balloon pilot. After all, the wind was at his back.

They could still see him for a while, after he ceased to be audible—he was flapping his arms. They could also see the hotel manager at his side. Not quite as flappy. But likely just as unhappy. Or even more so. He was watching a hundred and fifty thousand dollars float away before his very eyes. Meanwhile, the nine-year-old boy returned to the cake since everyone else was otherwise occupied.

A few more minutes passed, and then they could no longer see land in any direction. Julius finished cursing the red lever and threw it overboard, having given up trying to reattach it.

The gas and the flame were irreversibly on. And, in certain respects, that was a positive thing. Otherwise they would certainly fall into the ocean, basket and all.

Julius looked around. On the other side of the gas tank he found a GPS navigator. This was good news! Not that there was any way to steer the craft, but now at least they would know when land could be expected.

As Julius delved into geography, Allan opened the first of the four bottles of champagne they had brought along. "Whoopsie!" he said, as the cork flew over the edge of the basket.

Julius felt that Allan wasn't taking the situation seriously. They had no idea where they were heading.

Of course they did, Allan thought. "I've been around the world so many times that I've started to understand how it looks. If the wind keeps up like this, we'll end up in Australia in a few weeks. But if it turns a little that way we'll have to wait a few more."

"And where will we end up in that case?"

"Well, not at the North Pole, but you didn't want to go there anyway. Likely the South Pole, though."

"What the hell—" Julius said, but he was interrupted.

"There, there. Here's your glass. Now, cheers to us

on my birthday. And don't you worry. The gas in the tank will run out long before the South Pole. Have a seat."

Julius did as Allan said, sitting down next to his friend and staring straight ahead with a vacant gaze. Allan could tell that Julius was concerned. He was in need of comfort. "Yes, things look dark right now, my friend. But they've been dark before in my life, yet here I am. You'll see, the wind will change. Or something."

Julius found Allan's inexplicable calmness a little bit helpful. Perhaps the champagne could take care of the rest. "Pass me the bottle, please," he said quietly.

And he took four liberal gulps without bothering to use a glass.

Allan was correct: the gas did run out before land was in sight. The tank began to sputter and the flame danced irregularly for some time before it went out completely, just as the friends managed to drain the contents of bottle number one.

It was a gentle journey down to the surface of the Indian Ocean, which, that day, was practically a Pacific one.

"Do you think the basket will float?" Julius asked, as the surface of the water grew nearer.

"We'll soon find out," said Allan. "Look at this!"

The 101-year-old had been digging through the balloon's wooden box of supplies for unforeseen incidents. He held up a brand-new fitting for the red lever.

"Pity we didn't find this while there was still time. And look!"

Two rocket flares.

The crash landing in the sea went better than Julius had dared to hope. The balloon basket hit the water, plunging half a yard below the surface, thanks to its speed and weight, then tilted at a forty-five-degree angle, straightened again, and bobbed like a fishing float with ever-waning movements.

Both old men were knocked over by the strike and the angle, and they ended up in a communal pile along one of the basket's walls. Julius was quick to get up, a knife in his hand to separate the basket from the deflated balloon, which would no longer be of any use. It was temporarily spreading out on the water but would soon sink and take both basket and old men with it if it could.

"Well done," Allan praised him from where he lay.

"Thanks," said Julius, helping his friend back onto the bench.

Then Julius dismantled the heavy gas assembly and dumped it into the sea along with the four bracings that had held it up. With that, the vessel suddenly weighed at least 110 pounds less. Julius wiped the sweat from his brow and sank down next to his friend. "Now what?" he said.

"I think we should have another bottle of champagne so we don't sit around here sobering up. Can't you fire off one of those flares while I uncork it?"

Water was already seeping in through the sides of the basket, but it wasn't so dire that they would sink before a few hours had passed, Allan thought. Or even more, if only they had something decent to bail with. "A lot can happen in two hours," he said.

"Like what?" Julius wondered.

"Oh, well, a little can happen as well. Or nothing."

Julius unwrapped the first flare and tried to make sense of the Indonesian instructions. He was tipsy and didn't have the energy to be as desperate as he should have been. On the one hand, he knew he was soon to die. On the other, he was in the company of a man who was possibly immortal. A man who had not been executed by General Franco, had not been locked up for life by the American immigration authority, had not been strangled by Comrade Stalin (although it had been a close shave), had not been put to death by Kim Il-sung or Mao Zedong, had not been shot by the Iranian border patrol, had not had a hair touched on his ever-balder head in his twenty-five years as a double agent in the inner circles of the Cold War, had not been killed by Brezhnev's bad breath, and had not been dragged along into President Nixon's downfall.

The only thing to suggest that Allan might actually die, after having failed to do so for so many years, was the fact that he was sitting in a woven basket that was taking in water, in the sea somewhere between Indonesia, Australia, and Antarctica. But if the recently turned 101-year-old survived this too, one might reasonably expect that Julius could ride shotgun.

"I reckon you just have to pull on this," he said, tugging on the right string in the wrong position, at which the emergency flare shot into the water and kept going until it presumably extinguished at a depth of a few hundred feet.

Julius considered giving up. But Allan popped the cork on the next bottle, handed it to his friend, and asked him to take a few sips—with or without a glass—because he appeared to need it.

"Then I think you should try again with the other flare. But feel free to aim it upward—I imagine it will be easier to see that way."

The Indian Ocean

The official task of the North Korean bulk carrier *Honor and Strength* was to transport thirty thousand tons of grain from Havana to Pyongyang. A much less official task was to slow down the vessel southeast of Madagascar and, under cover of darkness, allow nine pounds of enriched uranium to be brought aboard. This cargo had changed hands from courier to courier, from Congo to Burundi to Tanzania to Mozambique and on to the island east of the African continent, which *Honor and Strength* had a legitimate reason to pass.

The North Koreans understood that they had eyes on them. Just a few years earlier their sister ship had been caught in a rebel-controlled harbor in Libya; the captain had managed to bribe his way out, that time with a ship full of oil. To make a stop in Somalia, Iran, or anywhere else with a similar reputation on the way home from Cuba would likely result in nothing but boarding by UN troops on the open sea. It had happened before, most recently outside Panama. That time there happened to be aircraft engines and advanced electronics under the grain, in violation of the current UN sanctions against the proud Democratic People's Republic. Upset, the Koreans had informed the world that it was the world, not the Koreans, who had placed the engines and electronics there.

This time, the journey home from Cuba was going in the other direction; the Earth was, after all, round. The official line was that the Democratic People's Republic refused to allow itself to be wronged again in Panama. What was not mentioned was that they had an errand along the way.

Thus far everything had gone right instead of wrong. Captain Pak Chong-un had a hold full of high-quality grain that the Supreme Leader didn't care about; he ate his fill anyway. But in addition there were now nine pounds of lead-shielded enriched uranium, secured in a North Korean briefcase. The uranium was a necessity for the continued crucial battle against the American dogs and their allies south of the 38th parallel. The amount, nine pounds, might not have been much upon which to build the nation's future, but that was not the point. This was a test of the distribution channels as such. If all went well, the Russians promised, their efforts would be doubled many times over.

Captain Pak could feel the imperialist satellites following the ship's path back to Pyongyang, prepared, as always, to find reasons to board, humiliate, and disgrace.

Pak kept the briefcase in the safe in the captain's quarters; the hooligans would find what they were looking for anyway, if it came to a boarding. But no sign of that yet. Still no mistakes made. Soon nothing could keep the captain from returning in triumph.

Pak Chong-un's thoughts were interrupted when the first mate entered the room without knocking. "Captain!" he said. "We've spotted an emergency flare four nautical miles to the north. What should we do? Ignore it?"

Blast! Just when everything was looking so good. Many thoughts flew through Captain Pak's head all at once. Could it be a trap? Someone who intended to seize the uranium? Best to pretend they hadn't seen it, of course, just as the first mate had suggested.

But some people were guaranteed to see it—the Americans. From space. And they were surely taking photographs. A North Korean ship ignoring someone in distress at sea—that would be a crime against maritime law, and an enormous PR disaster for the Supreme Leader (while Captain Pak himself would face a firing squad).

No, the least troublesome option would probably be to find out the reason for the flare.

"Shame on you, sailor!" said Captain Pak Chong-un. "Representatives of the Democratic People's Republic of Korea don't leave those in distress in the lurch. Set a new course and prepare for a rescue action. That's an order!"

The first mate gave a frightened salute and hurried off. He cursed himself for not doing a better job of watching his tongue. If the captain reported this, his career would be over. At best.

By now the water was up to the ankles of the friends in the basket on the sea. Allan sat with his black tablet, marveling that it worked in the middle of nowhere. "Listen to this!" he said.

And he told his friend that it wasn't only presidents who made fools of themselves out in the world, like Robert Mugabe of Zimbabwe, for example, the man who had defined homosexuality as "un-African" and decided that it ought to be worth ten years in prison so the homosexual would learn. Recently Mugabe's wife had allegedly used an extension cord to attack a girl who had spent time with the couple's son at a hotel room. Apparently in that family they had issues with heterosexuality as well.

Julius was too distressed to have any opinion on his friend's latest news and was just about to ask him to be quiet, so he could sit there and die in peace, when he was interrupted by a horn. In the distance he and Allan could make out a ship. Heading straight for the basket.

"Isn't that the damnedest thing?" said Julius. "You're going to survive this too, Allan."

"And so are you, it seems," said Allan.

The only items that accompanied the two old men onto the ship were Allan's black tablet and the last bottle of champagne. Allan was holding the tablet in one hand and the champagne in the other as he and Julius met Captain Pak on the foredeck.

"Good day, Captain," he said, once each in English, Russian, Mandarin, and Spanish.

"Good day," the astonished captain responded in English.

He had command of both Russian and Mandarin and, thanks to his many excursions to and from Cuba, he knew a certain amount of Spanish, but he was the only one of the crew who spoke English, and he felt instinctively that the fewer ears that listened and understood the better. At least until this mysterious situation cleared up.

Captain Pak informed the two castaways that their lives had just been saved in the name of the Democratic People's Republic of Korea and for the glory of the Supreme Leader.

"Say hello and thanks to the Supreme One, if you run into each other from now on," said Allan. "Where might we be let off along the way? Indonesia would be great, if it's not too much trouble. We didn't bring any identification papers, and it's always a little tricky to change countries, isn't it?"

Yes, Captain Pak knew how tricky it could be to change countries. It wasn't the sort of thing you did with ease where he came from. But that wasn't enough reason to fraternize with foreign gentlemen plucked from a bucket on the open sea. And certainly not in front of the crew, no matter the language.

"As commanding officer, I am bound by law to guard the cargo of this ship carefully during our journey, as well as watch out for the cargo owners' interests more generally. According to the same law, I am duty-bound to conduct the ship with due promptness."

"What does that mean?" Julius asked nervously.

"It means what I just said," said Captain Pak.

"It means he's not going to let us off before Pyong-yang," said Allan.

Julius had no desire to see North Korea. "But please, dear Captain," he said. "We happen to have a bottle of champagne here. We thought it might come in handy if we were picked up as we now have been. It's not quite as well chilled as it ought to be, but if the captain doesn't mind that, we'd be happy to share it. We can get to know each other and see what sorts of solutions might be hiding just around the corner."

That was well put, Allan thought, holding up the bottle in support.

The captain took it from his hand and informed them that it was being confiscated as no alcohol was allowed on board.

"No alcohol?" said Julius.

No alcohol? Allan thought, on the verge of asking to return to the basket.

"You gentlemen will be interrogated for information in two hours. For the time being you are not under suspicion of any crime, but that can always change. I intend to conduct the interrogation myself. The first two questions will be, who are you and why did you elect to float around in a woven basket on the open sea? With a bottle of champagne. But we'll deal with that then."

Captain Pak turned to his first mate, who was told he must take his belongings and move down with the crew, since he had just been relieved of his officer's cabin. He should instead have the two foreign men installed there. Furthermore, the first mate should make sure a sailor stood watch outside the cabin, unless he chose to guard it himself, to make sure the two gentlemen didn't come to any harm or, for that matter, get up to causing any harm.

The first mate gave a salute. He wasn't happy about this development. Forced to associate with the crew for the sake of two aged whites . . . No, the captain should have left them at sea. This could only end as poorly as it had begun.

Captain Pak Chong-un sensed trouble brewing. Once again he checked the contents within the otherwise securely locked door to the safe in the captain's quarters. He kept the key on a chain around his neck.

The safe contained all the mandatory ship's logs, a copy of maritime law, and a briefcase full of nine pounds of lead-shielded, enriched uranium.

The task he had *personally* been delegated by the Supreme Leader was now only three days from completion. There were no clouds on the horizon of this task. In a literal sense, that was. Which meant, as always, that the

American satellites were keeping a watchful eye on him. That was a cloud in and of itself, albeit a metaphorical one. Another was the two foreign men in the first mate's cabin just on the other side of the wall.

Captain Pak allowed himself to sum up the situation before walking the few steps to the neighboring cabin. "Ugh." He stared at the watchman until said watchman realized he should open the door for his captain. And then he stared again until the watchman closed the same door.

"Gentlemen, it is time to be interrogated," said Captain Pak Chong-un.

"Lovely," said Allan.

Congo

Congo is the second-largest country in Africa and has always been rich in two particular things: natural resources and misery.

The most miserable period of all was when King Leopold II of Belgium used the country as his private rubber farm. He enslaved everyone he encountered and had upward of ten million people killed. That's an entire Sweden. Or an entire Belgium, if you prefer.

When Congo gained independence many difficult years later, a certain Joseph Mobutu ended up in the president's chair. He became most famous for selling his country's resources to the highest under-the-table bidder, keeping the money for himself, and changing his name to "the All-powerful Warrior who, because of his endurance and inflexible will to win, goes from conquest to conquest, leaving fire in his wake."

This guy, thought the United States, was the future of Congo and Africa. And, with the kind aid of the CIA, the All-powerful Warrior remained in power for several decades. Uranium succeeded rubber as the most interesting natural resource. Indeed, the USA received the uranium for the atomic bombs over Hiroshima and Nagasaki from Congo and, as thanks for the help, assisted in the installation of a Congolese nuclear research facility under the leadership of the all-powerful one who left fire in his wake. It's possible that this was not the United States's brightest political decision in history.

In the country where everything was corrupt, no exceptions, large quantities of enriched uranium vanished. Some of it turned up here and there and could be secured, while an unknown amount remained missing.

Time passed. The most important security services in the Western world no longer had the energy to search for what couldn't be found. What remained was to try to keep any more from reaching the black market. Some of those with operational units found comfort in the fact that at least the missing uranium lost strength with each year that went by.

German Chancellor Angela Merkel, however, was in possession of knowledge that made her view of the whole thing rather less rosy. Frau Merkel had already been around longer than most of the world's leaders and she was counting on being reelected next autumn. Her background as a chemist told her that she would not be in her current position on the day the missing isotope no longer posed a potential threat to her country. To be sure, she still had a lot to give, even at the age of sixty-three, after twenty-eight years in politics. But even so, her own half-life was considerably shorter than that of enriched uranium: four point five billion years.

North Korea

Kim Jong-un had never asked to be the person he became. In fact, two older brothers were ahead of him in line, but one sealed his fate when he took his family under his wing and sneaked out of the country under a fake name to go to Tokyo for a lark. To *Disneyland*, to boot—he was 0 for 2. And their father, Kim Jong-il, considered his other son far too weak. That basically meant he was suspected of being gay. Here and there, it was considered questionable to love whomever you wished.

Their father Kim was quite advanced in age when he took over from Eternal President Kim Il-sung, and likely had plans for a similar run-in period for his youngest son. But the problem with life is that people both high and low die when they die. Suddenly there he was, the twenty-five-year-old son, expected to move forward the legacy of his just-deceased father. Or preferably further than that since his father had gone down in history as the man who had turned a hungry people into a starving people.

In the span of a few months, young Kim went from capable Game Boy player to three-star general. He wasn't given terrific chances by international analysts. A puppy, commander of a series of battle-scarred officers, including the puppy's own uncle? Surely that would never work out.

And it didn't. For the uncle and the generals. It's possible that they were scheming, but before they could finish they were purged, every last one. Young Kim proved to be a person not to be trifled with or herded about. The uncle was sentenced to death for, among other things, being unfaithful to his wife. Nowhere in the twelve-page verdict was there a word about the fact that young Kim's father had had five children with three different women.

Several years earlier young Kim had attended school in Switzerland under a secret name while his mother traveled around Europe to shop for the sorts of things the average North Korean had never even seen a picture of. Kim was more interested in basketball and video games than girls, but his grades were nothing to sneeze at. And when he hastily, and with a decent amount of enthusiasm, took over the entire nation his grandfather had created and his father had partially ruined, it was his grandfather he took after. He was an extrovert, liked to mix with his people, might thump the occasional citizen on the back when he was in the mood—he even *spoke* to them. Above all, he adjusted the dials of the homemade Communist system, after which the food didn't run out on as many tables as quickly as it had before.

So, as the world continued to titter in horror over the puppy, he made sure that the citizens were no longer starving even as he realized that the country he'd inherited must either curl up and die or pick a fight with the whole rest of the world, which was striving to make sure that the former occurred.

He chose the fight-picking.

But there was a slight issue with North Korea's inadequate finances. It would cost much more than they had squirrelled away to upgrade the aged Soviet tanks and ordnance. Better, then, to speed up the pace of the project Dad had helmed with a certain level of success.

Not *many* bombs. Just a few. But with a decent amount of oomph in them.

Nuclear weapons, in short.

By way of the development of the nuclear weapons

program and an eternal number of test-fired missiles, he informed the scornfully smiling world that North Korea was still in the game. Young Kim was rather satisfied when the world reacted with fear, sanctions, and repeated condemnations. Incidentally, he was no longer "young Kim" but Supreme Leader.

As a godsend, the United States replaced a Nobel Peace Prize–winning president with one who constantly fell into Kim Jong-un's traps. Each time Donald Trump ran his mouth about how North Korea would be struck by "fire and fury," he bolstered the Supreme Leader's position.

During his first years in power, Kim Jong-un had achieved more than his father had done in his whole life. There was really only one thing that concerned him: the fact that the domestic plutonium factory had such trouble making it. The downside to plutonium is that it does not occur naturally in the Earth. Anyone who wishes to play around with it, to build nuclear weapons for example, must first make sure he can create it.

And that's no small task.

Even the production of five tiny grams is a tough job. But say you succeed in that. Then it must be stabilized, preferably to 99 percent or greater, with the help of the element gallium, which in turn has the troublesome tendency to melt about as easily as a chocolate bar in the sun.

To stop the entire plutonium process slipping through your fingers, you must have a fancy centrifuge, and that is almost as complicated as the very process it is meant to aid.

All this for five grams of weapons-grade plutonium 239. For a nuclear charge worth mentioning, you need more like nine pounds.

Things would probably have worked out if only the Russians had stopped giving the North Koreans the runaround. They had quietly promised to deliver a centrifuge, but now they were making excuses this way and that. It was not an option to wait out their dillydallying for eternity upon eternity. Kim Jong-un hated being anyone's lapdog.

Incidentally, the Russians were masters of doubledealing. They might vote for sanctions against North Korea on Monday, half promise a centrifuge on Tuesday—and offer up valuable uranium contacts before the week was out.

For the alternative to homemade plutonium was enriched uranium. It could be had on the black market in the darkest parts of Africa. But the proud Democratic

People's Republic had many enemies out there. Half a ton of material for nuclear weapons was not the sort of thing you could ship intercontinentally by DHL.

And now the schizophrenic characters in Moscow had tipped them off about enriched uranium in Congo.

But could the supplier be trusted?

And would the delivery method work?

Both questions were currently under investigation.

USA, North Korea

The new President of the United States had been forced to fire his security advisor after it turned out the advisor was a security risk. Beyond this, his focus during the initial period of his presidency was to try to get the media to shape up. It was going so-so.

As a result it was basically a welcome interruption for President Trump when the Supreme Leader in Pyongyang allowed four mid-range Pukguksong-2 missiles to be fired three hundred miles straight out into the Sea of Japan.

On the initiative of the United States, Japan, and South Korea, the UN Security Council was convened, and it soon unanimously condemned the North Korean test. The American ambassador to the UN commented that "It is time to hold North Korea accountable—not with our words, but with our actions." What those actions might be, she was happy to hand over to the president, who in turn tweeted a number of suggestions.

It so happened that little Sweden was a member of the aforementioned Security Council that year. Margot Wallström, Sweden's minister for foreign affairs, was known for her outspokenness and enterprising nature. It was said, but not confirmed, that Benjamin Netanyahu had a picture of her on his office wall in Jerusalem and liked to throw darts at it each time he needed to work out his frustrations. This was because Sweden, on the urging of Margot Wallström, had upped and recognized the state of Palestine. A state without borders, without a functioning government and, as Netanyahu and others saw it, a state full of terrorists.

But Wallström persisted. And now, on the Security Council, she aimed high. Among her colleagues she promoted the idea that she should personally visit Pyongyang to establish a direct line of contact with the leader about the serious nature of things, as a representative of both Sweden and the UN Security Council. The visit must first be sanctioned by North Korea, and it must be completely unofficial. A high-level diplomatic game, but also a serious attempt to tone down the war rhetoric coming from both sides.

No Western country had as genuine a diplomatic

relationship with North Korea as Sweden did. The Security Council gave Wallström the green light. All that remained was to convince the Supreme Leader to do the same.

If Torsten Lövenstierna had been an athlete, he would have been world-renowned and a multimillionaire. But instead he was a diplomat, so no one had ever heard of him.

During his nearly thirty years in the Swedish foreign service, he had quietly performed his highly qualified services in Egypt, Iraq, Turkey, and Afghanistan. Among his merits were a posting to the UN in New York, being a special advisor during the Iraq inspection, taking on a leadership role in Mazar-e Sharif, and serving as the Swedish consul general in Istanbul.

What Torsten Lövenstierna didn't know about advanced diplomacy wasn't worth knowing. Now he was Sweden's ambassador in Pyongyang, perhaps the most complicated embassy posting of all.

According to some, he was a genius. Whatever, it was this man who had received the delicate task of bringing the North Koreans onto the track of discreet arbitration.

World peace was on the line. Torsten Lövenstierna

prepared himself meticulously, as always. Following his preparations he requested, and was granted, an audience with the Supreme Leader. The ambassador wasn't nervous—he'd been around far too long for that—but he was incredibly focused.

With great precision, deploying the right word at exactly the right moment, he conveyed the UN's argument for why quiet arbitration in Pyongyang would be in the best interest of the aforementioned world peace. He was so skilled at his job that he managed to finish his speech without being interrupted even once. What Torsten Lövenstierna accomplished in front of the Supreme Leader was nothing other than a feat of diplomacy.

When he had finished, he expressed thanks for being allowed to take up the leader's precious time, then awaited a response.

The leader looked the star diplomat in the eye and said, "A secret peace summit? Here? That's the dumbest thing I've ever heard in my life."

And with that, the audience was over.

"Then I ask permission to withdraw," said Ambassador Lövenstierna, backing out of the Supreme Leader's gigantic office.

And that would probably have been the end of that. If it weren't for Allan Karlsson.

The Indian Ocean

Captain Pak Chong-un took the only empty chair left at the table in the first mate's quarters. Allan and Julius were already sitting in the other two chairs.

The captain took out a pen and paper and began by inquiring what the gentlemen's names were, where they were from, and why they had chosen to float around in a woven basket fifty nautical miles from land.

This was the sort of thing Allan was best at, Julius thought, and said nothing. Allan didn't think much. Instead he said a lot.

"My name is Allan. And this is my best friend Julius. He's an asparagus farmer. I'm not anything, except old. I'm a hundred and one today, can you imagine?"

Captain Pak could imagine. He thought that this interrogation had got off to a difficult start. There was something carefree about the man who claimed to be older than should be reasonably possible. It made the interrogator both anxious and watchful.

"Well, Mr. Allan can be as old as he likes," said Captain Pak. "Where are you from and what are you doing here?"

"What are we doing here?" said Allan. "Please, dear captain, you're the one who doesn't want to let us off."

"No quibbling," said Captain Pak. "It's possible that I will let you off before you even know it. It probably wouldn't take more than ten, twelve days to swim from here to East Timor, if that's what you'd prefer."

No, neither Allan nor Julius would prefer that. Instead Allan explained that a birthday celebration on Bali had gone awry. They were supposed to take a hot-air balloon trip over the island, but instead the wind had changed and the balloon come loose. By the time the captain and his boat had done them the kindness of passing by, only the basket was left. Allan supposed it had looked very odd indeed, but there's an explanation behind everything.

"Isn't that so?" he said.

"What's that?" said the captain.

"That everything has an explanation. Everything really does—don't you sometimes think that too, Captain?"

Julius looked at Allan in concern. He tried to communicate that it might not be advisable to run his mouth so much: the captain still had the chance to throw them overboard.

"So you're saying you're Indonesians?" Captain Pak asked skeptically.

"No, we're from Sweden," said Allan. "A lovely country. Have you been there, Captain? No? Well, a visit would absolutely be worth considering. Snow in the winter and long days in the summer. Nice people too. Generally speaking, that is. There are certainly some we could have done without, even in our country. I had a frightfully bad-tempered director at the old folks' home where I lived before we ended up here. In Bali, I mean. I shudder to think of her. Perhaps you understand what I'm talking about, Captain?"

The captain was displeased that the old man was sending questions back across the table. If he didn't watch out, he would lose control of the situation.

"Let's start from the beginning."

And he wrote down Allan's and Julius's full names, nationalities, and business. Their business was, in fact, *nothing*. It hadn't been their intention to float around on the sea. As Captain Pak decided to believe their story, he also began slowly to believe he would survive this chapter of his life.

The interrogation paused at a knock on the door. The terrified sailor outside had been tasked with asking if there was a chance they would be serving the guests dinner. The captain thought that would be fitting. If fifteen or twenty minutes suited.

"Is there still a ban on alcohol?" Allan wondered, after the sailor had left.

The captain confirmed that there was. With their food they would be served water and tea.

"Tea," said Allan. "Captain, are you really sure you wouldn't like to drop us off somewhere along the way?"

"That would put both our cargo and my life in jeopardy. If you behave yourselves, you may accompany us to the Democratic People's Republic."

"If we behave ourselves?"

"Exactly. There, the Supreme Leader will take care of you in the best way possible."

"The way he took care of his brother not long ago?" Allan asked.

Julius swore internally. Couldn't the old man control himself? Did he *want* to become shark food?

Captain Pak might not have had a black tablet like Allan's, but he did have access to news from all corners of the world as long as he was at sea. He was aware of the accusations in the international media and said angrily that Mr. Karlsson had clearly allowed himself to be taken in by imperialist propaganda. "*No Korean leader would kill either relatives or visitors from other countries.*"

For one second, Julius entertained the vain hope that the 101-year-old would back down. When that second had passed, Allan said: "Oh yes they would. The only reason I'm sitting here today is that Mao Zedong saved my life a few years back, when Kim Il-sung intended to have me shot. As it happens, Mao himself had a change of heart at the last moment."

What was Captain Pak Chong-un hearing? So much was wrong, all at the same time. A Caucasian blaspheming the name of the Eternal President of the Republic. The president who had stepped into said eternity twenty-three years previously.

"A few years back?" said Captain Pak, waiting for his thoughts to fall into order.

"Oh, time flies. It was 1954, I think. When Stalin was putting on airs. Or was it fifty-three?"

"Mr. Karlsson, you . . . met the Eternal President of the Republic?"

"Yes, him and his angry boy both. But, of course, they've both sailed on since then—not everyone can simply grow healthier with age, like me. Aside from my memory, that is. And my hearing. And my knees. And something else. I've forgotten—the memory part, you know."

Captain Pak realized that the risk to his own life was not at all in the past. The man before him might constitute a direct threat to his health. For him to bring someone who might possibly have denigrated the Eternal President to Pyongyang could not reasonably lead to anything other than . . . other than what the imperialists claimed had afflicted the Supreme Leader's brother.

Then again: to take the life of someone who had sat down with the Eternal President without first double-checking with that leader's grandson . . .

Rock or hard place? Captain Pak weighed his options.

Julius was, to his own surprise, still conscious. Did Allan understand how high the stakes were, or was he just old? Whichever it was, the 101-year-old had talked himself into a state in which the captain's threat to throw them overboard was more topical than ever.

Julius considered how he might salvage the situation and heard himself saying, "Allan here is a great champion of freedom for the Democratic People's Republic. And an expert in nuclear weapons, too. Isn't that right, Allan?"

Captain Pak stopped breathing for a few seconds. He automatically brought his right hand to the safe key around his neck to make sure it was still there. *A nuclear weapons expert?* he thought.

Allan was thinking the same thing. He was afraid he had played a little too offensively against the suspected teetotaler across the table. And, as things were, it was best to play along with the make-believe his friend had started. "That was kindly put, Julius. Yes, I suppose we're experts just about to a man, but in different areas. My speciality happens to be slapping together what we called atom bombs in the good old days. I'm almost as good at that as I am at making vodka out of goat's milk. But, as I've understood it, vodka won't win me any points on this ship. And, anyway, I don't suppose there are any goats aboard."

Allan noticed the captain's hand seeking something around his neck whenever nuclear weapons were mentioned. That might, of course, have been mere chance. Or perhaps it explained somehow why he looked so tormented. The 101-year-old had done some reading on the North Korean atomic weapons program. Why, just a few days earlier, Kim Jong-un had sent a missile over the Sea of Japan, provoking fury from the rest of the world. This had prompted the old dynamiter to update himself via the black tablet, where you could read absolutely anything if you only knew where to look.

It turned out a lot had happened on the atom bomb front in the seventy-plus years since Allan had last had reason to delve into the topic. But the North Koreans seemed to be far from leaders in the field. "Beginners" would be a better word. International pundits guessed that the country's plutonium facilities hadn't yet succeeded in delivering what they were meant to.

Should Allan mention this to the captain and see what sort of reaction he got? With a tiny *promise* embedded to be on the safe side? His and Julius's options were no longer to be let off in Indonesia or North Korea, if they ever had been. Instead they would be let off in North Korea or tossed over the railing. North Korea sounded more pleasant. "Like I said, nuclear weapons and I are the best of friends. And you seem to have plenty of problems."

Captain Pak's hand immediately went back to the key.

Allan went on: "Judging by the puny strength of your country's first nuclear weapons tests, either you haven't quite figured out plutonium production or you have a severe lack of uranium. Or maybe both. One issue, when it comes to uranium, might be that you don't understand how to maximize it. That's what usually happens to nuclear weapons bunglers in general. No wonder people are laughing at you."

"Who's laughing at us?" Captain Pak said defensively.

"Who isn't?" Allan said, and Julius prayed silently to himself that Allan would stop there.

But Allan had caught a scent. The captain wasn't protesting at Allan's account of things: instead he was lamely arguing about the *laughter*. Had Allan hit the mark more accurately than he could have guessed? "Uranium," he said, feeling his way forward.

That was it. Nothing more. And once again.

"Uranium."

Now the captain's hand, clutching the key, almost turned white.

"Why do you keep saying 'uranium' all the time?" he asked angrily and uncertainly all at once.

"Because anyone who has two plutonium facilities at their disposal and still shoots off toy bombs likely has a problem. Anyone who can't produce their own plutonium must seek solace in—you guessed it— uranium."

Captain Pak tried to bring his hand to the key again, only to discover it was already there. Allan told the captain not to look so terrified. Surely it was no surprise that the world's leading nuclear weapons expert, all humility aside, would understand the situation.

One person who didn't was Julius. Had Allan become a mind reader?

"What situation?" said Captain Pak, fearing the answer.

Allan was on the verge of betting that the captain's boat was full of smuggled uranium. But if he was wrong, matters would deteriorate. "Let's not spend too much time on the obvious," he said. "This sort of thing is best dealt with discreetly. But the captain will have to make his decision soon. Either Julius and I will come to Pyongyang and whip your puny attempts at nuclear weapons into shape. Or you will have to throw us overboard and justify it to the Supreme Leader after the fact."

Captain Pak wanted to bury the two gentlemen a few thousand yards below the sea. At the same time, the older one knew so much. Perhaps more than the republic's own experts. How patriotic would it be to feed the fish with all that knowledge?

Allan could tell that the captain hadn't yet made up his mind. He gave it an extra go. "I believe this is your lucky day, Mr. Lackey of a Captain. Let's do this, for the good of everyone."

And he promised to tell the Supreme Leader of the Democratic People's Republic everything he knew about the technology behind the new hetisostat pressure.

"Hetistosat . . . ?" Captain Pak attempted.

"Almost," said Allan. "Twice the power for a quarter the uranium, in short. Or, alternatively, the same amount but eight times the power. With my help, you could blow half of Japan sky-high without losing more than a few pounds. Although I don't recommend it. The Japanese who were still around would be furious, I can tell you that much right now. And the Americans too, I'm sure, although they were once out to do the same thing. With a certain amount of success."

"Hetistosat . . ." Captain Pak tried again, but Allan hushed him.

"That's not something that should be said aloud, Captain, even if you could get the pronunciation right."

Captain Pak sat quietly in his chair, apparently awaiting Allan's instructions about what to do next.

Well, first of all the captain must immediately revoke that fussy rule against alcohol. If he wanted to join in and share the champagne with Allan and Julius he could; otherwise he didn't have to. If by chance there happened to be anything else good to drink hidden in the captain's quarters, he was more than welcome to bring it out so the champagne wouldn't feel lonely.

"Revoke the ban on alcohol?" the captain said.

"Be quiet and let me finish."

Julius closed his eyes as Allan snapped at the man who held their lives in his hands.

Allan went on to say that he would prefer to sleep in a separate room from Julius, as his friend tended to be a noisy sleeper, but in the interest of healthy cooperation he was able to overlook this. The captain should, however—once the bit about alcohol had been dealt with—get in touch with the Supreme Leader; Allan suggested doing so in an encrypted manner.

"Say that you've snagged the solution to all his problems, and that the Democratic People's Republic shall blossom like never before, thanks to hetisostat pressure and your resourcefulness. The Korean nuclear weapons program will reach heights you never thought possible. Given the part about the champagne, that is. And the rest."

Captain Pak made notes on his paper.

"Het-iso-stat pressure," said Allan. "Hetisostat pressure one thousand two hundred is between sixty and eighty GDM more than the USA itself can produce. And that is *double* the pressure of Russia's capacity."

"GDM," said Captain Pak, still writing.

"*Double*, Mr. Captain. Can you even comprehend such a thing?"

No, the captain couldn't. Neither could Julius. Nor even could Allan, as it turned out, once the friends were alone once more.

"I suppose I invented more than I actually needed to," he said.

"Oh? How much was that?" asked Julius.

"All of it."

Captain Pak made no promises as he left the friends' cabin. No more than that he would "process things."

To some extent he had already made his decision. The situation remained potentially fatal for him, but the potential upsides for the Democratic People's Republic, and by extension himself, were great. To touch a hair on the head of, or even displease, the man who possessed the solution of the hetisostat-something technique would presumably be very stupid.

The captain felt that he had reached his conclusion. As far as he could, anyway. Soon he would sit down and formulate the to-be-encrypted message to his Supreme Leader. There was only one thing he needed to take care of first.

Ten minutes after the captain had left Allan and Julius to do his processing, there was a cautious knock at the gentlemen's door. It was an on-duty watch sailor, who, with a greeting from Captain Pak Chong-un, handed over, first, the bottle of champagne, and, second, one of dark Cuban rum. Then he asked in Russian what else the gentlemen would like to drink with their meal.

"I think we have enough to get by for now, thank you," said Allan. "If you like you could have our tea."

The sailor bowed and made his exit. He left the tea. A few minutes later he was back with a meal of stewed meat and rice.

The friends gorged themselves. But the question was, with what would they wash down their food?

"I think we should start with the rum," said Allan. "And have the champagne for dessert. Perhaps we could have used the tea to brush our teeth, if only we had brought toothbrushes. We can save thinking up something clever about hetisostat pressures and GDM for tomorrow."

"We?" said Julius.

The Indian Ocean

The encrypted report from the captain of *Honor and Strength* was absolutely sensational. Kim Jong-un read it himself and drew his own conclusions. He had certain similarities to Trump in Washington in that he was reluctant to delegate tasks in his administration. With the possible difference that Trump drew conclusions without doing the actual reading.

The captain had managed to spell the nonexistent phrase "hetisostat pressure" correctly. And he had got the meaningless acronym GDM in the right order. But in the captain's formulation, the international expert Allan Karlsson happened to become Swiss instead of Swedish.

Perhaps this was lucky, given what was to come. A Swedish foreign minister who wanted to talk nuclear weapons, and an equally Swedish nuclear weapons expert a few days later, might have been too much for a conspiracy theorist's brain.

Instead the entire situation landed within the realm of likelihood, and Kim Jong-un could see potential.

Honor and Strength would reach the harbor outside Pyongyang in a few days. What if one were to . . . , said Kim Jong-un to himself. And agreed. A PR war was still war. With the help of the UN and the Swiss man, the republic could, within a few days, begin to matter extraordinarily in this area.

The Supreme Leader summoned his secretary from outside the door, with a curt order: "Get the Swedish ambassador here."

"Yes, Supreme Leader. When, Supreme Leader?"

"Now."

"The Supreme Leader wished to speak with me," said Ambassador Lövenstierna when, under an hour later, he found himself in Kim Jong-un's palace.

"Not so much *with* you as *to* you," said Kim Jong-un. "I have decided to invite the UN Security Council to informal talks. What was her name again, the one who wanted to come here?"

"Minister for Foreign Affairs Margot Wallström," said Ambassador Lövenstierna.

"That's right. Bring her here, as I said. Immediately."

Ambassador Lövenstierna nodded in acknowledgment. "Then I ask permission to withdraw," he said, for the second time in twenty-four hours.

And once again he backed out of the Supreme Leader's office. Whatever he was thinking, he kept it to himself.

Tanzania

Unlike their American colleagues, the Germans were not particularly good at outer space. But they were good on the ground—not least when it was African. The German equivalent to the CIA, the *Bundesnachrichtendienst*, had placed one of its many worldwide nonexistent offices inside a hairdresser's in central Dar es Salaam. Work there was led by a self-involved, unpleasant but capable male agent. For assistance he had a meek, depressed, and slightly more capable woman.

Through months of working on a dubious laboratory assistant in Congo, as well as patient network-building in environments where people were particular about portraying themselves as something other than they were, the BND had cobbled together some clear indications that a limited amount of enriched uranium would soon make its way out of Congo, through Tanzania, and on to the south.

But unfortunately, a couple of holidays got in the way. Among the few things that might be more important to the arrogant Agent A than saving the world was to travel home to Germany over Christmas and New Year's in order to salvage whatever he could of his family.

The meek Agent B reconciled herself to a break in their work and spent the holiday on her own inside the salon in Dar es Salaam. She had no family to go home to, since her spouse in Rödelheim had exchanged her for a younger woman with nicer teeth.

After the holidays were over they resumed their patient puzzle-piecing, day by day, week by week. The package seemed to have left Congo. And was transported on through Mozambique. This created plenty of concern, for the ruler there was a former freedom fighter, a Marxist-Leninist, and a buddy of Kim Jong-un in Pyongyang.

The arrogant man and the meek woman were getting closer to it. Apparently the uranium had been carried by fishing boat to Madagascar, off the east coast of Africa. This was a country that had formerly tight bonds with the blessedly late Soviet Union.

The trail went cold in Madagascar. And there were no further informants to turn to.

Agent A decided, in his capacity as the boss, that B should find out what was going on. The meek B did as she was told. After a brief period of analysis, she informed her boss that there were three potential scenarios for the uranium parcel in question. The least likely was that the isotope was still on Madagascar. Unless it had been sent on, either by plane or boat. Flying to or from Madagascar necessarily meant flying internationally. And to do this with more than a few pounds of uranium in your luggage would be tantamount to being discovered. Which left a boat—that was to say, the same method of transport by which the uranium had been brought *to* Madagascar. Repacking it and coming back the same way on a different fishing vessel didn't strike her as rational.

The meek woman's conclusion was that the uranium *had* left Madagascar by boat, but the size of the boat must be such that it could manage an ocean crossing. Either the Indian Ocean in one direction or the Atlantic in the other.

The arrogant man nodded, agreed, and made this line of reasoning his own in the subsequent report to Berlin, without protest from the meek woman.

The next step was to list all the cargo vessels that had

recently called at and sailed from the harbor in Toama-sina. When that didn't turn up any obvious hits, A and B expanded their search to encompass potentially sus-picious ships that had been anywhere near Madagascar during the period in question.

As a result, they were currently looking at a list of ships' names. It consisted of one: the North Korean bulk carrier *Honor and Strength*.

On its way from Havana to Pyongyang.

It had passed immediately south of Madagascar fif-teen days earlier.

The relationship between the Germans and the Amer-icans wasn't the best, ever since it had turned out that the Americans had bugged Chancellor Angela Merkel's cell phone, at which the chancellor picked up said phone and called President Obama to say she hoped the CIA was also listening to what she had to say now.

On the basis of his personality, as well as Germany's strained relationship with the United States, the BND's top central African representative had no problem lying through his teeth when explaining to his American col-league why he wanted help in determining the exact route and speed of the North Korean vessel *Honor and Strength*. As well as, of course, where the ship might currently be located.

The CIA, which was informed that it had to do with suspected industrial espionage on the car manufacturer Volkswagen in Brazil, told him what they knew. Without grumbling or delay, to boot. The blunder with the chancellor's phone meant that they would be indebted to the Germans for quite some time.

The North Korean ship had followed a route a little closer to the southern coast of Madagascar than was optimal. The various time stamps, as calculated from the CIA's satellite reports, also indicated that the ship had slowed down around there.

The German agents drew the conclusion that there was an immediate risk the uranium would soon wind up in North Korea, to be used for the nuclear weapons program that Germany, and the world in general, had condemned.

They had to hurry!

Or, as it turned out, they didn't.

Honor and Strength had, two hours earlier, reached North Korean waters and would arrive in the harbor at Nampo later that day.

North Korea

Uranium or plutonium? Plutonium or uranium? Kim Jong-un wanted the answer to be plutonium, and it would have been, too, if the Russians had kept their centrifugal promise, or if the only person in the Northern Hemisphere who was a bigger screwup than the director of the Institute of Nuclear Energy in Pyongyang wasn't his colleague at the plutonium plant in Yongbyon. What they had accomplished, at great cost to the Democratic People's Republic, was certainly enough to be a slight annoyance to the Americans and their puppets scattered throughout the area, but it was far from anything that could demonstrate real might.

Therefore the Supreme Leader had first removed the plutonium director north of the capital, citing his incompetence—that is, treason. It was, of course, a correct decision, as were all decisions made by the Supreme Leader, but in practice it had not led to anything but the removed director being replaced by a man who essentially deserved the same. And the one in Pyongyang mostly kept slinking around with his back to the wall, terrified, for some reason.

All these things a person had to do himself. The Supreme Leader gave the order to purchase enriched uranium on the free market. Just seven or nine pounds to start. The purveyor the Russians had mentioned had to prove himself, and the method of smuggling had to be run in before any meaningful deliveries could be fulfilled. It would never do to obtain uranium for maybe a hundred million dollars, only to see the load seized by the devil himself.

A few pounds (or even half a ton) were far from sufficient to win a large-scale war, but that was never the intent. Naturally, Kim Jong-un realized that an attack on South Korea or Japan could not end in anything but destruction for all. More so if he reached the United States, or even just Guam.

At the same time, nine pounds (unlike half a ton) was too little for the true purpose, which was to prove themselves and make the dogs in Washington drop their ideas about doing what they'd already done in Iraq, Afghanistan, and Libya. History showed that countries that couldn't bite back were devoured. A happy side effect of the armament was that it allowed for an ever-brasher rhetoric, which in turn brought local fighting spirit to entirely new levels. In this way, the Supreme Leader became even more supreme.

Deep down, Kim Jong-un didn't believe in anything but himself, his dad, and his grandpa. Religion in the wider sense was forbidden in North Korea. Yet he was close to thinking that a higher power was involved, in that the one person on Earth he needed more than any other, for his purposes, had been found floating in a basket at sea just days before. Only to be scooped up by the very ship that was on its way home with the trial cargo of uranium. If this person was who he claimed to be, of course. That was a detail that remained to be investigated.

Anyway, scooped up he had been. And by a captain who proved able to think for himself. For that, the captain would be awarded a medal. And scrutinized a bit more closely by the director of Domestic Security. *To think for himself.* From there, it was a slippery slope toward planning a coup.

There was plenty of uranium out there, if you only had the contacts. And nowadays they did. Further-more, Kim Jong-un also loved the fact that the main distributor of the necessary uranium was the director of a plant in Congo that had been created by the Americans.

The dream, of course, would be a hydrogen bomb, but for that they would need, first, a functional production line of plutonium (which, again, the screwups hadn't yet managed to create) and then something totally, uniquely complicated where deuterium and tritium melted together into helium atoms at the same time as . . . something. Kim Jong-un's brain was too valuable to the nation for him to weigh it down with the sort of thing his researchers ought to be able to manage in an afternoon.

The advantage of a hydrogen bomb was that it would erase Japan and South Korea from the map in a single bang. The disadvantage was that the Democratic People's Republic would cease to exist thirty seconds later. But as long as malevolent Americans, Japanese, and South Koreans didn't completely understand that Kim Jong-un realized this, it would fulfill its function. If only it were possible to build.

The hydrogen bomb would have to wait. The plutonium facilities could continue not to deliver. Kim Jong-un had uranium on the way now—*and*, possibly, the man who knew the best way to make use of it.

All that was left to do was to let the world know.

North Korea

Since Kim Jong-un was never wrong, naturally he had not rushed off in youthful zeal after that encrypted message from the captain of *Honor and Strength*, the one about how the solution to his ongoing nuclear weapons problems was 101 years old and would soon arrive at the harbor in Nampo, forty miles south of Pyongyang.

Instead he settled down for a bit of reflection with his evening tea. Because, really, what was to say that the Swiss man Karlsson was who and what he said he was, other than that he'd said so himself?

According to the *Honor and Strength* captain's second, more detailed, report to the Supreme Leader, Karlsson seemed to have demonstrated a surprising amount of insight into the Democratic People's Republic's ongoing woes when it came to the production of plutonium. This was, of course, one piece of circumstantial evidence. Another was the fact that he was Swiss. The Supreme One had lived and studied in Switzerland when he was younger. A lot could be said about the Swiss. They were, to be sure, detestable capitalists, like just about everyone else, and a bit more so than almost everyone else. And they worshipped their bloody Schweizerfranc. As if it had anything the North Korean won didn't.

But in addition they were always on time, as if they all had Swiss clocks surgically installed in their heads. And they succeeded in every undertaking. Quite simply, a Swiss nuclear weapons expert could not be a fraud. Right?

There would have to be a double-check before the Swiss man was allowed in.

Thus it came to pass that Kim Jong-un contacted the director of the laboratory at the plutonium factory in Yongbyon, the one who had just replaced the boss who had disappeared some time earlier. The new man could not yet be held accountable for all the shortcomings of the factory, but that was only a matter of time. Now he was tasked with meeting the Swiss man as soon as he set foot on North Korean ground, and not allowing him access to the Supreme Leader until it was clear that he was what and who he ought to be.

Allan and Julius were escorted ashore in the harbor at Nampo and met by a middle-aged man in civilian clothing, who was flanked by six young, nervous soldiers.

"Messrs. Karlsson and Jonsson, I presume?" the man said in English.

"Well presumed," said Allan. "I'm Karlsson. And you? We were supposed to meet the Supreme Leader to offer our services. It seems to me that you are not he. In which case he is not you, I imagine."

The man in civilian garb was concentrating too hard on his task to allow himself to be distracted by Allan's exposition.

"You are correct that I am not the Supreme Leader. I am the director of the laboratory at one of the development plants of the Democratic People's Republic. We'll leave my name out of it. I have arranged a place for us to sit down and speak undisturbed. If the conversation goes as it should, the Supreme Leader awaits you afterward. Circumstances dictate that time is at a premium, so would you please be so kind as to follow me?"

The laboratory director didn't wait for an answer

before he began to walk to the harbor offices, while the six young soldiers surrounded Allan and Julius and made sure they followed.

Soon the trio had settled into a conference room that the harbor had kindly made available after a proposal from the Supreme Leader's staff. The six young soldiers were left outside the door.

"Let's begin. I turn to you, Mr. Karlsson, since you are the one who claims to be a nuclear weapons expert, willing to put your services at the disposal of the Democratic People's Republic. For that reason I have a few questions concerning your commitment to our cause, as well as what you believe you can contribute more specifically. In short, my task is to find out if you're a charlatan or not."

A charlatan? Allan thought. Surely it doesn't make you a charlatan just because you invent as much about yourself as necessity demands. "No, I'm no charlatan," he lied. "Just old. And well-traveled. A little hungry and thirsty. And something more too, I'm sure. By the way, Julius here is an asparagus farmer. Green asparagus, primarily."

Up to this point, Julius hadn't said a word. What could he say? He nodded cautiously, longing to be somewhere else. "Asparagus," he said. "Green, as you heard."

The laboratory director was not interested in Julius. Instead he leaned across the desk and looked Allan in the eye. "Lovely to hear that you're a truth-teller. I'd just like to remind you, Mr. Nuclear Weapons Expert, that I'm an expert myself. Nonsense and empty phrases about asparagus or anything else will not suffice. Are you ready for my questions? The first is about your motive in helping the Democratic People's Republic."

Julius prayed to the god he appropriately didn't believe in, considering the country he was in. *Please don't let Allan go too far.*

"Well, if we're being honest here, Mr. Laboratory Director must not be much of a nuclear weapons expert. My services would not be required otherwise. By 'development plant,' I assume you mean a plutonium factory. Is it the one to the north of the city you work at? Perhaps it doesn't matter, because you can't have sorted out any measurable amounts of weapons-grade plutonium."

Within just a few seconds, the laboratory director had lost control of the conversation. Allan went on: "Although there's no reason to be too upset about it— this business with plutonium is terribly difficult. I think you should switch to uranium. And I imagine you've probably already come to this realization on your own."

Any charlatan worth his salt radiates a level of confidence that's hard to defend oneself against. The laboratory director now had very little left of his original certainty. "Would you please answer the question?" he said curtly.

"I would be very happy to," said Allan. "But I'm a bit advanced in age and I have to confess I've forgotten what the question was."

The laboratory director had very nearly done the same, but he racked his brains and repeated it.

The answer to the question about why Allan wanted to help was basically that he didn't want to help at all. However, he had nothing against surviving his repeat visit to North Korea. With that in mind, perhaps it was best to adjust his tone. "All you have to do is look around, Mr. Laboratory Director," he said, pointing through the windows of the harbor offices.

The view was of a rundown industrial area. To the left of the rustiest warehouse stood a dead maple, representing the only greenery the scene had to offer.

"It's hard to beat the beauty of your democratic republic. The abundant nature. The devoted people. The struggle against an ever-crueller world. Someone must dare to take the side of peace and love. A few days ago, your country saved the lives of me and my friend Julius. The least we can do is pay back the favor as best we can. Our services are fully at your disposal. If you would like advice on how to optimize your asparagus operations, there's no better man for the job than Julius. If you happen to want to prioritize your optimization of whatever enriched uranium you may have lying around, then I'm your man."

On occasion, people function such that they hear what they want to hear and believe what they want to believe. The laboratory director nodded, decently satisfied with this truthful description of his country, while he said that the Democratic People's Republic intended mainly to avail itself of Karlsson's services, not Jonsson's. But to be more concrete? The reports said that Karlsson was an expert in *hetisostat pressure*? No matter how hard the laboratory director looked, he could not find any confirmation that such a thing existed. Much less any information about how it might work.

Julius prayed to God again.

Allan responded. "I remember it from my relative youth at Los Alamos in the United States. The Americans toiled day and night to build that atom bomb, until at last I had to step in and tell them what to do. But there isn't a single word about *that* on the internet, is there?"

No. The laboratory director had to acknowledge that there wasn't. And he understood that this wasn't only because the internet hadn't been invented until over forty years later.

"Hetisostat pressure was created by me, in a secret laboratory outside Geneva. Though it's not as secret now as it was until just a moment ago, before I talked about it. As you will know, Mr. Laboratory Director, the critical mass of enriched uranium of the grade in question is fifty-five pounds—fifty-five point five, to be exact. With my pressure, the neutrons are held in place many times longer, and the chain reaction gets another burst of strength over and over until you have destroyed what needs to be destroyed with a considerably smaller amount of the key isotope. Particularly suitable for someone who prefers to stick the nuclear weapon into a missile rather than carry around a bomb that weighs a few tons."

Allan had read something about twenty-five point two and sounded sufficiently sure of himself to make the laboratory director equally sure.

"But in greater detail?" he tried again.

"Greater detail? How many weeks do we have? Perhaps the Supreme Leader has no problem being made to wait. Although I think I speak for both myself and the asparagus farmer here beside me when I say that, if we're going to do this, we'll have to start with some food and a bed on top of that, or rather, two beds. We may be good friends, Julius and me, but we prefer to sleep separately. Once we're full and rested I'll be more than willing, even genuinely eager, to tell you what you want to know, Mr. Laboratory Director."

The 101-year-old was a gifted talker. The laboratory director knew what Allan suspected: that Kim Jong-un absolutely did not want to wait a week or two. Or even much more than an hour. A decision had to be made, and soon. The director had been given sanction to supply the two Swiss men with a shot to the back of the head each instead of food and a place to sleep, should the situation so demand. But he also had orders to allow them through if it was likely to be in the best interest of the nation.

So what should he do? It was true that the old man was a chatterbox. It was also true that he'd hit the mark when it came to the critical mass of uranium, and to the decimal besides. And he appeared to be completely assured about this situation.

The laboratory director picked up a cigarette and looked around for his lighter. Julius fished the hotel manager's from his pocket and offered it to him. The laboratory director thanked him, lit up, and took a deep drag.

After another of the same, the laboratory director made his hasty decision. "Hasty" being the operative word. The Supreme Leader had extended an invitation to the UN envoy and he wanted to bring her and the Swiss man together; the envoy would be landing any minute. There was no time to do anything but decide.

"We will absolutely run through every part of your pressure system," he said. "Make no mistake about that. But first I will ask to send you over to the Supreme Leader."

The laboratory director was displeased at having misplaced his lighter, but pleased that his voice had sounded so confident. Much more confident than he actually was. Or ever would be again, as long as he lived.

He summoned the six nervous soldiers and had them lead the foreigners to a waiting car.

Allan and Julius had made it through their encounter with mortal danger number one on Korean ground, their good health still intact. All that remained was everything else. Now they were sitting on either side of a North Korean soldier in the back seat of a 2004 Russian GAZ-3111, one of the nine specimens the Russians had produced that year before giving up, sending the crap to North Korea, and signing a contract with Chrysler instead.

"Good day, my name is Allan," Allan said to the soldier in Russian. He received no response. He went on to offer the same greeting to the two soldiers in the row of seats ahead of him and was met with the same silence. Then he looked at Julius and said he hoped the Supreme Leader would be more talkative, or it might be a boring afternoon.

Julius didn't reply, but he thought anyone who could use the word "boring" in their current situation must be missing a considerable part of his common sense. What Julius was doing now, placing his life in the hands of a completely carefree 101-year-old, was trying. He breathed heavily as he mentally counted backward from 999; he had learned that this sometimes helped.

A change in the air told Allan that something was weighing on Julius; what it might be was unclear. As his friend passed two hundred in his countdown self-help, Allan asked if it might cheer him up if Allan read something exciting from the black tablet.

One hundred eighty-seven, one hundred eighty-six . . . No, that question was too much. Julius interrupted himself and opened his eyes. "Goddammit!" he said. "We're going to be world news ourselves soon, if we don't look out. How about you focus on your fucking hetisostat pressure? In ten minutes you need to have something to say to the man who is in charge of our lives. Can't you put that bloody tablet down for one second and think about something useful?"

Allan had been looking at Julius, but now he aimed his gaze slightly to the left and out of the window.

"The 'ten minutes' part was wrong. I think we're here."

Allan and Julius were led into the holiest of holies, the Supreme Leader's office, 360 square yards in area, with fifty-foot-high ceilings. An oak desk across the room, a briefcase, an intercom, a quill, and a few documents on the desk, four paintings of the Eternal President on the wall, and that was it. The Supreme One himself was not present; the old men were left alone in the room for a brief time after their escorts hurried off and closed the double doors.

"You could fly a kite in here, if you could just get a cross-breeze from the windows," said Allan. "Almost a hot-air balloon, too."

"Think hetisostat pressure," said Julius. "Do you hear me? *Hetisostat pressure.*"

It was difficult to think about something that didn't exist, but this was a reflection with which Allan didn't want to trouble Julius. His friend seemed unbalanced enough as it was.

At that moment, a smaller door just past the desk opened. A soldier with a holstered pistol stepped in and stood guard. Behind him came the Supreme Leader. Noticeably short of stature, thought Allan.

"Please have a seat," said Kim Jong-un, pointing at two chairs on the other side of the desk even as he himself sat down.

"Thank you, Supreme Leader," Julius said, his words as nervous as they were fawning.

"Agreed," said Allan. "Is there anything tasty to drink to break the ice? We can hold off on the food for a bit, if that would be too much trouble."

Kim Jong-un had no need to break any ice. But, still, he ordered a pot of tea by way of his Soviet intercom from the seventies. The order arrived under a minute later, delivered by a North Korean soldier who, with a certain amount of difficulty, tried to combine a straight back with a level tray and an apology in Korean that might have expressed regret for the delay.

The Supreme Leader sent the soldier away and raised his cup to the guests.

"A toast to a long and fruitful cooperation. Or the opposite."

Allan pretended to drink. Julius drank, and felt concerned about the Supreme Leader's part in what they had just toasted. But when the terrible tea had sunk into his soul, he decided to allow Allan to continue saving their lives on his own. The 101-year-old certainly had his issues, but if there was anything he was good at, it was surviving. Then again, better safe than sorry. Julius did his best to put the ball in Allan's court in the hopes of benching himself.

"Supreme Leader," he said. "My name is Julius Jonsson and I am the executive assistant to the world's leading nuclear weapons expert, that is, my dear friend Allan Karlsson here. I will hereby gladly hand things over to him."

"Oh no you won't," said Kim Jong-un, with a smile. "This is my meeting, and I decide who speaks. You're the executive assistant, you say? Where are the other assistants?"

Julius immediately lost the speaking ability he had so briefly managed to muster. Allan noticed, and rushed to his assistance.

"Supreme Leader," he said, "I hereby request the right to say something important while my friend the executive assistant gathers his thoughts. *Very* important, even. Depending on how concerned you are about your country's future, of course."

Kim Jong-un was extremely concerned about his country's future. Not least because it was inextricably linked with his own. "Granted," he said, and with that, his grip on poor Julius loosened.

"Good," said Allan. "Then I'd like to begin by praising you for your out-and-out battle against the evil that surrounds you. You are furthering the legacy of your father and grandfather in an exemplary manner."

Julius still didn't dare to speak, but he was regaining a faint hope of survival. Allan was obviously in his rubbing-up-the-right-way mood!

"What do you know about that?" Kim Jong-un asked, in a defensive tone.

The truth was, Allan knew very little about Kim Jong-un's doings—no more than he'd read on his black tablet. And it wasn't always pretty. "I know all about it," he said. "But to sit here and praise your many accomplishments would take up far too much of your precious time."

It was true that time was precious. Or, at least, short. At any moment, the Swedish minister for foreign affairs, UN envoy Margot Wallström, would land at Sunan International Airport and, in that moment, the Supreme Leader's PR plan would enter a critical stage.

"Well, then," said Kim Jong-un. "Tell me this important thing you had to say. I assume it has to do with hetisostat pressure?"

"That's exactly right," said Allan. "My humble suggestion is that my assistant and I teach North Korea everything worth knowing about hetisostat pressure and, in return, you help us reach Europe after our task is completed. As fantastic as your country is . . . well, there's no place like home, as they say."

Kim Jong-un nodded and gave the impression that he felt the same. An arrangement of that sort didn't seem like too much trouble to sign off on, especially given that he had no intention of keeping his side of the bargain. If this man was as competent as he was old, he couldn't be allowed to loaf around Europe or anywhere else with his knowledge. It belonged permanently in the Democratic People's Republic. Period.

"Agreed!" said the Supreme Leader.

And then he openly stated that Karlsson and his assistant had nine pounds of enriched uranium to play with, with another eleven hundred on their way. Incidentally, the first nine pounds had arrived on the same boat as the gentlemen.

"Properly lead-encased," said Kim Jong-un, and with that he placed his hand on the brown briefcase on the desk. Annoyingly enough, there was no time at the present to hear what hetisostat pressure might achieve with the contents of the briefcase. An assistant had snuck into the room to whisper something into the Supreme Leader's ear.

"Thank you," said Kim Jong-un. "I would have liked to hear more about your pressure, but we must get moving. We're going to KCNA. All three of us. No, scratch that, we have no use for the executive assistant there, so we'll send him directly to the hotel."

Kim Jong-un stood up and signaled the gentlemen to follow him.

Julius didn't know which was worse—being forced to visit a mysterious jumble of letters with Kim Jong-un, or not being allowed to come.

"KCNA?" he whispered anxiously to Allan. "What's that?"

"I'm sure it is whatever it is," said Allan. "I hope that, unlike the tea, it can be drunk. Or at least eaten."

North Korea

Korea had held together as a united empire for 1,274 years. Then it had gone downhill fast. After the Second World War, the Americans and Russians couldn't agree on what the Koreans wanted, and neither thought it was an option to ask the Koreans. The Russians placed a Communist in power in the north; the Americans, an anti-Communist in the south. The guy in the north thought he had the right to all of Korea. The one in the south thought the same thing, but the other way around.

This led to the violence that history books call the Korean War. Of course there had been wars on the peninsula before, but people have such short memories.

After two million Koreans (plus the occasional foreigner) had died in battle, enough was enough. They pointed at a line in the ground (the same line that had been there since before the war) and decided that, until further notice, they would keep to their own sides.

The Communist in the north invented "self-reliance" as a political ideology, while his counterpart in the south, sensibly enough, did not label the dictatorship he created with any honest name.

Years passed. Leaders on both sides came and went, as leaders tend to do. The dictatorship in the south gradually lost its hold, while the self-reliance in the north prospered so extensively that people began to starve.

It's easy for someone who trusts only themselves to become suspicious of others. When the south allowed American tactical nuclear weapons to be placed on their side of the border, those in the north took it all wrong. At least from an arms reduction perspective.

The Swedish manufacturer Volvo, outside Gothenburg, was full of celebration after the delivery of a thousand shiny new cars to Pyongyang. This celebration later turned out to be premature. For the North Koreans had rearranged their priorities. They chose to build test sites for nuclear weapons instead of paying what they owed. To this day, Volvo hasn't received a single North Korean won in return.

Despite one thing and the next, there were some cross-border talks. Surely a solution could be reached. Yes, perhaps. For a while, in the early childhood of the current century, things were looking very bright indeed.

But back to the part about how leaders come and go. In 2017, tensions were higher than ever between the north on the one hand, and most of the rest of the world on the other. The latest in the series of leaders who had come, but not yet gone, were named Kim Jong-un and Donald J. Trump. And caught in the middle was the Swedish UN envoy Margot Wallström.

She had no illusions that her task would be an easy one.

The envoy and her plane landed at Sunan International Airport ten minutes ahead of the scheduled time. The Supreme Leader was informed and, as planned, he immediately adjourned the ongoing meeting with Messrs. Karlsson and Jonsson.

Wallström was shown to a limousine and informed that the Supreme Leader awaited. Her baggage would be transported to the prebooked hotel or the Swedish embassy, depending on which the envoy preferred.

The journey took her south toward central Pyongyang. After forty minutes the limousine passed the

Supreme Leader's palace and continued toward downtown.

"Excuse me, but weren't we going to see the Supreme Leader?" said Minister for Foreign Affairs Wallström.

"That is correct," the driver responded, without expounding further.

Ten minutes later, in any case, the journey was over. The minister for foreign affairs was invited out of the limousine and led into an eight-story building.

"Where are we?" she asked her smiling female escort in bewilderment.

"This is the main office of the news bureau KCNA. The Supreme Leader awaits."

A news bureau? Margot Wallström felt ill at ease. After all, this trip was supposed to take place under the greatest discretion so that it didn't spur even greater polarization between the parties. On the other hand, this was probably a country where no news bureau would dare to report on her presence without first obtaining the blessing of the Supreme Leader. Perhaps her worry was unfounded.

Their journey continued three stories up, down a long hallway, to the left, right, and left again.

"Here we are," said the escort. "Please step in."

If Margot Wallström had been expecting crystal chandeliers and velvet chairs, she was disappointed.

This was more like . . . Well, what was this? The anteroom of a theater stage? A TV studio? There were cables running along the sides, two discarded spotlights in one corner, and . . .

There he was.

"Welcome, Madame Minister for Foreign Affairs," the Supreme Leader said kindly. "Was the trip okay?"

"Yes, thank you. Very nice to meet you, but I have to ask . . . Where are we, and what are we doing here?"

"Why, we're going to save the world together," said Kim Jong-un. "But right now, you must meet the man to whom I myself have hardly even had time to say hello."

Allan Karlsson was shoved out from behind a curtain and walked over to greet Minister for Foreign Affairs Wallström.

"This is the world's perhaps pre-eminent expert in nuclear weapons, Mr. Karlsson from Switzerland. He has come to the Democratic People's Republic out of love for our common cause."

Minister for Foreign Affairs Margot Wallström found herself in a situation out of her control. But she took the old Swiss man's hand on Kim Jong-un's urging.

"Good day," said the minister, hesitantly and in English.

"Good day yourself," said Allan, 100 percent in Swedish and with a faint Sörmland accent.

There was no reaction from Kim Jong-un when he didn't understand the nuclear weapons expert's greeting, but Margot Wallström realized to her horror that a *Swedish* man, not a Swiss, was apparently about to upgrade North Korea's nuclear weapons arsenal. What was going on?

Karlsson, was that his name? Minister for Foreign Affairs Wallström refrained from beginning to speak Swedish with him. He had, after all, been introduced as Swiss and the very best thing she could do right now was to feel her way through the situation.

The Supreme Leader lightly clapped both Allan and the UN envoy on the back and said he was looking forward to a dinner together in the palace that same evening. Karlsson's executive assistant Jonsson was invited as well.

Jonsson? That didn't sound particularly Swiss either.

"But we'll start with the press conference," said Kim Jong-un, signaling to a man with a headset who, in turn, spoke into his microphone.

Suddenly a round of applause began very close by. So they were backstage. *A press conference?*

"But, Supreme Leader, we can't talk to the media and keep our conversation discreet at the same time. I don't feel this is something we agreed upon," said Margot Wallström.

Kim Jong-un laughed. "Naturally we won't say a word about the contents of any conversations. How could we? We haven't had any yet."

No, this was well within the scope of the parties' common ambitions. As the leader of the Democratic People's Republic, Kim Jong-un had a responsibility to his people, the dignity of which perhaps Minister for Foreign Affairs Wallström did not fully comprehend. "It's called 'transparency,' Madame Wallström."

"Well, howdy-do," Allan said in Swedish.

Who *was* he? He was as old as the hills, clearly Swedish, alleged to be Swiss, and devoted to North Korea's nuclear weapons–related future. And his respect for his employer seemed to be moderate at best.

Out onstage, a woman had begun to speak Korean before the audience, which had temporarily stopped applauding. Then she switched to English.

"And with that I would like to welcome the UN envoy and minister for foreign affairs for the kingdom of Sweden, Madame Wallström—as well as the world's leading nuclear weapons expert, devoted friend of the Democratic People's Republic, straight from Switzerland: Mr. Allan Karlsson."

Kim Jong-un led Wallström and Karlsson to the

edge of the stage, where he stopped while the guests had to continue. Neither of them was given any choice but to step into the spotlights that shone down from four directions. They were guided to their respective marks on one side of a table and received polite applause from the audience. Margot Wallström was not at all a fan of the situation she found herself in.

Allan looked around and discovered at least three TV cameras aimed at them. "Why, this is my first time on TV," he said to the minister in Swedish, before they had made it all the way to the table and the microphones.

The host began by turning to the UN envoy.

"You're here, Madame Wallström, because the UN and the Democratic People's Republic share a common concern about the proliferation of nuclear weapons in the world, and about the tough rhetoric that so often flies from one side to the other."

Yes. Thus far Margot Wallström was more or less on the same page.

"Or from the other side to this one," she clarified. "It's a mutual problem."

"Tell me, Madame Wallström, what do you think of our country, from what you've seen so far?"

What Margot Wallström had seen so far was no more than the airport and a few glances at the North

Korean countryside and cityscape on her way into downtown Pyongyang. The countryside appeared poor but not shabby. In the city, the streets were wide, devoid of cars, edged by various monuments. The cult of personality was plain to see.

Like the diplomat she was, she responded by saying that she hoped to get the chance to enjoy the country before it was time to go home again; it struck her as both green and beautiful. The weather was also quite welcoming.

By the latter, the typical Swede means it's above freezing, which it was.

The host nodded. "Yes," she said. "Our motto is 'a powerful and prosperous nation.' I see that you understand why, Madame Minister for Foreign Affairs."

She did not wait for any response from Margot Wallström but turned to Allan. "And Mr. Allan Karlsson. The world's leading expert in hetisostat pressure one thousand two hundred. In possession of knowledge he would now like to share with the Democratic People's Republic in the name of peace. What do *you* think of our beautiful country?"

"Well, this isn't my first time here," said Allan. "I had business here way back in the days of the Eternal President. It seems to me the roadblocks aren't as numerous today as they were back then."

Kim Jong-un signaled that he wished to be called onstage. As it happened, the host had prepared another question for the Swiss man, but the Supreme Leader didn't trust that the old man would answer as he should. Roadblocks? What kind of talk was that?

The presentation of the Supreme Leader appeared to be magnificent. Exactly what was said was impossible to know for anyone who didn't speak Korean. But now the formerly lukewarm audience stood up and gave an intense round of applause.

Kim Jong-un nodded first at the minister for foreign affairs, then the Swiss man, and joined them at the table.

The audience continued to applaud.

And more applause. It didn't stop until the Supreme Leader ordered it to with his own hand. The host was able to make herself heard once more.

"Supreme Leader," she said. "You are the world's foremost champion of peace. How do you view the possibility that the aforementioned world would be a better place to live in under your leadership?"

Kim Jong-un nodded thoughtfully. A very good question. Almost as if he had come up with it himself. Which he had. "Peace between two parties presupposes cooperation by all. I cannot bring about peace on my own. I need help. Peace will come only when everyone wants it. It is with great sorrow I must say that the United States of America and its allies are instead trying to drive us all to destruction. But I do what I can, I do what I can. Hope is the last thing to abandon each individual in the Democratic People's Republic. And I am glad we have the United Nations on our side in this struggle, represented here by Madame Wallström, who is also the minister for foreign affairs in the neutral country of Sweden. With the help of the equally neutral nation of Switzerland—represented by Mr. Karlsson, as previously mentioned—the ultimate in nuclear strength can in the long term be relocated from the warmongers in Washington, Tokyo, and Seoul to here, the center of peace and love."

Minister Wallström was about to flip out. Was that bastard standing there and placing the neutral countries of Sweden and Switzerland on the side of North Korea in a nuclear arms race? And where was this being broadcast? Wherever it was, it would become an international story at any moment.

"May I say something?"

"Yes, that is certainly the intent here," said Kim Jong-un. "We will begin our demanding work this very evening. The Democratic People's Republic, the UN, and the countries of Sweden and Switzerland, which have so proudly refused to fall in line with the North American hawks."

The host realized that the show was over. She thanked her leader with a reverent bow and said she did not want to spend any more time standing in the way of the important work of the Supreme Leader and the others.

"Go, Supreme Leader, in the name of peace. And feel the love of your people. Take your friends with you. Our love extends to them as well."

Once again backstage, a very pleased Kim Jong-un said that everything had gone very well, didn't Minister for Foreign Affairs Wallström agree?

No, she did not.

"With all respect, Supreme Leader, what we just experienced was *not* part of our agreement, and it complicates rather than facilitates our upcoming talks."

Kim Jong-un smiled. "Oh, yes, our talks. I think one will be enough. As I said, you are welcome to the palace this evening for an early dinner. Now you will be escorted to your hotel and picked up again at around seventeen hundred hours. Do be sure to make the most of the fantastic service at Ryugyong until then. According to many reviewers, it is the best hotel in the world."

The minister, as annoyed as she was bewildered, was herded back through the hallways alongside the Swiss-Swedish Karlsson. At last they found themselves alone in the back seat of Wallström's limousine. There was no way the driver could hear what they said or in which language they said it. Once the car had gone a few hundred yards, the minister for foreign affairs thought the time was right.

"I must say I find myself curious about a few things," she said quietly to Allan, in Swedish.

"I can imagine," said Allan. "What might be the most curious part? We can start there and work our way down. Or up, whichever it is."

Margot Wallström had actually been planning to stay at the embassy, but she needed more time with the remarkable man beside her. "Then let's start with how it happens that a Swede pretending to be Swiss finds himself in Pyongyang on business, with a purpose diametrically opposed to the one I am here to represent."

"Good question," said Allan. "And well formulated. I don't think I'll start from the beginning, because we would never finish. That's how old I am. Let me instead begin with my hundred-and-first birthday on a beautiful white-sand beach on Bali in Indonesia."

And then came the story of the hot-air balloon. The crash into the sea. The rescue. The white lie about hetisostat pressure to survive at least in the short term, and the arrival in Pyongyang as recently as a few hours before her own. How he had become Swiss, he didn't know. As far as he could remember, he had never been to Switzerland. "But I hear it's lovely. And the Swiss are said to be orderly to a fault."

"Yes," said the minister. "But the question is, how happy will they be now that they've got a presumed traitor on their hands?"

"They have?"

"You, Mr. Karlsson."

"Oh, that's what you meant."

Ryugyong Hotel was an impressive creation, eleven hundred feet and 105 stories tall. The North Koreans had been building it since 1987 without ever finishing it. It was slow going, since the state coffers were substantially used up by the production of nuclear weapons and military parades. After three decades, they hadn't yet built more than the lobby and the first floor. At this rate, it would take another fifteen hundred years for the whole building to be finished.

Yet the ground floor was stylish. It consisted of a golden reception desk to the right, offering space for up to twelve simultaneous check-ins or check-outs, and a tastefully decorated piano bar to the left, with three pianists engaged to cover the better part of each day. Thus far the budget had not allowed for the acquisition of a piano, but it was a priority.

Julius was sitting on the edge of the bed in room 104, waiting for Allan to return from the alphabet soup KCNA. Since it was impossible to imagine what that place might be, he was succeeding, for the moment, in repressing the situation they had found themselves in. Instead he was thinking about his asparagus partner down in Bali. To be sure, that wasn't much fun either. Now Gustav had to handle the operation all on his own. What would come of it?

There was a telephone on the nightstand. Could it possibly be functional, in contrast to the hotel's eight elevators? It was worth a try.

He called his business partner, the Indian Gustav Svensson. The call went through, but instead of a ringtone followed by Gustav, voicemail took over.

Julius recorded a few irritated sentences. In his haste, he forgot to mention that he was still alive, but perhaps his partner would work that out for himself.

Then he took off his shoes and lay down on the bed. He yawned and closed his eyes, trying to aim his thoughts in a direction other than that of asparagus and alphabet soup.

It didn't work.

South Korea

How's the asparagus?

Three deliveries this month too?

Any return shipments?

Will we make it to five hundred million before the year is half out?

On the top floor of a fourteen-story building in the city of Goyang, northwest of the South Korean capital, a man and a woman wearing headphones sat in front of quadruple computer screens and various instruments. Both were civil servants. Nothing remarkable so far, except possibly the location: a simple two-bedroom apartment. And the fact that the state served by the civil servants was not the Republic of Korea but Germany.

The woman was a low-ranking diplomat; the man

was the same, only a little lower. Officially they were involved in a number of German-Korean housing projects, but they were seldom seen in such contexts. Instead they sat where they sat on order of the *Bundesnachrichtendienst,* the BND. They were distant colleagues to an arrogant site director and his meek colleague in Dar es Salaam.

The two fake diplomats' primary task, in the apartment in Goyang, was to make recordings of the Americans' wiretaps in North Korea. By doing so they avoided having to do the job themselves, and also got a dash of pleasure out of it. Winding up American intelligence services was one of life's little joys.

One of their easier targets was the permanently unfinished showpiece Ryugyong Hotel in Pyongyang. Seldom, bordering on never, did anything of interest come from there.

Today was an exception.

From room 104, a guest unknown to the BND had left a message on a powered-down cell phone in Indonesia that belonged to an equally unknown recipient. The message was in English, in code, and consisted of four questions.

How's the asparagus?

Three deliveries this month too?

Any return shipments?

Will we make it to five hundred million before the year is half out?

What asparagus was code for, the fake diplomats couldn't say. But the sum—five hundred million!—suggested narcotics or worse. The Germans knew that a small load of enriched uranium had just reached Pyongyang. It could hardly have cost half a billion. But what if this was a case of several ongoing deliveries? Such as three? Per month?

What was Kim Jong-un *up* to? Was he planning to start a war with the whole world? And where was he getting the money? Five hundred fucking million dollars! And 104 unfinished floors in the country's only luxury hotel.

More questions without answers. A return shipment? What, in that case, was supposed to be transported *out of* North Korea? And how? And where was it going? Indonesia? Well, shit.

North Korea

Julius was involuntarily imprisoned in the capital of North Korea, and he longed for the peace and petty thievery he had known back on Bali. His goal of five hundred million rupiah—almost forty thousand dollars—had been realistic once, but perhaps not now that he wasn't there to keep an eye on things.

On the other hand, his and Allan's debts to the hotel and the boat-renter were much greater than that. In this sense it was economically advantageous to keep their distance, although visiting North Korea was certainly overdoing it.

When this mess was all over, perhaps they could move the asparagus operation to an area where they didn't owe anyone any money.

"Thailand?" Julius said aloud, just as the door opened.

Allan held it open and allowed Minister for Foreign Affairs Margot Wallström to enter first. "Allow me to introduce my friend Julius Jonsson," said Allan. "He's single, if the minister feels so inclined."

Margot Wallström shot an angry look at Allan. "Thanks, but no thanks. I have been happily married for over thirty years."

Julius greeted the minister with the comment that she would have to forgive Allan. It must have to do with his age. The strangest things came out of his mouth sometimes. Most of the time, really.

Minister Wallström nodded and said she had noticed as much.

In the limousine after the horrid press conference, she had formed an approximate idea about Karlsson and Jonsson. The 101-year-old really did seem to be a nuclear weapons expert, or at least he had been once upon a time. The only good news of the day was that he aspired *not* to help Kim Jong-un.

The truly bad part was that he had no plans about how to avoid doing so.

The general impression in the UN building was that North Korea had the capacity for nuclear weapons but so far that capacity was limited; the Supreme Leader was trying to make such a rumpus that no one would notice. In any case, the threat was real. Nuclear weapons are so powerful, of course, that even a small, half-failed load could destroy an entire city. Like Seoul, for example. Or Tokyo. Or a whole island, like Guam.

Margot Wallström shuddered at the thought. And at the apparent truth that the man who could sort out the North Korean nuclear weapons program was in this very hotel room, digging through the empty minibar. And, furthermore, he was Swedish. Was *Sweden* going to be the primary reason behind a shift in the balance of worldwide power?

No, she had to stop it happening if she could. Preferably without ending up imprisoned in this country for thirty years or more, accused of espionage or whatever the Supreme Leader happened to dream up.

"Do you think you could come with me on my plane out of here?" she asked. "Twenty-nine of the thirty seats in the cabin are available."

Julius lit up.

Allan stopped looking for liquor. "As empty as the minibar in this hotel room," he said. "The whole hotel, in fact."

The minister for foreign affairs went on. "I can try

to help you get diplomatic passports. I'm afraid you'll have to sort out the rest on your own."

"The rest?" said Julius.

"Getting to the plane when it's time to take off."

Allan hadn't listened beyond the first part of what had just been said. "Diplomatic passports?" he said. "I haven't had one of those since 1948, when Churchill and I flew home from Tehran together. Or forty-seven. No, forty-eight."

"*Winston* Churchill?" said the minister.

"Yes, that's his name. Or it was. I suppose he's been dead a long time, like most people."

The minister for foreign affairs suddenly felt as if she was in a movie. And it made her stomach hurt to think of what she was about to do. Espionage wouldn't be an entirely inaccurate charge. But she took portraits of Allan and Julius with her phone camera and promised them passports within a few days.

"Sign the back of my business card so they'll have something to go on at home."

She's one results-oriented woman, thought Julius. And delightful. Shame she's taken.

The Swedish UN representative had been assigned room 105, next door to Allan and Julius. Once she was in the room, ostensibly to prepare herself for the evening's dinner, she spent more time pondering how she could rescue the two Swedes *and* trick Kim Jong-un out of knowledge he shouldn't have. It seemed as if the Supreme Leader didn't want her around any longer than necessary, but she had to give Karlsson and Jonsson time to come up with a plan. Plus the diplomatic passports had to make it over. She wouldn't be able to order them until she got to the embassy several hours later. Time seemed to be her greatest enemy right now. Although it was in serious competition with everything else.

She showered, changed clothes, spiffed herself up, and at last stood ready in front of the hall mirror. She looked at herself and said, "What am I doing here?"

Her mirror image gazed back but didn't respond.

Kim Jong-un asked his guests to have a seat at the dining table as he remained standing at one end, his hands on the back of his chair. He appeared to have something to say.

Two of the waiting staff came through the doors, their arms full of plates, and a third walked in with two bottles of wine. But all three immediately turned back after a glance from the Supreme Leader.

Allan watched the food and drink come and go in the span of one second and was disappointed.

"Friends," Kim Jong-un began.

"Could we perhaps talk *while* we eat?" Allan suggested.

The Supreme Leader pretended not to hear this comment. He launched into a speech about peace and freedom.

"Peace" seemed to involve supplying his country with ever more deadly weapons. What constituted "freedom" was not quite as clear. Except possibly that every single citizen had the right to love their leader, combined with the duty to avoid not doing so.

With that, the Supreme Leader expressed his contentment that Providence had supplied him with Mr. Karlsson, who had come all the way from Switzerland to contribute to the fight against American imperialism. And that UN Envoy Wallström had joined in for similar reasons.

"Well," said Margot Wallström, "as Mr. Kim is aware, my task is rather to try to open up lines of dialogue between different people, to begin *talking* to each other, like we're doing now, instead of putting on performances here and there, like the one that took place in front of the TV cameras earlier today. I have already expressed my displeasure with that, have I not?"

She's not only delightful, she's brave too, Julius thought. Now, if only Allan remains calm . . .

Kim Jong-un looked at the UN envoy without listening to what she said. And went on with his speech.

He started on how happy everyone was in the Democratic People's Republic, how well the crops were growing, and how much nicer the weather was in the northern half of the peninsula than in the south. Altogether, it was no wonder tens of thousands of Koreans fled from south to north each year.

Food and drink were turned away at the door once again, causing Allan to lose patience. On occasion it could be a wise strategy to hold one's tongue or express agreement, but right now it was time to say something before they all starved to death.

Julius sensed what Allan was about to do and desperately tried to make eye contact so he could say, using his hands and face, "No, Allan, don't do it!"

But do it he did.

"Forgive me, Mr. Supreme Leader. My name was mentioned not far into your speech about a bit of everything. And here I am. Old and frail, but ever at your service. However, I suspect I will be of far too little use if I'm dead, and I'm about to starve to death. Is there any way what you have to say can be wrapped up a bit more speedily than you had perhaps intended?"

Kim Jong-un's proud smile went chilly. "You will

soon be allowed to eat, Mr. Karlsson. But your presumed cleverness about nuclear technology doesn't give you the right to express yourself as you wish, here in the People's Palace."

Oh, so he was in that sort of mood.

"I certainly didn't mean any offense, O Supreme One, but it's possible that in addition to all the rest I haven't been sleeping very well lately. You see, my friend the asparagus farmer here has trouble being as quiet as he ought to be at night."

Kim Jong-un didn't follow. "What do you mean?"

"He doesn't mean anything—" Julius attempted.

"I mean he snores," said Allan. "Oh, how he snores. If the Supreme One had any idea at all how much he snores! The boat that picked us up was the size of an entire warehouse, but not big enough that we didn't have to share a cabin, and, well, there hasn't been as much sleeping as there ought to have been. But what were we talking about, again? Oh, that's right, food. And perhaps a drink alongside. Might it be on its way, perchance?"

With that, Kim Jong-un's train of thought was sufficiently derailed. When the staff dared to stick their noses out of the kitchen again, he gave the green light.

They were served entrecôte with mushroom sauce.

Not particularly Asian, but it appealed to the guests and was washed down with an Australian cabernet sauvignon.

Spirits rose around the table. Allan decided to tolerate the Supreme Leader's talk of this and that for a little longer. But when the Supreme One claimed the nation had detonated a hydrogen bomb the year before, Allan had to protest. He'd read about that on his tablet, and the truth was that the so-called hydrogen bomb had hardly made a bang.

"The fact that you're transporting nine measly pounds of uranium in a boat that could bring thirty thousand tons all the way from God-knows-where to Pyongyang is enough proof for me that, one, you aren't anywhere near having a hydrogen bomb, two, you hardly even know the first thing about plutonium, and three, your total stores of uranium fit into a briefcase. In short, you have nothing to use, except those nine pounds. And, as luck would have it, me. And I have nothing left in my glass."

Kim Jong-un waved over a waiter. The impudence of the Swiss man was really too much. Well, there were two options: either he would turn out to be useful, in which case there was no reason to send him home to Europe. Or he wouldn't, and then he would be sent nowhere but to his eternal rest. In either case he would come to regret his lack of respect.

The Supreme Leader decided to continue being amiable and generous. "You are outspoken, Mr. Karlsson, I must say. And I suppose you have every right to be, given your age. Although your primary reason for being here is to work, I'd be happy to make sure you do some sightseeing in our beautiful capital city. What do you say we arrange a visit to the city's most exclusive shopping center after work tomorrow? Unfortunately I won't be able to join you, but I'm sure you'll manage with the guide I'll put at your disposal."

By "most exclusive shopping center," the Supreme Leader meant the city's only shopping center.

Visiting department stores? That was more than Allan needed. But it seemed like a good idea to play along, so Julius could stop looking so tormented. "That's a kind thought," he said. "Sounds relaxing in every way, after a long day in the laboratory. I don't suppose we could borrow a coin or two? In all our haste we didn't bring anything with us but a few bottles of champagne, and unfortunately those are gone."

Kim Jong-un said that Karlsson and his friend shouldn't worry about the cost. If they found a souvenir or two to take home, they should consider it a gift.

When it came to the peace project, Karlsson could have six days in the lab. Time limits tended to promote creativity. Upon proven results, the Supreme One promised both a medal of valor and a first-class ticket home to Switzerland.

Julius still didn't dare to say anything, not after the failed attempt in the Supreme Leader's office.

Allan, however, was beyond daring. "A lot can be accomplished in six days. If only I manage to stay alive . . . I've been frail for a pretty long time. The last thirty or forty years, really. I suppose I'm singing my last refrain, as they say. Of course, Noah lived to be nine hundred and fifty. The difference is that I'm real."

"Who?" said Kim Jong-un.

"Noah. From the Bible. Exciting literature. Oh, but wait, what am I saying? I suppose you haven't read it, because you would have had to execute yourself, if I've understood your laws correctly."

Was this bloody Swiss man bringing up the *Bible*—a forbidden book—during dinner in the Palace of the People's Republic? Now he had crossed a line.

But Margot Wallström came to his rescue. She broke in and thanked the Supreme Leader for the opportunity to meet in private.

Kim Jong-un nodded, even though he hadn't promised any such thing. "Tomorrow I'm busy with important matters, but lunch the day after might work. And then you may leave, Madame Wallström. Go home and tell them that the world's leading expert in nuclear weapons is in my hands. That ought to prompt some humility in America. If that characteristic even exists there."

Margot Wallström took an extra large sip of her replenished wine to calm her nerves as she wondered what would happen if someone were to let Kim Jong-un and Benjamin Netanyahu into the same room. Monumental lack of humor and self-awareness against monumental lack of humor and self-awareness. All that would be missing was Donald Trump as a mediator.

Julius chewed Allan's ear off all the way from the palace to the hotel. Why on earth had he quarreled with the Supreme Leader like that?

"Quarreled? When has anyone died from a little honesty?"

"Here people have dropped like flies from honesty over the years! Where's the sense in it if we do the same?"

Allan allowed that he didn't see any sense in that particular result. "But, please, can you stop worrying about every tiny thing? This will all work out for the best, you'll see."

"How the hell do you expect it to work out? After tonight he'll never let us go!"

"He wouldn't have anyway. I have no intention of helping that chatterbox more than necessary. When that dawns on him, it'll be best if we've left the country. Preferably in the company of that briefcase he's so proud of."

"And how do you intend for us to disappear?"

"With the help of that charming Swedish minister for foreign affairs, of course. Have you already forgotten?"

"In greater detail, Allan."

"Detail, schmetail."

Margot Wallström took her limousine straight from the half-surreal dinner at the Supreme Leader's palace to the Swedish embassy to start the process of producing passports. It wasn't as simple as cobbling together a passport or two at the embassy. Sweden was Sweden and rules were rules.

The chief of the Swedish passport police wasn't happy about the call from Pyongyang. He wavered and balked and wavered some more, with a series of formal objections to the minister's request that he produce two diplomatic passports in extremely dubious accordance with the rules. He said he didn't understand how the minister could put him on this sort of spot.

It would never do, of course, for Margot Wallström to explain that she had two Swedes to smuggle out of North Korea in the interest of averting a third world war, so she decided to change tack. Thus she informed the chief of the passport police that there was no need for him to understand what he was doing: the important thing was that he did as she said. When the chief of the passport police responded by wondering once more if the minister was seriously suggesting he falsify signatures and produce passports for two people no one at the passport office in Stockholm had even met, she responded with a simple "Yes." And "Diplomatic passports, as I said."

"Diplomatic passports perhaps, but as for the rest . . ."

"As for the rest, either you do as I say or you do as I say. If necessary I can ask the prime minister to call you and repeat the request. If that's not enough, I have contacts in the royal court. The king could give you a ring, if you like. And the speaker. Whom else would you like to hear from? Secretary General Guterres?"

The chief of the passport police fell silent. What did the king have to do with this?

"Please, Mr. Passport Police Chief. There's not much time. The lives of Swedish citizens are at stake. And more lives than that."

At last he went along with her request, given that it would also be sent in writing along with the electronic transmission of photographs and signatures.

"Yes, yes," said Minister for Foreign Affairs Wallström. "But the passports must be produced at once and sent by diplomatic courier to Pyongyang within the hour."

"Within the hour? But it's almost lunchtime."

"No, it isn't."

USA

"What the hell?" said President Trump, to National Security Advisor H. R. McMaster, who had just replaced National Security Advisor Michael T. Flynn, who had, of course, turned out to be a security risk.

The issue was that Fox had just put up a clip from a so-called press conference in North Korea, and Breitbart News had followed up with an article on the same topic. And with that, the president knew all that was worth knowing about the issue, except for the whole situation as such.

That bitch Wallström from Sweden had nagged her way to a secret meeting with Kim Jong-something in . . . whatever the capital of North Korea was called. And then she'd stood up next to him on North Korean

TV! How stealthy did she think *that* made her, that goddamn nutcase? And as if that wasn't enough, she had hugged, on live TV, a Swiss Communist who was there to upgrade the North Korean nuclear weapons program.

"Well," said Lieutenant General McMaster. "She didn't *hug* the Swiss Communist. Breitbart might have been mistaken on that point."

The president waved away the security advisor's comment. He would have to twist that Wallström's nose when she got back, but who was the Communist she'd hugged?

"Didn't hug, as I said."

President Trump spent some moments swearing about the self-righteous Swiss before he realized he should give them a call. He picked up the phone and ordered his secretary to get him a line to the president of Switzerland on the double.

"And find out his name while you're at it," he said to the secretary, who said his name was Doris Leuthard and, given the first name, was likely a she. "Another bitch? You can bet your ass on it. Well, come on, make the call!"

"It's two in the morning in Europe, sir," said the secretary.

"Good," said President Trump.

Switzerland, USA

It had been a hectic day for President Leuthard. Which had turned into a hectic evening and night. She forced herself to go to bed just after one o'clock, in the hopes of being somewhat well rested by six o'clock the next morning.

She was able to sleep for forty-five minutes before she was woken by her assistant. There was an incoming call from the White House in Washington.

Doris Leuthard stood up, feeling dizzy, but prepared herself. When the President of the United States calls, you don't just flip your pillow over and go back to sleep.

"Good morning, Mr. President," said Doris Leuthard. ". . . Did you wake me? Oh, no, no worries."

"Great," said President Trump. "Because it's night already in Zürich, isn't it?"

Yes, President Leuthard could confirm that to be the case. Just as it was in Berne, where she was. But, anyway, why did he wish to speak with her?

Doris Leuthard posed the question and anticipated the answer. Ever since the previous afternoon, the federation she represented had been astonished and appalled that an unknown compatriot seemed to be in Pyongyang. Ever since, she and her Federal Council had been working intensively with their own intelligence service and its networks to find out what was going on.

It turned out that President Trump preferred to shout at his Swiss colleague rather than speak to her. He asked what they were doing and whether she realized the challenge she was giving the United States by initiating a collaboration on nuclear weapons with North Korea. This was completely at odds with the sanctions against the country the EU had ratified.

When Doris Leuthard spent a little too much time drawing a breath before responding, Donald Trump went on to say that he would make sure the EU kicked Switzerland out of the union unless she immediately withdrew all aid to that fool over there.

Now President Leuthard had no idea where to

begin. How many mistakes could a presidential colleague make in such a short time?

"Well, Switzerland isn't a member of the EU, so it will be hard for you to kick us out, Mr. President. Beyond that, I'm not sure your presidential powers extend so far that you can rearrange the European Union's roster of member states. Incidentally, the sanctions against North Korea are regulated by the UN, and we are a member there. If you'd like to alter that, I'll have to ask you to call and wake up Secretary General Guterres instead."

"But you said you weren't asleep," said President Trump.

Doris Leuthard had enough presence of mind not to get into a conversation with the President of the United States about whether or not she had been asleep at two in the morning. Instead she said she sympathized with his worries. "We have no idea who the alleged Swiss man is, but it's something we're working intensively to find out. I assure you."

"You'd better be," said President Trump. "And you'll have to do more than that. The moment you know something, you call me immediately. Is that understood?"

President Leuthard had already been tired; after two minutes on the phone with the American president she was exhausted. "When we know, we will take the proper measures. What those may be will have to be dictated by the circumstances. I cannot promise, but neither can I rule out, that I will inform you personally, especially now that you have expressed a wish thereof. The Swiss Confederation does, however, retain the right to come to its own decisions regarding national security."

President Trump hung up without saying goodbye. He muttered as he logged into Breitbart.com to see if the Swiss knew more than their president wanted to admit. But not even Breitbart seemed to have an ear close enough to the ground.

While Donald Trump was conversing with the terrible woman in Switzerland, two things happened outside his door. Retired CIA agent Ryan Hutton had called the White House and managed, via a few detours, to be transferred to National Security Advisor McMaster. Agent Hutton was almost eighty years old, but claimed he still had both intellect and vision intact. If the lieutenant general wished, Hutton could tell him who the Swiss nuclear-weapons expert in Pyongyang was.

"Please do," said H. R. McMaster.

Well, first off, the Swiss man in question was Swedish and nothing else. His name was Allan Karlsson and he had to be close to a hundred years old by now; during the seventies and eighties he'd been a paid agent of the United States, stationed in Moscow; he'd spent the fifties in a Soviet gulag in Siberia after he had, laudably enough, challenged Stalin. Prior to this he had been awarded the Presidential Medal of Freedom for his pivotal achievements in the building of the world's first atomic bomb.

"Another Swede?" was President Trump's first comment. "How many of them are there? What is wrong with that country?"

"He did receive the Medal of Freedom, Mr. President."

"Sixty years ago, sure. He's had plenty of time to forget what freedom is. What the hell else would he be doing in Pee-oy . . . Pyong . . . P . . ."

"Pyongyang, sir. We don't know. The fact is, we know no more than what was said at the press conference, plus these new pieces of the puzzle from former CIA Agent Hutton."

"Two Swedes and a North Korean. That makes three Communists in a row," said President Trump. "Get that fucking Wallström over here right now, before Sweden takes over the whole world. Was there anything else? I want some peace and quiet for a while."

Yes, the security advisor had one more thing. It so happened that the NSA had bugged a hotel in Pyong-yang. Since the hotel had hardly any guests, there wasn't much to overhear, but apparently they had just had a hit. There seemed to be regular transports into North Korea of something with the code name "as-paragus." The number five hundred million figured somehow. Dollars, one had to presume.

President Trump liked asparagus and was blissfully un-aware that the most exclusive variety, served at his many US hotels, was imported from Sweden. The brand was "Gustav Svensson."

"Five hundred million dollars for asparagus?" said President Trump. "It's not *that* good. Find out what that's code for."

North Korea

Allan and Julius met Minister for Foreign Affairs Wallström in the breakfast room before the friends' first workday in the plutonium factory north of Pyongyang.

As the three took their seats, she informed them that the diplomatic passports she'd promised were on their way from Beijing by courier. If all went well, she would be able to hand them over the next morning. "I've thought about it a lot, but I don't think there's anything else I can do for you."

"Even this much has made our situation a little brighter," said Allan.

Julius just nodded. The minister for foreign affairs was still wonderful, but no one could be so fantastic as to cause him to stop brooding about how his life was almost over and he would never get to see his beloved asparagus again. Or the money it generated.

"My meeting with Kim is tomorrow," Margot Wallström went on. "He's already indicated that he wants me out of here afterward, meaning that my departure will occur the next day at the latest. Have you had time to come up with a way to sneak out with me?"

"Have we, Allan?" Julius wondered.

But the 101-year-old's mind was elsewhere. Instead of responding he said that the black tablet seemed to be in the best possible mood at that very moment. First there was the Polish EU parliamentarian who maintained that women ought to be paid less than men on the ground that they were less intelligent. Speaking of male intelligence, Trump in the United States had just tweeted that one of the world's most beloved and award-winning actresses was incompetent. And in Brazil, President Temer stood accused of corruption after having replaced the corruption-tainted Rousseff, who had been removed from office after taking over from Lula, who was now waiting to be locked up for corruption.

"Wasn't there someone who wrote that humans are to be pitied?" Allan said, adding that, speaking of Trump, he didn't quite understand what "tweeting" was.

Julius gazed at his friend vacantly.

The minister said that, given the opportunity, she would be happy to explain to Karlsson the phenomenon that was Twitter, or for that matter let them delve into Swedish literary history. But for the moment, the more urgent matter at hand was whether the gentlemen had some plan for survival.

Allan said that if the minister was so determined to change the subject, then his response would be that "plan" might be an exaggeration.

"Then, Mr. Karlsson, what would you call what you do have, if it's not a plan?"

"Nothing at all," said Allan. "Except problems. And a certain amount of confidence. Mostly problems, or mostly confidence, depending on which one of us is asked."

Margot Wallström said she was addressing both of them. Since Julius appeared to have slipped into hopelessness, it was up to Allan to speak for them.

It seemed likely that much would clear up once they had completed their first workday at the plutonium factory. After all, sometimes solutions fall into your lap just when you least expect them, most recently when he and Julius were sitting with water up to their knees in a woven basket on the open sea. The water was warm, so they were doing fine in that respect, but they didn't have much else to be happy about.

"And then a ship came to our rescue. That was quite a stroke of luck."

"Was it?" said Julius, who had woken from his paralysis. "Couldn't that ruddy ship have been from a country other than this one?"

"Eat your breakfast, Julius. There are worse countries to end up in. Or maybe there aren't, but here we are. And the food may be strange, but it tastes good."

The table was laden with rice, fish, yellow soup of unknown ingredients, and something they called kimchi. The whole spread was completed with Western coffee and French croissants in an unholy alliance.

"I recall when I was in China just after the war, to blow up bridges. Coffee was out of the question back then. But they did have vodka made from rice. I can think of worse ways to start the day."

The minister for foreign affairs didn't know whether to be impressed by Karlsson's carefree nature or join Jonsson in his anxious state. Neither option was actually relevant to the gentlemen's situation, though, so she let it go.

"As the time of my departure necessarily approaches,

I will inform you of the exact hour. If you turn up you turn up. Otherwise I promise to cause the biggest diplomatic brouhaha I can as soon as I've landed in the West. I know better than to pull at any more loose threads around here. If our friend in the palace should get the idea that I'm breaking any laws, he might very well have me arrested. A representative of the UN Security Council imprisoned in North Korea! That would lead to a crisis beyond anything we've seen so far. Do you understand the fix I'm in?"

Allan noted that the minister had finished her breakfast and was about to stand up. "May I have that croissant? As long as the minister is leaving, I mean."

"Dammit, Allan," said Julius.

Minister for Foreign Affairs Wallström said that Allan could help himself. With that she excused herself: she had business to attend to at the embassy to prepare for her upcoming meeting with Kim Jong-un. To what end? one might wonder, but still.

So she went. As she waited in the lobby for the limousine to roll up, she heard Karlsson telling his friend about President Erdogan in Turkey, who had called the entire population of the Netherlands Fascists, Chancellor Merkel of Germany a Nazi, and Israel a terrorist state that devoted most of its resources to killing children.

"I don't give a crap about what's-his-name," Julius said, annoyed.

"Nor do I, actually," said Allan. "But don't you think he's exaggerating a bit, this Turk?"

Margot Wallström was invited into the limousine. As she settled inside, she asked herself if the world had made Karlsson crazy, or if it was the other way around.

While Allan seemed uninterested in anything but the contents of his black tablet, Julius shaped up and decided to do what he could to increase the odds of survival for them both. *Knowledge*, in this context, was not a stupid place to start. He decided to stretch his legs with the aim of studying.

Ryugyong had four public exits. At each stood two guards, although they were called guides, always ready to lead the Swiss man and his assistant back up to their room if they tried to take off on their own. It would not be as easy to escape this hotel as it had been the last one, with or without a balloon. What, incidentally, had they thought they would do next? Were they going to *stroll* all the way through Pyongyang to the airport? Call a taxi? At what phone number? In which language would they order a car? How would they pay? And what made them think the alarm wouldn't sound if they made an attempt?

How about a private driver then? The man who would drive them to and from the plutonium factory each day, over the next six days? Perhaps he would do them the kindness of swinging by the airport? If Allan charmed him as only Allan could . . .

Julius returned to the 101-year-old in the breakfast room. It was almost nine o'clock. Allan had eaten up his kimchi and the remaining croissants, except the very last one, which he had stuck into his coat pocket for future use. He welcomed Julius back and said he had found new information on the tablet. Before Julius could stop him, he said that the cost for the wall between Mexico and the United States was going to be four times higher than it would cost to end the famine in East Africa.

"The famine in East Africa?"

Julius hated Allan's black tablet and longed for the old man as he had been before all the misery of the world had overtaken him.

"And listen to this," Allan went on. The new hospital in Greater Stockholm had just been supplied with 165 faulty bathrooms. It turned out the water ran in the wrong direction. So they all had to be rebuilt, and surely doing that would cost half an African famine.

Julius blew up. "I've had enough of this. I sympathize with starving children and faulty bathrooms, but can't you get it into your skull that we're on our way to being shot within a few days? What if, for God's sake, we took things in the proper order?"

Allan pretended to be hurt. "Have you thought of something on your own, then, while I was updating myself on life? Or have you spent the whole time moaning and groaning?"

Julius told him about the guards at the exits and reminded Allan of the rules they had to stick to. These included, incidentally, that they must be sitting in a car outside the hotel in under a minute. That car might be the solution to their transportation woes. It, and the man behind the wheel.

"Then I suppose we should go and say hello to him. It's always exciting to meet new people. Come, my friend. And chin up!"

The driver welcomed the foreign guests with a salute. Then he asked the gentlemen to climb into the back seat, preferably without bringing with them any of the mud from the puddles.

"I'd rather sit in front, so we can chat," said Allan. "My, what fantastic English."

Julius climbed into the back, and the driver had no time to guide Allan into the same back seat before he was settling into the front.

"Not entirely proper," he said, once he was behind the wheel again.

"My name is Allan," said Allan. "What might our driver possibly be called? I understand Kim is common."

The driver said that his name was as inconsequential as he was. But he took his job seriously. As they knew, the gentlemen were expected to be ready at nine o'clock each morning to be transported to the laboratory, with their return journey scheduled for four o'clock in the afternoon. The nameless man was supposed to wait outside the laboratory each day in case of unforeseen incidents.

"I hear the airport is beautiful," said Allan. "Perhaps we could take a look at it tomorrow or thereabouts. Would that suit Mr. Nameless?"

It would not. The only departure from the route between hotel and laboratory would occur that afternoon, for the driver had orders to take the gentlemen to the leading shopping center in Pyongyang.

"But surely a little detour couldn't—"

"Yes, it could," said the driver.

He was not charming. Allan took his extra croissant from his coat pocket. The driver reacted with horror. He stopped the car and said that consumption of any sort was strictly forbidden in his car.

"Throw that food in the ditch immediately!"

Throw away food? Was that such a bright idea? If Allan understood correctly, food was less common in this country than military parades.

"No one starves in the land of the Supreme Leader," said the driver. "Now throw it away!"

Allan did as he said.

"But that doesn't mean you can't be hungry," the driver added.

Then no more was said in the car until the next time the driver opened his mouth.

"We have arrived."

"Thanks for a pleasant journey," said Allan.

Coming and going as one wished was as impossible at the plutonium factory as it was at the hotel. But security was limited to a strict door guard, who inspected everything and everyone who passed in either direction.

"Good day," said Allan. "My name is Allan Karlsson and I wonder if you—unlike our driver—might have a name as well?"

The guard assured Allan that he did. But right now his primary objective was to go through Mr. Karlsson's pockets. Nothing inappropriate could be allowed into the plant. Or out of it.

Allan said he hoped he and his friend Julius would

not be classified as "inappropriate," because that would lead to problems for all involved. But he hadn't caught the guard's name.

"Good," said the guard, allowing the alleged Swiss men to pass.

Allan planned to spend most of the day talking nonsense with the laboratory director who had, some time earlier, replaced the colleague who had passed away. This was the same man who had met him and Julius at the harbor in Nampo the day before.

Allan persisted in wanting to know what people were called, but the North Koreans were playing hard to get.

"You can call me Mr. Engineer," said the laboratory director.

"Oh, I see," said Allan. "If that's the way it's going to be, I want to be called Mr. Karlsson."

"You already are," said the engineer.

Once the titles were sorted out, Allan devoted a considerable part of the day to wasting time. He gave a speech on the importance of keeping the laboratory clean, another about the fact that nuclear weapons were serious business, and a third about how the approaching spring was worth looking forward to.

The engineer grew impatient. "Isn't it about time we got to work?"

"Got to work?" said Allan. "Just what I was thinking. I was thinking, Now it's about time we got to work."

Allan's acutely incomplete plan was, of course, that he and Julius would leave the country with the nine pounds of enriched uranium they'd arrived with. One positive factor was that they wouldn't have to search for the briefcase because it was no longer on the Supreme Leader's desk in the palace. Instead it was standing out in the open, against one wall of the laboratory, waiting to be needed.

"First I will ask permission visually to inspect the uranium I'm here to refine," said Allan.

"Why?" asked the engineer.

Allan didn't quite know why, but surely there was a good reason to know what the item you were supposed to steal looked like. "To make sure you haven't been tricked," he said. "If you only knew how much fake uranium is for sale, Mr. Engineer, you would be scared out of your wits. Although perhaps that's already the case."

"What is?"

"That you're scared out of your wits. Well?"

The engineer shook his head at the possibly senile

expert and went to fetch the briefcase. He placed it on the laboratory counter and opened it.

Enriched uranium has a high density and isn't terribly dangerous from a radiation standpoint. What Allan could see was a package the size of a brick, encased in a thin layer of lead. He measured its length and width. "Eleven by five inches. That should mean around ten by four inside the lead. That is perfectly correct! My congratulations, Mr. Engineer."

The engineer was surprised. Not so much by the pronouncement as how quickly it had come. "Have you already concluded your inspection? Don't you want to open the package?"

"No. Why would I? The measurements are correct. Now let's just weigh it, to be on the safe side."

Allan took it to the laboratory scale a few yards away.

"What would the correct weight be?" asked the engineer.

Allan didn't respond until he saw the number on the scale.

"Eleven and a half pounds. Exactly right, if we include the third of an inch layer of lead. My double congratulations, Mr. Engineer. You seem to be a man who knows what he's doing, after all."

The engineer didn't follow. "After all?" he said.

"Let's not quibble over words. Why don't we put

the briefcase back where it was, and then perhaps we can finally move on? We have a lot to deal with and far too little time."

The engineer wondered inwardly how it could have become his own fault that they weren't getting anywhere.

"So, where were we?" Allan asked. "Have we discussed how important it is to keep the laboratory clean?"

"Yes," said the engineer. "Twice."

"And how important it is to make sure the uranium is the right weight?"

"Wasn't that what you just did?"

Julius looked on in silence. A greater natural talent than Allan's could not reasonably be expected to exist.

The newly appointed director engineer was having a tough time. His future was entirely dependent on the results of Allan Karlsson's work. Even more so since the engineer had put in a good word for him to the Supreme Leader after the brief meeting at the harbor.

The plutonium factory had, up to that point, not delivered what it should, and the Russians were hemming and hawing about their promise to provide a centrifuge. As a last resort, the engineer had requested enriched uranium as an ingredient that would enable them to fulfill the Supreme Leader's expectations.

To the engineer's relative horror, the aforementioned Russians had arranged for a contact in Africa and now he had received a test shipment with which to prove himself. And into the bargain he'd got an ancient expert who was said to know how one could achieve a result multiplied five- or tenfold using the same amount of raw material. *Hetisostat pressure one thousand two hundred?* The engineer was no dummy, but no matter how hard he tried he couldn't follow this concept to any comprehensible conclusion. Well, he still had five days. Tomorrow, he intended to keep a much tighter rein on the conversation.

As Julius dozed off in the back seat, on their trip to the shopping center, Allan sat in front, thinking. After all, he had no one to talk to. And then he thought a little more. And after a while, he said to Julius: "Do you know what I have?"

Julius cracked open an eye. "No, I don't. What do you have?"

"A plan."

Julius immediately woke up.

"For us to get out of this country?"

"Yes. That was what you wanted, after all. Or have you changed your mind?"

His friend in the back seat assured him that he had not. He wanted to know more this minute.

Allan's idea was to trick the engineer into leaving so they could sneak out, take the briefcase of uranium with them through the security check, and convince the waiting driver to leave the car, since he would probably never agree to give them a lift to the airport.

Julius absorbed what Allan had just said.

"That's your plan?" he said.

"In short, yes."

"Aside from all the rest, how are you planning to get the uranium past the guard at the door? What will make the driver leave his car? And how do we get into the minister's plane without being caught by the personnel at the airport?"

Allan said that was too many questions all at once for an old brain.

The largest department store in Pyongyang, and the only one worthy of the name, consisted of four stories very full of wares and very empty of people buying them. The nameless driver guided Allan and Julius from floor to floor.

On the ground floor was men's and women's clothing. They already had the former; they didn't need the latter.

The second floor sold shoes, coats, gloves, and bags. Why not a coat each, as long as the Supreme Leader was footing the bill? It was chilly out.

On a shelf near the coats stood a row of around forty briefcases, all identical to one another—and to the uranium briefcase in the laboratory. It appeared that North Korea produced one model of briefcase alone.

"Communism has its upsides," said Allan. He picked one up.

Julius realized that the 101-year-old had just made up his mind to switch one briefcase for the other.

The third floor contained nothing of interest. For sale there were toys and various types of stationery and art supplies. Allan was first, Julius a few steps behind him, with the apparently bored driver a few steps behind Julius.

On the fourth floor, Julius picked up a roll of lead tape. "What do you say about this, Allan?"

"Clever boy. I think we've finished shopping now."

Back on the ground floor, a young woman stood at the cash register, waiting for customers. When Allan and Julius placed their coats, briefcase, and lead tape on the counter, the driver said she should send the bill to the Supreme Leader, at which the woman fainted. The driver picked her up off the floor, apologized to the Swiss men, and said he ought to have known better.

On the brief trip back to the hotel, the driver had time to emphasize to Julius in the back seat and Allan, who still insisted on sitting in the front, that it was strictly forbidden to bring anything from the breakfast table into the car the next morning.

"Not even kimchi?" said Allan.

"Especially not kimchi."

"We hear what you're saying, Mr. Nameless. We'll get up extra early to make sure we're full and in fine form next time we see one another."

Allan spent the rest of the evening sitting at his desk in the hotel room with the black tablet. This time he had paper and pen as well. He seemed to be writing down chemical formulas. And giving a contented "Hmm" now and then. Meanwhile Julius searched the room for a suitable object to wrap in lead tape. At last he settled on the black box of toiletries he'd found next to the sink.

"Good choice," Allan praised him. "The right size and everything."

The shape and appearance of the box were rather like the engineer's enriched uranium. It weighed a good deal less, to be sure, but what would the guard at the door know about that?

Just before midnight, Allan had finished surfing and writing. "There we go. Now the engineer and I will have a lot to avoid talking about tomorrow."

North Korea

It was clear that Allan had some sort of plan, after all. And, what was more, Julius had partly gathered what it would involve. But only partly.

In the breakfast room the next day, Allan found a lidded plastic box full of teaspoons under one of the serving tables. He dumped its contents onto the table with the aim of keeping the box, at which point a waitress who had heard the clatter hurried over and asked what he was doing.

Allan instructed Julius to bribe the waitress with the gold lighter he'd stolen from the Indonesian hotel manager.

"I didn't *steal* it," Julius protested, as he made a quick deal with the woman. "It just ended up in my pocket."

Allan didn't bother to start a discussion on the definition of kleptomania. Instead he gave instructions to the overjoyed waitress: "Fill this box with muesli and milk, please. Then put the lid on good and tight and leave the rest to the man whose lighter you have just inherited."

The young woman stopped looking at her reflection in her new possession and dashed off.

"Muesli and milk must be the last thing our driver wants in his car," Julius said.

"We're on the same page," said Allan.

The mixture was necessary to lure the driver out of his car. Neither Allan nor Julius had the muscles to *lift* him out, and two things were certain: first, the driver would never leave his car voluntarily; second, he was not going to drive them to the airport, no matter how hard they tried.

Minister for Foreign Affairs Wallström joined them. She had a cup of coffee and a French-Korean croissant while standing at the gentlemen's table, saying she was in a rush. The diplomatic passports had arrived as they should. The minister handed them over, wrapped in a napkin.

"Much obliged, Madame Minister," said Allan. "When might the departure take place? We have a few things to take care of today. It wouldn't be a bad idea to know."

Minister for Foreign Affairs Wallström was just getting to that. Kim Jong-un had conveyed the message that their next meeting would not only be their last but would be followed by her departure from the country that very afternoon.

"In short, he doesn't want anything to do with me. In contrast to President Trump, whose staff have given me orders to come and explain a few things. The airport has confirmed that my plane will take off at fifteen thirty."

"Today?" Julius asked anxiously.

"What is it the American president wants explained?" Allan asked.

"I can't rule out the possibility that your name may come up, Mr. Karlsson."

The minister looked sad. Julius felt sorry for her. But mostly he felt sorry for himself.

"As I said, fifteen thirty," said the minister. "I hope you will be there." She wasn't sure she would ever see Messrs. Jonsson and Karlsson again.

Julius wasn't either. "Today?" he repeated. "How on earth are we going to have time—"

"Don't start, Julle," said Allan. "Either this will all work out or it won't. I have a hard time envisaging any other option. Come on, it's already nine, and we have a job to mismanage. And bring the muesli."

"My name is not Julle," said Julius.

The guard at the entrance to the plutonium factory had strict and detailed instructions. Everyone who came and went got the same treatment.

On day two, Karlsson and Jonsson showed up, each in a new coat. The guard went through all the pockets and corners but found nothing remarkable.

Karlsson, in addition, was carrying a briefcase that contained a silver package of some sort, as well as a few documents full of handwritten formulas.

"What are these?" the guard inquired, of the formulas.

"These are the proud Democratic Republic's nuclear future," said Allan.

The guard put back the papers in horror. "And this?"

He held up the package.

"Those are toiletries," Allan said truthfully. "Wrapped up as a gift for Mr. Engineer. But please don't say anything—it's supposed to be a surprise."

This was extraordinary and mundane at once. On the one hand, the nation's future, on the other . . . What?

The guard allowed himself to become suspicious. He carefully unwound the tape until he was able to confirm that the strange old man had told the truth. In the black box he found a razor, shaving cream, soap, shampoo, conditioner, a comb, a toothbrush, and toothpaste. He opened a few of the bottles to sniff their contents.

"Do you think he'll like it?" Allan asked.

The toothpaste smelled like toothpaste; the shampoo smelled like shampoo. The razor was clearly a razor.

"I don't know . . . ," said the guard. Could it truly be proper to bring in unfamiliar liquids like this?

"I'm going to have to ask you to tape this up again," said Allan. "Mr. Engineer might arrive at any moment, and it would certainly be a nuisance if . . ."

And then he arrived. Peevish. "What is going on? We were supposed to start ten minutes ago."

The guard, in all haste, taped up the gift again as Allan entertained the engineer with the story of how what was going on was quite simply that the guard was just doing his job, and honorably at that. Mr. Engineer ought to think seriously about whether it wasn't time to promote the man. As far as Allan could tell, the guard was primed to take on greater tasks. Lead guard, at the very least. Although that would necessitate increasing the number of guards by at least one or he would have no one to lead.

Was Karlsson planning to talk about nothing today as well? This could not continue.

"Come along!"

While Allan was prattling, the guard had time to return the engineer's present to its original condition, at which point he handed the closed briefcase to the Swiss nuclear weapons expert. He hadn't found anything more of which to make note (the muesli mixture was still on the floor in the back seat of the car). He spent a long time gazing after Allan, Julius, and the engineer as they went on their way.

Lead guard, he thought. Now that would be something.

The engineer led Karlsson and Jonsson into the laboratory. He had, after the first day, reported to the Supreme Leader that the task of draining the old Swiss man of knowledge was moving slowly, but in the right direction. After all, the fellow was over a hundred years old: perhaps it would be best if he was allowed to work at his own pace? The Supreme Leader agreed. The engineer had five more days to get everything the man knew out of him. This still seemed like plenty of time.

"Now let's see," Allan said, placing his many pages of freshly written formulas on the engineer's desk. "In my day, of course, fission was the answer to all problems.

These days, fission and fusion go hand in hand, but perhaps Mr. Engineer is already aware of this."

The engineer squirmed. That bit about fusion belonged in the category of "stating the obvious." Oh, well, at least the old man had come up with some notes that might be worth studying.

"No peeping, Mr. Engineer. If we move too quickly, it will go wrong."

The engineer felt there was no risk of moving too quickly, but he decided to be patient for a little longer.

Allan went on: "What we see before us is the issue of how much we can compress the uranium you have so successfully gathered."

"I know that's the issue," said the engineer. "I also know you are expected to have the answer. Is that in these documents?"

Allan looked at the engineer, affronted. Wasn't it obvious that he had the answer? But they were going to hold off on the documents for now: Had the engineer already forgotten this? Allan reiterated that his greatest worry was that his pupil wouldn't be able to follow their conversations. In which case there was no point in having them.

The engineer said that Mr. Karlsson shouldn't worry about that. A child could follow, at the speed Karlsson went. And the engineer, for his part, had devoted nearly a decade to these issues.

"With limited results," Allan said, then excused himself. There was something he needed to discuss with their private driver, outside the door. "I'll be back soon," he said, walking off.

Julius realized that Operation Create Confusion had just begun. He shrugged reassuringly as he met the engineer's gaze. "He has his own way of doing things," he said. "But it always works out in the end."

With any luck, he thought.

The 101-year-old walked straight past the guard, coat, briefcase and all, and the guard bounced up off his chair and cried, "Stop! Where are you going now, Mr. Karlsson?"

"To see my driver," said Allan. "About an important matter."

The guard had appreciated Karlsson's earlier suggestion of a promotion, but that didn't mean he had any intention of shirking his duties. Thus Allan would have to submit to having his coat and briefcase searched once more. The contents of the briefcase were the same as they had been a few minutes before, minus the documents full of formulas. That was fine: formulas could be taken in but not out.

The driver was polishing the dashboard with a white cloth when Allan knocked on the window to attract his attention. "Back to the hotel, sir? Already?" said the driver.

"No, I just wanted to check on things here. It's not too warm? If it is, roll down the window, and there will be improved ventilation."

The driver looked at the old man. "It's three degrees outside," he said.

"Not too warm?"

"No," said the driver.

Allan's black tablet was waiting for its master on the passenger seat.

"If you like, Mr. Nameless Driver, you may borrow that while you wait. There's quite a bit of nudity in it, I've noticed."

Horrified, the driver informed Allan that he had no such plans.

"That's that, then," said Allan, turning and walking back to the entrance. He almost made it past the guard. But only almost.

"Give me the coat, please. And the briefcase."

Allan said he hadn't taken anything from the car, if memory served, but added that Mr. Guard shouldn't take his word for it. "I've noticed that at my age things are likely to go wrong when I mean them to be right, and not necessarily right just because I was thinking wrong. Check whatever you need to check. Caution is a virtue. I know the Supreme Leader is of the same opinion."

The guard became nervous each time the Supreme Leader was mentioned.

Back in the laboratory, Allan said: "Listen, I thought of something."

"What's that?" the lead engineer wondered.

Allan appeared to brace himself before rattling off, at a rapid pace: "$MgSO_4$—$7H_2O$ $CaCO_3Na_2B_4O_7$—$10H_2O$."

The engineer did not follow. "Say that again," he said.

"That is, if we'll be satisfied to double the explosive charge. But I'm talking more along the lines of a tenfold increase."

"Say that again," repeated the engineer.

"Of course," said Allan. "But we have to do everything in the right order. Haven't I mentioned that already? Otherwise, in my experience, something will go wrong. And wrong is the wrong way to go, don't we agree?"

The engineer mumbled that he agreed that wrong would be wrong, while Julius stood next to him, rendered totally mute. Where had all that come from?

It had come, of course, from the black tablet. To the untrained eye (Julius) or the unprepared one (the engineer), it might well have been the solution to the proud nation's every nuclear weapons–related problem.

But it wasn't. It was a formula that, in the right hands, described the makeup of bath salts, toothpaste, and bleach, respectively. Allan had looked for something nuclear, but instead ended up on a site run by a Canadian hobby-chemist. The chemist wanted to tell the world what he had in his bathroom and cleaning closet. In contrast to what Allan proclaimed far and wide, there was nothing wrong with his memory. Beyond what he'd already said, he still had in reserve formulas for aspirin, baking powder, oven cleaner, and a few more. All thanks to a young man in Missisauga on the shores of Lake Ontario.

The engineer could have used an aspirin (but hardly baking powder or oven cleaner). He was back in his impatient mood.

"Now, once and for all, can we make some progress here?"

"Of course we can," said Allan. "I just have to . . ."

And then he went to the bathroom, where he remained for fifteen minutes.

By the time the great breakout was at hand, Allan had gone on another errand to the nameless driver (to ask if the driver was freezing, considering that it was only three degrees outside) and had guided his conversations with the engineer another few steps forward, or at least sideways. Meanwhile, Julius did his best to keep the engineer and himself in a decent mood.

In all his haste, Allan had forgotten to brief Julius on his most important contribution that day: keeping the engineer's attention elsewhere at a specific moment so that Allan could switch one briefcase for the other. The 101-year-old made up a reason for the engineer to visit the cold storage room next door, and took the opportunity to give his comrade some brief instructions.

"Distract him when he comes back."

"Distract him?" said Julius. "How?"

"Just distract him. So I can switch the briefcases."

"Why not switch them now while he's not here?"

Allan looked at his friend. "Because I didn't think of that. I don't always manage to get as far in my reasoning as those around me feel I ought to. For the most part, this suits me just fine, but on certain occasions . . ."

That was as far as he got before the engineer returned.

"We have eight hectograms of gallium in storage," he said. "Now, in what way is this relevant to compressing the uranium? Please explain it to me as if I were an equal, not an idiot."

"Only eight hectograms," said Allan, a look of concern on his face.

Then Julius fell headlong to the floor. "Help, I'm dying!"

The engineer was thoroughly frightened. Even Allan was startled, although he was the one who'd put in the order.

"Ow!" Julius cried, where he lay. "Ow!"

Allan stayed where he was as the engineer hurried to Julius's aid.

"What's the matter, Mr. Jonsson?" he said, kneeling beside the possibly dying assistant. "Aren't you feeling well?"

Julius realized that Allan had already managed to exchange one thing for the other.

"Yes, thank you," he said. "I'm fine. I just had a sudden bout of homesickness."

"Homesickness?" said the engineer. "You collapsed in a heap on the floor."

"Severe homesickness. But now it has passed."

The engineer, who had thus far considered Julius the more sensible of the two foreigners, had the feeling he was just as bad as his colleague. "Shall I help you up, Jonsson?"

"Thank you, kind engineer," said Julius, putting out his hand.

The engineer found himself in a desperate situation. First, because he'd had only a few short minutes at the Nampo harbor to determine whether Karlsson was a charlatan, aware that if he found he *was*, the engineer himself would have been forced to produce results faster than he might have been ready for. So he had decided Karlsson was the genuine article, the most pressing reason being that the engineer wanted him to be so out of sheer desire to survive. Then had come the painful realization that he was probably neither a charlatan nor in full possession of his mental faculties. And that the assistant's situation might be equally unfortunate.

The engineer toyed with the idea of explaining to the Supreme Leader that the original question was one of charlatanry, and that nothing had been mentioned about the potential levels of senile dementia. But he realized that wouldn't work. It left the option of lying to the Supreme Leader (a mind-boggling thought) and saying that the gentlemen were no longer needed: the engineer had come to understand the mechanics of pressure and within a few weeks would be able to convert that knowledge into practical results. In which case he either had the given number of weeks left to live, or he would have to deliver on his promise.

Karlsson had proved to have chemical formulas in his aged skull, and he'd put some of them on paper. When the Swiss men left for the day, the engineer planned to take a closer look.

During lunch he'd lost his temper with Karlsson, who had been reciting from his black tablet by memory about an American TV show host who had first committed a series of sexual harassments, then said he was angry with God, who hadn't rushed to his defense. The engineer roared his displeasure and said he didn't give a damn about God or all the Americans in the world, or about hetisostat pressure and what it could do, because he was about to have eleven hundred pounds of enriched uranium to deal with. When that shipment arrived they would no longer need Karlsson. The engineer promised to *drag* the old man out of the laboratory if he didn't shape up immediately.

Eleven hundred pounds? That was the second time Allan had heard this. Even nine pounds was bad enough.

"There, there, Mr. Engineer," he said. "We don't want to take that tone with one another, do we? Comrade Stalin in Moscow was once angry with me too, and for that sole reason sent me all the way to Siberia. But all that brought him was a stroke. A bad temper is no good for your health, I like to say."

The engineer was not feeling well. But he didn't drop his battle with the muddle-headed Karlsson.

At some point, the 101-year-old took a closer look at a photograph on the wall in which the grinning Supreme Leader stood next to a midrange missile. The Swiss man seemed to be focusing his attention on the tip of the missile; he was contemplatively mumbling another formula. Properly deciphered, it was a combination of vitamin C and smelling salts, but the unprepared engineer thought there might be hope after all.

At one minute to two, it was time. Allan had buttered up the engineer to such an extent that he didn't even protest when the self-proclaimed expert asked him to run yet another pointless errand to the cold storage room. It was something about the use-by date of the distilled water. Bottle by bottle.

When the engineer had vanished, Allan said: "I think it's time to take off. He probably won't be back for a few minutes."

———————

"Wrong shampoo," said Allan, placing the briefcase on the guard's table and opening the lid. "It didn't smell as much like lavender as it should have. Or whatever it was. The engineer is a quality-oriented gentleman. You can count on another package tomorrow."

Before the guard had time to take a closer look at the package he recognized, Allan wriggled out of his coat.

"But you had better check this properly. More than once I have stuck things into my pockets without remembering what or why. Once when I was out shopping I found a padlock in one. To this day I can't imagine where I had been planning to hang it."

The guard dug through Karlsson's pockets and soon had Jonsson's coat.

"I'm the same way," said Julius. "Although I'm more inclined in the direction of cigarette lighters."

The guard's eyes darted from coat to coat as Allan calmly closed the lid of the briefcase.

"We can't stand here chatting all day, no matter how pleasant it may be. The Supreme Leader is waiting. Done with the coats? That's good. Come along, Julius."

The old men walked toward the waiting driver, Julius very eagerly, Allan at his usual pace. They got into the vehicle, which drove off while the guard stood there pondering padlocks, cigarette lighters, the Supreme Leader, and what had just happened.

Thirty seconds later, the engineer came to the entrance. Angrier than ever.

"Where did those damned idiots go?"

"Why, they left, Mr. Engineer."

"Lovely. Tomorrow I'm going to throttle Karlsson."

The nameless driver was surprised that the international guests wished to return to the hotel when it was only two o'clock.

"Not the hotel, my dear Whatever-your-name-is. First we're going to the palace to pick up the Supreme Leader. Important meeting. Exciting, isn't it?"

The driver went totally pale. To a North Korean civil servant, having the Supreme Leader in your car would be the equivalent of a pastor riding around with Jesus Christ Himself. In fact, the man had orders to drive the guests to the hotel and nowhere else, but the palace was on the way.

"I understand if this is nerve-racking," Allan said. "But I know the Supreme Leader well. He's very amicable. There's really only one thing that irritates him. Or two, if you include the United States."

The nameless driver nervously asked what it might be.

"Filth," said Allan. "Filth, dust, trash, and messes. I recall one time when a poor assistant happened to spill a glass of juice on . . . Well, we don't need to discuss that any further. Rest in peace. Now I'll have to ask you to speed up. We don't want to keep the Supreme Leader waiting."

The trip went ever faster. Allan asked Julius, in Swedish, to become part of the action.

"Not so fast," he said. "I get car sick."

"Did I mention we were in a rush?" Allan said.

It was, of course, impossible to speed up and slow down simultaneously. The driver judged that the Supreme Leader was more important than the less elderly man in the back. Many times more important.

Once they reached the deserted highway, Julius complained about the high speeds again. The nameless driver continued to ignore him, encouraged by Allan, who spoke uninterrupted about all the fine qualities of the Supreme Leader, as well as how upset he became when faced with a mishmash of messiness.

"I must say, your car is in fantastic condition," he said. "The Supreme Leader will be very pleased with you. One pleasant thought is that he might ask you to introduce yourself by your name, and then we'll finally learn what it is."

The nameless man was now steering the car with

one hand and wiping the already clean dashboard even cleaner with the other.

"I feel sick," said Julius, cautiously picking up the box of milk and muesli from the floor. It had become terrifically mushy during the day.

This was immediately followed by the absolute worst sound the nameless man had heard in all his fifty-two years. Julius feigned noisy vomiting and splashed the muesli mixture across the seat back, between the front seats, and onto the driver's neck. The nameless driver completely panicked, according to plan. He swerved 180 degrees into the other lane, braked hard in a parking spot, and threw himself from the vehicle. How big a catastrophe was this?

When you're 101, you are no longer a flexible wonder, if you ever were in the first place. Even so, Allan managed to reach across, close, and lock the door after the driver. This occurred even as Julius locked the doors in the back and crawled into the front. That only went so-so too—after all, he was nearing seventy. But after a few seconds, he was in the driver's seat. With the most astounded driver on the Korean peninsula outside.

"Now let's see how this machine works," he said, putting it into gear and driving off.

"We need to go in the other direction," Allan reminded him.

So it came to be that the friends turned the car around not far down the deserted road and happened to pass the nameless driver where he stood without having worked out what was going on. Allan rolled down the window to say goodbye.

"Farewell. We won't need to be picked up tomorrow morning. Although you wouldn't have anything to pick us up in, now that I think about it."

The journey continued southward, toward Sunan International. Allan said that they were in good shape timewise, and that Julius did not need to drive like the car thief he had once been. Also, the risk of traffic jams seemed small. Or the risk of traffic at all.

Julius nodded, and wondered if Allan had considered how they should proceed once they arrived. That was a matter both of them had repressed while so much else was standing in the way.

But Allan had already fallen back into the clutches of his black tablet.

"Oho. Speaking of being out driving, apparently women are going to win the right to do the same in Saudi Arabia. Prince Abdulaziz seems to be a pragmatic fellow. No wonder the Saudis have a spot on the UN women's commission."

"Can't you put down that goddamn news machine

and devote just one second to our survival?" said Julius, who recognized this very type of frustration from earlier.

"On the other hand, everything is relative," Allan went on. "The prince is a Wahhabi and Wahhabis are against most things, as I've understood it. Such as Shiite Muslims, Jews, Christians, music, and vodka. Have you ever heard anything so awful? To be against vodka!"

Julius swore at Allan's further exposition.

"Would you tell me what we're going to do? Should we drive straight through the fence and up to the minister's plane? If we get caught, it's all over! Or should we drive in the regular way? What will we say to the guards at the sentry gate, in that case? Should we shoot them? With what? Jesus Christ, Allan!"

The 101-year-old turned off his black tablet and thought for a moment.

"Wouldn't it be best to leave the car in the short-term parking, take our briefcase and our diplomatic passports, and check in?"

One of the check-in desks was different from the rest. It was off to the side and had a gold-framed sign above the counter with Korean words and an explanation in English below: Premium Check-In.

Allan greeted the man at the counter with "Good day," introduced himself as Special Envoy and Diplomat Karlsson from the kingdom of Sweden, and wondered if Minister for Foreign Affairs Wallström's plane had already pulled up for boarding.

The man behind the counter took Allan's and Julius's passports and looked at them.

"Okay," he said. "I have not received information that you . . ."

"Information isn't exactly in keeping with the spontaneous nature of hush-hush diplomacy," said Allan. "People like us stay in the wings. Would you please be so kind as to show us to the plane?"

No, the man did not wish to be so kind.

"One moment," he said, and left to find his boss.

Julius thought Allan was behaving admirably at the airport, but they hadn't accomplished anything yet. After a minute or so, a man in uniform arrived to ask how he could be of service.

"Good day, Colonel," Allan said to the man, who wasn't a colonel at all, but the head of airport security.

"What is this about?" asked the head of security.

"Are you the one who will be taking us to Minister Wallström's plane? Wonderful! Would you please carry this suitcase for me? We're traveling light, but I'm old and worn out," said Allan, placing the briefcase of uranium on the counter.

"I won't be leading you anywhere, not before we've found out who you are," the head of security said defensively.

At that instant, a miracle occurred.

"Attachés Karlsson and Jonsson! Are you here already? Splendid!" said Margot Wallström, as she strode toward them from the main entrance. "I've just come straight from lunch with the Supreme Leader. We talked almost exclusively about you, Mr. Karlsson, and he sends his kindest greetings to you both and offers you a warm welcome back as soon as possible."

The head of security went pale. He knew who Madame Wallström was—he was the one who'd met her two days earlier and welcomed her according to his orders.

"Now, where were we?" said Allan. "Will you be helping me with my briefcase?"

Two seconds of reflection. Five. Ten. Then the head of security said: "Of course, my dear sir."

At which he guided the minister-slash-UN-envoy, her two attachés, the envoy's suitcase, and the one attaché's briefcase past all the checkpoints and all the way to the freshly refueled airplane, ready and waiting.

Eighteen minutes later, thirty-six minutes ahead of schedule, the Swedish minister for foreign affairs' plane exited North Korean airspace, carrying two more passengers than it had when it landed two days earlier.

Three hours after that, the North Korean leader Kim Jong-un flew into a rage the like of which was seldom seen. And he hadn't even yet been informed, by the engineer at the plutonium factory, that the briefcase of enriched uranium now contained instead a diverse selection of pleasantly scented toiletry articles. This, in turn, was because the engineer had just hanged himself in his cold storage room (right after he had deciphered Karlsson's first formula as the main ingredient in a nylon stocking). The name- and limousine-less driver, for his part, had to spend twenty-five minutes waiting at the edge of the highway before, at last, a truck approached for him to step out and plant himself in front of. The head of airport security did not share this death wish. Even so, he was allowed to live for only two more days, before being summarily charged in court and duly executed by firing squad.

USA

The service on board was excellent. Allan had a vodka and Coke, Julius a gin and tonic, and Minister Wallström a glass of white wine.

"Nice plane you're flying around in," said Julius. "The Swedish government's plane, I assume. It will be nice to go home again."

The minister for foreign affairs sipped her wine and replied that the plane didn't belong to the Swedish government but the UN. "And you'll have to long for Sweden for a little while longer, Mr. Jonsson. We're on our way to New York. President Trump is waiting for us there, at the UN building. I just learned he wants to meet you too, Mr. Karlsson. My colleagues on the Security Council have hinted that he's not in the best mood. Unless angry as a hornet is his best mood."

"My, my," said Allan. "Just think, getting to meet another American president before turning up one's toes."

"Have you met one before?" asked Minister Wallström in surprise.

"No, two."

The UN plane landed at JFK and was treated with the respect every UN plane deserved. Margot Wallström, Allan, and Julius were guided a few steps to a black Lincoln that took them to the VIP area for entering the United States of America. There stood the president's chief strategist, Steve Bannon, stamping his feet impatiently. He was annoyed for any number of reasons. Partly because he was being made to play errand boy, but mostly because Donald Trump had chewed him out earlier that day when he had flown into a rage and accidentally kicked the president's son-in-law in the backside during a conversation about proper policy on the Middle East. Since it wasn't possible to shout back without getting fired, he'd had to yell at someone else instead. He had to let off steam somehow.

"Don't make any trouble here," said Steve Bannon, to the border control officer. "The president is waiting."

The officer became nervous when she realized she

was creating a delay for the president, but she still made sure to do her job. Two of the three diplomats did not have ESTA authorization.

"But they're diplomats, for fuck's sake," said Steve Bannon.

"That may be," said the border control officer, "but I still have to do my job."

"Then do it," said Bannon.

It took a certain amount of digging in the immigration computer, plus one phone call, before the officer was able to rubber-stamp the diplomats Jonsson and Karlsson. There was nothing in their backgrounds to suggest they might be enemies of the state. Neither of them had even been born in Tehran.

"Welcome," she said at last.

"Thanks," said Allan.

"Thanks," said Julius.

"Now come on!" said Steve Bannon.

"Hope the president isn't this irate," mumbled Minister for Foreign Affairs Wallström.

He was.

Perhaps their carry-on luggage should have been included in the inspection of Allan and Julius, but typically carry-ons are inspected at the departure airport. And the journey had been taken in a UN plane.

And all three were diplomats. And then there was ranting Steve Bannon.

These reasons weren't sufficient, yet the fact was that the United States of America had just been saddled with nine pounds of enriched uranium, carefully packed in a North Korean briefcase, without having any clue that it had happened.

This occurred to Julius in the limousine on the way to the UN building. He also realized that Allan had never told the minister for foreign affairs what he was carrying around. "What are you going to do with that?" he whispered, while Margot Wallström was engrossed in a phone call.

"I suppose it could make a nice present for the president," said Allan, "as long as he's so eager to meet with me. But why don't you hold on to it for now? It doesn't seem quite right to barge into the UN building carrying enriched uranium without letting them know in advance."

Julius squirmed.

"Don't worry," said Allan. "I've thought it all out."

The minister for foreign affairs finished her call and the limousine arrived at their destination. Julius was assigned to a nearby park bench and Allan promised to be back soon.

As Karlsson and Wallström approached the security checkpoint at the main entrance, the latter took the opportunity to give the 101-year-old a piece of advice. Or perhaps it was more like a plea. Given what she had seen him evoke during their dinner with Kim Jong-un, she suggested he consider being a bit more agreeable this time.

It was obvious that she was on edge about what was to come.

"Agreeable," said Allan. "Of course. That's the least I can do, Madame Minister, since you saved our lives and everything."

USA

Donald John Trump was born in New York on June 14, 1946, a year to the day after Swedish citizen Allan Emmanuel Karlsson solved the last problem facing the United States in its struggle to create the atomic bomb.

Allan and Donald had more in common than one might at first think. For example, both had received inheritances from their parents. Allan had taken over a cottage with no insulation or running water somewhere in the forest outside the Sörmland village of Malmköping, while young Donald's father had left him twenty-seven thousand centrally located apartments in New York City.

Subsequently things went equally poorly for the sons. Allan accidentally blew his cottage sky-high and as a result became homeless. Donald did more or less the same thing with his father's business empire and was only rescued from bankruptcy by the help of a number of benevolent banks.

Another common denominator was that Donald and Allan had sat around sighing over their existences at more or less the same time, but on opposite sides of the globe: Allan on Bali, before he was bewitched by a black tablet and let himself be carried off by a hot-air balloon, Donald in a big white house in Washington, surrounded by idiots and malevolent characters.

It wasn't as pleasant to be President of the United States as Donald Trump had expected. Firing people was just about the most fun thing in the world. When he did it in the business world and on TV, he was met with fear and respect. But as soon as he set a head or two rolling in the White House (or thirteen: it sort of depended on how you counted them), the corrupt media insinuated that he was mentally unstable.

Another horrible experience was that the Republicans—*his* Republicans—didn't do as he said. And that apparently the law was written in such a way that he couldn't fire them too.

And all this goddamned talk of racism. Like how his father Fred had allegedly been arrested at a KKK march in Queens at some point back in the beginning of time. For one thing, it had never happened. For another, he was released right away, so what was the big deal?

Worst of all, you could no longer tell the truth in this country. Not if you were the president. Like saying Mexicans were rapists. And Muslims were something even worse, every last one.

There were bright spots too, of course. After all, the president had a lot of say. He could start wars if the necessity arose. Real ones and verbal ones. His war against the fake media was ongoing. Donald Trump praised himself for having invented the word "fake" on his own. Anyone who invents new words can make them mean whatever he wants. In practice, it meant that fake news was anything Trump didn't like reading, listening to, or watching.

But it was trickier with the real wars. Heads of state in other countries turned out to be as difficult to remove from office as any given House member or senator. The best remaining option was to threaten to bomb the shit out of them. This tactic worked in the business world, if you switched out the word "bomb" for "sue." But when your opponent was a pint-sized, narcissistic madman with the capacity for nuclear weapons, you really had to think twice. This wasn't exactly one of Donald Trump's strong suits. He had to admit that to himself. His time was far too precious for it. And, also, the North Korean narcissist reminded him of someone—he just couldn't think who it was.

Anyway, Trump knew he had half the country on his side as long as he played his cards right. Since the other half was beyond salvation, it was mobilizing his own people that counted. Talking about new gun laws would, for example, be a bad strategy. Donald Trump had always taken care of his friends, especially the ones who couldn't be fired. Like the gun lobby, for example. It was a nuisance that a psychopath had just killed sixty or so people in Las Vegas with the help of twenty-three different guns. According to Murphy's Law, he would probably also have a school shooting on his hands soon.

Furthermore, the president had to continue to remind the country of all the external threats they faced (aside from the mass shootings, that was). To be on the safe side he added a few on his own. Everyone on his elite squad, of course, had to be on board with building a wall to block the country that consisted solely of rapists.

War was also a good mobilizing factor. He won his ongoing Twitter war just about every day. That left the other one, the one against the tiny rocket man. The narcissist.

Who *did* he remind him of?

———

White House Chief of Staff Reince Priebus had reason to come along on the president's trip to New York to meet with UN Ambassador Nikki Haley, among others. The developments in North Korea were worrisome on all levels, including that Priebus himself had to do everything right from now on in order to keep his job. He had just made the mistake of correcting his boss—the armada of American ships the president said was heading for North Korea was not in fact an armada and, what was more, they were on their way in the other direction, toward Australia. His boss had lost his temper and blamed Priebus for the fact that the lying *New York Times* had published the truth.

Aside from the part where the president wasn't always as exact in his pronouncements as the world might wish, there was also the fact that he only made things worse each time he insulted Kim Jong-un. But the worst thing anyone could do was try to tell him that.

In any case, Priebus informed his president that the representative of the Security Council, Minister for Foreign Affairs Wallström, had arrived at the UN building and was ready for a meeting. In addition, she was—in accordance with the president's wishes—in the company of the Swiss nuclear weapons expert, the Swede Allan Karlsson.

"Shall I ask—"

"Bring them here," said President Trump.

"Hello, Mr. President," said Margot Wallström.

"What she said," said Allan.

"Sit down," said the president. "We'll start with you, Mrs. Wallström. What body part were you thinking with when you began your visit to Pong . . . Piyong . . . North Korea with a *press conference*? Press conferences are awful, and North Korean ones are worse."

Margot Wallström said that there had been no time to think with any body part at all. She had been driven straight from the airport to the live TV spectacle that the president and the rest of the world had been privy to.

"We were all fooled by Kim Jong-un. It's as simple as that," said Minister Wallström. "In my capacity as representative of the United Nations, let me be the first to apologize."

"*You* were all fooled," the president contradicted her. "*I* will not be fooled by that little rocket man."

The minister apologized: it had not been her intent to insult the president. That said, she wasn't sure an epithet like "little rocket man" would benefit the conversational climate between North Korea and the rest of the world. She had devoted a whole chapter in her report to the secretary general on the importance of proper linguistic usage. "If you would like a copy, Mr. President, I will immediately make sure—"

"A chapter? Who would ever read that? Who would read that? Just answer my question."

Minister for Foreign Affairs Wallström could not recall the president having asked any question other than with what body part she had been thinking. Although she couldn't say so.

"I'll do my best, Mr. President. May I take this opportunity to introduce you to Mr. Allan Karlsson? He's not Swiss, as has been claimed, but Swedish. And he has *not* helped North Korea in its struggle to build—"

"Who are you?" the president interrupted, turning to Allan.

Allan was already wondering the same thing about the man across from him. Was he the president, or just strange? Oh, well, history proved it was possible to be both.

"Who am I? I'm Allan Karlsson, as the minister mentioned. And I'm Swedish. I believe she mentioned that as well. And, like she said, I did not help North Korea. In fact, it's possible I threw a wrench in their works. In short, that's who I am. I can, of course, tell you more."

"They say you received the Presidential Medal of Freedom," said Donald Trump. "But that president is history. This one is going to take it back if you don't answer my questions right. Take it back."

"I promise I'll do my best, if you'll only start asking questions," said Allan. "But giving the medal back would be difficult. It vanished somehow in a submarine on the way to Leningrad in 1948. It's possible that the Russians have been keeping it hidden since. You can always ask that guy in Moscow, Putin. I understand you're on good terms."

President Trump was thrown off balance. A submarine? 1948?

This afforded Allan the opportunity to keep talking. "But I will answer as I'm able. I must say, I'm in the habit. Truman wanted to know all about the atom bomb. Soon after that it was Nixon. He was more curious about the practice of politics in Indonesia, wiretapping and such. I told him what I knew, and apparently it had an impact on him. Whatever the current president wishes to know, I'm ready to be of service. I expect that the art of making vodka out of goat's milk is not at the top of the list. It seems, in any case, that the goat's milk would be the more interesting part anyway."

Allan had read on the black tablet that the poor

wretch of a commander-in-chief was a teetotaler and always had been.

Trump remained quiet for a moment. "You talk too much," he said. "Why don't you tell me what you were doing in North Korea instead, and why you helped that idiot over there with nuclear weapons?"

"I didn't help any idiot," said Allan. "Unless we're counting Nixon. I ended up in Korea by chance, along with my friend Julius. We were rescued at sea by a ship. Unfortunately enough, it was on its way to its home harbor outside Pyongyang. And as if that wasn't enough, alcohol was forbidden just as much on that boat as it seems to be here. The captain's name was Pak, by the way. Perhaps you know each other."

President Trump tried to find something of substance in the old man's exposition but didn't succeed. "Would you get to the point? What do the Koreans know that they didn't know before you told them?"

Allan was beginning to dislike the cross man in front of him. What was wrong with him? He was just about to ask when he recalled his promise to the delightful Madame Wallström. He was supposed to be *agreeable*. How did one do that? "Anything I may have told the Koreans is more likely to have had the result that they know less today than they did before. I gave them a few formulas, that's true. Among others, one that tells how best to purify wastewater, if memory serves. That's not the sort of knowledge one can start a war with."

"Wastewater?" said the president.

"You can bleach clothing with it too. In any case, with the exemplary aid of Minister for Foreign Affairs Wallström, we managed to flee before they could discover that the formulas I'd patched together would not be of any use in nuclear weapons. My only crime, as I see it, is probably that I ended up in peril at sea off the coast of Indonesia. If the president considers this reason enough to take back the medal, then all that's left to do is find it."

Even Allan thought this last bit didn't sound sufficiently agreeable.

"Speaking of nothing much at all, might you allow me a personal reflection, Mr. President?" he said, as the president was still pondering his next step.

"What is it?"

It was worth a shot.

"That's a tremendously nice hairstyle."

"A tremendously nice hairstyle?" said the president.

"Well, actually, all of you looks very nice. But the hairstyle has something a little extra."

President Trump adjusted his reddish-blond mop. His internal rage ebbed away. "You're not the first to say so. Not the first."

Clearly pleased. It was a wonder how easy some things were. Allan vowed to practice this "agreeable" idea again the next time he met an American president.

The Swiss-Swede was decently likable, now that Donald Trump thought about it. And a little exciting. With good judgment, it seemed. He looked at his watch. "I have to go see to some important business. No more time for you."

Margot Wallström stood up to leave the meeting she would have been more than happy to do without. Allan, due to his age, was considerably slower.

"Hold on," said Donald Trump. He had an idea, and it never took him long to move from thought to action. This old man was long-winded and strange, but he definitely had taste. What he'd said about the hairstyle was right on target. "Do you play golf, Karlsson?" he said.

"No, I don't," said Allan. "I once had a Spanish friend who played the harmonica. But that was before he died. After that he didn't play anything. Got his head shot off in the Civil War. A real shame. That was a while ago now."

Donald Trump wondered which civil war Karlsson could be referring to. Surely he wasn't old enough for it to be the American one. Oh, well, whatever war it was, it didn't matter. It would be interesting to keep him around for a while yet.

The problem was, the president had a round of golf planned outside New York, by invitation of one of his better friends, a real-estate magnate who'd invested seven hundred thousand dollars in Trump's presidential campaign, and was now poised to get six point two million dollars in lowered real-estate tax in return. This was best celebrated over eighteen holes, but unfortunately a virus had sent the magnate to bed with a high fever. Trump was loath to cancel the game just for that. Golf was golf, and remaining at his borrowed desk at the UN building didn't seem like a viable alternative. Each time he made himself available, it seemed the whole world wanted a piece of him.

So golf it would be, and Trump informed Karlsson that he was welcome to join in, so they could chat a little more. If he wanted, in addition, to make himself useful he could keep an eye on the Puerto Rican caddy. Perhaps Puerto Ricans weren't any more likely to be thieves than anyone else, but they did have a tendency to drag their feet.

"I don't know what sort of talent I have for keeping Puerto Ricans in line," said Allan, "but I suppose we can find out. If the president desires my modest company, I won't be the one to upset the apple cart. I must confess that I have done just that at certain junctures when I happened to end up involved with various leaders from the many corners of the world. It's seldom ended well."

The old man was being difficult again. But he still had his charm. Had his charm. "Then that's settled," said the president. "Nice!"

He asked Minister for Foreign Affairs Wallström to leave, with the comment that she should watch herself from now on. "Thanks for coming. Now go."

"I should be the one to thank you," said Margot Wallström.

Once a diplomat, always a diplomat.

The President of the United States doesn't take a taxi, or even an Uber, from Manhattan to a nearby golf course. He takes a helicopter. It was waiting on the roof of the UN building. Trump and Allan were escorted to it by five Secret Service agents, three of whom followed them on board. Another five had long been on-site at the golf course, to secure the area, along with a large number of local police officers.

Allan spared a fleeting thought for his friend Julius as he stepped into the helicopter. The weather was pleasant for the season and he would have nothing to complain about, sitting on a park bench in the sunshine; he'd just have to sit there a little longer. How long could a round of golf take? An hour?

During their journey over Manhattan and Queens, the president pointed out all the buildings he'd inherited, bought, or sold throughout the years. And a few he'd neither inherited nor bought nor sold, but which had slipped in nonetheless. Then he talked about what he planned to do with the real-estate tax, that vile health-care reform, various free-trade agreements, and the general level of decadence. He unintentionally gave the unemployment rate as double what it currently was and promised Allan he would halve it so it reached actual levels.

Allan listened. He already knew enough of the contents of the black tablet to observe that the president was exaggerating or making things up as often as he hit the mark.

The helicopter landed; the president and his 101-year-old Swiss-Swedish companion stepped out just a few yards from the first tee. There was no waiting time for the president. Hole number one was a par four and 339 yards. It bent slightly to the left, with a wide fairway and a deep bunker on the right side.

"Well?" was Trump's first and only word to the Puerto Rican, who informed the president that he would do best to play it safe and put the ball in the middle of the fairway so that he would be in the optimal position to hit the ball into the green.

The president's golf skills were not, however, so great that the ball always went where it was supposed to. Like this time. A more forceful hit than intended, plus a crosswind.

"You goddamn worthless good-for-nothing," said President Trump to the poor caddy. "Worthless good-for-nothing."

Clearly it was the caddy's fault that the wind had taken the ball and sent it into the bunker.

Allan knew not a whit about golf, but it seemed to him that the guy holding the club must be at least partially responsible for his own stroke. Above all, he had grown tired of the president's habit of repeating himself, like a scratched record. It probably wouldn't count as agreeable to bring this up, but Wallström wasn't present any longer, so what would happen?

Given that things were as they were, he supposed whatever happened would happen.

"Why do you always say everything twice?" Allan asked the man who had just put his ball into the bunker.

"Huh?" said the president.

With that, the 101-year-old found himself in a bind.

"At the risk of becoming guilty of the same crime, I will ask again. Why do you say everything twice, Mr. President? And most of the time something that isn't even true?"

"Not true? *Not true?*" said the president, and in an instant he was back in the same mood he'd been in when they'd first met. "Oh, so you're the *New York Times's* errand boy, you rat!"

Some golfers are more sensitive than others, immediately after hitting into a bunker.

"I'm not running errands for anyone," said Allan. "At my age, you don't run at all. I'm just wondering why, first, the president has such a hard time telling the truth, and second, how it could be the potentially lazy Puerto Rican's fault that the man holding the club just shot his ball into a deep pit, and third, why the president has to make almost all of his stupid remarks again right after saying them the first time."

Some golfers are more sensitive than those who are extra sensitive immediately after hitting into a bunker. It's possible that President Trump belonged to that category.

"You goddamn fucking I-don't-know-what," he said. "Here I invite you to . . ." (play a round of golf, he was about to say but, of course, Allan was nothing more than a supervisor of Puerto Ricans).

"To what, Mr. President? To what?"

Allan's repetition put the president in an even worse mood. He brandished his five-iron at the old man, unable to form words.

"It seems to me the president ought to do a better job of reining in his impulses," said Allan, upon which the president failed to do so.

"My impulses? No one has better impulse control than me. No one!" said the president, and threw the five-iron over the head of the Puerto Rican, who might have been as lazy as the president suggested, after all, for, luckily enough, he had just sat down. "I am more stable than anyone!"

"Well, I counted seven foolish things during our brief journey in the air. Eight, if we count hitting the ball into the bunker just after we landed. If you avoid saying the same thing twice in a row, that's cutting down on lies by half."

Donald Trump couldn't believe his ears. So he was a Communist, after all, this bastard. The President of the United States certainly couldn't fraternize with that type of person.

"Get out of here!" he said.

"Happy to, Mr. President. But I'll send you off with one last thought. I don't know anything about therapy or other such modern conveniences, but if I were you I would try having a drink. Aren't you past seventy by now? I suppose seventy years without vodka could make anyone crazy."

With that, the encounter was over. A Secret Service agent moved to stand between the president and his guest; another tugged at Allan's arm and said he would immediately be flown back to the UN building.

"I'll help you on board. Come on!"

"Can we wait for just a minute?" said Allan. "It would be fun to see how this guy is planning to get out of the bunker."

USA

Allan found his friend on the park bench outside UN headquarters where he'd parked him just over an hour earlier. Julius was still sitting there, the North Korean briefcase on his lap. The switch from North Korea to the United States had been a step in the right direction, but the realization that this was a country where the possession of enriched uranium could bring you a few hundred years in prison had captured his anxious attention all over again.

"How was the meeting?" he asked Allan by way of a greeting.

"Agreeable."

"Good. Does that mean you've finally made sure we'll be rid of this?"

He held up the briefcase as if Allan didn't already know what he meant.

"No, it wasn't quite that agreeable. That Trump is not getting our briefcase. He seems awfully close to exploding all on his own."

"What? Then what are we going to do with it? And with ourselves? You said you had everything worked out. Exactly what have you worked out?"

"Did I say that? Well, you say a lot of things when you're my age. I don't know, dear Julius, but it will all sort itself out. May I have a seat here next to you?"

Allan didn't wait for a response, assuming one wouldn't be forthcoming anyway. He sat down and said it felt nice to rest his legs a bit, because the hallways in the UN building had been both long and plentiful. Add to that the time difference and other oddities . . .

But Julius did not allow himself to be sucked in. Didn't Allan understand that they were in the United States with nine pounds of enriched uranium, and that there was no way they could leave the country with the briefcase in hand? It would immediately set off alarms at the airport no matter how hard they waved their diplomatic passports.

Allan said he did understand, now that Julius had reminded him.

Julius went on: "If the president was angry today, what do you think is going to happen when he finds out what we're strolling around his country with?"

"Then we'll have to try not to tell him," said Allan.

At which he felt around a bit, asked Julius for the briefcase, and placed it on one end of the bench with the North Korean coat on top. This provided a temporary bed with nine pounds of enriched uranium and a coat as a pillow. He lay down and closed his eyes in the fresh air.

"So now you're just going to lie down and die?" Julius said acidly, shifting in the other direction to keep his trousers away from the dirty soles of Allan's shoes.

No, Allan had no such plans. He was just going to recuperate a little; it had been a long day. After all, it was not much later than it had been half a day earlier, such was the design of the Earth.

As he lay there, the 101-year-old looked both tired and pathetic, on top of how extremely old men look in the first place. In under a minute a passing woman had already asked if he was okay and if she could help somehow. She was probably South American. The surroundings in the UN district were fairly international. Allan politely declined the offer of aid, saying that he felt fine and would soon be on his feet again.

Julius kept up his anxious talk of the briefcase and

the future, but Allan stopped listening. Julius seldom came up with any new ideas when he was worried, and the old ones brought no joy to anyone.

After a few more minutes, a man stopped. He was perhaps sixty years old and wearing a hat. Just like the woman, he wondered if everything was as it should be, and if he could be of any service.

Julius was grumpy and said nothing, but Allan realized what he was missing. He looked up and inquired if the gentleman had something to drink. The fact was, he had just suffered through a meeting with the American president and *there* was a man about whom one could say a lot of things. An ill-natured scoundrel. With a temper as uneven as a rural North Korean highway. Who apparently had never had a drink in his entire life.

"The president?" said the man in the hat. "The American one? Trump? That's terrible. Let's see if I have anything for comfort." He dug through his shoulder bag and brought up two small bottles wrapped in brown paper. "It's not much, but it's something. Underberg. Good for the stomach."

"There's nothing wrong with Allan's stomach," said Julius. "Don't you have anything for his head?"

"Yes, there is," said Allan. "Depending on the alcohol content, of course."

The man in the hat thought it might be 40 percent or more; he hadn't checked. In any case, he never traveled abroad without a few of these brown bottles in his luggage. Good for the stomach. Had he mentioned that?

Allan sat up with a certain amount of difficulty, accepted the hat man's offer, unscrewed the cap of the small bottle, and drained its contents in one gulp.

"Brrrr!" he said, his eyes sparkling. "You'll want to hold onto your hat before having any of that."

The hat man smiled. Julius saw what good the little bottle seemed to do for Allan and quickly reached for the other. Soon he had caught up and both men gazed contentedly at their new acquaintance.

"I'm Ambassador Breitner," he said. "Representative here at the UN for the Federal Republic of Germany. I have one bottle left in my bag, but I think I had better keep it, because you gentlemen might fight over it."

"Maybe not fight," said Allan. "We're not violent. Violence seldom leads anywhere. Julius here certainly tends to take a dim view of most things, but it always stops there."

Julius was on the verge of taking a dim view of what Allan had just said, but chose to smile along with his friend and the man in the hat.

"So, another UN employee. Then we're colleagues," said Allan. "I myself, and this fellow here, who doesn't seem to be quite as surly anymore, are diplomats and assistants to UN Envoy Wallström from Sweden. My name is Allan and this is Julius. A good man, deep down."

Ambassador Breitner shook hands with them.

"Might you be hungry, Mr. Breitner?" Allan asked. "The miracle cure we were just served has whetted my appetite. We'd love you to keep us company at some venue, especially if you might be so generous as to foot the bill, because it has just occurred to me that we have no money. We once had a gold cigarette lighter, but we had to exchange it in Pyongyang for muesli with milk."

UN Ambassador Breitner had already come to enjoy his new companions. Also, he was curious about the frail man who had apparently just had a disastrous meeting with President Trump. The other, too, might have an interesting story to tell. But above all he was an experienced diplomat and as such he was always on the job. Pyongyang? These two gentlemen might be sources of information.

"Why, it so happens I can spare an hour or two for a couple of diplomat gentlemen. And the Federal Republic will pick up the tab. We can afford that."

———

The German knew a nice place on Second Avenue. It wasn't far to walk, even for Allan. There they were served schnitzel, German beer, and fruit vodka, and the mood was so cheery that with their second toast, Ambassador Breitner suggested that Allan and Julius could call him Konrad.

"Of course, Konrad," said Allan.

"For once I agree with Allan, Konrad," said Julius.

During dinner the ambassador learned first how an iPad works (he chose not to mention that he already owned two) and then how best to cultivate asparagus. After their second toast, the conversation turned to how Allan and Julius had ended up in North Korea and managed to sneak out with the help of Minister Wallström and the diplomatic passports she had conjured up.

Konrad Breitner was able to connect Allan and Julius's story with the news he had been following for the past few days. So the Swiss nuclear weapons expert was Swedish! He didn't appear to be much of a traitor, but he was quite a rascal when it came to downing fruit vodka. He had already had three, though he had complained all the while, saying he didn't understand what business fruit had being in vodka.

Julius didn't have Allan's talent for taking the day

and early evening as they came, not by a long shot. He was tormented by the fact that he had a briefcase full of enriched uranium at his feet, and the more vodkas he consumed, the more his imagination convinced him that Ambassador Konrad was sneaking repeated glances at it. All in his mind or not, he decided to be proactive.

"We are certainly happy that we managed to get away with all of Allan's technical design plans in the briefcase here. It would have been terrible if they'd got into the hands of the Supreme Leader."

For a moment Allan thought his friend was about to ruin a carefree night at the pub, but then he caught on to what Julius was up to. The asparagus farmer wanted nothing more than to be rid of the uranium, and it wasn't as if they could just put it down somewhere between Fifth and Sixth Avenues and walk away. Konrad might be the answer to their problem!

"I'm glad you revealed what the briefcase contains, Julius. We'd been planning to hand it all over to President Trump, but . . . well, as I said, he was about to explode even without any blueprints for how it should be done. Now we're wondering if we might find terminal storage for the documentation in safer hands."

"Have you discussed the matter with Minister Wallström?" Konrad wondered, sobering up.

Allan said that Madame Wallström was extraordinary in every way, but at the end of the day she was Swedish and had, like all Swedes from 1966 onward, a pathological fear of touching anything nuclear.

Julius understood that Allan understood, and hurried to his rescue. "Safest of all, of course, would be if the knowledge was kept with the EU, wouldn't you say, Allan?"

"There you go being so clever again, Julius, as only you can be. When you choose to show that side of yourself. Please feel free to do so more often. But finding a strong EU leader who is prepared to take responsibility for world peace is easier said than done. Perhaps that new Frenchman, Macron?"

"Macron?" Julius said earnestly, although he was still playing along.

"Yes, he won the presidential election the other day. Didn't I mention that? No, of course not. You only get surlier when someone tries to enlighten you. The special thing about Macron is that he's neither left nor right. Or he's both. I'm not quite sure how that works, but it sounds nice and balanced."

UN Ambassador Breitner was no dummy. What was more, he had been on his guard ever since a few minutes ago. Yet he fell into the trap. "Well, it just so happens that Chancellor Merkel is coming to Washington in two days. Do you suppose she would suffice as guarantor? Of world peace, I mean?"

Julius let Allan get in the crucial jab.

"Why, Konrad! You're a genius! Are you saying you're prepared to hand over our nuclear weapons–tainted briefcase to Angela Merkel? Why didn't we think of her?"

Ambassador Breitner smiled humbly. "What are friends for? Cheers, boys."

The ambassador was the only one with anything left in his glass, but it still worked.

Now, the contents of the briefcase might have been encased in lead, but who knew what sort of instruments could be found at American security checkpoints? No one would be surprised to find that radioactivity warning lights started blinking here and there. A potential life sentence at Guantánamo was not something Allan and Julius wished upon their newfound friend Konrad. Especially since he was picking up the tab for the evening.

"But we have a problem," said Allan.

And he explained that the nuclear weapons–related documents had been hidden in a lead-lined package and that it might cause problems for the ambassador at airport security. Not to mention what would happen if officials at JFK got it into their heads to take a closer look at said package.

"Oh?" said Ambassador Breitner, doubtfully.

"Given what we've just said, may we suggest that you take a taxi to Washington, Ambassador? Julius and I can cover the cost, but that will likely require a payment plan. We're a bit hard up just now."

"Extremely hard up," said Julius.

If the ambassador went by road to the German embassy, Allan and Julius's white lie wouldn't be discovered until he arrived. Once he'd carried the briefcase through the gates, it would be too late. A global scandal would have been averted (since no one would expect the Germans to call a press conference on the matter) and Ambassador Breitner would get off with an internal scolding. And perhaps dismissal. But *not* Guantánamo.

"A taxi?" said Ambassador Breitner. "Why not? Certainly, now that I think about it. And don't worry about the fee. I'll be saving the cost of the flight."

"Wonderful," said Allan. "Then I think that's enough saving the world for today. Time for another round before we all get stiff."

It had taken six fruit vodkas each to accompany the beer and schnitzel. When Ambassador Breitner excused himself to visit the cloakroom, Allan and Julius had the chance to exchange a few words.

"Imagine you coming up with something like this," Allan said encouragingly.

"Although he's a good man, is Konrad. It's too bad we're making trouble for him," said Julius.

Allan absorbed his friend's musings. "That can be remedied," he said.

Then he swiped a paper napkin and asked the waitress for a pen. Julius wondered what Allan had cooked up and was told that it might help their newfound friend Konrad if the briefcase contained not only enriched uranium but also a greeting to the big cheese.

"Merkel?"

"Yes, that's her name."

Allan composed a letter on the napkin.

Dear Chancellor Merkel, I have come to realize via my black tablet that you are a lady to be reckoned with. With my friend Julius, by trade an asparagus farmer, I happened to bring nine pounds of enriched uranium with us when we left North Korea after a short visit. By luck and cleverness both we and the uranium ended up in the United States, and the plan was to hand it over to President Trump.

I had the dubious pleasure of meeting him. He shouted and squawked, and, in fact, his demeanor was rather reminiscent of Kim Jong-un's. So the asparagus farmer and I reconsidered. Trump must already have plenty of enriched uranium. What he could possibly do with another nine pounds would probably be a mystery even to him.

In any case, we met your eminent UN Ambassador Konrad outside the UN building and decided to join ranks for a very pleasant dinner. Konrad is off answering nature's call at the moment, and I'm writing in all haste behind his back, so to speak. Excuse the penmanship (continued on the next napkin).

So, after a schnitzel and a few rounds of beer and vodka that for some reason had to taste like apple, Julius and I became more personal with Konrad than perhaps we should have. Unfortunately enough, the resulting words fell in such a way that Konrad was given the impression that the briefcase you have now inherited contains a variety of instructions for building nuclear weapons. Instead, the package you have just received contains those nine pounds of uranium I mentioned on the previous napkin. The fact that they are now in the secure

hands of the Federal Republic of Germany is a re-
lief to Julius and me. Perhaps it's not so much fun
for you but, after all, life is full of hardships. We
trust that you will handle the uranium in the best
way possible (continued on the next napkin).

My friend Julius says, by the way, that you
Germans are good at growing asparagus too, if,
that is, German asparagus is actually grown in
Germany, in contrast to

At that instant, Julius yanked the pen out of Allan's
hand and told him to get a grip.

"Konrad will be back at any moment! For God's
sake, hurry up!"

He gave Allan the pen back, so he started a new line
and kept on writing.

The long and the short of it is, we ask you not to
be too angry with Ambassador Konrad; he seems
to us to be a fine representative of your country. If
you must be angry with someone, Donald Trump
is a better choice. Or perhaps Kim Jong-un over in
North Korea. By the way, they say they have their
sights on over one hundred times as much uranium
as we managed to fool them out of. With eleven

hundred pounds they could afford to keep on failing
at their undertakings until they hit the mark. Kon-
rad will be back soon. Better wrap this up.

With kind regards, Allan Karlsson and Julius
Jonsson

Allan placed the three napkins on top of one another
in the proper order and asked Julius to stick them into
the side pocket of the briefcase.

Julius did as he was asked, assuming there was no
time to edit out the silly part about his relationship to
German asparagus. Given the circumstances, Allan
had actually done a rather good job on the napkins.

Konrad, however, didn't return for some time.
Bathroom visits could, after all, vary by nature. This
one was clearly of the longer sort. Julius had a sudden
inspiration. He took a scrap of paper from the inner
pocket of his worn summer jacket. There he had Gustav Svensson's phone number. On the table was Konrad's phone.

"Do you suppose . . . ?" said Julius.

"I absolutely suppose," said Allan.

Julius called. And found himself speaking to the
same voicemail as last time. This was deeply annoying.

"Gustav, for God's sake! What was the point of the
phone if you're going to keep it turned off all the time?

Allan and I made it to New York from Pyongyang and next we're going . . ."

"Here he comes," said Allan.

Quick as a wink, the phone was back on the table.

"Well, then, my friends, I suppose we should be thinking of getting along," said Konrad, taking out his wallet.

The bill was already on the table, next to the phone. Germany was about to become 620 dollars poorer, plus a hundred dollars in tips (plus the cost of a fifteen-second call to Indonesia). Konrad placed seven hundred-dollar bills and two twenties on the table, stood up, and said it was time for the friends to part ways.

"And for me, I suppose, all there is to do is take over this exciting briefcase and catch a cab," he said.

"Yes, I suppose that's true," said Allan, standing in the way so Konrad wouldn't notice Julius commandeering the tip.

USA, Sweden

While Allan and Julius used part of the tip money to outfit themselves and most of the rest to take the bus to Newark airport, President Trump sat in the clubhouse at the golf course, feeling a frustration he couldn't put into words.

What *was* that meeting he had suffered through? Had Minister for Foreign Affairs Wallström sat in the UN building sneering at him while old man Karlsson babbled away? Maybe that was what had happened. That was definitely what had happened. Yes, it was.

And Karlsson himself. Who on earth was he? Talking about goat's milk with the President of the United States? In front of the hysterically sneering, almost mockingly laughing Minister Wallström?

Not to mention what had happened next.

The president was seething. The Communist had questioned his impulse control. He should have walloped him in the head with his golf club. Trump mused, self-critically, that now and then he went too far in his attempts to arrive at a compromise in every situation.

What should he do now? The seething went on. The president opened his laptop and signed into Twitter.

Three minutes later, he had ridiculed a television host, insulted a head of state, threatened to fire one of his own cabinet members, and declared that his declining approval numbers had been made up by insert-the-newspaper-of-your-choosing.

He felt better.

Minister for Foreign Affairs Wallström had kept her promise: Messrs. Karlsson and Jonsson were booked in business-class seats to Stockholm that very evening.

"Any bags to check?" asked the woman at the check-in counter.

"No, thank you," said Allan.

"Just carry-ons?"

"We just gave our carry-on away."

Their journey to the motherland was a pleasant experience. It began even before the plane took off, when Allan and Julius were offered something to drink.

"Champagne? Juice?" said the flight attendant.

"Yes, please," said Allan. "And no, thanks."

"Same here, please," said Julius.

Later came a three-course dinner (not that the old men were hungry, but free was free) and if you pushed the right button after dessert you could lie down without even having to go to bed first.

"What will they think of next?" said Allan.

"Mm-hmm," said Julius, who had already covered himself with a blanket.

"Shall I read aloud to you from the tablet?"

"Not unless you want me to take it away and throw it out of the window."

Sweden

Allan and Julius stood in the arrivals hall of Terminal 5 at Arlanda airport, looking around. Julius summed up the situation: they were freshly outfitted, well rested, full—and had twenty dollars in assets.

"Twenty dollars?" said Allan. "That ought to be enough for a beer each."

Two small beers. Then they were out of cash.

"Now we're freshly outfitted, well rested, full, and not quite as thirsty as we just were," said Allan. "Do you have any ideas about what to do next?"

No, Julius didn't, not off the top of his head. Perhaps they should have considered this before drinking the last of their money, but what was done was done. The bit about personal finance was probably at the top of the agenda.

The 101-year-old nodded. Money made life easier in many ways. How were the asparagus funds? They had reached Sweden: Didn't Julius have a whole bunch of asparagus contacts here? Allan wasn't familiar with the details of how Indonesian Swedish asparagus was sent this way and that, all over the world, but he assumed it made a stopover in this country. Wouldn't anything else have been verging on unethical?

Brilliant! Julius didn't have a whole bunch of contacts, but he did have Gunnar Gräslund.

"Who might he be?" asked Allan.

Gunnar Gräslund was an acquaintance from the past. Most people knew him by the name "Gunnar Grisly" because that was what he was. He never showered; he shaved once a week; he did snuff and swore. And he had spent his entire life swindling people (Julius didn't blame him for that last part). He was the one who'd been handed the task of selling Gustav Svensson's locally grown asparagus onward and, however grisly he was otherwise, he fulfilled his commitments.

"All we have to do is travel to Gunnar, explain our situation, and he'll take out his wallet."

"Travel on what?" asked Allan.

"On foot," said Julius.

Sweden is 990 miles in length, but not quite so wide. A relatively enormous surface for a trifling ten million people to share.

In most of the country, you can wander for hours without meeting another person, or even a moose. You can buy yourself a valley including your own lake for an amount that wouldn't get you more than a shabby studio apartment on the outskirts of Paris. The downside to this purchase is that you will soon discover it is seventy-five miles to the nearest store, a hundred to a pharmacy, and even longer to limp if you step on a nail and require a hospital. If you want to borrow cream for your coffee from the nearest neighbor, there's a good chance they're a three-hour walk away. And three hours back. The coffee will have gone cold long before you return home.

Not everyone wants that sort of lifestyle. Those who want it least have made a silent pact to gather in Stockholm and its immediate surroundings. With them come the businesses. H&M, Ericsson, and IKEA prioritize the areas where two and a half million potential customers live over places like the village of Nattavaara north of the Arctic Circle, where seventy-seven people still haven't left.

So it wasn't particularly surprising that the regional warehouse for Julius Jonsson and Gustav Svensson's asparagus operation was located outside Stockholm and nowhere else. For a firm that has no need of direct contact with the consumer, yet moves imports and exports by plane, the area around Arlanda airport poses an advantage. More specifically, Märsta. Even more specifically, a two-hour walk from Arlanda airport. Two and a half if you're old.

The alternative was a fifteen-minute taxi ride, but that possibility had been drunk for breakfast.

Indonesia

Gustav Svensson had already had to manage with-out his partner for far too long. First Julius had disappeared, on Allan's birthday and everything. Gustav had unfinished business with their hotel and couldn't go there to look for him, but by asking around he discovered that Julius and Allan had gone to sea in a hot-air balloon.

After a few days, Gustav assumed Julius was dead, but almost a week later his cell phone received a call. He was alive! And asking questions about the operation, without leaving a call-back number.

Then came a few days of quiet before the next sign of life. Another message on the voicemail. Gustav prom-ised himself he would get better at charging the phone. This time, his friend said he had traveled to New York from Pyongyang! He'd gone to America? In a hot-air balloon? Via North Korea?

Even so, the question of where Julius was and when he planned to return home was subordinate to the necessity of having someone to make important daily business decisions. Gustav didn't know what to do other than sit down at his partner's desk and make those decisions in said partner's spirit. Without Julius, he listened to the Swedish importer/exporter who suggested that they call the so Swedish-sounding asparagus Swedish in Sweden as well. That would bring an even higher price.

Gustav had some vague memory from his conversations with Julius that this was something to look out for. But only a vague memory. The advantage of arak was that it freed your thoughts; the disadvantage was that they were not only freed but also, by the next morning, gone.

Julius would have put a stop to further Swedifying Gustav Svensson's asparagus, if he'd had the chance. The last time it had happened, a stupid middleman had laid waste to the entire operation by doing that very thing.

Sweden

Thus it came to pass that Allan and Julius, after two and a half hours of slow walking, arrived at the warehouse of the Swedish partner, the day after the police had raided the place and arrested the partner in question. The door of the warehouse bore a yellow sign with a red outline and black text: "Sealed in accordance with Code of Judicial Procedure Chapter 27, Paragraph 15. Trespassing is punishable by law." Signed: "The Police."

"What happened here?" Allan asked a woman passing by with her dog.

"A raid on an illegal vegetable importer," said the woman.

"Bloody Gunnar Grisly," said Julius.

"Nice dog," said Allan. "What's its name?"

The friends were once again at a loss. And as penniless as before. Furthermore, Julius had a blister. He limped alongside Allan toward central Märsta, and had trouble keeping up with the 101-year-old's pace. At last he had to give up.

"I'm not taking another step," he said. "I'm about to die of this blister."

"It's not that easy to die," said Allan. "I know from my own personal experience. You'll just have to take a few more steps."

He pointed at a corner shop across the street; it appeared to share a wall with an undertaker. "Won't that be nice? Inside the door on the left you can buy bandages, and if they don't have any for sale you can die inside the door on the right."

Allan stepped into the corner shop with his limping friend two yards behind. A woman of late middle age with three different kinds of amulet around her neck sat at the cash register. She looked up in surprise; she wasn't exactly drowning in customers.

"Good morning," said Allan. "Might there be any bandages for sale here? My friend Julius has grown weary of his blister."

Yes, there were. The woman pointed at the shelf of personal hygiene items. Julius staggered over, found what he needed, and staggered back to the amulet lady, who scanned the item and informed him of the price.

"Thirty-six kronor, please."

"Well, that's the thing," Julius thought up. "I forgot my wallet today. Can I come back and pay tomorrow?"

"That's fine. I'll put the bandages aside for now," said the woman, snatching the box back so fast her amulets rattled.

"No—that is, I have a blister now, but money later. I want to take the bandages with me, come back tomorrow and pay."

The woman was more than just a cashier. In fact, she owned the store. She aimed a grave look at one of her first customers of the day. "I am a hardworking business owner. I've been here since eight this morning for almost no reason. Are you suggesting that I should start handing out my wares for free, once someone who needs something finally appears?"

Julius sighed, not sure he had the energy for the dialogue he could see coming. But he responded that he understood the woman's point of view, and that he wished she could come to understand his own. This was a very special situation. He was an honorable person, a diplomat, in fact, who had just returned from America on an urgent matter. He had accidentally left his wallet at the embassy.

"Then why not go and get it?"

"In the United States."

The amulet lady took an extra look first at Julius, then Allan, then Julius again. One of them was older than her; the other seemed older than was possible. Neither of them looked like a diplomat, whatever one of those looked like.

"Then how about calling a friend?"

Julius's left heel was bleeding. His right heel was calling attention to itself as well. And it had been several hours since he'd had any food. "I have no friends," he said.

"That's not true," said Allan, who was standing nearby. "You have me, Julius."

"And how much money do you have?"

"None, but still."

The lady with the amulets followed the gentlemen's conversation.

"I'm sorry. No money, no bandages. That is the policy of this poor little shop. Put into place by me, the owner, Sabine Jonsson."

"But that's Julius's last name too," said Allan. "Isn't that reason enough to make an exception?"

The amulet lady shook her head. The amulets followed. "There must be close to a hundred thousand

Jonssons in this country. What would become of my finances if I handed out free bandages to them all?"

Allan said he supposed her finances would go to pot if she did that, but right now they were talking about one Jonsson, not a hundred thousand. To be on the safe side, of course, she could put up a sign on her door later, which clearly stated that all the country's Jonssons shouldn't bother asking.

The amulet lady was about to reply, but Julius was in absolute despair. He couldn't deal with this any longer. It was impossible to consider limping away without bandaging himself first.

"Give the bandages here," he said. "This is a robbery!"

The amulet lady looked more surprised than scared.

"What do you mean, a robbery?" she said. "You don't have anything to rob me with. Not even a water pistol. If you're going to rob someone, at least do it properly."

Julius had never robbed anyone before, but he felt insulted on behalf of all the professional robbers of the world. How could a robbery victim be so disrespectful?

Allan asked if the woman had water pistols for sale. It might be just the thing to get them out of the impasse in which they were currently stuck.

She did not. What was more, how was he planning to pay for the pistol? If he had money, wouldn't it be better to pay the ransom for his friend's bandages?

Allan realized she was right. But he also sensed a note of forgiveness in the air. Perhaps the woman with the amulets didn't want to argue anymore. He quickly worked out a plan for peace.

"I see you have a small café corner over there. If my friend and I have a seat with the bandages, might you keep us company over a cup of coffee, ma'am? Wouldn't that be a decently unexpected turn of events?"

The amulet lady smiled for the first time. She handed the box of bandages to Julius with the comment that he and his friend weren't thirty-six kronor in debt, but another twenty on top. The coffee was ten kronor a cup.

Julius nodded gratefully and shuffled over to the closest empty chair. Allan wondered if there would be an extra charge for a sugar cube.

"Both sugar and milk are included. Have a seat. I'll be over in a sec."

Sweden

Sabine Jonsson arrived with three cups of coffee, a bowl of sugar cubes, ten ounces of milk from the fridge, and three cinnamon buns she'd just warmed in the microwave. Julius had finished bandaging himself and decided to stay in socks for a while longer.

"Just so we can keep our accounts in order," said Allan, "what do we owe for the buns?"

"Oh," said Sabine Jonsson. "They might as well be as free as the rest of it. My finances are going to pot anyway. I am, as you will have noticed, hopeless at running a business."

What Allan noticed above all was that Sabine wanted to talk. Perhaps it wasn't much fun for her, alone behind a counter all day long. Surely it didn't help, having customers who couldn't pay their way.

"It seems to me you're a generous person, Miss Sabine," said Allan. "Tell us a little about yourself, and I'll eat this bun in the meantime."

Allan's analysis of the situation proved correct. It was like pushing a button.

What did he want to know? That she was fifty-nine years old, unmarried, and had neither friends nor relatives? At least, not on this side of existence.

"On which side, did you say?" Julius wondered.

"This one. There's another side too, if you ask my mother."

Allan said he wanted to know more about the other side, and that he would be happy to ask her mother. "Where might she be?"

"On the other side."

"Is she dead?"

"Yes."

Allan finished chewing his bun and swallowed. "In that case, would you mind, Miss Sabine, trying to summarize what your mother would have said if she were somewhere other than that?"

By all means. The spirits' side was unfamiliar to most. But, as a child, Sabine had learned from her mother that, like her mother, she had gifts others did not. Her mother, Gertrud, was no longer alive, but until her death she had spent many years running Other

Side AB, assisted by her daughter, who kept to herself the fact that she never saw what her mother seemed to see. Their speciality was consultations in the field of clairvoyance. This meant that mother and daughter held séances upon clients' request and offered courses in finding spirits, handling malevolent spirits, and the best way to reward friendly spirits that watched over old houses. In their communications work they used pendulums, crystals, divining rods, sounds and scents, all with the aim of establishing a bridge between the world as we know it and the unknown on the other side. Hence the name of the business.

"And the amulets around your neck?" Allan asked.

"Inheritances from Mom. Just about all she left behind. They're symbols of earth, fertility, and gifts. Or nonsense, nonsense, and nonsense, if you prefer."

"You don't believe in the other side?" Julius asked.

"I hardly believe in this one. My life is fairly miserable."

Sabine had more to get off her chest. There were a lot of things that wanted to come out. But she thought it was her turn for something to nibble at. Time to hear from the gentlemen. What were they, besides shop robbers? Diplomats? No matter how much Sabine appreciated a good story, in this case she preferred to hear the truth.

Julius nodded in shame and apologized for the attempted robbery. But he'd been in such pain, both of sole and soul. And, incidentally, it hadn't gone away.

"There's ibuprofen in a rack by the register," said Sabine. "You can put the money you don't have on the counter."

Julius thanked her and hobbled off. Meanwhile, Allan began his story. In certain respects, they were in fact diplomats—at least, they had diplomatic passports. The part about the wallet, though, wasn't true. Happenstance had brought them on an involuntary journey from Indonesia, where they worked as vegetable merchants. On their journey they had met the Swedish minister for foreign affairs, who had helped them along the way and promoted them to diplomats, mostly for practical reasons, but still. In the United States, Allan and the minister had met President Trump, at the president's own request. After that, it seemed best to return to Sweden. Earlier that day they had been standing at Arlanda with twenty dollars in their pocket. Unfortunate circumstances had led them to run out of that money. Without a single ore to their names, all they could do was walk. Until they could walk no more.

Vegetable merchants who had come to Sweden on diplomatic passports, after a meeting with the American president, but with no wallets: Sabine suspected there was more to the story, and Allan admitted that there was. "But perhaps we don't have to cover it all at once?"

No, certainly not. Sabine was glad she hadn't chased Allan and Julius off with a broom, an option she had weighed for quite some time.

"It's high time it was your turn again," said Julius.

He had already managed to become almost as enamored of this woman as he had been of Minister Wallström. "What happened with Other Side AB? I assume business isn't booming, given that you're running a shop."

What had happened was that her mother had died the previous summer. Eighty years and a few days old. She had been the driving force of the operation for all those years, communicating nonstop with spirits while high on LSD.

"Was that often?" asked Julius.

"Nonstop, like I said. But then one trip went particularly awry last summer, and she took her life. Or else she just switched sides."

"Oh dear. How did the switch itself happen?"

"She was supposed to go to a séance in Södertälje, and I thought I'd better go with her because she was really tripping and would never find her way there or back without me. On the platform she caught sight of a ghost no one else could see. She said it was hostile, and she chased it onto the track before I could stop either of them. And she was run over by the eleven twenty-five train from Norrköping."

"Oh dear," Julius said again.

"How did the ghost fare?" Allan asked.

That's the kind of thing that can come from the mouth of someone who has never in his life thought before speaking.

Sabine aimed a weary gaze at Allan. "Ghosts are hard to kill."

She went on, in a subdued tone, about how the income from Other Side AB had gone constantly toward tiny, sweet LSD pills or toward the somewhat larger but equally sweet LSD stamps, with happy characters on them. Even so, mother and daughter were able to take care of themselves since they lived for free in a small cottage on Sabine's grandmother's land. Her grandmother had also passed on the previous summer, at the age of ninety-nine, and before her mother realized she'd inherited a whole house to blow on drugs, she had ghost-hunted her way to the other side, or wherever she was nowadays.

"Ninety-nine," said Allan. "That's not old at all. But, tell me, what sort of relationship do you and narcotics have?"

"None," said Sabine. "That's probably why I was such an incompetent student for Mom. She always said you had to *free* yourself. Maybe I think too much."

"Hmm," said Allan. "Julius here thinks just about all the time, but I've seldom noticed that it helps."

The accused thinker ignored Allan's comment. "So you inherited a whole house from your grandmother?" he said instead.

Sabine nodded. "Once it was sold, and the funerals and everything were paid off, I had two whole million left over. I thought about what I wanted to do and came to the conclusion that being an entrepreneur was the life for me. I'm terribly good with numbers. It's the most beautiful word in the world, if you ask me. 'Entrepreneur!'"

Julius agreed. There were some words and expressions that stood out above the rest. "Entrepreneur" was one. "Without a receipt" was another.

But then everything had gone wrong. For one thing, of course, the money wasn't enough for a location in central Stockholm, where all the customers were. Which was why she now sat where she was, twenty-five miles north of all the action. For another, she had led herself astray doing what Allan had warned about: she had *thought* too much.

"May one inquire what sort of thought led to a corner shop in Märsta?" Allan asked.

"I think you just did," said Sabine. "I sat down at my grandmother's kitchen table with a paper and pen. I was thinking, you know, that the broader the potential target audience, the greater the chance of success. This led to two universal truths. One: all people eat food for as long as they live. Two: despite this, they die eventually. All of them, no exceptions."

"Except possibly Allan," said Julius. "He turned a hundred and one not long ago."

"Wow," said Sabine. "That's what I call having one foot in the grave. It's too bad you don't have any money, or I would have sold you a coffin."

Allan looked around. There was no coffin section.

"Hold on," he said. "Is the funeral parlor next door part of this business as well?"

Sabine smiled at Allan's deductive reasoning skills. "Well done!" she said. "To live, you need food, hence the corner shop. And when you die, you get buried. Hence the production of coffins. Simple as that. Selling coffins."

Sabine's story caused Allan to become downright philosophical. "Life and death," he said. "And ghosts in between."

"But you could make money from the ghosts, or you

could if you were prepared to kill yourself with drugs in the process. Life, at least in my version of a business plan, was useless even before you two started emptying the shop of goods without paying. And death has been even worse."

Julius felt sorry for their new acquaintance. And he was slightly ashamed about his failed attempted robbery. "Didn't you say you were terribly good with numbers?"

"I am! If you like, I can tell you exactly how big my loss will be next quarter. And how much bigger, as a percentage, it will be the quarter after that."

"I see."

Sabine went on: "It turned out that those who are alive don't want to accept that it's a transitory state. People don't expect to die, which means they don't arrange for a coffin ahead of time. Once they find themselves dead, to their own astonishment, it's hopeless doing business with them."

"But they must at least have bought food before they died, right?" Julius said. "To keep death at bay, I mean."

"Yes, I assume as much. But seldom from me."

A first, last, and only ad campaign ("Comestibles and coffins at low cost") in the local free paper had ended up as the beginning of a rumor that spread all the way to the municipal health and safety inspector, who paid a surprise visit to make sure no corpses were being stored with the dairy products.

"That campaign was my worst idea yet, in a parade of bad ideas."

Julius wondered what she would do now, if business was so bad on both sides of the wall. Sabine didn't know. All she knew was that she was tired of everything. If only her mother hadn't hammered all that supernatural stuff into her. What she really possessed, aside from her skill with numbers, was artistic talent.

"Artistic talent?" said Allan.

"Yes, I can paint your portrait, if that might be of interest. Shall we say four thousand? Oh, no, of course not."

Allan apologized for what Sabine had just remembered: he had no money.

"But speaking of that, I feel responsible for this little youngster Julius and his well-being. The blister he's been whining about incessantly ever since just before it appeared was not a pretty sight. Is there anything we could assist you with, Miss Sabine, that you might allow us to stay a night or two? We can sleep on the floor over there by the yogurt, if we must. I promise not to die in my sleep and cause more trouble with the food-safety authorities."

Julius caught on. "And I'm good at carpentry. Perhaps the collection of coffins could use some new additions."

Let them stay overnight? That would be moving fast, from customers with no money to overnight guests in under half an hour. But Sabine noticed again what she'd suspected early on: she enjoyed the old men's company. So . . . why not? She turned to Julius. "Little youngster," she said. "Well, where else could you go, with those heels? If I understood correctly while you were robbing me, you don't have anywhere to go even if you could walk."

The truth was, she didn't want to be rid of Allan and Julius, not at all.

"I have a two-room apartment upstairs. One of you can sleep on the spare bed in the hall there, the other on the sofa in the coffin store. Or in one of the coffins if it would be more comfortable. You'll find toothbrushes and toothpaste next to the bandages, and you already know where those are."

"Perhaps a razor too?" said Allan. "I can't imagine that will make a difference either way in the impending bankruptcy."

"Oh, take two. I'll add it to the tab."

Sweden

When Sabine came down from her apartment the next morning, Julius was in full swing building coffins. Allan was still on his sofa, watching.

"What is he doing?" she asked in surprise.

"I don't know," said Allan. "Preparing for his departure?"

"Good morning," said Julius. "I'm compensating you for our room and board. I've always been good at carpentry. Did I mention that? Shouldn't we go ahead and varnish the coffins as well? That might increase sales."

"From nothing to almost nothing?" said Sabine. "Did you have time to grab some breakfast from the shop?"

They hadn't dared. But Julius felt that if they were allowed to stay in the guest room and the carpentry shop for a few more days, he would be happy to open up each morning. That way Sabine could sleep in. Perhaps she didn't often get the chance?

She responded that this was an offer worth considering, but that sort of decision shouldn't be made on an empty stomach. "Come on, let's eat."

Breakfast consisted of a roll with cheese, juice, and coffee from the machine. Meanwhile the shop received four whole morning customers, each of whom made a small purchase. Julius seemed to be something of a lucky charm. And he proved that he could handle the cash register.

"Fifty-eight kronor, please. Thanks. Two kronor change. Have a nice day."

Sabine thought the fake diplomat seemed like a better sort than you would have expected at first. And so far his labor wasn't expensive. Altogether, the cost ran to a box of bandages, a few cups of coffee, a bun, a roll, ten ounces of juice, and one or perhaps two ibuprofens. The one called Allan wasn't quite as useful, but then again he was even cheaper.

So there were objectively good reasons to let the old men stay. Beyond the fact that she enjoyed their company.

"Of course you can stay here for a while," she said. "But don't build too many coffins—that will only drive up the cost of storage."

USA

Chancellor Merkel had just finished her first meeting with President Trump in Washington. In it she had been informed that NATO was useless. And that NATO was fantastic. That Trump loved Germany. And also that Germany had to get its act together on a number of issues. That the bonds between the countries were strong. And that the only thing that united them was that they had both been wiretapped by Obama.

Now she was back at the German embassy, where she was immediately shown to a situation room that was protected from bugs. Waiting for her there were the German ambassador, the German UN ambassador, and the director of German intelligence in the United States.

The chancellor, who had thought her day couldn't get any worse, realized that it absolutely could. The intelligence officer was leading the meeting.

The issue was, as the chancellor had already been informed, that North Korea had succeeded in smuggling nine pounds of enriched uranium to Pyongyang via a ship called *Honor and Strength*. The Swiss nuclear weapons expert, whom Kim Jong-un had put on display at a press conference, had turned out to be Swedish. His name was Allan Karlsson and he was not on Kim Jong-un's side, as they had feared earlier. Instead he had managed to leave Pyongyang and make it to New York. And he'd brought the enriched uranium with him.

"To America? The uranium is *here*?" said the chancellor.

"Yes," the intelligence officer confirmed. "It's very much here."

A few days earlier, Allan Karlsson had met President Trump, with Swedish Minister for Foreign Affairs Margot Wallström, who was also Sweden's representative on the UN Security Council.

"Yes, I know who she is," said Angela Merkel. "A competent woman. Do we know what was said during the meeting?"

"Not exactly. It seems President Trump stated that

Wallström and Karlsson had not done anything wrong, and warned them not to do it again."

"Sounds like President Trump," said Angela Merkel. The chancellor had been around the block. She could sense in the air that there was more to come. "And?" she said.

"Well, after that meeting, Ambassador Breitner ran into Allan Karlsson outside UN headquarters. Admirably enough, the ambassador recognized a possibility for gaining intelligence and invited him and his friend Jonsson to dinner."

The intelligence officer looked unhappy. But not as unhappy as the UN ambassador at his side.

"And?" said Angela Merkel again.

"The ambassador promised to help Karlsson and his friend with a briefcase they wished to turn over to the Federal Republic. They said it contained important nuclear weapons–related information that Karlsson had originally intended to give President Trump, but he changed his mind after meeting the president in person."

The chancellor felt a certain sense of solidarity with Karlsson. They seemed to have had similar experiences with the American president. "And now you're going to hand the information to me so that I may consider sending it on to our analysts in Berlin."

"Well," said the intelligence officer, "the briefcase turned out to contain . . . the nine pounds of enriched uranium. And a letter to you, Frau Chancellor. Written on three napkins."

"Three napkins?" said the chancellor.

But what she was thinking was, *Nine pounds of enriched uranium? Here? At the German embassy in Washington?*

By the time the intelligence meeting concluded, the chancellor had also learned that the previously intercepted code word "asparagus" referred to actual asparagus, nothing more. And that Karlsson, by his own word, had heard Pyongyang was expecting a larger shipment of enriched uranium, eleven hundred pounds' worth this time. The intelligence officer in Dar es Salaam had already been duly informed. Since the test shipment had made it all the way to Pyongyang from Africa, there was reason to believe the North Koreans would try the same route again.

Chancellor Merkel knew most things but she didn't know whether UN Ambassador Breitner should be considered a national hero or one of the greatest idiots in the Federal Republic. She decided, for the time being, to view him as something in between.

Sweden

The days came and went. Julius opened the shop each morning, while Sabine laid out breakfast for herself and the gentlemen one hour later. Then Julius and Sabine spent some time outdoing each other with sighs, as Allan took out the black tablet for reading-aloud time. After the meal, Sabine sat at the cash register while Julius went to work as a coffin-producer and Allan settled in on his sofa.

Now that the diplomats were making themselves at home, Sabine saw fit to come up with a few rules. Especially when it came to hygiene. She put out four sets of clothes, left behind by her grandfather, and required a shower followed by a change of clothes each day.

Quite strict, thought Allan and Julius. But they obeyed.

The luck Julius had brought, attracting four customers during one single breakfast, turned out to be temporary. The stream of people who thought they needed food to live was limited. As for customers who wanted to prepare for death instead, not one turned up.

Julius walked around in his socks while his heels healed. With Sabine's permission, he did some product development on the coffins: he painted them different colors, because he had seen somewhere that some people did so. He decided there was nothing to lose, aside from the cost of paint. Sabine adjusted her calculations so the budget would continue to be the right shade of red for the coming quarter.

The shop window was now arrayed with five coffins of solid pine, in white, pigeon blue, pink, olive green, and gray. There were also a few finished but untreated coffins in the carpentry shop, and another two in production.

The market for coffins north of the northern suburbs of Stockholm, however, seemed to be dead. When Julius asked Sabine about her reasoning behind the pricing and positioning, he received an evasive answer. When he wanted to know about nearby competition, she said she would be thrilled to know the same.

After two weeks, Julius's blisters had healed, while total coffin sales remained at zero. Via the internet he identified Berglund's funeral parlor as the closest competitor in a geographical sense. Sabine promised to take care of all the customers who wouldn't appear, and he set off on a reconnaissance mission.

It was a comfortable twenty-minute walk to Berglund's. Julius stepped inside and was greeted by a woman in a black jacket and checked skirt. She welcomed her customer, introduced herself as Therese Berglund, proprietor of the business with her husband, Ove, who was, unfortunately, unavailable at the moment. Julius took her hand but saw no immediate reason to give his own name.

"How may I be of service?" asked Therese Berglund.

"I'm curious about your coffins," said Julius.

Therese Berglund was not used to such a start to her client relationships. Usually the first thing that happened was that she was told who had died and countered with a suitable amount of condolences. "Okay," she said, rather uncertainly.

"I see you offer them in various colors. May I ask what you use for material?"

Therese Berglund said that the caskets the gentleman was pointing at were made of Masonite and were therefore a very good bargain. But no shortcuts had been taken on the surface treatment, and in that way Berglund's was always able to offer caskets that radiated the utmost dignity yet didn't cost as much as you might think.

"And how much do they go for? The pink one and the blue one?"

"Six thousand four hundred kronor apiece."

"Oh, damn," Julius said spontaneously.

His and Sabine's coffins of solid pine had to be priced somewhere around fifteen thousand to break more or less even. The Masonite coffins looked just as nice.

"Although we're happy to offer complete solutions, with various funeral packages including the casket, of course, but also such things as invitations, programs, casket decorations, and thank-you cards. There's a lot to think about when a loved one has passed away, and you're weighed down with sorrow. The level of our engagement and therefore the cost is determined with the bereaved."

"Well, there you go," said Julius. "Although in this case there is no deceased loved one."

Funeral director Therese Berglund looked at the customer, who apparently was no customer. "So why . . . ," she began.

"Oh, well, death is always just around the corner, so it's wise to be prepared. Do you make the coffins yourselves, by the way?"

"Or, again, the caskets," said Therese Berglund. "No, they're produced for us in Estonia. For special orders there's a two-week delivery time, but we have most items in stock. I just don't quite understand your interest in our caskets if no one—"

"I won't trouble you further," said Julius. "Thanks for the peep. Very nice coffins, really. Fun to see. And a good price! See you once I've pegged it. Or I won't, exactly, but you know what I mean."

The bad news was that the quality of the coffins at Berglund's was equal to their own, but for less than half the price. The even worse news was that the package deals Berglund offered made it even more irrelevant to turn to Julius, Sabine, and the guy with the black tablet. And apparently they couldn't be called coffins anymore: they were caskets.

Sabine felt they could call them whatever they wished, as long as they upped their sales. The two participants in the emergency meeting were unanimous that there were two paths forward. Either they buried the coffin idea or they expanded it.

"Let me think," said Julius.

"Ugh," said Allan, from his sofa.

Julius thought.

He thought that someone who ordered a pink coffin, for instance, did so for a reason. The funeral industry liked to call it "powder pink."

A coffin you could identify with . . . Julius kept thinking. Different *theme* coffins: might that be an idea?

A rainbow coffin for someone who, even in death, would defend their right to prefer embracing someone of the same sex?

A Harley-Davidson coffin for someone of that persuasion?

A Jesus coffin, even?

A protect-the-environment coffin?

A soccer-team-of-my-heart coffin? To many people, soccer meant win or die. And maybe, when one died, one would prefer it to look like a win.

An Elvis Presley coffin? In his youth, Julius had known an Elvis impersonator whose singing was uniquely bad and who also looked more like Gustav V of Sweden than the King. There were rumors that someone had beaten him to death at a karaoke bar for that very reason many years later. But if he was still alive, and starting to think about rounding it off, he would obviously be an example of a potential client.

"Now we're starting to get somewhere," Sabine said, when Julius shared his thoughts. "I could paint everything you've listed. And much more besides. I could handle a Harley-Davidson coffin in two or three days. Elvis might take a week. Early Elvis would be preferable, I think—he wasn't quite as fat when he was young so it wouldn't use up as much paint."

Julius was delighted with the indirect praise he had received from Sabine. The next step would be to find a way to get their message out. An ad in the local Märsta paper probably wasn't worth another shot, was it?

"No," said Sabine. "I think our concept is rather more international. Do you think there might be a trade fair for us? A coffin fair?"

Julius had never heard of a coffin fair, but the world was nuts, so why not?

"Let me do some searching," he said, and asked to borrow Allan's black tablet.

"I beg your pardon?" said Allan from his sofa. "Then who would tell you about what is and is not happening in the world?"

"How about no one?" said Julius.

Sabine warded off a fight between the old men. "I'll fetch my laptop. Back in a minute."

An international trade fair it would be. It was reasonable to expect that 99 percent of the potential in an Elvis Presley coffin was to be found outside the borders of Sweden. Just as one example.

Julius found what he was looking for. In the German city of Stuttgart. The world's biggest travel and tourism fair would take place there in the near future. It fitted their purpose, like a hand in a glove: two thousand exhibitors from ninety-nine countries. Travel agents, hotel chains, tourist organizations, RVs, camper trailers, campgrounds, tents, backpacks, and a couple of hundred more items.

"Coffins?" said the German fair organizer, when Julius called to book a booth. "We don't usually get involved in what the exhibitors wish to communicate, but it really should be somehow relevant to the overarching theme of the fair."

"Oh, but it is," said Julius. "The final journey is, of course, its own sort of travel—perhaps the most important one of all. Don't you agree?"

The fair organizer, who earlier that day had received an application from a Slovenian manufacturer of shoehorns, realized that nothing could surprise him anymore. "Of course, sir. I'll send over the documents. We look forward to giving you and your . . . coffins a warm welcome."

Now it was time to prioritize. They would have to take a number of samples. Which theme would be best from an international perspective?

Sabine wondered what Germans in particular might get excited about. A "Say No to Nuclear Power" coffin?

Allan had been listening with one ear. Now he interfered to say that this wouldn't work. Not in Germany, and not anywhere else. The Germans had already decided to do away with nuclear power, so what would be the point of protesting against it? To everyone else, the nuclear accident in Fukushima was already old news. People preferred to worry about things to come, as opposed to what had been or, in this case, was utterly ongoing.

Perhaps, however, they would be able to market an anti-nuclear-weapons coffin in Japan. There, the half-life of what people remember is not quite as short. After all, the level of radioactivity in ocean fish off the coast of Fukushima was still two thousand times the allowable limit. And recently levels of more than five hundred Sieverts per hour had been measured in the destroyed reactor.

"So what does that mean?" asked Julius, who didn't really want to know: he had already dropped the anti-nuclear-power coffin idea.

"If the level had instead been three, it would have been survivable," said Allan.

"Three hundred?"

"No, three."

Sabine muttered that this sounded cheerful. Was there anything in Allan's black tablet that could benefit their business instead?

"Maybe," said Allan.

What the tablet offered was, essentially, news from every corner of the world, a little bit of music, and some naked ladies. For his own part, he focused on the first. "The prevailing sentiment right now is that those of us who have it good want to avoid dealing with those who have it bad."

"And what does that business model look like?"

Allan wasn't sure, but any number of people were drowning in the Mediterranean each day, and when they floated ashore here and there, they would certainly need a coffin.

Sabine said that even *living* refugees probably weren't their primary target group. Drowned ones, even less so.

Allan tended to agree.

Julius was impressed by the words Sabine was tossing around. "Business model" and "primary target group" within the span of a few sentences. "I think you have a nose for business," he said.

"A nose for *bad* business," Sabine corrected him.

"Do you have any experience with trade fairs?" Julius wondered.

"Yes, as a matter of fact."

Once, twenty years earlier, her mother had taken her on a trip to Las Vegas. There, they had attended a "spiritual insight" fair, which, loosely translated, involved a giant meeting between her mother and twenty-five thousand like-minded people from all over the world.

The main attraction for her mother had been the presentation on "Healing with Spiritual Energy" but she'd managed to miss it—and just about everything else—because she had immediately discovered that LSD was sold in all imaginable forms in the neighborhood. The Americans called it "acid," and Sabine's mother had explained to her daughter that she had no choice but to try out all the American varieties to see what sort of new spiritual insights she could find.

What happened next was that her mom stayed in their hotel room for three of the four fair days in a series of attempts to teleport herself and Sabine back to

Sweden. She'd managed to get there time and again, she'd said, but her daughter, ever the rigid thinker, kept being left behind in Vegas.

Julius thought he was almost on his way to falling in love. "Poor wonderful you," he said. "The things you've had to deal with!"

"Oh," said Sabine, blushing.

LSD trips over there hadn't been much different from those at home. While her mother—or at least her spirit—was traveling back and forth across the Atlantic, Sabine had walked around the booths at the fair, learning the basics of how to communicate with your own guardian angel. She was offered an entire starter package for twenty-eight hundred American dollars, including a DVD, a handbook, and a CD containing ninety minutes of silence.

Angel Talk, the CD was called. The cover explained that it was empty because angels, in general, don't talk.

The involuntarily retired asparagus farmer was reminded that the world was full of endless business ideas.

"If our coffin project fails, maybe we can breathe new life into your mother's operation," he said.

"Maybe," said Sabine.

Russia

Gennady Aksakov grew up in 1950s Leningrad. His father taught philosophy; his mother worked at a bank. His loving parents doted on their only child. On his tenth birthday, Gena received a hockey stick and a new pair of ice skates, but ice hockey wasn't for him. It felt too collective. The same went for soccer.

Instead he became enamored of the combat sport of sambo, self-defense without weapons. It was man to man, with no one but yourself to depend on. It was a much better match for Gena's temperament. What's more, he met Volodya at the gym. They were the same age, an even match on the mats, they laughed at the same things and had a similar outlook on life. In short, they became best friends and still were, fifty-five years later.

Gena came and went as he pleased at Volodya's workplace. He was the only one who was spared the extensive security routine at every entrance. The fact was, he didn't even knock before stepping into his friend's private office. Such as on this day.

"Hi, Volodya," he said. "I just spoke with our friend from Chabarovsk. An ambitious young man, I must say. Who has, unfortunately, begun to sound a lot like the little big man in Pyongyang."

"How so?" asked President Putin.

"He wants that centrifuge. He says he needs it to make the Americans and Chinese start gasping in chorus."

Putin smiled at the picture his friend had painted. A gasping Chinese and an equally gasping American, side by side. Lovely.

The "friend from Chabarovsk" was the new director of the plutonium factory north of the North Korean capital. It so happened, of course, that the man formerly responsible for the operation had been put to death after failing at his task, and had been replaced by the man who, to those around him, had never been called anything but "Mr. Engineer." After the engineer in question had hanged himself from an extension cord in the cold storage room of the laboratory, the position had stood vacant for a few weeks before Kim Jong-un managed to get Putin in Moscow to have mercy on the Koreans and their situation. At least, that was how the Supreme Leader wanted to see it, that the Russian apostates of the True Way still had a little bit of Communist spirit left.

The truth was that Putin and his secret right-hand man, Gennady Aksakov, had no other agenda than to destabilize certain parts of the world, with a view to indirectly strengthening Russia. Then, as now, Volodya and Gena had not been about to send any plutonium centrifuge to the nut in Pyongyang. Instead they offered a highly qualified Siberian engineer. From Chabarovsk, not too far from the border between North Korea and Russia.

The man from Chabarovsk had a rough start, but soon turned out to be the asset the Russian president knew he was. Just a few weeks after stepping in, he had found success in his first underground detonation. This, of course, provoked an unholy fuss from the hypocrites in the rest of the world, all according to plan. Part of Putin's agreement with the Supreme Leader was that Putin himself, and Russia, would sound as upset as everyone else.

The new guy's loyalties lay with Moscow above all, and the uranium used was Russian. The man from Chabarovsk regularly reported to Gennady Aksakov.

Thus Volodya and Gena knew everything worth knowing about the 101-year-old Swede who'd had a cameo in the laboratory and made a mess of things. Kim Jong-un had nagged President Putin nearly to death on the topic of how the Russians, with their global network of agents, ought to track down Karlsson and slit his throat, but Putin was secretly amused by the old man. Imagine being more than a hundred years old, coming to Pyongyang and getting the little big man all worked up like that. Even if the old man hadn't vanished, the president would have let him be. The problem seemed likely to solve itself within the not-too-distant future.

In any case, the news of the day was that the man from Chabarovsk had joined Kim Jong-un in whining for a plutonium centrifuge. Volodya could see Gena's opinion written on his face.

"Hmm," said the president. "Send the damn thing over, then. But we won't go too far, will we, Gena?"

Sweden, Germany

The rainbow coffin joined a Harley-Davidson coffin, a Ferrari coffin, a golf-is-the-best-thing-ever coffin, a John Lennon/*Imagine* coffin, a white-doves-in-flight-on-a-pale-blue-background coffin, a dancing-fairies-in-a-meadow coffin, and a sunset-at-sea coffin.

Sabine was quick on the draw and found a used hearse for sale. Very quick. At the conclusion of the sale she realized that the eight coffins they were planning to bring to Stuttgart wouldn't fit into it. It would take at most two, preferably just one. Julius offered comfort by pointing out that it would be useful for years to come, when it was time to deliver completed orders. Then he sent her to rent a small truck at the nearest service station. Before it was time to take off on their trip, she managed, on Julius's advice, to paint a VfB Stuttgart coffin in red, white, and a little yellow, with the words "Love since 1893" in German, thanks to Google Translate.

"VfB Stuttgart? What's that?" Allan asked.

"The local soccer team," said Julius. "Might work."

Sabine locked up and put a sign on the door: "Closed. You all shop somewhere else anyway." Then they aimed southward, all three of them, with nine coffins in tow.

It took two days, with overnights in Copenhagen and Hanover. Pleasant dinners for three in both cities. As pleasant as they could be, at least, with Allan stubbornly reporting the latest news all the time, as if Sabine and Julius weren't already aware of the state of the world. Allan's latest charming story was about a former winner of the Nobel Peace Prize who might currently be pursuing genocide instead of peace.

After dinner in Hanover, Allan went to bed. Julius promised to join him soon, but this was a promise he wouldn't keep. Instead he slept in Sabine's room; it turned out this was something they had both been considering for some time.

"Well, then," said Allan, when the trio gathered for breakfast the next day. "The Minister for Foreign Affairs is no longer good enough."

"Idiot," said Julius.

He and Sabine had spent time together every day and night since they'd first met a few months ago. Of course, Allan was always there in one corner, but he seldom left his sofa and in no way did he pose a threat to the love between the much-younger Julius and the even-younger-than-that Sabine.

It would be an exaggeration to say they just clicked. After all, their love affair had begun when Julius tried to rob his future intended of a box of bandages. But from that point on, their relationship grew steadily. And the evening in Hanover turned into a night neither regretted the next morning.

Julius felt that Sabine made him a better person. She didn't just take, she gave too. He felt . . . proud of her.

"Better late than never," said Sabine, apropos of the fact that she'd fallen in love shortly before her sixtieth birthday.

"Much better late than never," said Julius, raising a glass of breakfast milk in a toast.

"Okay, okay," said Allan. "Do you know what Trump did overnight?"

Germany

The trade fair was a success. Few of the two thousand exhibitors were met with as much interest as Booth D128, the one with nine coffins and banners that said things like "Heaven Can't Wait," "Ticket to Paradise," and "The Last Journey." Sabine wasn't quite sure what message she was trying to get across, but she was in charge of designing the booth and wanted everything to be as lively as possible around the death they were marketing.

The first to go was the VfB Stuttgart coffin. A die-hard Karlsruhe fan offered three thousand euros; his goal was to humiliate Stuttgart somehow, with the help of the coffin, when the occasion arose. If no such occasion presented itself in a reasonable amount of time, he planned to charge ten euros per Karlsruhe fan who wanted to relieve themselves on the coffin in a public place. Then he could set it on fire and put the video online as a potential viral success.

"Does you-know-what really burn?" Sabine asked the customer, who had shared more of his plans than the salespeople truly needed to know.

Julius stepped in and said that the purpose of the coffin had been to honor the organization that was VfB Stuttgart, not to deride it. Furthermore, Julius went on, he understood now, if he hadn't before, why the concept of peace on earth seemed so remote. Last but not least, he sincerely pitied the buyer of the coffin for putting hate above love.

"All that said: three thousand euros, it's a deal."

The second coffin to sell was a preorder for a Karlsruhe coffin. It so happened that a Stuttgart fan, in all the fuss, had happened to overhear the preceding conversation and acted accordingly.

"He who pisses last pisses best," he said to the Karlsruhe fan, once the coffin was ordered and the agreement signed.

At which the two fans began first to bicker and then to scuffle, until they were carried off and ejected by security.

Before the day was over, they had sold twelve more coffins, including preorders. The only coffin they'd brought that didn't move was sunset-at-sea. Sabine believed this was because it was 370 miles from Stuttgart to the nearest sunset at sea, but Julius thought it might be because the sunset had turned out an awful lot like a sunrise.

Fourteen coffins at three thousand euros each made forty-two thousand. The company Die with Pride wasn't even formally established yet, but it seemed to be headed for a fruitful future.

If only it hadn't been for that damned bad luck.

Denmark, Sweden

Povl Riis-Knudsen was the chairman of the National Socialist Movement of Denmark, until he happened to get it on with an Arab and was forced to leave the party. Caught red-handed, he tried to argue that the Arab had awfully white skin. That wouldn't do. An Arab was an Arab.

Yet, as the leader of the movement, he'd managed to leave his mark. He appeared on Danish TV to argue that all foreigners should be forced to leave the country, and advocated the death penalty for anyone who spread AIDS. He wanted to place political opponents in labor camps and sterilize everyone with the wrong skin color. In accordance with some extra-complicated logic, he also had a passion for fundamentalist Islam, even though he wouldn't touch Muslims with a ten-foot pole (unless they were white Arabs). More recently he had published books in which he attempted to prove that the concentration camps of the Second World War had never existed.

This Danish man was a main source of inspiration for the Swedish neo-Nazis in the Nordic Resistance Party. It wasn't Denmark or Sweden under threat: it was the Aryan race and, in the long term, all of humanity—that was, biology and ecology over geography.

Within the movement were those who masqueraded as quiet Sweden Democrats and those who wanted to take quick and drastic action. Kenneth Engvall was of the latter category, to such an extent that one day he took his brother and created the Aryan Alliance instead. The last straw, for Kenneth, was when the Nordic Resistance Movement applied for a demonstration permit. What kind of resistance was that? And whom did they have to apply to? The same corrupt Jewish power elite they claimed to be resisting!

For Kenneth, it was simple. Real democracy meant, among other things, the right to hound out everyone who didn't belong in the Nordic countries. If they didn't leave voluntarily, there were other options. Popular government, in the true sense of the phrase, meant that the people the National Socialists put in government actually governed. The *right* people.

And yet Kenneth's lack of respect for the Nordic Resistance Movement didn't give him any immediate reason to wage war on two fronts. The Resistance could remain. Anyway, they weren't all bad. During the most recent demonstration in Gothenburg, several had raised their right arms in the air, toward the spectators, palms flat. That was the way to do it! It was just annoying that they later called the whole thing a "friendly greeting to allies" and said that only the power elite would read anything else into it.

Many people saw the humor in denying the obvious. Kenneth saw nothing but cowardice. The only thing worth denying was the Holocaust. After all, that was how the Jewish Mafia got their fuel. It wasn't the neo-Nazis' problem to account for where six million Jews had gone during those years. Why would it be? Weren't people allowed to do whatever they wanted with their lives?

To argue with power was to legitimize it. And Kenneth refused. The people's courts that would soon replace the faux-justice system the power elite had wrapped around their little finger had no task more urgent than purging all the race traitors of Scandinavia. And the Arabs, Jews, and Gypsies, of course. And owning it! At long last, those who remained would be pure and white, the people the current elite worked around the clock to destroy. *That* was genocide. It could not stand. And yet it did.

So what did the Nordic Resistance Movement do? Demonstrated! And denied themselves.

An objective onlooker would have placed Kenneth Engvall high on the list of Sweden's most dangerous people. He had once been schooled in the Los Angeles branch of the Aryan Brotherhood, where he had made a career out of being a Nazi and Fascist, without quite knowing the difference between the two. He climbed rapidly through the ranks by using a chainsaw to cut in two a man with the wrong attitude and the wrong race. For this he was locked up for four years, and no more, since the group's extraordinary attorney managed to get the brutal murder defined as gross negligence.

After just a week in prison, Kenneth killed a fellow prisoner, a Mexican who happened to have an opinion about his heavily tattooed back: across the top it said, "In memory of Adolf Hitler," with a swastika underneath. This was followed by the cross of the Ku Klux Klan with the words "white supremacy."

The Mexican thought that only someone *brain-dead* would identify with Hitler and the KKK. For this he received a ballpoint pen shoved into his skull via one eye, at which he too became a member of the group "brain-dead."

All seven people in the room with the perpetrator and the victim had managed to look the other way when it happened. No witnesses, no one to punish. But in the three years and fifty-one weeks that remained of Kenneth Engvall's sentence, no one complained about his tattoos or any other of his undertakings.

For a long time now, Kenneth had been free and back in the country of his birth. With his little brother Johnny he had joined up with and made something of a career out of the Nordic Resistance Movement. But he'd never managed to get to the top, where he belonged. He was thought too "outspoken." What the fuck kind of word was that? Surely if this country needed anything, it was outspokenness.

And that was how the Aryan Alliance came to be, in cooperation with the Aryan Brotherhood in Los Angeles. The operation had only just begun; there was no structure to speak of yet. Kenneth and his little brother were putting the finishing touches to a plan of action to overtake power and devoted their free time to homicide and gross assault of the foreign element. Mostly assault. A string of murders at this stage would risk waking the current powers and their yes-men on the police force.

Spending twenty or thirty years inside was hardly the quickest path to a new order.

Money was an issue as well. The Americans contributed a certain amount each month, but they had already sent word that in time the cash-flow must start to come from the other direction. They recommended that Kenneth take over Stockholm's cocaine trade from the Turkish-Italian coalition that currently had the market cornered. Of course he would. But there were more than eight well-guarded targets and only two people to do it. They needed a plan. "Take your time," was the Americans' response. They trusted Kenneth.

Russia

It was almost as if Gennady Aksakov didn't exist. He had no title, no employer, no official tasks. He did, however, have two passports: one Russian and one Finnish. He'd obtained the latter in 1998, with some difficulty, but with support from the then-director of the Russian Federation's Federal Security Service, one Vladimir Vladimirovitch Putin.

Since he was a Finn when it suited him, Gennady Aksakov could travel around the Nordic countries as he pleased. He was perhaps the best in the world at what he did. Of course he had more important things to do than destabilize Scandinavia, but it was a decently large market in which to test new ideas.

These days, there were established nationalist parties in all four Nordic countries. All four opposed the EU. As such they were Gennady's tools without knowing it. At the same time, it was clear that their political momentum had stagnated. Take, for one example, Swedish populists. They amplified existing problems or invented ones that didn't exist, polarizing and making people fearful of one another. Then they pointed to what they'd created and said they were the only ones with solutions.

This method wasn't new. Back in 1933, Hitler, Goering, and Goebbels had succeeded in inflating a simple case of arson to an international Communist conspiracy. They scared people one day and came up with the solution the next. After all, fright demands might. Instead, it wasn't long before almost four thousand had been imprisoned without trial, emergency laws put in place, and competing political parties forbidden, along with select parts of the press.

And that was only the start. But, above all, that was *then*. A new century demanded new solutions. Certainly the Sweden Democrats, Finns Party, Golden Dawn, PVV, BNP, AfD, FPÖ, and other flavors of alphabet soup could try what had worked in 1933, if they wished. But they would never take it all the way.

After all, only one in five Swedes could imagine voting for a party leader who clearly stated that simply being born and raised in Sweden, and having the ability to play soccer, did not make you Swedish. In the reborn north, you weren't named anything that started with Z. The Sweden Democrats' current leader had originally been attracted to the party by a woman who first shared with him her political vision, then took off for a pro-Nazi demonstration, wearing a uniform with shiny boots, leather pants, a shirt, and a scarf. The future party leader joined the movement, made a career of it, and polished their political arguments almost beyond recognition. He had his teeth fixed, and was now reaping the fruits of many years of hard work. He had done everything right. Yet four out of five Swedes turned against him. To Gennady Aksakov, this was the ultimate proof that the established right-wing populists would never split the EU wide open.

Not without help.

Money wasn't the issue. Gennady and his friends had billions, if you counted in kronor. Several hundred million in euros or dollars. How much it amounted to in roubles was less relevant. But to pump up the Sweden Democrats, Finn Party, and others financially would be risky and, most importantly, not a viable way forward. Human logic functioned such that very few people considered themselves extremists. As long as the Sweden Democrats were the most extreme party Sweden had to offer, there would always be plenty of people who refrained from voting for them, even if those voters agreed with their platform. Nothing about that would change just because Gennady managed to fortify the party coffers, so they could tell the same truths even louder.

If, however, he contributed to an alternative voice, to the right of those who were furthest right, two things would happen: first, the Sweden Democrats would point fingers at the neo-Nazis and say, "Look how terrible they are! *We* are certainly not like *them!*" Second, people would agree. In one fell swoop, voting Sweden Democrat would become more socially acceptable. Fifteen percent voter support might become thirty; the third-largest party could become the second-largest, or perhaps even the largest. A Sweden Democrat prime minister wouldn't necessarily mean Sweden would leave the EU, because that would take a majority vote in Parliament. But the political map would be redrawn. The conservatives, Liberals, and Social Democrats would all have reason to overhaul their foreign policy. Few wish to die, after all. That went for political parties as much as it did people.

And, above all, if the experiment worked in little Sweden, then in the future a person would only have to do the same thing where it would truly matter.

Like in Germany.

Gennady Aksakov had to choose between the established Nordic Resistance Movement and the newly formed Aryan Alliance. The problem with the former was that it was generally known in Gennady's circles that the Swedish Security Service had infiltrated the organization to the extent that it was no longer possible to know who was what. The problem with the Aryan Alliance, on the other hand, was that thus far they were absolutely nothing.

But Gennady wasn't in much of a hurry. Better done right than done fast.

He met with Kenneth Engvall and his brother on a Monday. Under a fake name, of course. By Tuesday he had put four million euros at the disposal of the Aryan Alliance's honorable mission. The Engvall brothers believed what they wanted to when it came to Gennady's origins and devotion to the good cause. And with that everything would probably have gone just fine, if only those idiots had managed to stay alive.

Sweden

Investee Kenneth Engvall perished suddenly in connection with a spontaneous political manifestation.

It began when the brothers arrived at a shopping center in Bromma, not far from Stockholm's domestic airport. Little brother was behind the wheel, looking for parking. Big brother beside him caught sight of a beggar at one of the entrances to the shopping center. He was monumentally displeased and made a snap decision.

"Wait here with the engine running. We'll go shopping somewhere else. I've just got to . . . make a point."

Johnny understood more or less what Kenneth was getting at and agreed with his analysis: that, as a result, it would be best to find a different place to shop.

Big brother left the car and approached the Romanian who was sitting by the entrance in the hope that passersby would give him a krona or two, since the Roma minority's life back home in Romania was far beyond hopeless (even as those in Sweden preferred to discuss the legality of being a beggar rather than that EU member-state Romania ought to shape up).

"Hi," said the Romanian, when he caught sight of Kenneth Engvall.

"Hi yourself, you fucking Gypsy!" Kenneth said, as he pulled his cap down on his forehead and walked faster, intending to give the needy man a powerful kick in the throat with a boot, as if *that* was the primary need of the needy man.

Except it so happened that someone had tossed a circular, advertising sale-priced minced beef, on the ground into a puddle. Kenneth planted his foot on the meat (organic, country-of-origin Sweden, 109 kronor per pound), slipped, lost his footing on the other leg, spun ninety degrees above the ground, missed the beggar, landed on his back, and hit the concrete base of the waste-bin the beggar was huddled behind to keep out of the wind. Kenneth Engvall cracked open his temple, was struck by a massive brain bleed, and died in the ambulance on the way to the hospital.

Sweden's perhaps most dangerous person was no more. In one blow, the Aryan Alliance had lost half its members. All that remained for the other half to do was plan a funeral.

Johnny had just returned home from such an event. The interred was an acquaintance as well as a courier of hard drugs. He was an underling of one of the eight in the cocaine cartel that was on Kenneth and Johnny's secret kill list. Phase one in the takeover, according to Kenneth, was to infiltrate. He hadn't had time to say what phase two would be.

But now, in any case, the underling no longer had to worry about getting smoked when the day came, for smoked he already was. It happened when he turned his back on a desperate junkie, a tiny woman, light as a feather, incapable of harming a fly.

Or not.

The courier had just informed her that there would be no replenishment of drugs unless the woman coughed up some money. Since he was sure she would be unable to cough up anything, except maybe blood, he walked off. And was extremely surprised to feel a stabbing pain in his back. The featherweight woman had had the nerve to stick him with a knife. Well, she was about to fucking . . .

That was as far as he got. You can't get much further when you've just had your subclavian artery severed. Loss of consciousness occurs after five seconds, and soon thereafter permanent cardiac arrest.

Johnny's acquaintance was buried two weeks later and consigned to the annals of eternity. The remarkable thing about the funeral wasn't that the courier had been killed by a junkie—that sort of thing happened on occasion. No, it was the *coffin*. It was a shiny black-lacquered Harley-Davidson coffin with the words "Highway to Hell" on both sides. Johnny had never before seen anything so tasteful and dignified in a church.

Johnny Engvall was not as strategic a thinker as his older brother Kenneth, but he had a reputation almost as authentic. There'd been at least three murders over the years. A fag, a wog, and a policeman who was a wog besides. The last one happened after a Nazi demonstration in downtown Stockholm. One of the uniforms came a little too close, grabbed Johnny by the arm, and started to say something.

"Don't touch me, you fucking pig!" said Johnny.

"Take it easy, dammit," said the cop. "I just want to . . ."

But Johnny had already taken his 1984 Colt Trooper

from his inner pocket. With it, he shot the police officer in the throat from a distance of a few inches.

Johnny was later able to admit to himself that he had acted rashly. But no one is perfect. There was quite a hullabaloo, of course. And the cop didn't even have an old lady or any brats at home to cry in the newspapers. He was probably a fag.

The advantage to things turning out the way they did was that ever since Johnny had enjoyed great respect in the right circles for so much more than being his brother's brother. The disadvantage was that he would never ever find out what that *blatte*-fag actually wanted.

The police killing was never cleared up. None of those who could testify about what had happened wanted to risk becoming a victim of the same thing. The police investigators didn't even get as far as an unofficial finger-pointing behind closed doors.

To shoot a cop in the throat in public, and get away with it, was something special. But little brother remained little brother: nothing could beat having done time for sawing a man in half with a chain saw. Furthermore, Johnny hadn't spent as much time in the United States as Kenneth had in his day. The USA really built up your image.

Sweden

The corner shop had been permanently closed since their homecoming from the trade fair in Germany. Out with the old, in with the new, and away with the separating wall. The coffin store had suddenly doubled in size. Sabine put up a new sign on the door of the former corner shop: "Closed forever. Buy your food elsewhere. PS: Don't forget you are mortal. Right now, ten percent discount on coffins. Next door."

They never got any walk-in clients from the street, but the list of orders from Sweden and Europe was extensive. Julius received praise from Sabine for his organizational skills and swiftness. In return he offered her loving words about her artistic talent and beautiful eyes.

"Yeah, yeah," said Allan.

Sabine was in charge of deliveries. She either drove them around herself in the hearse or used DHL for the more distant corners of the world. While she was out on the road, Julius took over the role of answering machine.

"Die with Pride AB, how may we be of service?"

"Well, I guess we'll find out. My name is Johnny. Do you make coffins to order?"

"Yes, and we're happy to personalize them. That's our speciality."

"Then I need your help."

"Things are a bit hectic at the moment . . ."

"You've got five days."

"Hectic, as I said. I don't think . . ."

"How much?"

Julius could smell cash. He had done so uninterrupted for at least sixty years. Here he had a customer on the line for whom money was no object.

"Well, I suppose it wouldn't be impossible to . . . We typically list our prices in euros, but we're an international player, so to speak. Four thousand eu—"

"I'll give you five if you make the coffin the way I want it, no grumbling."

"Of course," Julius said, thinking he could milk the client a little more. "Five plus tax, that is."

"No, five without tax or a receipt. Or grumbling. Cash."

The asparagus farmer already suspected that the motif was not going to be sugary-sweet. Even so, over the next few minutes, he found himself gasping repeatedly. The customer, Johnny, had only a vague idea of what he wanted on the coffin, so he listened to the supplier's artistic opinions. After almost fifteen minutes, Julius was able to summarize what they had come up with. He certainly didn't want any mix-ups.

"Now let's see . . . The majority of the coffin will be black. On the top we'll paint a red swastika. You're sure about that, then? Right. Moving on, along each side it will read, 'Our blood is our honor' in red on a white background, followed by a Celtic cross. And on the ends it will say, 'White power' in white, followed by the SS logo. That seems right as well? Okay. On the rest of the empty areas we'll make sure to put flames. Have I captured this all accurately?"

"Yes," said Johnny Engvall. "That's totally accurate, I would say."

"So we're striking the stuff about how cops and race traitors must die, and the various phrases about homosexuals and Jews?"

"Yes. You said that would be a little too much?"

Julius tried to find words. For quite some time, all of this had been not a *little* too much but *much* too much. Yet there was something about Johnny that made you not want to say no to him. And Julius wasn't even thinking primarily of the money.

"Well, it's important for the coffin to maintain a certain degree of dignity. For example, I hesitate to send a message about who should die along with the already dead person in the coffin."

"I'll take it," said Johnny Engvall. "Deliver it to the morgue I mentioned in time for the funeral on Saturday, okay? I'll send the money in a bag, by taxi, right away."

Taxi? Julius thought. But he said something more down-to-earth: "On Saturday? That's an unusual choice for a funeral. Typically—"

"Typically people listen to me and to whatever I say," said Johnny Engvall.

He was tired of all these questions. The funeral guests were coming all the way from America and had no time to wait for a proper burial day according to Swedish tradition.

"I hear what you're saying," said Julius. "It's fine."

That last part wasn't true. It wasn't even half fine. They'd apparently attracted a Nazi for a customer. It would never do to deliver slipshod work on this order.

And Sabine didn't.

And still, what happened happened.

Sweden

"Your job is certainly full of variety," Julius stated, as he studied the three latest coffins, all ready to be delivered.

The one on the left was black with swastikas and white-power symbols. The one in the middle was yellow, red, and blue in homage to Djurgården hockey. And the one on the right was pale blue with white rabbits on each of its sides, hopping in a dignified manner through a green meadow. On the lid were fluffy white clouds and the words "God who holds His children dear, watch over me as I sleep here."

"Yes," Sabine said, as she washed her hands. "Today swastikas, soccer, and bunnies. Tomorrow Lenin awaits. Apparently the last Communist is not yet dead. Unless he was the one who just died. Can't we go out and celebrate at a restaurant tonight?"

"I'd love to! But what are we celebrating?"

"Anything. You decide. That we found each other? That we're starting to do well financially? That you haven't had a blister in several months?"

Julius thought the best reason was that they'd found each other. "Shall we take the hearse or a taxi?" he wondered.

To make a Lenin coffin, Sabine began by lacquering the entire thing in the proper shade of red. As the paint dried she began practicing Lenin himself. It turned out right every time. He was easy to make: his face was the right level of angular.

"It's no Picasso, but it's close," she said to herself, pleased.

Then she took off her painter's smock and spiffed herself up to perform the week's deliveries. Two coffins were going to a single morgue south of the capital, and a third to a different one just eighteen miles away. As the money flowed in, she sent more and more of her deliveries via DHL. Once, in the early days, she had driven all the way to Sundsvall and back, but now she outsourced anything that needed to go beyond the Mälaren Valley and its immediate environs.

It was Friday, and there was just one day left to disaster.

Sweden

D ressed in a white shirt, his most attractive black leather jacket, black leather trousers, and black gloves, Johnny Engvall stood outside the church to greet the funeral-goers. He had planned a small, dignified gathering. The four leaders of the Aryan Brotherhood in Los Angeles were the guests of honor. The only guests, actually. Four angry, dangerous men. Plus Johnny himself, who was also angry and dangerous.

Johnny knew that after the funeral he would be faced with troublesome questions about how the Aryan Alliance's only member planned to take over Stockholm's cocaine cartel and thereafter bring down the government. But the Americans had already said, "Take your time," once. If Johnny played his cards right, they might say it again. They still didn't know about the four million euros from the secret Finnish financier. Kenneth had delayed sharing this information: he wanted to find the right way to say it. Now he no longer existed and Johnny was wondering how the right way would have sounded, coming out of Kenneth's mouth.

To some extent the Americans weren't needed now that the Finn had joined the righteous cause, but they lent stability to the operation. Johnny felt that, through them, he was part of a greater whole. Anything might happen if they reacted poorly to the alternative financier, including the execution of Johnny.

All in good time. Right now, it was time for a funeral.

His little brother wanted to honor Kenneth in every way. Therefore he had arranged to serve drinks to the guests as they approached the steps to the church. Kenneth had had a particular passion for Irish whiskey. It had to be a double, with four drops of water. There was a story from his California years about how a bartender in Malibu ended up with a knife through his hand after mistakenly serving Johnny's big brother a Jim Beam Kentucky Straight Bourbon. And without any drops of water.

Back in Sweden, Kenneth had broadened his preferences a little. When it was cold enough outside, he might mix his whiskey with coffee, brown sugar, and cream. That was warm, delicious, and inspiring. As long as the main ingredient came from Ireland and nowhere else.

So Irish coffee it was; it seemed more ceremonial. Once the four men had gathered and warmed up, Johnny gave a short welcome speech. First he explained why they had gathered at a church, of all places. This was where Kenneth would be interred, in the family plot, just as he would have wanted it. Yes, this meant that a *pastor* would preside over the proceedings, but Johnny had talked to him and explained that he must not bring God and Jesus into the ceremony unless he wanted to meet them both earlier than he expected to.

"You all know how much I loved my brother. I welcome you to step inside. And imagine how proud Kenneth is in the coffin I chose."

A curious murmur rose from the men. A few nodded in surprise. Clearly Engvall's little brother knew what he was doing.

Johnny placed himself strategically on the church steps to shake each man's hand as he entered. He did what he was doing out of genuine respect for his brother, but there was an additional aspect in the background. Something Johnny hardly wanted to admit to himself.

The Americans had not yet formally identified

Kenneth's successor. Of course, there was no one but Johnny to choose, but the pronouncement had yet to take place. The other option was for the Swedish branch to be closed now that their founder was no longer with them. But it was hard to believe the American leaders had come all the way across the Atlantic just to share this information. Perhaps Johnny would be upgraded that very evening.

The Swedish branch leader-to-be was so absorbed in his thoughts that he didn't hear the buzz from within the church. When he entered, the last to do so, he was met by a dreadful sight.

The four guests had not sat down in the pews. Instead they were all in a row, up by the pastor and the coffin. Two on the left, two on the right. Between the groups, Johnny had an unobstructed view of the unimaginable.

The pastor smiled at Johnny and his companions. He nodded at the coffin and agreed that it was lovely. If the gentlemen would take their seats, the ceremony could begin.

No one listened to him. Everyone was waiting for Johnny, who was walking slowly past the men and all the way to the front. He cautiously touched the coffin to confirm that what he saw was real.

And it was.

What Johnny had arranged, as a mark of honor and respect, turned out to be a pale blue coffin, not a black one. Instead of swastikas and fire, the sides of the coffin were covered with white bunnies hopping in a green meadow. The lid was decorated with fluffy white clouds and gold lettering: "God who holds His children dear, watch over me as I sleep here."

"I understand you are all moved," the pastor went on uncertainly. "Please have a seat."

The leader of the Aryan Brotherhood broke the group's silence. He had chosen to tattoo his swastika on his forehead instead of on his chest, like the others.

"Not that it matters, Johnny, but what does the writing on the lid say?"

"It says . . ." said Johnny, but he couldn't finish. "You don't want to know what it says."

Actually, out of sheer curiosity, he did. But there was no need. The bunnies were enough. And the fluffy clouds against the pale blue background.

"I'm leaving now," he said.

And he did. Americans two, three, and four followed.

The pastor was bewildered. The dead man's brother had given him ten thousand kronor in exchange for a promise that he would neither complain about the design of the coffin nor bring up God. Why would he complain about this coffin? It was hard to imagine anything more tasteful.

Only now did Johnny wake from his mental paralysis. Were the Americans about to blame *him* for this?

"Hold on, boys. Surely you don't think . . ."

It was at this point that the pastor made the biggest mistake of his career thus far. He felt that the dead man's little brother needed comforting and took a few steps forward to give him a long, tender hug.

One minute later he was so thoroughly battered that even his own mother wouldn't have recognized him. Johnny beat him and beat him to make the coffin and the situation disappear. Yet the only result was that the four Americans left before Johnny could explain himself. The coffin was where it was. The pastor lay where he lay.

Little brother returned to reality. He wiped his bloody hands on his trousers as he took a fresh, pained look at the monstrosity of a coffin.

If Kenneth was in there, it was a catastrophe. If he wasn't . . . then where the hell was he?

Johnny's life as Sweden branch leader was over before it could begin. And that was that. Now he had bigger fish to fry. Like how someone had to die for what his brother had been subjected to. And how he had to figure out where on earth Kenneth was.

Oops, the pastor was moving. Johnny bent down to whisper in his ear. The bloodied man nodded. He and Johnny were in agreement that the pastor had slipped and fallen down the stairs.

Johnny left him where he was, got into his car, and took out his phone. He found the number to the morgue and called it.

One Beatrice Bergh answered. Johnny introduced himself and said he wanted to know where Mrs. Bergh was since he intended to come over and beat her to death.

Beatrice Bergh was as frightened as she had reason to be.

Sweden

Business was booming. The order phone even rang on weekends. Like now, a Saturday afternoon.

"Die with Pride, but perhaps not immediately," said Allan, who happened to have the business phone on a small table beside the sofa he so seldom left.

Beatrice Bergh from the morgue in a neighboring town introduced herself in a panicked tone. She and Allan didn't know each other. But he knew Sabine had delivered coffins there a few times, most recently the day before.

"Why, hello and good day, Madame Morgue Manager. Calling on a Saturday? Is someone in a hurry to get underground?"

Beatrice Bergh didn't respond. She said something, but it was hard to get a grip on exactly what it might have been. The woman seemed thoroughly out of balance. Her words came all in a jumble. At last she gave up and began to cry. "Forgive me," she sobbed. "Forgive me!"

Allan had sat up on his sofa. This didn't seem to be just another typical call. "I'm sure I'll forgive you, Mrs. Bergh," he said. "But that will be easier to do if I know what I have to forgive. Is it calling on a Saturday? In that case, just hang up and we'll let bygones be bygones."

He let her cry a little longer, figuring that she needed to get it out. But at last he grew weary of her. "I think it's about time for you to pull yourself together, Mrs. Bergh. Otherwise I may have to reconsider the forgiveness. Tell me what's going on."

"Thank you, okay, well . . . Oh dear," said Beatrice Bergh.

And did, in fact, manage to tell the tale.

It was easy to work alone on the Saturday shift at the morgue. Still, on that particular day there were two deceased to distribute for burial, which was two more than usual. One was a young girl: the family had chosen Saturday so her classmates could come. The other . . . something entirely dreadful.

"Well, I'm sure you know which coffins I'm thinking of, sir, since your colleague Sabine Jonsson painted them both."

Allan didn't know the details of Julius and Sabine's doings, but he did recall the twelve-year-old girl's coffin: it was lovely. Allan had thought, when he saw it, that he would have been happy to donate some of his 101 years to the twelve-year-old if only it were possible, which of course it wasn't. What the morgue manager was referring to by a *dreadful* coffin, he didn't know.

"Was it Elvis?" he said.

"No!" said Beatrice Bergh. "It was one with swastikas and white power and God knows what. I've worked here for eighteen years. *Eighteen years.* There's never a mistake!"

"Until now?" Allan guessed.

"Until now." Beatrice Bergh was on the verge of crying again. But she did manage to report that transport one had received number two's coffin while transport two had received number one's.

"That's all?" Allan said. "Can't they just be redirected?"

No. What's done was done, and it was too late to fix it.

She had received two phone calls within a few minutes of each other. The first was from an outraged pastor, who had stopped the twelve-year-old girl's funeral before her family could see the most horrid coffin imaginable. And a minute later one from . . . Beatrice Bergh dropped off midsentence.

"From?" said Allan.

"From a man who said he was on his way over to kill me! He was calling to find out where I was."

And she sobbed again.

But Allan had no intention of suffering through another round of tears. "There, there, Mrs. Bergh. If someone is on his way to kill you—which is not to be believed—then isn't it better to leave, instead of sitting there making phone calls without quite getting to the point?"

"I'm not the one who has to leave," cried Mrs. Bergh. "You are!"

Allan summoned the lovebirds Jonsson and Jonsson from upstairs. Because he was standing up, instead of lying on the sofa when they came down, they surmised it was important.

"Apparently we made a coffin with swastikas and Hitler and that sort of thing?" he said.

Sabine and Julius nodded.

"Not Hitler himself, but in that spirit," said Sabine.

"I was just speaking with the morgue. The swastika coffin went astray and was replaced by the lovely one you made, Sabine, with doves and clouds and all that. The purchaser of the swastikas is now upset, as I understand it. He called the morgue some time ago and wanted to kill the woman behind the mix-up."

"And?" Julius asked, worried.

"And . . . Well, she saved her own skin by blaming us. Complete with the address. It seems we have an angry Nazi on the way. As I recall from history, one must watch out for angry Nazis. Or Nazis in general."

"What the hell?" said Julius. "Couldn't you have led with that? We have to get out of here! Now!"

"That sounds like an accurate analysis," said Allan. "I suppose we should gather up—"

He was about to say "the essentials," by which he meant the black tablet he already held. But he didn't have time to finish his sentence before all hell broke loose. The three shop windows shattered, one after the next. A loud rat-a-tat suggested that someone was out on the street, shooting straight into the shop with an automatic weapon. Allan, Julius, and Sabine survived the first salvo and managed to crawl through the door to the courtyard, all in a line. After a brief interlude, the shooting on the other side of the building resumed.

Julius helped Allan into the back of the hearse as Sabine got behind the wheel. A few seconds later, Julius settled into the passenger seat.

"Go!" he said, a second after Sabine had set off.

"It's crowded back here," said Allan. "Is someone in the coffin, or can I climb in?"

The hearse raced away from Märsta, heading south on the E4 highway. Allan moved into the white coffin painted with red roses that would never be delivered the following Monday. With a few minor adjustments, it would be truly comfortable. If they could only arrange for sufficient oxygen intake, he might close the lid and keep it that way each time the lovebirds got cozy with each other. But it would be best to hold off on suggestions of that sort. The man in the front seat seemed thoroughly shaken by the hail of bullets that had rained over them. That must have been Julius's first time. Allan recalled Guadalajara in 1937 as if it were yesterday, where you'd had to keep your head down if you wanted it to stick around. Those were the days. Franco had taken quite a pasting. And then what happened had happened, until it was over. That was life.

While Allan let his mind wander eighty years back in time, Julius sat next to Sabine in silence, his heart pounding, his mind a total blank.

Sabine speeded up a bit. Allan wrestled his way out of his jacket and placed it under his head. Then he took out his black tablet—what luck that it had escaped without a scratch.

"Shots fired in Märsta!" he reported, after some time.

"Really?" said Sabine.

Allan had his tablet; Sabine had the wheel. Julius had nothing more than a slowly recovering brain. He forced himself to recount the trio's situation, as self-therapy.

"Here's where we stand," he said to the others, and took a breath.

Die with Pride AB was now a business without operations and couldn't expect any further income. The firm had perhaps a hundred thousand untaxed kronor in the bank, and there they were welcome to remain. Untaxed. Further, the three representatives of the company were on the run from a Nazi who evidently wanted nothing but to kill them. Their escape was being undertaken in a vehicle recognizable from many hundred yards away. The Nazi was probably after them on the same road.

"We're not switching cars, are we?" Allan said nervously. "I'm comfortable here."

"Let's start by switching roads," Sabine said, exiting the E4 in Upplands Väsby, without seeking approval from the others.

Sweden

It had simply become too emotionally charged. Johnny stood on the pavement, shooting from the hip, instead of calmly and quietly walking in among the coffins and making funeral fodder of everyone who got in his way.

The only thing he managed to kill was a laptop that had been left on a table near the coffins. The store was otherwise devoid of anything of value. Above all, it was devoid of people.

Still, Johnny glimpsed a black hearse leaving the courtyard, an old lady behind the wheel and an old man beside her.

Five minutes had passed since their departure. It was impossible to know where they were heading, but a reasonable guess was the southbound E4. He ought to be able to catch up with a hearse, even if it had had a five-minute head start.

He got into his BMW and drove toward Stockholm at 110 miles per hour, staring straight ahead and keeping a lookout for the back of the black car.

Just south of Upplands Väsby, he was able to take a more sober look at his situation. He should have caught up with them by now if they were planning to use central Stockholm as their hideout. But he hadn't.

Somewhere between Sollentuna and Kista, he gave up and slowed down. He realized he'd already passed a dozen exits that went in all different directions. It would be pointless to continue. Better to head home and plan his next step.

Their journey took them down Mälarvägen to Highway 267 and onto the E18 headed for Oslo.

"I've never been there," said Allan.

"And so it will remain," said Sabine. "What would we do in Oslo?"

The question was where they would go instead. And what would they do with their lives?

After a few dozen miles in the direction of the Norwegian capital, Sabine aimlessly turned south again. Twenty minutes later, Allan discovered a serious news item on his tablet. A possible terrorist attack was under way in Stockholm. An out-of-control truck had driven into a crowd and there were scattered reports of shots fired.

For once, Julius and Sabine wanted Allan to tell them more.

Well, it had happened a few hours ago and the driver of the truck had managed to escape. It seemed no one had been apprehended. Blockades everywhere; the police were evacuating the city center. Several were feared dead. The tablet didn't have much more to say on the topic.

It sounded terrible. Julius was ashamed when he not only allowed himself a full-body shudder but also had the thought that if there had to be a tragedy, at least it had come at an opportune time. With police and blockades everywhere, the Nazi ought to be lying low, while they were putting increasing distance between themselves and the beleaguered capital.

He had just finished that thought, but had come no further, when Sabine drove straight into a police checkpoint.

"I'll close the lid," said Allan.

One of the two officers saluted and informed them that the checkpoints had been set up to inspect vehicles and people on account of a dramatic incident in Stockholm.

"We just heard about it," said Sabine. "Truly awful."

The police officer looked at her and Julius. His gaze moved to the coffin in the back and he said he understood that they were out on official business.

"Yes," said Sabine.

"Official business," Julius confirmed.

It was just that the female driver and the man at her side were not dressed for a delivery of this sort. He was wearing a colorful jacket, a crumpled shirt, and shabby gabardine trousers. She looked more like a retired hippie with medals around her neck.

Caution was not only a virtue, but also a police duty.

"May I see your IDs, please?"

"Of course," said Sabine. "Of course not, now that I think about it. I'm afraid I left my wallet at the funeral parlor. Some tasks are more urgent than others, even in our line of work."

But Julius had discovered Sabine's handbag on the floor at his feet. A stroke of luck. He dug out her driver's license and handed it over with his own passport.

"You're a diplomat?" the officer asked Julius, sounding as surprised as he was.

"Just home from the embassy in New York," Julius said.

"Isn't the embassy in Washington?"

"Just home from the UN building in New York, and prior to that the embassy in Washington."

The policeman looked at him for a long time. "One moment," he said, walking back to his colleague. They exchanged a few words, then both returned to the hearse.

"Good day," said the colleague, who was just as much of a police officer.

"Good day," said Sabine. "We have an urgent delivery, so to speak. Is there a problem, Constable?"

"Inspector," said the colleague. "There's no problem, certainly not, but we have to follow orders. Would you please open the back?"

That was just about the last thing Sabine wanted to do.

"Oh, please, Inspector!" she said. "Think of the sanctity of the grave!"

The inspector said that what he had to think of first and foremost was the nation's security. And then he opened the back and studied the white coffin and the rails it rested on. He pulled the coffin out, apologized for what he was about to do—and opened the lid.

"Peace be with you, Constable," said Allan. "Or Inspector, I mean. Please excuse me for lying down while I greet you."

The inspector stumbled backward and landed on his rear. His colleague swore in shock. When the smoke cleared, the two alleged undertakers and their far-too-animate corpse had been escorted to the police station in Eskilstuna for questioning.

After a strained opening, the tone of the interrogation became rather milder. Credit for this was due to lead interrogator Holmlund, who understood that while the situation was beyond strange, in all likelihood it had nothing to do with the terror attack in Stockholm.

Sabine explained that the members of the group were producers of coffins, that they had business to attend to in the south, and that it had taken creative problem-solving to fit three people into the two-seat vehicle.

"Not just creative," said Holmlund. "Illegal. All passengers in a vehicle must be belted in. In the front seat since 1975, and in the back seat since 1986."

"Of course, I wasn't sitting," Allan said. "I was lying. And what is the definition of a back seat? I'd say I was in the trunk."

But this wasn't Holmlund's first rodeo.

"Karlsson, was that your name? I had been about to let it go this time, but if you think backtalk a good idea, perhaps I should reconsider."

"No, no," said Julius. "Karlsson here is a hundred

and one years old, but he's as daft as a hundred-and-eleven-year-old. Pay no attention to him. We'll definitely belt in the old man, we promise. The fact is, we've already considered a straitjacket."

"Come now," said Allan. "But certainly, Mr. Interrogating Officer, I hear what you're saying although my hearing is pretty bad. I apologize on behalf of myself and young Jonsson here."

Lead interrogator Holmlund nodded. He had no time for fools on a day like this. And there was no reason for a more thorough investigation. It had been proved that the woman owned a company in the coffin industry.

"Off you go, then," he said. "And if Karlsson's going to crawl back into that coffin, he damn well better be strapped in. As long as he's alive. After that I don't give a hoot what you do with him."

Back at the car, Julius pointed out that they had to find some sort of belt for Allan in the back.

"Oh," said Allan, "forget about it. I'll just play dead next time."

Sweden

Too much had happened for one day. East of Eskilstuna, Sabine found a pension where they could check in to catch their breath and take stock.

The problem was, they had just lost their home, workshop, business, and future. All that remained: one hearse.

The manager of the pension, Mrs. Lundblad, was a plump woman of around seventy-five. She was glad to receive unannounced guests. "Of course I have available rooms for Messrs. and Mrs. Undertaker. There are five rooms in all and all five happen to be empty, so take your pick. Would you like dinner? I can offer pea soup with ham, or . . . Well, pea soup with ham."

In Allan's opinion, pea soup with or without ham had never brought anyone joy. But perhaps there was something to wash it down with. "That sounds good," he said. "What will be served in the glasses? Beer, perhaps?"

"Milk, of course," said Mrs. Lundblad.

"Of course," said Allan.

After the soup, Sabine called a meeting in the room she was sharing with Julius. She began by stating what Julius had already realized: their coffin operation was as dead as someone out there wanted them to be. One had to assume that the Nazi at least knew Sabine's name: she was, after all, the firm's frontwoman. Unless he was totally useless he would have found Allan as well, via the Companies Registration Office. But not Julius.

"We need a new source of income," said Sabine. "New lives altogether. Preferably before we run out of money. Any ideas?"

Julius had touched upon an idea earlier, without being very serious about it. At the time. But now? "What about honoring the memory of your mother and starting again in the clairvoyance industry?"

Allan was on the verge of becoming excited. He thought it sounded thrilling to talk to the dead: what came out of the living was seldom of much interest. There were exceptions, of course. At the old folks' home back in Malmköping, the man in the neighboring room had dug trenches in Finland's Winter War. An intriguing job. Or not, really, but the man told a good story. They'd had one ten-minute break per hour, which they devoted to more digging so they didn't freeze to death.

Sabine turned off her ears to Allan while she thought.

"Would that be a feasible path?" Julius asked.

"Trenches?"

Sabine glared at the 101-year-old and replied to Julius. "No," she said. "Or maybe. It depends."

If their assumption was that her mother had truly been clairvoyant, there was no way for them to move forward. After all, Sabine hadn't inherited an ounce of her mother's talent.

But if in fact she had been a charlatan or, alternatively, believed in her own fantasies, thanks to her regular intake of happy pills, well, that put things in a different light.

Julius belonged to the small group of people who think that charlatans are a lovely thing. So he said encouragingly that Sabine shouldn't worry that her mother had been anything but.

Sabine thanked Julius for his kind words but said that the fantasy explanation was the most likely. "And it's possible to copy those. Or even develop them further."

For all those years, her mother had talked about how she wanted to take her operation and herself to new heights; Sabine knew her stories by heart. There were reasons nothing ever happened on that front. Toward the end, she could hardly get out of bed.

Her favorite story was the one about Olekorinko.

What if he was still alive? And she could find him and his operation via the internet?

"You're not touching my tablet," said Allan.

"Oh yes I am."

Sweden

The Americans returned to Los Angeles without touching base with Johnny and without letting him touch base with them. There is nothing you can say to a person who has buried one of the brotherhood in a pale blue coffin with bunnies on it. Perhaps you could beat the bastard to death, but that was the problem. Kenneth's little brother was spared because he was Kenneth's little brother. With that, the Stockholm branch closed; it died with its founder. All planned future payments to the Aryan Alliance would be immediately canceled.

Yet Johnny still wanted to be optimistic about the future. Once those guilty of the coffin mix-up were properly executed, he would try to contact Los Angeles again.

Via the thoroughly distressed woman at the morgue he came to learn that Kenneth had at least ended up in the right coffin, but the coffin had ended up in the wrong place. Now that it had been returned, it was time for a new funeral. Unfortunately the pastor in charge was indisposed after sustaining injuries from a bad fall. Johnny dropped the idea of finding a new pastor. There was no time. He bought a bouquet of tulips at the closest corner shop and paid an evening visit to the battered man at the hospital. The pastor thanked him for his concern, told him of his fractured nose and the crack in his right cheekbone, and said he could probably be back in service within six to eight weeks.

"You've got two and a half," said Johnny.

Meanwhile, Kenneth would stay at the morgue. Johnny, seeking to comfort himself, reasoned that it was no colder there than in the ground.

His priorities were clear. Before anything else, the coffin marauders must float in a puddle of their own entrails. Thanks to the coffin shop's website, he knew he was looking for one Sabine Jonsson. But he'd spoken to a man on the phone when ordering the coffin— probably the man next to her in the car when they'd fled. If Johnny could just find Sabine and the hearse, he would get the strange man too.

It didn't take long to learn more about the woman, via the internet.

She was the CEO and only permanent board member of Die with Pride AB. The other member was one Allan Emmanuel Karlsson, who had to have been the man next to her in the car; he could no longer hide his identity. Sabine had also been a board member of Other Side AB, which had since been liquidated. Other Side AB? What the hell was that?

Oh, right, the internet. Other Side had specialized in clairvoyance! They talked to people who had departed life on Earth. Johnny brushed aside the sudden urge to spend one more moment with Kenneth. One last conversation. No, dammit! There was no point in believing all that nonsense.

Sabine Rebecka Jonsson and Allan Emmanuel Karlsson. In a black hearse registered to the company. With a residential address they seemed utterly unlikely to return to. He would find them, he knew it. He just didn't know how.

Russia

"Good morning, Volodya. How are things? You look concerned."

Yes, that was true. President Putin had some thinking to do. His colleague Trump was about to go entirely off the rails.

"That idiot in Washington has seriously riled that fool in Pyongyang," he said. "What will we do, Gena?"

Gennady Aksakov took a seat at his friend's desk. They were an unbeatable pair. Not just good, they were the best. Just as they had once been on the sambo and judo mats.

But, as they say, it's possible to be too successful. That was more or less what the Russian president was brooding over now.

Under Gena's discreet leadership, Russia had started

a war with the United States without telling anyone. A whole army of young men and women had marched onto the internet, literally donned American baseball caps, opened a Dr Pepper, and gone on the attack.

From within.

The battles took place on Facebook, Instagram, Twitter, blogs, and websites. From those positions, the fake American web soldiers aimed shots in every direction: they undermined left-wing movements one day and right-wing movements the next, supporting NFL players' right to kneel before the flag on Facebook and calling those same players unpatriotic on Twitter. They expressed support for stricter gun laws and protested against the very same thing. They demanded walls against Mexico and the opposite. They praised and cut down every new attempt at health-care reform. Opined every possible opinion on LGBTQ issues. They fired up the masses, no matter who the masses were and what they stood for.

The point was to set American against American. A divided country was a weakened country, after all.

When the dust of war settled, the president and his friend found that their troops had won every single battle. But what about the war itself?

Putin wondered if it had all gone *too* well. Gena had even managed the impossible: placing the extreme divider Trump in the White House. Was it a Pyrrhic victory? Had they created a monster that could no longer be reined in?

The United States was definitely going to pieces; that part was good. But nations are like the Siberian tiger: a wounded one can be lethal. The USA was still the greatest military power in the world. The man who was running his own country into the ground, with Russia's help, might now, in his monumental unsuitability for the job, be on his way to a nuclear war with North Korea. Which was in the immediate vicinity of eastern Russia.

That hadn't been part of their calculations. And it was impossible to predict what it might lead to. In hindsight, they never should have sent over that goddamn plutonium centrifuge.

"Perhaps not," his friend admitted. "But what's done is done."

What had once seemed like a good idea was about to bite them in the butt. One or more true nuclear weapons tests in North Korea, while the United States and China were talking trade agreements, was meant to mess things up for them. It was not in Russia's best interest for the Americans and the Chinese to enjoy each other's company.

The risk now was that they would realize they had

a common enemy. And Xi Jinping had found a way to talk to Trump. Or maybe he'd just made sure to lose by the proper number of strokes on the golf course. Whatever he was doing, it appeared to be working.

"What's done is done," Gennady Aksakov said once more. "Let it go, Volodya. Let's focus on Europe."

Putin nodded. "You swung by Sweden, then? How are things there?"

Gena made a face. "You don't want to know. Let's talk about Spain and Germany instead. I have some good German news for you."

Putin smiled. "Oh, really? Does that mean Merkel isn't sitting as securely on her fat ass as she thinks?"

Sweden

Journalist Bella Hansson with *Eskilstuna-Kuriren* wanted readers. What was the point of her job, otherwise? To realize this goal on a day like today meant delivering something terrorist-related. People didn't want to read about anything else anyway.

She browsed through the incident reports from the police. A bar fight from the day before? No. Alleged maltreatment of animals on a farm? Upsetting just about any other day of the year, but not this one.

Nor was it possible to make terrorism out of two cars that had backed into each other in the car park outside a department store, even if one of the drivers was Muslim.

But perhaps here was something.

A hearse had been searched just a few hours after the attack in Stockholm. No measures taken, case closed.

But there had been an interrogation.

Why?

In Sweden there's something called the principle of public access. It means that everything a public official does, writes, says, and almost thinks must promptly be reported to any citizen who wishes to know. Citizens in general seldom go to the trouble. But journalists are a different matter.

The pockmarked lead interrogator-slash-Inspector Holmlund was on his way home after a long day— a Saturday, to boot—but had the misfortune of running into young reporter Bella Hansson at the door. With an inaudible sigh he invited her into the office.

He was far too experienced to lie to the reporter's face. However, he did elect to leave out parts of the truth. In doing so he imagined she would lose interest in the story and he would be spared extra work with troublesome follow-up questions.

The truth was, then, that a car transporting a coffin had been stopped at a routine checkpoint, and an interrogation had been held. No, the coffin had not contained any deceased person: the inspectors had ascertained this on-site. But at least one of the people had been unbelted.

"You brought in an undertaker for questioning because he or she wasn't wearing a seat belt?" Bella Hansson asked.

The fact was, they weren't undertakers but coffin manufacturers, yet Holmlund opted not to correct the reporter. "It's been a very special day, as you know."

Bella Hansson gave Inspector Holmlund a skeptical look. "Where did the interrogation lead? Were you in charge of it?"

"Yes, I was. Honestly it led to nothing but a talking-to from me to the man who'd neglected to use a seat belt."

Of course, it wouldn't be possible to turn this story into terrorism either, but after Bella had asked a few more questions, and received answers, she changed perspective. She'd had an idea that felt even better. The article she'd almost finished composing in her mind was really too good to be put online. The problem was that the physical copy of the paper didn't come out on Sundays.

Online it would be. But Bella sat on her story until the next morning so it would remain at the top of the news feed for as long as possible. In the new world, it was important to amass clicks.

Sweden

Yes, indeed, Olekorinko was more active than ever. It appeared a lucrative business to be a witch doctor of his caliber. But to copy his ideas Sabine needed to study them on-site. And since Africa wasn't exactly next door, she would have to stick to what she already knew for the time being.

First they had to find out what the clairvoyant competition looked like. Sabine spent the evening and half their night at the pension on market analysis. It was depressing work. Not just because Allan whined non-stop about how she had stolen his toy, but also because it was all there in black and white, how the market for various types of clairvoyance had just about exploded in the past year. The supply was enormous. It would be easy to enter the branch anew, but it would be hard to position herself for financial viability, even ignoring the fact that Sabine had no talent for running economically viable businesses.

Julius left her in peace, partly because he believed she needed it and partly because he was busy wondering about the bloody asparagus. The old lady at the pension had an old-fashioned telephone on a table in the hall. It would have been possible to borrow it for an intercontinental call while she was out shopping, if the scrap of paper with Gustav Svensson's number on it wasn't missing. It must have been left behind on the table at the restaurant in New York.

Without Gustav's number, and without Gustav having a number at which to reach Julius (who didn't even have a phone), there was a considerable risk that the friends and business partners would never meet again. Julius thought some more and realized it was almost certain they never would. This was tragic on several levels. After all, he liked the Swedish Indian. And he also felt the need to hit him on the head with something hard.

While Sabine and Julius were otherwise occupied, Allan found a sofa in the pension's common room upon which to settle himself. He lay there waiting for Sabine's short breaks from the tablet so he could catch up on his surfing. Among other things, about the Swedes' fury that postal delivery wasn't working as it should. Far too many letters took two days to arrive rather than the stipulated one. The postal service's solution was to change the rules rather than the routines. Now *all* letters would take two days, in accordance with the new regulations. Suddenly, delivery assurance was approaching 100 percent. Allan guessed the director of the postal service had a considerable bonus coming.

In other news, a leader of the National Front in France had sat down at a North African restaurant to eat couscous. And liked it! This was considered beyond unpatriotic. Soon the leader had been kicked out of the party, or perhaps he had stepped down of his own accord. Allan wasn't sure what couscous was. Perhaps the Arab world's answer to pea soup with ham. Too much of that stuff and he, too, would probably have stepped down. From what, however, was unclear.

Before Sabine demanded the tablet back, Allan also managed to read about the Swedish military's investment in a fleet of helicopters so expensive that there was no money left to use it. But the helicopters looked nice sitting on the ground.

After the night's work, Sabine had a list of forty-nine women and one man who all offered services in the same arena as her mother had.

"How's it going?" Julius wondered, as they breakfasted together. He noticed how grim Sabine looked.

"Not great."

She expounded her statement. The world outside was swarming with angel cards, tarot cards, and pendulums. Women devoting themselves to long-distance healing. Breaking up blockages in the soul. Speaking with animals. Telling love fortunes. Giving telepathic guidance. Having the universal laws of energy down pat. Seeing the past, present, and future in glowing ash, coffee grounds, or crystal balls.

"It can't be that hard to see the past," said Allan. "I could, before my memory got too bad. And isn't the present the present?"

It wasn't quite that simple. The past was made up of parallel events that together created an individual's now and would do the same with said individual's future.

"Without the proper knowledge of the guardian angels, you are spiritually lost. With the wrong energies in the room, it's still worse."

Julius had known for a long time that Sabine was as

spiritually lost as he was. Not to mention Allan. But business was business. What sort of focus did Sabine think they should have, in this clairvoyant muddle?

Well, that was the thing. The reasonably good news in all of this was that few of the mediums focused on ghosts, driving out ghosts, or conversations with the other side. Sabine saw potential market success in what had once been her mother's speciality.

Allan delivered the good news that the ranks of those on the other side had recently increased by one. He read from the tablet about the 117-year-old Uzbek farmer's wife who had just passed away after her only cow happened to sit on her.

Sabine was growing more tired of the old man with each passing day. Perhaps on his hundred-and-second birthday they could buy him a cow, and hope for the best.

Sweden

The day after the terror attack in Stockholm, *Eskilstuna-Kuriren* revealed evidence of surprising incompetence at the local police station sixty miles away. In the hysterical hunt for the terrorist, they had not hesitated to terrorize the most innocent of citizens. Not even the dead were spared (Bella Hansson chose not to mention that there had been no dead person in the coffin, and the fact that there had been a living corpse within it was beyond her knowledge).

The individual inspectors and police leadership were portrayed, in her article, as a bunch of nitwits who didn't understand the concept of prioritizing. Cracking down on an innocent hearse! What next?

The article was sharp, even if it did peter out a bit

toward the end. It was also rather long. Thus, at the last second, Bella cut the sections in which the police assured her that the crackdown, which incidentally was not a crackdown, had occurred due to suspicion that there actually *was* a link to the terrorist act in question.

Foolish police make good local-paper reading.

Foolish police make good national-paper reading too.

In no time, the Stockholm papers' online editions had cranked out a recap of the hearse story.

As a result, two things happened.

One was that a clearly not-so-foolish police officer in Märsta noticed a possible connection. He was investigating a reckless shooting in a coffin shop from the day before, and this new clue might move the investigation forward. He would just have to make a phone call or two.

The other was that the membership of Aryan Alliance—that was, Johnny Engvall—now knew for certain that those who must die at any cost were on a trip through Sweden.

"You're heading south, you pigs," he said to himself. "On back roads?"

At first he smiled at his own great intelligence. Then

he realized that there were many back roads to choose from in southern Sweden. And the trail had already gone cold.

Johnny needed to know more than the article's reporter had given him.

Sweden

The concept development continued. While Allan, aged 101, showed Julius, aged sixty-six, how to maximize one's reach to the proper target group via Facebook ads, Sabine drove around in the hearse to obtain pendulums, crystals, divining rods, and nasty-smelling myrrh. She respected the group's limited budget. For a pendulum she used a plumb line she found on sale at Byggmax. She whittled her own divining rod with the help of a stick stolen from the pension's garden. Ordinary sea salt would do for crystals. And she produced myrrh with the help of an oil lamp, whose fuel consisted of one part shrimp soup and nine parts oil. The rest of the secret was double wicks: one to burn and one that just glowed, spreading smoke and smell.

The pension manager looked curiously at Sabine's many tools of the trade and cautiously asked what Mrs. Undertaker planned to use all that for. Sabine told it like it almost was: they weren't only undertakers but had an additional speciality in which they established contact with those they had just helped send into the ground. At this Mrs. Lundblad's enthusiasm was set aflame. Did Mrs. Undertaker mean to say she could establish contact with Börje?

The old woman had brought up her deceased spouse time and again in the short period they'd been in her company. In under twenty-four hours Sabine knew everything worth knowing about the spouse's previous doings, like, for example, that he had been dead for fifteen years. Background knowledge was, after all, everything in the field of clairvoyance.

Why not? A dress rehearsal could only be an advantage before they started their operation for real.

The performance that followed made quite an impression on Allan and Julius. If they hadn't known better they would have believed that the dead man really was talking to his widow from the other side, via Sabine. The husband swore his eternal love to his widow and sounded distressed when he learned that the cat had died eight years earlier at the age of sixteen. When asked point-blank, he promised he had stopped smoking.

It would have been a resounding success if only the manager had avoided being struck with heart failure when her deceased husband said he pined for her so badly that he cried himself to sleep each night.

"Oh, my," said Julius, as the old woman pitched forward and landed with her nose on the table.

Sabine jumped out of her séance chair in horror and turned on the ceiling light as Julius took a closer look at the old woman.

"Is she dead?" Sabine asked.

"I think so," said Julius.

The only one who remained calm was Allan.

"Then they'll soon be together again," he said. "If the old man was lying about his smoking, he'd better snuff it out soon."

Sabine snapped at Allan and his lack of respect, saying that now she was sure there was something wrong with him. Then she gathered up her things and called an urgent crisis meeting in the kitchen. For the time being they would leave the old woman where she was.

They sat down at the kitchen table: Sabine, with creases on her forehead, Julius, with pen and paper; and Allan, with a ban on speaking.

"We can't stay here," said Sabine. "But where will we go, and why?"

Julius praised her for the brilliant performance she'd just given; he imagined they could rake in some good money from it. Somewhere the customer base was sufficiently large. Time for a snap decision. He wrote "Stockholm" on his paper. Under that "Gothenburg." And under that, "Malmö."

Stockholm was ruled out immediately: there were far too many Nazis there. Julius wrote *No.*

What about Gothenburg? Sweden's second-biggest city. *Hmm.*

Or Malmö? With its proximity to Copenhagen. Almost four million people lived there, if you counted both sides of the bridge.

Julius wrote *Yes.* Their destination was determined by a vote of two to nil, with one vote declared invalid. All that was left was to decide what to do with the dead woman.

"Not call the police," said Julius.

No, presenting a dead elder to the police the day after they'd found a living one in a coffin seemed like asking for trouble.

Julius took a peek at the woman's ledger. Two guests from Greece were booked two days later. The woman wouldn't have to be alone for longer than that.

"When you're dead, you're dead," said Julius. "It's not as if she'll suffer more."

And that was that. Mrs. Lundblad remained where she was.

"Good decision," said Allan.

"Weren't you supposed to keep quiet?" said Sabine.

Inspector Holmlund's weekend had been ruined. He almost wished he hadn't stopped those three coffin marauders. Even before his Sunday afternoon coffee break, they had cost him time and mental effort in the form of two phone calls, one stranger than the next.

The first was from an old woman who ran a pension outside the city. She was upset and wanted to know if it was possible to report three specific people for attempted murder. The trio had spent one night at her pension and offered her a séance, the possibility to converse with her husband. When she had fainted in shock, they left her there at the table and had since vanished.

"Hold on," said Inspector Holmlund. "Who is it they tried to kill? You? Your husband? Or someone else?"

"Me, of course. My husband is already dead."

"Since when? Didn't you speak to him?" The inspector wasn't entirely familiar with how clairvoyance worked.

The woman explained. When her husband, who had died fifteen years previously, told her how much he missed her, it was as if all the oxygen vanished from her brain, and that was the last thing she recalled. The medium and the others must have thought she had died too, but she wouldn't go that easily. The old woman was tougher than that and now she demanded justice.

What Inspector Holmlund wanted was to focus on the essentials. But he didn't say so. Instead he explained how the law works: speaking with someone who is dead, at which point someone who isn't faints, does not fall under the definition of attempted murder. It does not, as far as the inspector could understand, fall under any definition at all. There was no scale of penalty for general tomfoolery. "Unfortunately," he added.

And he'd hardly hung up when the phone rang again.

This time a man introduced himself as a "concerned citizen." He wished to know more about what had happened during the crackdown against a hearse the previous day.

The inspector told him, since concerned citizens had a tendency to transform from concerned to displeased, which increased the workload many times over for those who only wished to get away relatively unscathed. It had been a case of three people in a hearse who found themselves at a routine checkpoint, which had led to a brief interrogation in which all uncertainties had been cleared up. It could not in any way be described as a "crackdown."

The concerned citizen would not be deterred. He wanted to know where the hearse had gone after the interrogation.

What was wrong with people? The inspector didn't have time for this! But perhaps if he tossed the concerned customer at the old woman they could bother one another instead. Good idea!

"I can't rule out that the people you're inquiring after spent the night just outside Eskilstuna. For further information I recommend you call Mrs. Lundblad at Klipphällen Pension. A lovely woman. I'm sure you'll have much to talk about."

Click. The concerned citizen hung up. He didn't seem as concerned any longer. Great.

Johnny had no intention of calling Mrs. Lundblad. But he would pay her a visit. Along with her three guests, if they were still there. *Three,* incidentally? Sabine Jonsson, Allan Karlsson, and who else?

Oh, well, he could always ask the third to introduce himself before he slit his throat.

One week had passed since Kenneth's accident; one day since the canceled funeral. Johnny missed his brother something fierce.

Next stop, Malmö. Two of the three were in the front seats of the vehicle; the third was on his back with his black tablet in the coffin at the rear, with a closed lid and freshly drilled ventilation holes. They made their way down Highway 55.

South of Strängnäs, Allan opened the lid for a moment. "I lived around here before they tried to lock me up in the home in Malmköping. I blew my house sky-high, or else we could have swung by to take a look."

"You blew up your own house?" said Sabine.

"Ignore him," said Julius.

After Malmköping, the trio ended up on the E4 again, north of Norrköping this time. From there they headed south along Sweden's busiest highway.

Allan noticed that Sabine and Julius snapped at him no matter what he said, unless he talked about the terror attack. They were all upset by what had happened in the capital city.

He told them that the country seemed preoccupied by the tragic and bewildering incident. Several people had died. The terrorist had been apprehended, to be sure, and had confessed, adding that Allah was the greatest of them all. Allan wasn't sure how much blame could be placed with Allah for the attack: you never know with gods—they all have their issues. According to the Bible, one deliberately took the lives of ten children in a bet with Satan.

Sabine had never heard of this, but Julius had. "The Book of Job, Old Testament," he said.

And then he said no more. He shuddered at the memory of his tyrannical father, who had forced him to be confirmed fifty-two years earlier. Even if the boy had spent most of that time stealing Bibles to sell (twenty-five ore per Bible, two for forty), something had stuck with him.

The international press was reporting that Sweden had lost its innocence, that this heaven on earth had been punished for its generous attitude toward the so-called refugees.

Allan muttered over what he read. In just his brief time on Earth, Sweden had been afflicted with leftists who blew up boats, right-wingers who blew up editorial offices, and Red Army factions who blew up embassies. And then there was the guy who wanted to kidnap a Swedish minister and lock her into a box. And those who wandered around here and there, shooting foreigners at random until they could be arrested and put behind bars.

What they all had in common was that they had their reasons—including the one who heard voices and killed the Swedish minister for foreign affairs because of them. What the man who'd shot the prime minister on the street was thinking, however, was impossible to know. Partly because he himself was dead now, partly because it might have been someone else.

It was all genuinely sad, of course. But when it came to Sweden's *innocence*, Allan suspected that had gone out of the window back in the days of the Vikings.

"What are you mumbling about back there?" Julius wondered.

"I don't know," said Allan.

Everything had been so much easier before the tablet.

Duller. But easier.

The 101-year-old surfed on. That was what he did, these days.

It turned out that the trash collectors had run into problems in Alvesta in Småland. Someone had discovered that the municipal company Alvesta Refuse AB had been abbreviated as ARAB for thirty-five years. The citizen complained, in a petition to the local authority, that this abbreviation suggested that Arabs, in general, smelled bad.

This was a news item to Allan's liking, and perfectly necessary to share with the group.

"Don't people have lives anymore?" Julius wondered.

"Alvesta isn't too far from here, is it?" Allan said. "Should we head over and have a look?"

"At what?" Sabine asked.

Allan didn't quite know, so he didn't respond. But he did give his black tablet a kiss to thank it for the refuse truck news. All was forgiven.

The journey continued southward. As they approached Värnamo it began to get dark. With the aid of Allan's tablet, Sabine found another pension, of the more rustic sort. It was run by an older woman, rather like the one who had just landed on the table nose-first.

"We're not holding any séances with this new one, right?" said Julius.

Sweden

It was already nighttime when Johnny Engvall arrived at Klipphällen Pension. There was no hearse parked outside; he was too late.

The manager of the pension, who had not, in fact, died at the séance table, was in the kitchen cooking a new batch of pea soup when she received a surprise visitor.

The Nazi made an effort not to scare the old woman too much. Before he squeezed what she knew out of her, he would try to get her to tell him voluntarily.

"Good day to you!" he said, hating himself for his pleasant tone.

"Good day to *you*," said Mrs. Lundblad. "Are we looking for a place to spend the night?"

Pea soup was Johnny's favorite. It was delicious, Swedish, and authentic. Especially with some mustard on the edge of the bowl, a piece of *knäckebröd*, and a big glass of milk.

"Maybe," he said. "And perhaps even a bit of food?"

Mrs. Lundblad invited him to the table. The soup was almost ready. As she set two places, she said she was happy to have company, for she'd had a perfectly horrible day, she would like her guest to know.

And she told him the tale. Johnny didn't even have to ask.

Three horrid people—with a hearse!—had arrived the day before. Just a few hours before the young gentleman arrived they had invited her to a séance, offering her the chance to speak with her dead husband. It had all gone well, but when she happened to faint with the excitement those louts had taken off. It was so unchristian as to be beyond words.

Johnny really wanted to ask right away whether she knew where they had gone, but something else took precedence.

"A séance?" he said. "Did you really speak with your husband, ma'am?"

"Oh, yes. He's happy up there in heaven, I now

know. And imagine! He's stopped smoking. My darling, clever Börje stopped smoking!"

For the second time, the Nazi was struck by the thought, as absurd as it was wonderful, that he might be able to contact Kenneth on the other side. This time it took longer to put out of his mind.

The soup was marvelous. And the old woman had probably been blond before her hair turned white, which only made it that much better.

"You're a fantastic cook, I must say. Tell me, do you know where those horrible people went?"

No, of course the old woman didn't know. She had been unconscious when they left.

"I understand. Did they take anything? Did they leave anything?"

No, apparently they weren't thieves. The only trace of them was a note left on the counter. She handed over a sheet of A4. It read:

Stockholm—no.
Gothenburg—hmm.
Malmö—yes.

Malmö!
That was where they were going.

"Would the delightful gentleman like seconds?" asked the old woman.

"No, I wouldn't, you old bitch," said Johnny Engvall, and left.

That last bit felt good.

Sweden

"And what has Trump done since last time?" Julius started off the next day's breakfast.

It was time to leave: ninety miles to Malmö. Where they would stay once they arrived remained to be seen. One thing at a time. On that note, Julius thought if they got Allan's news from the black tablet over with now, they might get out of there and to the point much quicker.

"Glad you asked," said Allan. "And I'd thought we could skip that for today, considering the difficult situation we're in. But, of course, a thing or two did happen while we were sleeping, or whatever you two were doing instead. I thought I heard something through the wall."

"Get to the point," said Sabine.

Right, Trump. He had appointed a new communications director, who immediately communicated that he intended to fire everyone around him, at which point he himself was dismissed.

"Thanks for the update," said Julius, "so shall we—"

"Hold on! I only told you that for context. They say the man behind the president's fire-as-many-people-as-possible-in-as-little-time-as-possible strategy is our friend Bannon."

"Our friend who?"

"Steve Bannon. The chief strategist. The surly red-faced man who met us at the airport in New York."

"Oh, that was his name. I didn't know he's the president's chief strategist."

"Well, he's not. Not anymore."

Malmö was getting closer and closer. Julius had dozed off in the passenger seat. Allan was snoozing in the coffin, always ready to play dead should the need arise. Sabine was alone with her thoughts. She wasn't happy about starting a new business in Sweden, the country where they'd managed to rile a Nazi. A foreign country would be safer. But which one? It wasn't enough just to make contact with someone on the other side: she would also need to understand what they said. Plus it was uncertain how economically viable this might be.

Which brought her back to her original thought.

Olekorinko. The witch doctor. Or *mganga*, in the local language. The man her mother, Gertrud, had spoken of so often. With a business model unlike any other.

In Africa.

Shit, shit, shit.

She'd sworn inaudibly. But Julius heard the silence and woke up. "What are you thinking about?" he asked.

"Nothing."

She saw no other solution than to follow the path and the Facebook campaign Allan and Julius had already prepared, where Sabine's abilities would be advertised as "Medium Esmeralda," based in Malmö—370 miles from the angry Nazi in Stockholm, but just one bridge from the gigantic Copenhagen market.

It's not easy to find a business location when you're living under the radar. Or, for that matter, a place to live. Their solution was to expose Julius to a certain amount of risk: he was the only one of the group who didn't appear in any registry of firms. There were empty rental apartments scattered around the area, among others a two-bedroom place in southern Rosengård for just over six thousand kronor per month, only four miles from central Malmö. It wasn't the most attractive part of the city, but for that very reason it was a good option for the friends. Buying a centrally located place for three or four million was, of course, out of the question.

Julius was dropped off outside the offices of the public housing authority (which, unlike the available apartment, was not in Rosengård) to express their interest.

And, to his surprise, he got a *no.*

"We have rules," said the representative of the authority, a woman in her forties.

"And what are those rules?" asked Julius, who, as a rule, hated rules.

"Well, as I understand it, you are unable to provide a current address or steady income, and that makes things difficult."

Julius looked at her. "When it comes to a current address, that's what I'm currently trying to obtain. I can't exactly report myself as living in one of your apartments until I have access to it, can I?"

"That's true," said the woman. "But your age leads me to suspect that you may have lived somewhere else previously but that is not evident from the form you filled in and there are no hits when I search your name in the system."

This country! Couldn't *anything* be kept private? Was he even allowed to choose a toothpaste on his own? But he didn't say this.

"Young lady," he said instead. "As a diplomat in the service of the Department for Foreign Affairs, I have not had an address in Sweden since the Cuban Missile Crisis. I have struggled on many occasions with extreme homesickness. But never have I felt it as strongly as now, when a municipal authority turns its back on me in this manner."

And then he placed his Swedish diplomatic passport on the table.

The woman looked at it. Then opened it. At first, she said nothing. Then: "And a steady income? You must understand, sir, that—"

"Naturally I have not taken an income in Sweden," said Julius, who felt that he was really getting into the swing of it. "Please search for me in the Bank of Investments in the Seychelles, and I'm sure you will find what you're after."

Fortunately for Julius, the woman capitulated at once. He had made up the name of the bank, and he couldn't have spelled "Seychelles" if she'd asked.

"I believe I understand the dilemma, sir," she said hesitantly. "I'll see what I can do."

"Please hurry, I'm jet-lagged," said Julius. "Just back from a quick trip to the Swedish embassy in New York. I mean Washington."

She spoke with her boss for under a minute. However odd it was for a diplomat to wish to reside in Rosengård, the housing authority would welcome him. Furthermore, it was a feather in their cap.

"We've decided to overlook the fact that you can't provide proof of income, Mr. Diplomat. You're welcome to rent the unit in question for three months' advance rent. That's not too much, I hope?"

The two-bedroom apartment was on the first floor of a five-story building. One room for Allan, one for Julius and Sabine, a kitchen, and a living room that would function as a location for séances and spiritual exercises. They bought furniture secondhand; it took two full hearse-loads before everything was at home. Prior to this, Julius and Sabine had carried the white coffin with red roses into the apartment, under cover of darkness.

"It looks nice in the séance room," Sabine said, pleased.

"I can't decide where I want to sleep," said Allan.

"There are blinds in my room, but on the other hand I'll miss the coffin. Then again, I can always close the lid . . ."

"You will sleep in the bed we bought for you," said Sabine. "With the door closed."

Sweden

When it was a weekday again, Inspector Viktor Bäckman with the Märsta police contacted his colleague Holmlund in Eskilstuna, who didn't even have the energy to be surprised when he heard that the coffin people had been shot at. In fact, he felt a certain amount of sympathy for the perpetrator. Consequently, he answered his colleague's questions politely and accurately and wished him good luck.

Allan Karlsson, Julius Jonsson, Sabine Jonsson.

Viktor Bäckman absorbed this new information.

Two were members of the Swedish diplomatic corps. At least two had also been involved with the coffin shop in Märsta. Which had been fired upon with at least sixty shots. Whereafter the diplomats had not reported the incident to the police, but taken off for Eskilstuna, only to land at a traffic checkpoint. With one of the three lying in a coffin. Extremely alive.

What was going on?

None of the three was suspected of any crime, but Inspector Bäckman wished to question them for information.

Sabine Jonsson and Allan Karlsson were listed as living at the same address as the shop in Märsta, while Julius Jonsson had, earlier that day, listed himself at an apartment in Malmö. A visit for clarification purposes was in order. But first he wanted to finish digging through what was available for digging.

Viktor Bäckman elected not to contact the Security Service; they never responded to the regular police's questions anyway. Instead he called the Ministry for Foreign Affairs to confirm that there truly were diplomats by the names of Allan Emmanuel Karlsson and Julius Jonsson, no middle name.

The inspector was transferred from the operator to someone else and then another someone else. Then he had to wait one minute, and then another three. At last his call was taken.

"Margot Wallström, how may I be of service?"

Inspector Bäckman was perfectly astonished, but recovered quickly. He began by apologizing for bothering the minister for foreign affairs; that had not been his intention. It was just that he needed to confirm two identities, those of Diplomats Karlsson and Jonsson.

It wasn't as if Margot Wallström picked up the phone for each incoming call to the ministry, but her ears had pricked up when Karlsson's and Jonsson's names began bouncing off the walls and the civil servants couldn't find them in the system. She found it best to break in before anything unmanageable broke out.

"I can confirm that those gentlemen exist and that they are diplomats," said Margot Wallström. "Is there a problem?"

"No, no," said Inspector Bäckman. "Just that someone seems to have shot at them with an automatic weapon, and they have been missing ever since."

Margot Wallström was immediately struck by a vision of her career falling to pieces. Should she have left those strange beings to their fate in Pyongyang? No, no matter what was happening now. The alternative would have been that Kim Jong-un risked being supplied with more powerful weapons than he already had. That must be of more value than . . .

"What did you say? *Shot* at them? Did they shoot back?"

Inspector Bäckman explained in greater detail. The diplomats hadn't fired any shots. Neither was there any indication that they had been harmed. However, eight coffins had been perforated. Plus a laptop.

The story was as unbelievable as its main characters. A good offense is the best defense, Margot Wallström thought, praying to a higher power that she would land on her feet.

"Bäckman, is that the name? Great. First, I will tell you, Inspector Bäckman, that in my capacity as minister for foreign affairs I have no intention of doing your job for you. If Diplomats Karlsson and Jonsson are under suspicion of any crime, it is certainly your right—or, rather, duty—to investigate further. If not, I have a bit of discreet information to share."

Inspector Bäckman reiterated that, for the moment, the gentlemen were not suspected of anything, but that he would appreciate the opportunity to speak to them.

"Unfortunately I can't help you there," said Margot Wallström. "The last time I saw either of them was during a secret meeting with President Trump in New York. You are, of course, free, Inspector, to do whatever you see fit with that information. But I will permit myself to hope that you keep it to yourself, in the name of world peace."

Viktor Bäckman regretted his call to the Ministry for Foreign Affairs. Margot Wallström had just placed the responsibility for world peace at his feet, and that was more than he would wish upon his worst enemy. "I hear what you're saying, Madame Minister," he said. "Once again, since the diplomat gentlemen are not suspected of any crime, I have no reason to begin a search for them. May I just take the opportunity to ask if you might have any suspicion about who would have shot at them?"

The truth was, Margot Wallström had no idea. "I have no idea," she said. "But I would consider checking with President Trump and Secretary General Guterres to see if they know. Shall I ask either of them to contact you, Inspector, if it turns out that they do?"

She was taking a chance. But it worked.

"Oh, shit, no," Viktor Bäckman let slip.

Enough was enough! Viktor Bäckman was recently engaged. He and his girlfriend were planning a golfing trip to Portugal. In his free time he coached a girls' soccer team for Märsta IK, which, the previous autumn, had found success in the Märsta Games tournament. Once a week he attended an evening class in leadership and organizational theory, in the low-key hope that this would help him secure a promotion in the future. On the last Saturday of each month he and the guys met for an evening of beer and poker.

He was *not* prepared to sacrifice all of this to go

down in history as the person who had started the Third World War.

"Please excuse my accidental use of a swear word, Madame Minister. But I think I will refrain from any further investigation. At least for now. I do, however, have a possible address for Mr. Jonsson if you would be interested. It's an apartment in Malmö."

Margot Wallström mostly wanted to forget about Allan Karlsson and his asparagus-farming friend. But perhaps that would seem suspicious. "Extremely interested," she said. "It's possible that Theresa May will want something from Jonsson moving forward, so it would be nice to have an address."

The British prime minister? What was this? No, Viktor Bäckman didn't want to know. He. Didn't. Want. To. Know. Instead he gave Minister for Foreign Affairs Wallström the address and hurriedly bade her farewell before hurrying off to soccer practice. He arrived at the sports facility forty minutes before anyone else.

Margot Wallström felt a bit guilty about the part with Theresa May. But she hadn't lied, even if the odds that May would want something from Julius Jonsson were small. Partly because she had no idea he existed, partly because she was extremely busy dismantling her country.

Sweden

The extensive Facebook campaign in Swedish and Danish brought seven hits in the first week, which in turn led to four appointments. One from Denmark and three from Sweden.

The offer involved two options: contact with the other side or help with troublesome spirits. The séances were held in the medium's apartment in Rosengård and priced at three thousand kronor per session. Driving out spirits and the like was, of course, best performed where the spirit actually was; in such cases there were additional charges for travel and lodging for Esmeralda and her assistant.

Of the first four bookings, all concerned wishes to establish a dialogue between the customer and a deceased loved one. All four came to Rosengård. Three of the séances went well. The fourth case involved a recently drowned fisherman. His despairing girlfriend wanted one last conversation with her beloved. Esmeralda established contact with him, but at that very moment so did the girlfriend. The drowned man had not drowned at all, but had floated to shore on Bornholm with a broken-down boat engine. The first thing he did when he was rescued, of course, was call his sweetheart, who cried with joy, before demanding her money back.

Sweden

Johnny was sitting at a café on Gustav Adolfs Torg in Malmö, having his morning cup of coffee. With it he ate a salad, which he'd asked to have rinsed an extra time, since he belonged to the group of neo-Nazis who accepted the research that said the rampant levels of homosexuality in society were caused by toxins in food.

Perhaps Gustav Adolfs Torg was not the best place to take one's meals, but you can't get hung up on every detail. Gustav IV Adolf had been generally useless as king. He'd picked a fight with Napoleon, suffered a resounding defeat, and by the time it was all over he had lost both Finland and his own royal title. He was dethroned, exiled, and died a few years later penniless and alcohol-soaked, at a pub somewhere in Switzerland. He began as a king, was demoted to count, lived for a few years as Colonel Gustavsson, and ended up a drunk. Not exactly an illustrious career.

After his salad, it was time to take out his city map again, as he'd done every morning for the past few days. Johnny had already worked his way through downtown, the harbor area, and Arlöv and its environs. Next up were the western and southern neighborhoods. His task was to drive up one street and down the next until he found the hearse, either parked or on the move.

But it wasn't easy to concentrate. Johnny kept thinking about his brother. And he couldn't drop his musings about the pension bitch outside Eskilstuna. Had she really spoken with her dead husband?

Sabine Jonsson was, after all, chairperson of the board of something called Other Side AB, specialists in clairvoyance. She'd obviously moved from that to the coffin trade, but she had demonstrably returned to the clairvoyant at the pension.

One idea might be to force her to contact Kenneth while holding a knife to her throat. But could he trust her? What if big brother said, during the séance, that little brother ought to let the medium live? In that case, who would be speaking? Kenneth or Sabine Jonsson?

No, the woman who must die was not an option as a point of contact between the brothers. But there had to be others, right? On the one hand, it was impossible to believe in all this. On the other, Johnny felt that Kenneth was still around, always by his side. That must mean he was out there somewhere, in another dimension. It *had* to mean it.

Johnny searched online and got hits all over the country. When he limited the search to southern Skåne, only about two dozen remained. Most could be ruled out because they didn't offer what Johnny was after. As he sifted through them, it struck him that Sabine Jonsson might show up in an ad. She was already dumb enough to drive around in her hearse, but that extra step of actually *informing* the person who was searching for her of her whereabouts? No, no one was that stupid.

At last he had four names left: Bogdan, Angelique, Harriet, and Esmeralda.

Bogdan went out of the window right away. Harriet didn't sound enough like a medium. Angelique? That name gave Johnny porn-star vibes. And obviously the porn industry was run by Jews.

That left Esmeralda. Might be a wog, but he could always find out.

Sweden

Nine thousand kronor in, minus half that in start-up costs. It wouldn't cover the payments to Facebook by a long shot, and since the results of the ad had quickly died down it was obvious that this business idea was not viable in the long term.

A few days later, though, they received three new inquiries. The first two led nowhere; the third was a request for a séance, a man who wanted to contact his brother, who had died in a tragic accident. As always, background information from the customer was the key to a séance's success. Esmeralda sat down in the kitchen and called the man via the computer. Her face was white when she joined the old men in the living room. Julius was in the easy chair; Allan had his tablet and was on his back in his white coffin with red roses.

"What's going on?" Julius asked.

Sabine didn't respond. But Allan did.

The new president of France had used ugly language when he thought no one was listening. And the German chancellor had given Putin in Moscow a talking-to on the topic of various LGBTQ issues. Allan didn't know what LGBTQ was. It sounded like a North Korean news bureau, but he assumed that couldn't be right.

Julius snapped at his friend: he hadn't been talking to him. Couldn't Allan see that Sabine was completely distraught?

No, Allan said, he couldn't. The lid of the coffin impeded his view. But if Sabine wished to clarify it would be to everyone's advantage. Was he correct in thinking that her primary concern lay somewhere other than with this LGBTQ question? If so, she had Allan's full support, especially if she told him what it meant.

Sabine tuned Allan out: she'd learned to do so when necessary. Instead she said she had just booked a séance for one Johnny, who wished to contact his brother Kenneth.

"Great," said Julius. "What do we know about Kenneth?"

"Too much," said Sabine. "He's the one who was supposed to be in the Nazi coffin we made."

"The one who shot at us later?" Allan asked.

"No, he didn't do much shooting. That was his brother. He's coming here tomorrow. At one o'clock."

Sweden

Johnny Engvall didn't have any luck south of the city either. Eastern Malmö awaited him the next day, but he decided to perform a preinvestigation now. He was on his way to see the medium Esmeralda, as a cry for help with his genuine sorrow over Kenneth.

What if she really had the gift she claimed? What if Johnny could at least send one final greeting to his brother, and receive one in return? Just think: What if the brothers could even open a two-way line of communication, so that neither would have to feel lonely ever again?

Johnny was making good time. Apparently Esmeralda's office was also her home. It was in Rosengård, just four or five blocks away now. But—what on earth?

Suddenly, there it was.

The hearse.

Parked.

It was the right vehicle. But the nearby buildings were numerous and tall, so he couldn't just go knocking on doors.

Johnny climbed out, walked over to the hearse and felt the hood, which was warm. It had recently been driven. Since the parking permit displayed on the windshield was valid until the next morning, it had probably finished moving for the day.

The plan would just have to be to keep watch until Sabine Jonsson and crew appeared.

"No rash decisions, Johnny," he said to himself. "No rash decisions."

It was almost one o'clock. Esmeralda was waiting just blocks away.

Johnny decided to carry out the visit. Again: "No rash decisions."

For some unfathomable reason, then, the Nazi with the automatic weapon in Märsta had now surfaced in Malmö and hunted down Esmeralda the Medium. It couldn't be a coincidence. Unless it was a coincidence. It had to be a coincidence!

No matter how the friends racked their brains, they couldn't find a single crack in their facade. There was no link between Sabine Jonsson on the one hand and the apartment four miles southeast of central Malmö on the other.

Julius was the one listed on the rental contract. There was no connection anywhere between him and Sabine. Not in her company, not for the apartment in Märsta.

"There's literally no way . . ." said Julius.

At which point he realized that Allan, Julius, and Sabine had presented ID, all three of them, to the police in Eskilstuna. And with that, he was listed on the police system along with his friends. But did this Johnny have access to that?

Still, their conclusion was that the Nazi had booked an appointment with Esmeralda in order to execute as many of them as he could during the séance.

But in that case why the hell had he booked it under his own name?

Their revised conclusion was that it was impossible to draw any conclusions. The friends decided to go with the flow. Perhaps the Nazi really had just sought out one of many mediums and only happened to be in Malmö. There was really no way they could believe this. But it wasn't possible either to believe the alternative.

"I'm going mad," said Julius.

"Me too," said Allan, to appear supportive.

"You already are," said Sabine.

So this was how it would go.

During the séance, Sabine, a.k.a. Esmeralda, would receive Johnny the Nazi on her own while Allan and Julius hid in the apartment, as armed as the circumstances would allow. If the mood turned threatening, they would step forward and . . . Well, what?

A weak plan, as all three were aware. Still, Julius went shopping and returned with a baseball bat and an air gun.

"Not exactly Kim Jong-un, are we?" Allan said. "And I can't lift the bat. Hand over the pistol!"

Meanwhile, Sabine prepared herself in her own way. She made coffee and ground four sleeping pills into a mug. It couldn't hurt for their potential murderer to become sleepy before he started murdering. She became dizzy just from taking a test sip of the mixture. She couldn't taste anything funny.

At the last moment, she thought of moving the hearse four blocks away. On the off chance that luck was on their side, they might as well let sleeping dogs lie.

The minutes crept by. Eleven. Quarter past. Seventeen past. Ten to twelve. Twenty past. Twenty to.

At one on the dot, the doorbell rang.

This was it.

Allan in the kitchen with the air gun. Julius with the baseball bat in the hall cupboard. Sabine, fully equipped with medallions and all. The séance room was reasonably dark, with a tasteful coffin in one corner, and myrrh, a crimson cloth, and warm stones on the table.

Sabine opened the door nervously, and welcomed—

"Minister Wallström? What are you doing here?"

"Oh, I see you recognize me. I'm looking for a Julius Jonsson. And his friend Allan Karlsson. We're acquaintances, and I have a few questions I need to ask."

Sabine thought she'd been ready for anything. But not this. Had the minister for foreign affairs used a fake name to request . . .

Before she could ride that train of thought any further, another person popped up behind the minister. Her bodyguard? No.

"Hi, I'm Johnny. Am I in the right place?"

Sweden

The minister for foreign affairs had scared Inspector Bäckman off any further investigation of Karlsson and Jonsson. But that didn't mean she could let the matter go. What had happened to them since their return to Sweden? Someone had fired an automatic weapon into a shop where they were presumed to be?

The minister was struck by a dizzying thought. What if the North Korean security service were operating in Swedish territory and trying to execute Swedish citizens? After all, it was only recently that the life of a North Korean had been taken in Malaysia—it was a big step from there to doing the same to a Swede in Sweden, but perhaps not *too* long?

But . . . the method? Going from poison to shooting wildly?

And why hadn't Karlsson and Jonsson reported the incident to the police? Because they were afraid? They hadn't seemed particularly terrified in front of either Kim Jong-un or Donald Trump. Who could be worse than them?

All of this and more nagged at the minister. She had a Malmö address for Julius Jonsson, but couldn't see herself traveling all the way from Stockholm for some sort of private investigation of two diplomats to whom she herself had wrongly supplied diplomatic passports.

Not until she happened to have reason to go there on business.

For more than a year, border patrol between Denmark and Sweden had been a source of irritation to both nations. Refugees in need journeyed all the way through Europe, and when they arrived in Denmark, the Danes gladly helped send them on across the sound to Sweden.

That worked, until it didn't anymore. Once little Sweden had accepted more refugees than all the rest of Europe combined, with the exception of Germany, the system collapsed. There was nowhere for the refugees to live. The country was unable to investigate their refugee status within a reasonable amount of time, much less offer them a dignified future. What was more, a frighteningly large percentage of the children who arrived alone were seventeen-year-old boys, whether or not they were seventeen. They had been sent off as vanguards by family somewhere in the most miserable corner of the world, whose head of household had, as the only remaining source of pride, the task of making sure the whole family survived. Others had grown up on the street and were schooled in crime but nothing else. Still others were heroin addicts: How else could they have endured?

The rest of Europe laughed at silly Sweden. Few came to the inverse conclusion: that if the rest of the EU countries had followed the lead of Sweden and Germany, the refugee situation would have been manageable. Trying to collect gold stars in heaven, before the Day of Judgment, was out.

Anyway. At last Sweden forcibly closed its border with neighboring Denmark. No one was let across the bridge without first being thoroughly inspected. Thousands of people who commuted between the countries experienced terrible delays.

This got immediate results. Sweden lost its reputation as heaven on earth and the number of asylum-seekers decreased from everyone to almost no one. Meanwhile daily life between the big cities of Malmö and Copenhagen was disrupted. For the first time in decades, it became clear that Sweden and Denmark were two different countries that you couldn't randomly travel between as you wished. No matter the color of your skin.

But now, however, it was time for a thaw in the relationship. Sweden planned to stop requiring ID from everyone who wanted to come over from the Danish side. This would be replaced with more effective border control in Sweden. Thus the Swedish border police needed fresh resources, and the long and the short of it was that the prime minister had asked Minister for Foreign Affairs Wallström to travel to Malmö to speak with the border police about the new government policy. And, if possible, reassure anxious civil servants who didn't understand how they could be ready in time. She would strike a tone of international perspective and help the hardworking civil servants understand that they were an important part of a greater whole.

Marking oneself present, as politicians called it.

The minister took a commercial flight between Stockholm and Malmö, and after the meeting with the border police was over and had even gone well, she had three hours of free time. After considering it for a while, she informed her security team that she was planning to take a brief private side trip in Malmö before their journey home.

A side trip? Just like that? The bodyguards wanted

to know more. The minister told them that the people she wished to see were old acquaintances (exactly how old, she didn't say), and posed no threat to her. At this, they all agreed that she would be escorted to the desired address but left alone from the front door of the building onward. Security was important, but so was personal integrity.

Sweden

Johnny Engvall thought he recognized one of the two women in the hall. It was obvious which one was Esmeralda—the one with the knickknacks around her neck. The other looked more like a businesswoman, and she was the one who seemed familiar somehow.

Margot Wallström had done an about-face. Suddenly she didn't feel quite so secure in this situation. The man who'd come up behind her was wearing a lot of leather and gave a generally rough impression. She turned back to Sabine.

"As I was saying, I'm looking for Julius Jonsson and Allan Karlsson. But I see you have a visitor, so perhaps it would be better for me to return later."

Sabine thought fast. "There's no one by those names here."

But Johnny Engvall had overheard. And he was on his way to understanding.

"Allan Karlsson?" he said slowly.

The hearse *was* parked just a few blocks away. What an idiot he was.

"I know an Allan Karlsson," Johnny went on. "He's on the board of a company north of Stockholm that makes coffins. And it has a connection to another company in the clairvoyance industry . . ."

"I have no idea what—" Sabine said, but she was interrupted.

"And Karlsson's hearse is parked around the corner."

"Hearse?" Sabine tried.

"Hearse?" Minister Wallström said, more genuinely.

But by now the strange man had produced a knife.

"May I ask you ladies to back slowly into the apartment? We have a few things to discuss. I think today is my lucky day."

That last bit wasn't accurate, but there was no way he could know it.

Johnny felt sad inside when he realized that the rest of the day would lead somewhere that didn't involve making contact with his big brother. His sadness turned to rage. He got into gear and changed his tone.

"I haven't stabbed anyone to death for several years,

so this will be nice. But first you'll have to tell me where the man who took my coffin order is. His name was Karlsson, right? I want to do away with both of you at the same time, if possible. And you, into the bargain, I think," Johnny said, turning to the minister for foreign affairs. "Have we met before?"

Margot Wallström had learned the hard way that Allan Karlsson and his friends were to be avoided. But it was too late now. Suddenly the bodyguards down on the street seemed very far away. The question was, would she increase or decrease her chances of survival if she told him who she was? At last she made up her mind.

"Interesting," she said. "I recognize you too. Is there any chance you were once the Swedish ambassador in Madrid? If so, perhaps we're colleagues. I'm the head of the Ministry for Foreign Affairs in Stockholm."

Johnny Engvall was flustered. For one second.

"You're the minister for foreign affairs?" he said. "What the hell is going on?"

Sabine seized her chance. "Can you two be quiet, please? I can feel that I'm making contact. Kenneth? Is that you, Kenneth?"

Her distraction had the intended effect. Johnny's eyes went wide as Sabine raised both hands in the air and looked up. Her movements were almost eerie in the dim light. And long shadows were falling on a nearby coffin.

It's possible it wouldn't have taken Johnny more than ten seconds to see through Sabine's trick, but since the minister for foreign affairs needed only half of that time to think through the situation, things went as they did. She spent the first two and a half seconds wondering if she could scream so loudly that the bodyguards outside would hear and come to the rescue. She spent the next abandoning that idea in favor of grabbing the table lamp off the bureau next to her and slamming its base into the Nazi's head.

Johnny Engvall dropped to the floor, unconscious or dead—which it was remained to be seen.

"Hands in the air!"

Allan had entered the room by way of the kitchen door, with his air gun.

"You were supposed to distract him *before* I got him in the head with the bat, not after," said Julius, who had just come in from the other direction.

"And you were supposed to bat him in the head *before* the minister for foreign affairs did the same with the lamp," said Sabine.

She had really scored quite a hit, that minister. Now she stood there with the table lamp in hand, feeling totally empty.

"Well done, Margot," said Julius. "If I may call you Margot?"

The minister nodded. "By all means," she said.

Questions of etiquette were way down her list.

Allan and Julius had heard the drama playing out from their respective positions. Where on earth had the minister for foreign affairs come from?

According to the original plan, Allan was to make use of one of the entrances to the living room, the one from the kitchen, and wave his gun. During the seconds it would take the Nazi to realize the gun was as harmless as the 101-year-old holding it, Julius would knock him out with the baseball bat.

"Well, it all turned out okay in the end," was Julius's summary. "No thanks to slowpoke Allan."

"Or to you," said Sabine.

"It all turned out okay?" said Minister Wallström. "There's a potentially dead man at my feet. And I potentially killed him."

"There, there," said Allan. "Let's not allow our moods to be darkened by so little."

"I can hear him breathing," said Sabine. "By the way, we didn't get to say a proper hello, Minister. My name is Sabine Jonsson. I'm not married to Julius, even though we have the same last name. But it's never too late."

The minister numbly took Sabine's extended hand. "Margot Wallström," she said.

"Yes, I know."

"Do you really want to marry me?" Julius said, his whole face lighting up.

"Oh yes, dear Julius."

This sparked new life into the dumbstruck minister. "Please," she said. "Could you propose to each other some other time, before I completely lose my mind?"

In the company of a minister for foreign affairs on the verge of a breakdown, and two lovebirds who had eyes only for each other, Allan felt it was up to him to take control of matters.

"I think it would be best for Madame Minister to look away as the rest of us clean up as best we can. I imagine it would be of no benefit to her personage or career to be forced to explain to Sweden and the world what she was doing in a séance room in a Malmö suburb along with an unconscious Nazi."

"But surely I can't just . . . ," said the minister.

"Leave? That's a good idea," said Allan. "Not least because it was Sweden's leading diplomat who single-handedly took out the Nazi. There is much good to be said about what you just did, but it wasn't very diplomatic. Have you ever heard of such a mess, Madame Minister?"

No, she hadn't.

Allan thought she at least deserved an explanation before she took off. He gave her the short version of how he and Julius had ended up in Märsta, met Sabine, joined forces with her in a brilliant business idea about coffins with a little personality, how it happened to go wrong one measly little time, and how the man now asleep on the floor became upset with them beyond all measure as a result, started shooting wildly, and sent them fleeing.

"Why didn't you just call the police?" Margot Wallström asked.

"Not the police!" said Julius. "You don't call the police unless it's necessary. And hardly even then."

"But . . . ," said the minister.

That was as far as she got. For now the so recently unconscious man on the floor had begun to stir. He groaned and said something unintelligible. Sabine hurried over.

"Sit up now, Mr. Nazi, that's right, here on the floor is fine. Here's a cup of coffee to perk you up. Can you believe that lightning struck you in the head like that?"

"Coffee?" said the minister for foreign affairs. "Is that really so . . ."

Wise, she was going to say, but by now Johnny Engvall was sitting up with mug in hand.

"Lightning?" he said, trying to remember where he was.

He drained the mug with all the sleeping pills and was still out of it enough that he allowed Julius to pin his hands behind his back, albeit under some protest.

"What are you doing?" said Johnny. "Who are you? Where am I?"

"There we go," said Sabine. "He just took four sleeping pills, so in a few minutes he'll have mumbled his last for some time."

And with that, the minister had reached her limit. She didn't want to know any more. She didn't want to be a part of any more. She turned to Allan. "May I hear your plans for how to move forward, Mr. Karlsson? I have two representatives of the security service outside . . ."

"Not the police," said Julius.

Allan's suggestion involved the minister for foreign affairs' immediate departure, preferably in the company of the bodyguards she didn't appear to need since she could obviously take care of herself. The rest of them would do their best to deal with the ever-sleepier Nazi on the floor. And there was no reason for Madame Minister to worry. Although it was true that an accident or two had been known to occur in Allan's vicinity over the years, they would make sure that this character survived the day. Not because he deserved it, but out of general decency.

General decency? Minister for Foreign Affairs Wallström closed her eyes. She sensed that her career would soon be over. Yet she couldn't figure out what she'd done wrong. At least, not from a moral standpoint. How could it turn out like this when her sole ambition had been to bring about a little peace on earth?

When everything came to light, no amount of apologies or explanations would be sufficient. If everything she'd learned about the inherent dynamics of the media was accurate, she would instead be ripped apart by newspapers and on TV.

Oddly enough, the realization that all was lost made her feel calmer. She would stand for what she had done and fall into the abyss with her head held high.

But she could still do good, before reality caught up with her. The very next day would bring a meeting of ministers for foreign affairs in Brussels. The next week she had a full day scheduled with the prime minister to analyze the new French president's first days in office and how they might relate to the upcoming election in Germany. Back when the meeting had been scheduled, the assumption had been that the future of the entire European Union was at stake. Later had come the realization that the sitting President of the United States of America had a screw loose. Thus the future of Europe became increasingly that of the world. Sweden had an important role to play in all of this. Even as the country's minister for foreign affairs, as well as representative to the UN Security Council, stood in a room in a Malmö suburb with a knocked-out and drugged neo-Nazi at her feet.

"Listen to this," said Allan, who had found the time to grab his black tablet after having been separated from it for several minutes. "Donald Trump has just ordered his own secretary of state to undergo an IQ test."

What had she just heard?

No, she would not simply give up. The world still needed Margot Wallström, and that was that. "I'm leaving now," she said.

She met her two bodyguards outside the car on the street.

"Everything okay, Madame Minister?" said one.

"Of course," said Margot Wallström. "Why wouldn't it be?"

The minister for foreign affairs and her bodyguards took off. Allan, Julius, and Sabine stood in a semi-circle around the sleeping Nazi on the floor. He must be moved out of there and dumped somewhere before he got it into his head to regain consciousness.

"Can we roll him up in a rug?" said Julius.

"If we had one," said Sabine.

"He can borrow my coffin," said Allan.

Sabine's face lit up. "Imagine! Something sensible finally came out of you, Allan."

Julius and Sabine lifted the unconscious man while Allan walked alongside, digging through the Nazi's pockets.

"What are you doing?" Julius asked.

"Getting to know the enemy," said Allan.

He found car keys, a tin of snuff, and a wallet containing a driver's license, credit cards, and thirty-seven hundred kronor in cash.

"Thanks, Johnny Engvall," he said, to the picture on the license.

He kept the Nazi's money and tossed the rest into the bin.

When the lugging was over, Sabine stationed the 101-year-old at the kitchen table with his black tablet and ordered him to remain there until he received further instructions. This was a solution that suited Allan.

Julius was given the task of stuffing the trio's belongings into the newly bought suitcase while Sabine went to fetch the hearse. They couldn't exactly stroll four or five blocks in broad daylight with a coffin between them. Sabine designated herself and Julius pallbearers, while Allan would be in charge of the wheeled suitcase.

One and a half hours after the séance with the minister for foreign affairs and the Nazi, the trio were leaving the apartment. Julius and Sabine struggled with the coffin full of sleeping Nazi, Allan humming a few paces behind them. It was only a half-flight of stairs down to the front door, but it was difficult. Naturally they met a neighbor, a woman holding double grocery bags. She looked at the coffin in horror.

"Overdose," said Allan. "Heroin. Terrible stuff."

The woman didn't respond. Perhaps she was a foreigner.

"Heroinski," Allan clarified.

Sweden, Denmark

Allan, Julius, and Sabine crowded into the front seat of the hearse, since the Nazi was hogging the back.

Ten minutes later they had managed to divorce themselves from their unconscious problem. Johnny Engvall was now sitting on a bench in a decently empty park not far from downtown. While Julius and Sabine did the grunt work, Allan found a white plastic cup between the front seats in the car. He placed it in the Nazi's hands, instantly transforming him into a presumed beggar who had fallen asleep on the job.

"Don't sit here too long, Mr. Johnny, or you'll catch a cold," was Allan's farewell.

The situation remained intensely complicated. The Nazi problem was, of course, far from over. But with all the carrying-around and the fresh air, Sabine had her brain function back.

Now was the time to use it to think new thoughts. Or, at least, big ones. Best-case scenario, also good ones.

Sabine made up her mind.

Julius noticed that she seemed to know where she was going. He didn't say anything, for he thought the next move should be hers.

They left Malmö, ended up on a highway, and soon found themselves approaching the bridge to Denmark. Sabine slowed and prepared to pay the bridge toll.

"In light of what has happened, it's best if we switch countries," she said.

"Denmark," said Julius.

"I love Denmark," said Allan, who had returned to his coffin and made himself comfortable. "I think. I've never been there. Or have I?"

"Denmark won't be far enough, if we're going to keep away from everyone who wants to kill us," said Sabine. "And assuming we want money to put food on the table, our current business model will never do."

She continued by saying that she had, in tandem with other topics, put a great deal of thought toward their future. It had all come to a head when the Nazi turned up to get a table lamp to the head.

"That lamp knew where to land," Allan said. "If I'm alive next year I'll be danged if I don't vote Social Democrat."

"You vote?" Julius asked.

"Not that I know of."

Sabine asked the old men to keep quiet for a bit and went on: "Anyway, I had time to do some thinking. We can't drive around in the hearse anymore. It will be recognized by the Nazi who, we know with all certainty, is angrier with us than ever."

Allan was on the verge of gauging the Nazi's presumed rage in comparison with that of Kim Jong-un and Donald Trump but realized he had been asked to keep quiet.

"So, no more hearse," Sabine reiterated. "And no Sweden."

Allan sat up in the coffin. This conversation looked promising. He couldn't keep not saying anything. "It sounds to me as if young Miss Sabine has an idea."

"Agreed," said Julius.

She did. If their séance operation was to blossom, and they were to survive for more than a week, they had to think internationally. The Nazi and his gang would have a much harder time finding them out in the big, wide world. On the other hand, the competition in the spiritual branch would be much tougher than it was in their homeland. It wouldn't be enough to hawk ghosts and the chance to speak with those who had already spoken their last.

"So what do we need?" Julius wondered.

"Product development," said Sabine.

"And where on our good green Earth can we best develop our product, do you think?"

"Are you sitting down?" Sabine asked.

"I am sitting, as you can see," said Julius.

"I just lay down again, but by all means," said Allan, and sat up.

"Good. Right now we're driving to Kastrup, where we'll permanently park the car and buy three plane tickets to Dar es Salaam."

"Dar es what?" said Julius.

Russia

After a series of setbacks of a varied nature, Gennady Aksakov could smell the scent of victory once more. And a sensational one at that. He appeared to be the only one who realized that Merkel, in Germany, was on her way to defeat. After all, a victory was no victory if it wasn't possible to rule after winning.

Gennady administered grotesquely large sums of money for himself and his best friend. The capital was safely held abroad, made even safer in that it was protected by Gennady's Finnish passport. No matter what sorts of sanctions the world decided to slap on Russia and its citizens, no one could freeze the Finnish Aksakov's assets. He was financially secure, and so was the president.

Lately they'd had varying levels of success. With

the help of 116,000 Twitter accounts, Aksakov and his army of internet soldiers had worked on the voters of Britain before the Brexit referendum. Only an amateur would allow all the accounts to be automated bots: people would notice that. The secret was a perfectly balanced mixture of fully automated, half-automated, and 100 percent human accounts. The message, however, was relatively uniform—namely, that the Brits should turn their backs on Europe.

Volodya cackled with joy and thumped Gena on the back when the results turned out to be 52–48 "leave." Gena responded humbly that, even without his help, it might easily have been 51–49.

Not long after Brexit there was the American presidential election, which had gone so frightfully well that by now it was just frightful.

The parliamentary elections in the Netherlands and France, though, showed that Gena and Volodya weren't invincible after all. Despite massive support from Moscow, the numbers of the Dutch PVV didn't increase enough to bring about political chaos. It took over two hundred days for the center right to put together a coalition government, but in the end they succeeded.

In France, the Russians nearly lost in a walkover. The plan was to take sides on both right and left and polemize to the extent that Marine Le Pen would dash past all but one competitor, at which point the Russians would sink said competitor. But when that bastard made a complete fool of himself *before* Moscow was ready to sink him, a new middle-of-the-road candidate popped up out of nowhere. Gena had no time to reposition, and France ended up with an EU-friendly president. The trolls' disinformation about Macron's secret life as a homosexual only fired up Macron and his voters. If there was anything you were allowed to devote yourself to in France, it was diverse alternative romantic encounters.

Up next after that blunder was the fiasco in Sweden: the four million euros in support of the neo-Nazi whose thanks for the financial aid involved getting himself killed. The neo-Nazi's brother had, according to unanimous intelligence reports, been the one subsequently to shoot a funeral parlor to hell. What was absolutely inconceivable about this story was that the brother (who was just as much a Nazi) had tried to take the life of *Allan Karlsson* of all people! The 101-year-old who had caused such a kerfuffle in Pyongyang had been promoted to diplomat, at which point he had evidently entered the funerary trade and, for the second time in a brief period, acted in direct opposition to Russian state interest. All of these conclusions had been drawn from an intercepted conversation between an individual police inspector and the Swedish minister for foreign affairs, who had, carelessly enough, used a nonsecure phone within her department. Perhaps Kim Jong-un was right: they should have tracked down that old man and slit his throat. But now, in any case, he had disappeared again.

Gennady decided to wait a week or two, then get in touch, once again, with the dead neo-Nazi's living brother to repeat the terms and conditions, or, alternatively, remove him from the equation.

While he waited, he would have to try to relish the thought that it would soon be time for revenge. Everyone said Merkel was the obvious victor in the German election, that the Social Democrat candidate was too weak. No one wanted to see what Gennady saw: the Social Democrats would refuse seats in Merkel's government if they did poorly in the election, for anything else would be political suicide. The Russian tactic was to further weaken what was already weak, combined with genuine but secret party support to the right-wing nationalist party, AfD. This way they were attacking Merkel on two fronts without actually touching her. So she would win the election, but she wouldn't be able to build a coalition government. When this dawned on her, she would finally give up. The last thing Russia needed was that hopelessly strong bitch in Berlin.

"The Social Democrats lost three more percentage points in the latest poll," Gennady Aksakov told his president. "Two of them landed with our friends in AfD."

"You're a genius, Gena," said President Putin. "Have I mentioned that before?"

"Many times, Mr. President." His best friend smiled. "So many times that I'm starting to believe you."

Denmark

S abine sat quietly behind the wheel as they crossed the bridge and drove through the tunnel on their way to Copenhagen's international airport. She thought through her decision to emigrate one more time.

Olekorinko in Tanzania had been in her thoughts so long that she had just about exalted it to a truth that he was the solution to everything. The country in and of itself also brought many advantages. For example, Tanzanian Nazism had not yet been invented. There probably weren't many snakes to speak of either, up at that high altitude. Snakes, in general, were among the few things Sabine disliked more than Nazis. She disliked snakes, Nazis, wars, and deadly illnesses. In that order. With Karlsson a close fifth. War and violence were not on the list of things the country had to offer.

That left deadly illnesses, but it seemed likely they'd have cures for such things down there. Not least with Olekorinko's help, if everything her mother had told her about him was to be believed, which of course it was not.

Sabine had done her homework. There were further sources of inspiration to be found nearby. The Kenyan side of the border was the domain of a businesswoman named Hannah. She called herself the Queen and spent Monday through Friday curing clients' ailments, breaking curses, and giving life advice based on what could be read in the coals left by a fire. For extra money she also took on the more serious cases of cancer and AIDS. She spent Saturdays resting and on Sundays she went to church, to be on the safe side.

Hannah was happy to show off her luxury home and her fifteen cars to anyone who wanted to see them. "I'm a witch and I'm good at it," was her standing refrain among the cars. "In the name of the Father, the Son, and the Holy Spirit."

Hannah was impressive in many ways. But, still, Sabine didn't find her sufficiently attention-grabbing. Sabine already knew how to scrape through glowing coals.

The retired evangelical pastor Olekorinko and his concept were wildly different from what the Queen practiced. The pastor had built up a tent city on the savannah in the Serengeti. He kept a laboratory in an annex to the main tent, and there he created his miracle medicine, according to a precise and partially secret recipe.

He took only very limited payments, focusing instead on the masses. For the medicine only worked there, in the tent city, and only in the moment when it was blessed by the pastor.

Sabine wanted to know more about his process. Mass meetings would be something new in modern European clairvoyance. Her mother had understood this. And it was the way forward for Sabine, her beloved assistant, and the 101-year-old who came with them, whether they wanted him or not.

Sweden

Johnny Engvall woke up when someone placed a five-kronor coin in the white cup he was apparently holding. Where was he? Why was he freezing? Who had just given him a coin, and why?

He was suffering the side effects of a table lamp to the head and an overdose of sleeping pills. He didn't remember the former; he could only guess at the latter.

He realized he was sitting on a park bench somewhere, but he didn't have time to grasp where before someone bent over him.

"What's the matter, my dear?"

A woman. Her face was only a few inches from his own. Who was she? What was going on?

His vision returned, along with his personality.

"What's the matter?" he said. "What business is that of yours? Plus, you're ugly."

The woman had taken pity on the beggar sleeping on the park bench, found a coin in her purse, and seen that the sleeping man was waking up. He looked dreadful, the poor thing.

"Well, good heavens," she said. "There's no reason to be angry with me, is there? Walk with me for a bit and maybe we can find somewhere for me to treat you to a bowl of hot soup."

Soup? repeated Johnny's muddled mind. He tried to stand up. The woman helped him.

"Move it, you goddamn dispensable woman," he said, shoving the Good Samaritan so hard she almost fell over.

Johnny's vocabulary had returned. He informed the woman of what he and his knife wished to do to her. She backed away in horror, first one step, then another. But she was braver than most. "I'm moving, as you can see. But where do we stand on the soup?"

Johnny took out his American army knife with its well-polished eleven-inch blade, and aimed it at her throat. "Say 'soup' one more time," he said.

But the woman didn't. She didn't say anything. Johnny left without harming her. He had too bad a headache for anything else.

A few blocks away, the still-dizzy Nazi found a café where he could order a sandwich and a cup of coffee, and collect himself.

Until just now, his struggle to kill those who had so seriously degraded his brother on the day of his burial had been plagued by something quite akin to tunnel vision.

But just as he was about to fulfill his self-assigned task, a bolt of lightning had struck him out of the blue. He couldn't just let it go. Or could he? He had four million euros and a cause to advance in Kenneth's memory.

Johnny's brainpower was not so limited that he didn't understand he had been vanquished by an old woman and a minister for foreign affairs. There was no brushing it aside. It couldn't even be dropped down the priority list. The four million and what could be accomplished with it would have to wait. The minister might be allowed to live if she didn't cross paths with Johnny again, but that bitch and her crew? Never.

All he had to do was find them. It might take days, weeks, or months, but so be it, thought Johnny, even as his phone flashed with an important news item.

Another suspected terrorist attack! This time at Kastrup, Copenhagen's international airport.

Coffee and sandwiches could wait.

Denmark, Sweden, Germany

For the second time in a short period, Sabine had to admit that Allan had made himself useful. She was behind the wheel and had instructed him to search on his tablet to find out how soon they could hop onto a flight to Dar es Salaam. What Allan found first was very soon. It would be a little circuitous, with stopovers in Frankfurt and Addis Ababa, but it would work. If only they made it to the airport in time. Sabine speeded up a little more and decided to park as creatively as possible once they arrived.

She found a suitable spot on the pavement immediately outside the correct terminal at Copenhagen's international airport. It took some slaloming between double no-parking signs and traffic cones, but she made it. Even Julius, who'd never had a soft spot for the legal, was impressed.

They bought tickets at the counter; they only had carry-ons and hardly even that, since Allan had forgotten to bring their joint suitcase from the apartment when the other two had their hands busy.

"You had one thing to remember," said Sabine. "*One thing.*"

"The silver lining is, there wasn't more," said Allan.

But check-in went even faster for this reason, and they were in their seats in the second row on the plane, destination Frankfurt, twenty minutes after their arrival at the airport.

"Champagne?" asked the flight attendant.

"Are you a mind reader?" said Allan.

Lufthansa Flight 831 was the last one that managed to take off before the airport closed. The security threat was already elevated, but it had been raised even higher after the attack in Stockholm. And now a suspicious vehicle was parked in a particularly rule-violating manner immediately outside the entrance to Terminal 3.

A common belief in Denmark was that their neighbor Sweden had made a full-time career of importing suicide bombers. During the war in Syria, more people than the entire population of Denmark had fled tanks, bombs, and aerial attacks with chemical weapons. Most of them ended up in Turkey, where they weren't welcome, so many wended their way north, doing their best to avoid traps, like Hungarian electric fences and well-aimed tear gas.

Those with six thousand dollars in their pocket could avoid tear gas in favor of the chance to keep moving toward even more distant nations, where they weren't welcome either. Like Denmark, for example. Which in turn guided them onward to Sweden. Where no one knew which way was up. Still, the Swedes decided against electric fences and tear gas in favor of roofs over heads, since it had not been established that all of those who said they had fled for their lives were in fact terrorists (a select few Swedes knew better, though, and did their best to burn down as many refugee camps as they could, to teach the terrorists a lesson).

The result of all this was that the Danes concluded that the hearse with a Swedish license plate was full of explosives, meant to cause great destruction. All departures were immediately canceled; approaching planes were rerouted; the terminal was evacuated; the police brought in their bomb robot.

Just a few minutes after the alarm had sounded, the

news hit the internet, an unidentified black hearse, strategically placed perilously close to thousands of travelers.

"Oho! So that's where you are," said Johnny Engvall. "And you made sure that you won't get away. You fucking idiots."

He assumed that Sabine Jonsson and her crew were as stuck at the airport as everyone else. Since his own car was several miles away, he flagged down a taxi on the street.

"Rosengård, please."

Once they arrived, of course, the driver wished to be paid, but Johnny realized he had neither wallet nor car keys in his possession. He asked the driver to wait as he broke into his own trunk. With the help of the automatic weapon he stored there, he changed the driver's mind.

"What's your name?" Johnny asked, the barrel of the gun pressed to the driver's forehead.

"Bengt," said the driver. And started to cry.

"Nice to meet you, Bengt," said Johnny. "Do you think you and I can come to an agreement where you will drive me to Kastrup airport with no compensation?"

"Please don't kill me."

"I'll take that as a yes."

When they reached the Øresund Bridge, Bengt made an attempt to slow down to pay the toll.

"Surely you're not about to fatten up the Swedish state with a bridge toll?" Johnny said angrily.

During the journey Bengt had managed to become more terrified than he had been when they'd started out. After all, the radio was broadcasting the news that a suspected terror attack was under way at the very airport to which he and the man with the automatic weapon were driving. The only logical conclusion was that this man, too, was a terrorist.

So Bengt did as he was told: he stepped on the gas and drove at seventy-five miles per hour toward the tollbooth as the security cameras took pictures.

And even faster over the bridge. Kastrup was only a few minutes away now.

Thus far, the collected intellect of the Aryan Alliance had not analyzed the situation in the least. But, with just a few miles left to the airport, he ordered his involuntary chauffeur to slow down. It was crucial to take the right steps now, not the wrong ones.

No rash decisions, right?

Okay, so the trio who had besmirched Kenneth's memory had got stuck at Kastrup, for reasons they'd orchestrated themselves. According to the live updates from the Jew media online, no one had yet been apprehended. So they had to be with all the other evacuated travelers in the hangar the radio had mentioned.

Priority number one was to find that hangar.

People fled from war, terror, and desperate poverty. For reasons not difficult to comprehend, if at all possible they sought refuge in places where war, terror, and desperate poverty for the most part didn't exist. After all, there would have been no point in fleeing otherwise.

Sweden lacked all three aforementioned characteristics; thus it was a country people fled to rather than from. This meant, in turn, that the Swedish-Danish border patrol on the Swedish side of the Øresund Bridge was more or less one-way. Each vehicle that came to Sweden was subjected to inspection, while those going in the other direction had only to pass a pay station.

But that didn't mean it was possible to drive through such a station at, for example, seventy-five miles per hour and expect no reaction. In such cases, the police on the Danish side were supplied with the make and color of the car, as well as its license plate number. If, at the time in question, there also happened to be a suspected terror attack under way at, for example, the international airport of Copenhagen, no other measure was taken than to enter the fee evasion into a database of ongoing investigations, where it would be labeled "inconclusive investigation results" and written off.

One exception to this might be if the driver of the suspicious vehicle were imprudently to encounter a police checkpoint and stop for it.

Half a mile from the international departures terminal at Kastrup, the police had set a boom across the road, put out cones, and allowed you the chance to turn around and go back where you'd come from. The driver of each vehicle was met with a salute and given a brief statement about police activity at the airport, which was closed until further notice. The driver and potential passengers were advised to follow media reports for information about when it might reopen. While a constable shared this message, a more junior constable took the opportunity to check the license plate, purely as a matter of routine.

The more senior Constable Krogh found himself on guard as soon as he initiated contact with the driver of the Swedish-registered taxi he was dealing with now.

The man behind the wheel looked terrified. And beside him, in the passenger seat, a very focused customer was obviously hiding something under his leather jacket. Then, when the more junior Constable Larsen cleared his throat, he realized that the license plate had suggested something and he had a case on his hands.

"May I see your ID?" asked the senior constable. "Yours too, please," he said to Johnny Engvall.

Almost two dozen heavily armed colleagues nearby took notice that something might be going on.

Bengt had his cab-driver ID.

"Unfortunately I left my driver's license at home," said Johnny.

Constable Krogh received a brief from Larsen. The vehicle had just neglected to pay the bridge toll on its way over from Sweden.

That was all? Oh, well, closer scrutiny was still in order.

"May I ask you to step out of the car? Both of you, please," said Constable Krogh.

Bengt opened the door, set one foot down, then the other—and threw himself headlong to the ground. "Terrorist!" he shouted. "The guy in the car is a terrorist! And he has a rifle!"

The last bit was not a correct description of Johnny's automatic weapon, but still.

A violent life had taught Johnny that thorny situations were best handled with weapon in hand. Since the Danish police are not nearly as trigger-happy as, for example, their American colleagues, he therefore had time to bring out his automatic weapon and almost release the safety before he was scrupulously fired upon by the twelve of twenty officers who had not been struck by inability to act. The other eight stood there at a loss, but that had no effect on the end result. Johnny was gravely injured by the first shot and killed by the next; he died an indeterminable number of times more from the next thirty-five.

Fifteen minutes later, the hearse was secured. It contained none of what they had had reason to fear.

With that, the attack against Copenhagen's international airport had been averted, the suspicious vehicle taken into evidence, and a heavily armed terrorist eliminated. And, for what it's worth, the hero of the day was Swedish. His name was Bengt Lövdahl and he was a taxi driver.

During their stopover in Frankfurt, Sabine, Allan, and Julius bought themselves a new wardrobe before they sat down to wait for the next flight. Allan had his tablet, of course.

He said it was a good thing they'd left Scandi-

navia behind because, believe it or not, the terrorists had struck for the second time in a short period.
This time it was at Kastrup, where they had been just
hours earlier.

"Wow," said Sabine. "What is the world coming to?"

Germany

When the leader of the free world had spent long enough devoting his workdays to bullying selected portions of his own citizenry on Twitter, the world had to look for a replacement. This ended up being sixty-three-year-old Angela Merkel. As the daughter of a Lutheran pastor, she didn't live in a palace but in an apartment in downtown Berlin.

She slept four hours a night from Monday to Friday, but sometimes on the weekend she would sleep all the way to sunrise. Among her excesses was a special passion for cabbage soup. She enjoyed a beer to wash it down; she was German, after all.

In her free time she worked a little more, or took her husband by the arm and went to the opera. On special occasions they went further—for a walk in the Italian Alps.

She was among many other things a physicist, he a professor of physical and theoretical chemistry. The physical chemistry between them had emerged sometime in 1984.

As chancellor, Angela Merkel was President Trump's opposite. She was soft-spoken, thoughtful, and analytical. She understood, more than anyone, the import of this in a troubled world. She'd been planning to retire in the coming autumn. But then what would happen, with Trump and Putin and everything?

So she decided: four more years, if the voters would have her. After that, they and the world would have to take care of themselves.

The German Security Service in Berlin had a few tricks up their sleeve. One was to make sure they were automatically notified if anyone they were keeping an eye on chose to travel with Lufthansa.

The Swiss-Swedish nuclear weapons expert Allan Karlsson had gone off the radar after dumping nine pounds of uranium at the German embassy in Washington and thereafter jetting to Sweden.

But now the old man was on the move again. He had

just traveled from Copenhagen to Frankfurt. Why on earth would he do that?

A closer look revealed that his full route would be Copenhagen–Frankfurt–Addis Ababa–Dar es Salaam. The question remained: *Why on earth would he do that?*

The nine pounds had originally come from the enrichment facility in Congo that had once been sponsored by the CIA, in violation of all sound reason. Thanks to an on-site laboratory assistant, the BND collected enough puzzle pieces to follow the uranium's route through Africa, with a certain amount of delay.

It was transported through Tanzania and south through Mozambique and Madagascar. There it was snatched up by the North Korean bulk carrier *Honor and Strength*, which, it so happened, was out on a new journey even now, another trip to Cuba and back. The same detour again, too, via the Atlantic and the Indian Ocean.

Was it time for a refill of depleted North Korean uranium stores? If it was, what role did Allan Karlsson play? He clearly knew something was up: he had told Chancellor Merkel so himself by way of a handwritten napkin. Eleven hundred pounds this time!

But the entire issue was difficult to analyze. If Karlsson was planning to smuggle out the greatest amount of uranium the world had ever seen, why tell the German chancellor so in advance? On a napkin?

The director of the BND wished to give a personal report to Chancellor Merkel, who really didn't have time for him. The closer to the parliamentary election she got, the busier she was doing nothing. And saying nothing. The poll numbers were to her advantage. The fear that the Russians would try to meddle in the election with disinformation about her doings had also come to naught. In fact, the general view on social media seemed to be that the Social Democrat Schultz was incompetence personified. Plus that the ultra-right was getting grabby, of course, but it wouldn't be enough.

Political analysts judged that Merkel's relative success in the opinion polls was due, to a certain extent, to the fact that the opposition leader hadn't found any weak point at which to attack the Merkellian façade, since they held more or less identical views. Just like the Germans in general. But for the most part it was considered to be due to the chancellor's general competence, in combination with the fact that the rest of the world had become what it had become. The United States had a president who should be diagnosed with something. In Great Britain they had held an election a year earlier based on Cameron's rhetorical question "Surely we shouldn't kick out all foreigners?" which received a "Why not? That's a great idea!" in response. In Poland they were protesting against democracy as best they could. In Hungary, they had already finished that job. Add to this Madrid's inability to knock Catalonia into shape (or Catalonia's to knock Madrid into shape), and the man who would soon be as wide as he was presumed to be dangerous: Kim Jong-un.

In the midst of it all: Chancellor Merkel, steady as an ancient oak in a field. The crops waved around her, but she stood where she stood.

If only world events and the debate over domestic politics would freeze solid until election day, she would have four more years ahead of her. To the relief of the entire world, except maybe Russia. And maybe the guy in the United States, who didn't know what to think or why at one moment, and changed his mind at the next.

The director of the *Bundesnachrichtendienst* was expected. He knocked on the chancellor's door and was duly admitted.

What he had to report was that the Swede and troublesome element Allan Karlsson had popped onto the radar again. In Frankfurt. On his way to Tanzania, of all places.

The chancellor was provided with the details, to the extent they existed, and reminded of the eleven hundred pounds of enriched uranium. She responded by raising the BND's total budget by ten million euros on the spot.

Merkel added that the director of the BND must get back to her *immediately* with regard to whatever nuclear weapons–related activities Karlsson might be planning to take on (eleven hundred pounds of enriched uranium could not be thought out of existence, no matter how close to the election they were). The director blushed and admitted that he and his family were planning a trip to the Bahamas a few days later, but naturally he would be at her service during every minute of his vacation. It was just that he would be on a plane for at least ten hours, from Berlin to Nassau, and it wasn't certain that he could keep in constant contact with the agents on-site from up there.

"Forgive my boldness, Chancellor, but might it be reasonable to ask the East African director in charge to contact you directly in the event anything critical happens while I'm out of touch? If not, I will of course cancel my trip."

Angela Merkel had a heart behind her chancellor mask. She didn't want to make the director of the BND go home to his wife and children and tell them their holiday was canceled because he had to sit by the phone.

"Give my private number to the agent in charge in Dar es Salaam," she said, "with orders to call day or night as soon as Karlsson gets within two hundred miles of an enrichment facility or a suspected smuggler. Have a nice trip. Say hi to the wife and kids."

Among the last things the director of the BND did, before taking time off for the first time in six years, was send a report to the two BND representatives who used Dar es Salaam as their base of operations. Karlsson and his crew would land at 1:20 P.M. the next day, on Ethiopian Airlines from Addis Ababa. The attached phone number went straight to the chancellor, in case of any drama, and should only be used if he couldn't be reached.

Russia

Gennady Aksakov put down the phone following the informal intelligence call from Stockholm. Or, rather, he slammed it down. And kicked the empty chair by his side.

"What is it, Gena?" asked President Putin, across from him.

"Allan fucking Karlsson, that's what."

"The 101-year-old?"

"Yes. That bastard killed the second Nazi too. Four million euros, down the drain."

Putin said it wouldn't bankrupt anyone, but what had happened?

The Nazi had challenged a great number of heavily armed police officers with the Danish antiterror force and was immediately shot to bits.

Putin quietly wondered what this had to do with the 101-year-old. Hadn't the alarm been sounded because of a hearse full of explosives in Copenhagen?

"The hearse wasn't full of anything. It was just illegally parked."

"Illegally parked? By whom? No, hold on. Don't say anything. I understand."

Tanzania

Olekorinko's miracle-medicine tent city was in the Serengeti, right on the banks of the Mara River. When Allan, Julius, and Sabine got into a taxi outside the airport in Dar es Salaam, they learned from the cheerful driver that it would take a day to get there by car, then half a lifetime to find their way. The Mara River had the peculiarity of being 250 miles long, and the Serengeti about fifty-eight hundred square miles in size.

"They have *Lebensraum*, those lions," said Allan.

"We need a more accurate address," said Julius.

"And some form of transportation other than a car," said Sabine.

It was a third of a mile from Julius Nyerere International to the domestic terminal.

Since the trio were already sitting in the taxi, they changed their order from a one-day journey to a two-minute one. The driver was no longer quite so cheerful: he'd hardly had time to switch the meter on before it had to be turned off again. He ought to have driven first and explained later.

Behind the taxi a black Passat contained two highly focused agents from the *Bundesnachrichtendienst,* whose task was not to let Karlsson out of their sight. And immediately to inform the top director of the BND, or alternatively the chancellor, if the elderly man got up to anything stupid.

Congo

The Congolese mine in Katanga had officially been closed for several years. The UN had seen to it. With that, the supply of uranium was cut off to the immediately adjacent nuclear research center, which the country had once had the blessing of the United States to open as thanks for the delivery of uranium for the bombs over Hiroshima and Nagasaki, back in the forties.

No one but the United States had ever thought it was a good idea to have that type of capacity in a country where everything could be bought for the right money. But since the Americans had more of that particular commodity than anyone else, their interests came first. They had essentially bought the entire country. With money.

Eventually, however, even the USA got behind the rest of the UN's demands for law and order in Congo. It followed that the Katanga mine and its laboratory no longer posed a threat to fragile world peace.

Or did it?

A local watchdog force, financed by none other than the UN, was tasked with making sure that no uranium prospecting activities occurred. The immediately adjacent laboratory was sealed.

At the end of each month, the head of this force, Goodluck Wilson, faxed a report to the International Atomic Energy Agency in Vienna. It always read the same: *Everything is quiet, trust us.* More or less.

Goodluck Wilson had handpicked the entire rest of the force, which was made up of his three brothers and their seven most trustworthy cousins. They all had the same goal with their watchdog mission: to get filthy rich. There was no discussion of how the world would end up feeling as a result.

Each morning, four former laboratory assistants crawled up out of an underground tunnel, through the floor of the sealed center for atomic research, to enrich whatever could be enriched. All in all fifteen people should theoretically have been sharing the profits, but in practice there were only eleven. The four assistants didn't know that in fact an accident would befall them when they were no longer needed. The gross profits as budgeted were fifty million dollars for Goodluck and another five million each for the ten brothers and cousins. The nonexistent miners received eight dollars per day, and were satisfied with this, until the western shaft collapsed on several of them six years after the mine was closed. This would likely have passed unnoticed if it hadn't been that seventeen workers who shouldn't have been there had demonstrably been there. And now they were dead. This was impossible to hush up. The IAEA wondered what the miners had been up to in the shaft, if everything was so quiet. Without listening to the answer, they sent observers down for a closer look.

Goodluck and his men had been planning to wait until the amount of enriched material was up to an even half-ton; that was what the North Koreans had ordered via the Russians. But now the first 880 pounds had to be hastily encased in lead and hidden in a hut in a nearby village. There were plenty of empty huts after the latest landslide. The four laboratory assistants (including the one on the BND payroll) also managed to become victims, when the underground tunnel to the nuclear research center collapsed, as planned, the morning before the observers from Vienna arrived.

The representatives from the IAEA found no irregularities. But they were cautious enough to exchange half the watchdog force for people who could be trusted. Or people who were *not* to be trusted, in Goodluck Wilson's estimation.

Everything comes to an end sometime. The head of the watchdog force knew he couldn't squeeze any more out of this operation. The profits topped out at eighty million dollars, more than half of which went to Goodluck. There wasn't much to be done about it. You had to be content with the little you could get.

Tanzania

On a bench in the departure hall at the domestic terminal of Julius Nyerere International Airport, Sabine delved into the geographical research she thus far hadn't had time to perform. Allan had involuntarily to give up his black tablet for this purpose (with the roaming data charges still covered by an already sufficiently duped hotel manager in Bali).

The resulting decision was to take the first flight they could get to Musoma in the Serengeti, then ask their way to their destination. Olekorinko's miracle-medicine tent city was famous throughout Africa; finding someone in Musoma to show them the way shouldn't be difficult.

The plane had a single engine and seated thirteen passengers. Nine were from an Italian consulting firm that was celebrating its twenty-fifth anniversary by taking the staff to the Serengeti for a few days of safari (tax-deductible, since they made sure to have a fifteen-minute conference every day). Three more seats were reserved just prior to departure by a small group of Swedes.

The two agents had, on the one hand, been tasked with keeping an eye on the suspected uranium delivery to *Honor and Strength*. Last time, the much smaller cargo had traveled through Tanzania and Mozambique, then on to the south. On the other hand, Berlin had ordered the agents not to let Allan Karlsson out of their sight. And Karlsson was heading in the wrong direction.

Tailing someone, even a 101-year-old, was not the sort of thing anyone wanted to do on their own. The risk of being discovered was too great. The egocentric and arrogant Lead Agent A disliked the idea of leaving in the wrong direction in relation to the uranium—just because the old hag in Berlin had got some bee in her bonnet. And why, incidentally, did *he* have to carry around the folder for this operation? He was the boss, unlike the woman at his side.

"Take this," he said, to his meek colleague. "And book us two tickets. I'm going to get some coffee."

The carrier Precision Air seemed to be on the arrogant man's side that day. There was only one seat left. The arrogant agent was able to hand the short end of the stick to the meek one with a clear conscience (and a scornful grin). Meanwhile he intended to keep the border of Tanzania and Mozambique under surveillance. If you wanted to climb in the ranks, you had to be where the action was, when the action was.

The short end of the stick, in this case, meant tailing Karlsson to see what kind of foolishness he got up to, far away from the center of the action.

As it happened, the loser had the misfortune of ending up in the sole empty seat, right next to the target she was absolutely not supposed to reveal herself to.

Agent B elected to enter into service rather than a deepening depression. She started a conversation with Karlsson; perhaps she would get something useful in return. She said hello and avoided giving her name but told him she was a businesswoman.

"Well, there you go," said Allan. "Hope business is good."

"It is, thanks," said the agent, immediately turning the conversation in the other direction.

She fished for what might be bringing the gentleman to . . . to . . .

"Musoma?" Allan said. "We're on our way to Musoma. And so is the businesswoman, I expect."

Agent B cursed herself. Forgetting the name of their destination! But it had been such a whirlwind at the terminal. This was a big country, three times the size of Germany. She knew Dar es Salaam like the back of her hand. And the capital, Dodoma. And Morogoro, of course. And Arusha.

But Musoma, way up to the northwest? She hadn't heard of it until today.

Allan unreservedly told her that Sabine—that lady two rows ahead—worked as a medium and was seeking fresh inspiration. There was meant to be an extraordinary healer up in the Serengeti, his name was Olekorinko, and there was nothing wrong with that—everyone had to be called something. His friend Julius, the man in the seat next to Sabine, might have changed other people's names the way some people change shirts, but that didn't suit Allan.

"A healer?" said Agent B.

"Or maybe a witch doctor. I seldom commit difficult words to memory. I have trouble enough with the easy ones."

The plan was to visit Olekorinko, learn from him, and gain new spiritual energy. Sabine could surely tell her more, if the businesswoman was interested. "I don't suppose you're in the clairvoyance trade yourself? Or in tourism, perhaps?"

What was this? Atomic bomb expert and potential uranium smuggler Karlsson was on his way to see a witch doctor in the savannah to get spiritual energy? If he had to sit there telling lies, couldn't he at least do so with finesse?

No, the agent did not work in clairvoyance. She said she was a real-estate broker.

That was the cover A and B used in Dar es Salaam.

But that didn't have the desired effect either. Allan thought it sounded interesting. He said that there must be many exciting mud huts to bid for on the Tanzanian savannah.

Was the 101-year-old being sarcastic or just hard to read? The agent felt ill at ease in his presence. Pretending to be a real-estate broker in the largest city in Tanzania was one thing. That story would not work nearly as well in areas where there might not be any real estate to broker. Musoma?

"Well, the mud huts there are not my primary target," she said, trying to sound self-assured. "But there is the occasional safari camp to look at."

"Oh, so you are in tourism after all?"

Few more words were exchanged between Allan and the agent during the rest of the flight. The German needed the time to work out the details of her cover story. Thus far it had not gone as expected. Neither did it get any better when the plane came in for landing and it turned out that Musoma was a real city with what had to be over a hundred thousand citizens and a great number of European-style buildings.

"Look!" Allan said, pointing out of the window. "There's quite a bit to sink your teeth into around here after all, Mrs. Real Estate Broker. Imagine! You didn't know about that *or* where you were heading."

The agent already hated herself. And now she hated Karlsson too, damn him.

The runway was made of earth. It was narrow, and not a single yard longer than necessary. It was in the middle of the city that turned its back on the southern shores of Lake Victoria.

Outside the small terminal building there were several taxis, whose drivers were hoping for fares. Everyone knew where Olekorinko could be found, but no one was so desperate for money that they wanted to drive the three foreigners out to see him. It was a journey of around ninety miles and the roads were in such poor shape that it was just about 100 percent certain that a Fiat, Honda, or Mazda would get stuck along the way.

But Sabine caught sight of a man unloading passengers and luggage from a Land Cruiser not far away. It was an open car with three rows of seats and heavy tires that didn't look as if they would get stuck anywhere. When the man had finished and said farewell to the owners of the luggage, Sabine approached to ask if he was available for hire.

No, he was not. He wasn't from the area and was about to head back to camp at Maasai Mara. There would be more guests arriving in two days, and he had to be back at work by then.

Sabine didn't give up immediately. Continued conversation indicated that the place where the man worked was in Kenya, bordering the Serengeti—and just a few dozen miles from Olekorinko's camp. Suddenly the three foreigners' suggestion was of interest. Being paid for a journey home you had to undertake anyway was a bonus, even if it did involve a short detour.

The German agent stood ninety yards away, looking on unhappily. There were no other Land Cruisers within view, and she had already come to understand the limitations of the taxi cabs.

B called her boss in Dar es Salaam to discuss the situation. He updated her on the latest news. The Americans had just sent information on the latest position of *Honor and Strength*. The vessel had only a few days left to reach the southern tip of Madagascar.

If nuclear weapons expert Karlsson's earlier information was correct, there was a good chance a new delivery of enriched uranium would be made there and then. This load would be much larger than the first. The smuggling route was more or less known, thanks to the now-vanished laboratory assistant. The greatest challenge for the smugglers would be to cross the border between Tanzania and Mozambique. That was to say, about eleven hundred miles from where Agent B was currently located.

B thought Karlsson might be part of the smuggling operation, after all, and that his earlier information had been meant to throw them off the trail. If anything could bring B joy, it was the chance to show up her boss.

"What did you say he said he was going to do up there, that Karlsson?"

B reproduced portions of the conversation.

A chuckled. "Clairvoyance wouldn't be a bad thing for you to have right now. Can't you borrow a little of his?"

"He's *gone*, dammit!" said the meek agent, in a slightly less meek tone than usual.

Lead Agent A lied and claimed to be suffering alongside his underling. For his part, he was about to pack his bags and head for the Mozambique border, where he planned to intimidate the head of border control. A man who was on their payroll.

"You just stay up there, keeping Merkel happy. It's not much fun for you but that can't be helped. Same goes if it turns out I get all the credit when those eleven hundred pounds are neutralized. We all have our roles to play, now don't we?"

Agent B sighed. There were only taxi cabs here. Surely very good on asphalt. Useless on the savannah, as she'd been made to understand.

"Buy yourself a Land Cruiser, then," said her boss. "Or a helicopter."

At least there was one positive thing about Karlsson: the BND had been given more money to play with.

Buy an off-roading vehicle? thought B. What she wanted most was to buy herself a new life. "I'll see what I can do," she said, and hung up without saying goodbye.

They still had six miles left to Olekorinko's tent city for miracles when the traffic came to a standstill. That can easily happen when ten thousand people try to reach the same place at the same time and the road to get there is so narrow it can barely handle two-way traffic. Cars were constantly passing in the opposite direction because just as many freshly treated people were heading away from the camp.

Far from everyone arrived by car. Many were driving motorcycles or mopeds. Others were on bicycles. The very poorest ones walked. Each time the oxpecker twittered from the sky, everyone knew a herd of Cape buffalo had come too close for comfort. Those who weren't already in a car climbed onto the nearest four-wheeled vehicle—onto the hood, the roof, or someone's lap. When the birds disappeared, the chaos returned to its original level. There was no reason to worry about lions or leopards. They slept during the day. And elephants could be seen and heard from a distance.

Now and then the traffic eased and the Land Cruiser with the three Swedes and the driver might advance a third of a mile or more before it had to stop again.

The man they'd hired as a driver was named Meitkini and he was worried he might not get back to camp and his job as a safari guide in time. Nevertheless, he didn't regret his decision. The three travelers were pleasant. And they paid well.

Allan was in the passenger seat up front and had borrowed Meitkini's binoculars. He gave a running commentary on everything he saw, from warthogs to giraffes, read aloud from the black tablet about what was going on in the world beyond the savannah, and got Meitkini to tell the better part of his life story. Julius and Sabine were in the next row of seats and did their best to contribute to the cheerful atmosphere. When Julius asked, Meitkini responded that he wasn't sure, but he didn't expect the climate of the Serengeti was optimal for asparagus.

Their driver was a Maasai from Kenya; it was unusual for him to spend time on this side of the border. The recently departed guests had insisted on flying out from Musoma. They refused to listen when their guide advised against it, and in the end he gave up caring. If not before, they would realize when they tried to leave Tanzania from the airport in Dar es Salaam that they had entered the country illegally.

"One week in a lockup and a few thousand dollars in fines," Meitkini guessed.

"Or a few extra thousand and no lockup at all?" Allan suggested.

Yes, that might work, but the Tanzanians were proud. Meitkini recommended Karlsson obey the laws of the land.

"I would never dream of doing otherwise," said Allan.

Julius squirmed in the back seat. This general law-abiding attitude was spreading from continent to continent like an epidemic.

Meitkini didn't believe in hocus-pocus or miracle cures. What he did believe in was God, and in humankind's ability to live in harmony with wild animals. The Maasai didn't hunt anymore; those days were several generations in the past. Back then, you hadn't been a *man* until you had killed your first lion. Nowadays the coming-of-age ritual involved first being circumcised, then surviving under the open sky for a whole year. Those who succeeded were upgraded to real Maasai warrior. That's what they called them, even though they never actually made war.

"It seems Merkel is on her way to winning the German election," Allan said, referring to his black tablet. "That should keep Europe together for a while. Unless there's a civil war in Spain. The Catalonians are thoroughly tired of Madrid. I know how they feel—I was there the last time this happened."

"In 1936," said Julius. "It's possible some things have changed since then."

"Perchance," said Allan.

Julius turned to the driver. "Are you sure it wouldn't work to grow asparagus here, Meitkini?"

Agent B was at the wheel of the Land Cruiser she'd just rented. Traffic was almost at a standstill, and at regular intervals people climbed into her car without asking.

They stayed there for fifteen minutes or more with no explanation, then jumped down again as if at some sort of signal.

Absolutely everything had gone wrong. There was the part where B was likely thousands of miles from the action. But there was also the part where Allan Karlsson now knew who she was. How was she supposed to explain her presence among those miracle tents, if she ever arrived and had the misfortune of running into the very target of her surveillance? Then again, if she *didn't* find the old man, what was the point of it all?

Incidentally, what *was* the point of it all?

Oh, well, they were starting to move now. Maybe this jam was about to break— No, it wasn't.

"I think we're here," said Meitkini, waking Allan, who had been taking a nap.

Their trip was far from well planned. It was starting to get dark and the friends had nowhere to stay. The thousands of hopeful Tanzanians around them appeared to be preparing fires to sleep next to, in anticipation of a meeting with the miracle doctor the next day. Fire was something wild animals had avoided throughout time. A fire, along with a guard armed with spear and club standing watch in two-hour shifts through the night, increased the chances of survival to almost 100 percent.

Allan took things as they came, but Julius and Sabine didn't like the fire plan. Not least because they would first have to head out onto the savannah to gather up dry branches to burn, and it was getting darker by the minute.

Sabine checked with Meitkini to see what he intended to do. Could he stay until the next day, so they could all sleep in his car?

Well, the trip hadn't taken as long as Meitkini had feared it would. But what would they do afterward? They probably wanted to go back to Musoma, and Meitkini wasn't headed that way. As he'd said, a fresh group of tourists was en route to him, and he had to entertain them for four days. He wouldn't be available for a jaunt back across the Tanzanian border before then.

"We're not really in any big hurry," said Allan. "It might be pleasant to see what things look like where you live."

Meitkini said that the kingdom of the Maasai looked the same on both sides of the border but, by all means, the friends were welcome to come along to camp for a few days. It was the off season, and he would make sure their visit was priced accordingly. But they would have to make this stop quick. They needed to leave by dusk the next day, at the latest.

Allan, Julius, and Sabine thought a full day of miracles should suffice.

Everyone was in agreement. Meitkini drove the car to the side and handed out blankets to all. No one had considered food, but that problem solved itself. When ten thousand people gather in a given place, some form of commercial activity will automatically arise out of sheer human nature. Women walked two by two with baskets full of a variety of delicacies. Julius made an offer for eight sandwiches and four Coca-Colas.

"I suppose you don't have any liquor?" Allan asked.

"Is that all you ever think about?" said Sabine.

"They only speak Maa and Swahili, so they didn't understand you," said Meitkini. "But I can answer for them. Coca-Cola is what's on offer."

"You can't have everything," said Allan.

"Well, maybe you can," said Meitkini, opening the glove box to take out a full-sized bottle of Konyagi.

"Look at that! What sort of delight is this?"

It was the most popular alcoholic drink in Tanzania. Best enjoyed with a slice of lime and a few ice cubes. Or with cranberry juice.

"Or as is, straight from the bottle?"

"That's how I do it," said Meitkini.

"I think this is the beginning of a beautiful friendship," said Allan.

"Cheers to that," said Meitkini, tossing the cork over his shoulder.

"Will you accept company?" Julius wondered.

It was totally dark when Agent B finally reached the tent city. The women and their goodies were gone. B had to set up camp in the middle row of seats, with no food or blankets. Nearly a year before, she had been offered a transfer to Singapore. Now she wondered what life would have been like if she'd accepted. Since it was too cold to sleep, she was forced to spend time with her thoughts for most of the night.

She had declined the offer in Southeast Asia for Franz's sake. He loved his job as a dentist and had refused to go. Just three weeks after B had told her employer "no thanks" on his behalf, it turned out that Franz had also loved his hygienist since a few months back. Her and her now-perfect teeth.

The breakup was tumultuous. Franz said he was beyond tired of never knowing where his wife was or what she was working on. She had told him all along that she was in the employ of the state and could say no more than that. For a long time he thought this sounded exciting, but once they'd been married for three years, and she kept repeating the same thing, it was just wrong. Was he supposed to have kids with a secret woman? What would their son or daughter write when they were assigned a school essay about their mother's job? "She does things no one is allowed to know about?" The teachers would think she was a prostitute. Sometimes Franz suspected as much.

In the midst of all this she wanted to move to the other side of the world with him. "In the employ of the state." From Rödelheim to what? It was bad enough having a secret wife. A secret wife in a foreign country was just too much. Plus there was the hygienist. And her teeth. B realized it wouldn't help to punch them in, even if she had been so inclined.

Since then she was not only secret, she was alone too. The nearly impossible task of finding enriched uranium on the lam in Africa was an escape from everything else. She had been offered the job in Dar es Salaam at nine o'clock on a Wednesday. At five past, she'd said yes.

The next day's ceremony would begin at eleven and last until one, when it got too hot. The camp came to life at seven A.M. The women with baskets of food were back. Everywhere signs in English and Swahili explained the rules. Each person who paid five thousand shillings (or, alternatively, two dollars) would receive a sip of the miracle drink, with Olekorinko's blessings and incantations on top. Those without money would have to settle for the incantations.

"Two dollars isn't much," said Julius. "No more than the wholesale price of a bunch of asparagus."

"No," said Sabine. "But ten thousand bunches of asparagus per day will make you some money."

Besides the twenty thousand dollars Olekorinko raked in during the big gathering, he offered private consultations in his own tent, twenty minutes for a thousand dollars or sixty minutes for twenty-five hundred. The demand was huge.

Sabine wasn't first in line, but second. She booked the shorter version at three o'clock. She expected she would be fully educated by the end.

Olekorinko spoke into a microphone to reach his audience. It was hooked up to two giant amplifiers that were run off eight car batteries. His organization was impressive. Sabine estimated two hundred women were walking around handing out *kikombe cha dawa* (a spot of miracle medicine) to all who could pay, and to the occasional person who couldn't but looked sufficiently desperate.

Julius and Sabine tried what was on offer. The drink

tasted bitter and didn't have any immediate effect in any direction. Allan discovered that there was still a little of the Konyagi in the corkless bottle. He thought that was miracle enough.

The medicine man stood on a raised platform far away, and now he was singing something in Swahili. When he stopped, his assistant took the stage. She explained what was already on several of the signs: that the medicine worked only in the presence of Olekorinko, and only if he blessed it (which he had just done) and, above all, only for people who were free of doubt.

"If you don't believe in Olekorinko, his medicine doesn't believe in you," the assistant said in English, Swahili, and Maa. "Let us pray."

And then she prayed. First in English.

"Dear God, fill the *kikombe cha dawa* with the energy of your servant Olekorinko. Let that energy in turn fill body and soul of those who believe without doubt. Focus on asthma and bronchitis. On rheumatism and mental deficiency. On depression and unemployment. On HIV and AIDS. On cancer and pneumonia. On bad luck and poor love-life performance. On childlessness and on more children than the family can handle. Oh, dear God, lead Olekorinko and his students along the right path. Show us your goodness, Lord. You are our everything! Amen."

A man next to Sabine was disappointed that his bacterial prostatitis hadn't been included in the prayer, but from almost every other direction came great raptures.

Now Olekorinko began to sing in Swahili again. It was rhythmic and monotonous and accompanied by drums. And it lasted for at least half an hour. Meanwhile the two hundred women walked through the audience, gathering more requests for the additional prayers to follow. The man with prostatitis was able to call attention to his malady and was satisfied.

All in all, the ceremony lasted under an hour, not the promised two. The assistant's explanation was that Olekorinko was more filled with spiritual strength than usual that day so he transferred a greater amount of healing energy per minute. No one had been cheated.

Olekorinko stood in the background, nodding in agreement with his assistant's words, and concluded with a "Hallelujah."

Scattered hallelujah responses came from the field before ten thousand people simultaneously got ready to start the difficult journey back, more content and possibly liberated from inflamed prostates and AIDS.

The only ones who remained were those who had

booked one-on-one time with the healer. And one meek, depressed agent from the German security service.

Sabine's twenty minutes with Olekorinko began with him meditating silently to himself. Allan, Julius, and Meitkini were on chairs at the very back of the tent and had been instructed not to take part in the session. If they did, Olekorinko would have to release more energy and this would cause the fee to increase accordingly.

"He knows how to get paid," said Allan.

"Quiet!" said Julius.

After the meditation, Olekorinko opened his eyes and met Sabine's gaze. "What can I do for you, my child?" he asked.

Sabine did not feel in any way as if Olekorinko was her father. But she was finally where she needed to be. She would have loved her mother, Gertrud, to be at her side.

"I have a few straightforward questions," she said. "The first is, what does your magical drink contain, aside from your own soul and the support of God?"

Olekorinko observed her cautiously. He had encountered journalists before. Was she another? Some had even smuggled out the miracle drink and analyzed it in a laboratory. This had led all the way to a government decree stating that the drink "is not harmful to human health and is therefore permitted to be sold." Even back then, seven members of Parliament with various afflictions had made the round trip to the miracle man by helicopter.

"The active ingredient is just what you said: the energy of God, by way of me, his servant. But the Lord and I work in symbiosis with nature. The bitter sweetness comes from the *mtandamboo* bush. Is that something you're familiar with?"

No, Sabine wasn't. But she realized that the miracle man wasn't referring to any secret ingredient. Such a thing could be found, given a history, and exported to become a suitable business model in Europe. But God wouldn't be so simple. His advantages and shortcomings were already well known at home. And, by the way, God? Wasn't Olekorinko a witch doctor?

"At home I work with clairvoyance and the driving out of ghosts. What experience do you have with those?"

Olekorinko's four bodyguards were suddenly on edge. Olekorinko himself fixed his gaze on his guest. Sabine had just said something terribly wrong.

"Witchcraft is of the devil," he said. "If you're a witch, drinking *kikombe cha dawa* is associated with death. It is reserved for people who have chosen the right path."

What was this?

"The right path," Sabine mumbled, noticing how tense the atmosphere in the tent had become. What had she missed in all her research?

"The right path," Olekorinko repeated. And he went on, in a low, hostile tone, to give her something much like a lecture. It was about witchcraft and how best to fight it. Happily, five hundred Tanzanian women were killed each year for being witches. But that wasn't enough. Evil was always a step ahead. The only solace was that witches and wizards killed each other. Recently a magic man in Ngorongoro had killed a witch and cut her up into decently large pieces, each intended to bring him luck. Now he himself was imprisoned for eighteen years. That was all his luck had brought him so far. Nevertheless: wizards shouldn't end up in prison; they could too easily continue their depravity there. They should die along with the witches.

Sabine was confused. Was this character honestly sitting there and distancing himself from sorcery in general? But he was the reason she had come. And brought her friend. And Allan.

She was flooded with the feeling that their trip to Tanzania had been pointless. Or had they merely sought out the wrong representative of what might be possible for development and export? If drinking a holy liquid extracted from the roots of nature to rid oneself of prostatitis wasn't witchcraft, then what was?

Unwisely enough, she posed this very question. But instead of responding, Olekorinko signaled his bodyguards. Each took one step forward, then another. Were they about to . . .

At that instant, Meitkini stood up. He said something in Swahili. It sounded stern, and the bodyguards stopped in their tracks. They glanced around, across the bush outside the tent. It was below Olekorinko's dignity to follow suit, but he sat with his back straight, watching Meitkini intently.

The Maasai man had somehow bought time for himself and his friends. He instructed Allan, Julius, and Sabine to leave the tent immediately and get into the car.

"But I have a question," said Allan.

"No, you don't," said Meitkini, as he continued to keep an eye on Olekorinko. "Do as I say. Now!"

A minute or so later, they were driving away from the miracle man's camp. After a little longer, Meitkini was able to relax. The first thing he did was apologize for sounding so harsh, but the situation had been more threatening than Sabine and the others had likely been aware.

"May I say something now?" Allan said.

"Go ahead."

"Does that character believe in himself?"

Meitkini allowed himself to smile. "I'm glad you didn't venture to ask that in the tent, Mr. Karlsson. You wouldn't have got much older if you had."

"I probably won't anyway. What did you say that made them stop what they were doing like that?"

"I said that the African poison-arrow tree was watching them and would give them a jab if they didn't calm down."

"The African what?"

"They knew what I meant. I unbuttoned my collar so they could see from my necklace that I'm Maasai. They found it believable enough that a nearby kinsman could have them in his sights. There were at least ten bushes, rocks, and hollows to choose from. By now I'm sure they know I was lying, but it's too late."

"Unless that's them behind us," Sabine said anxiously.

Meitkini glanced in the rear-view mirror and recognized the model of the car and the decal above the windshield. "No, that's a rental car. The kind tourists drive around in, but not Olekorinko and the likes of him."

"The African what?" Allan said again.

"Poison-arrow tree. That's where we extract the poison we dip the tips of our spears in. A good hit will kill a fifteen-hundred-pound buffalo in ten seconds. For a slight man like Olekorinko, it wouldn't take more than a scratch."

"Who's the 'we' in this context?" Sabine inquired.

"The Maasai."

"But didn't you say you're peaceful?"

"Sure. Until someone is nasty to us."

"Like a buffalo, for example?"

"Yes. Or a charlatan."

Tanzania, Kenya

Sabine still couldn't come to grips with what had gone wrong. Olekorinko was a *witch doctor*. And she had passed herself off as a witch.

"Well, it's more complicated than you seem to think, Miss Sabine," said Meitkini. "Would you like me to explain?"

"Very much."

So Meitkini did.

Being a *witch* was considered a bad thing all over Africa. The best way to deal with witches was to beat them to death. Or, even better, pour gasoline all over them and set it alight. Which, incidentally, was what Olekorinko's men had been about to do to Sabine. Hence their hasty departure.

Sabine shuddered. "But I read about the Queen in

Nairobi. A witch with a luxury home and fifteen cars. A proud career woman, it seemed."

Meitkini looked at her appreciatively. Oh, so Miss Sabine had heard of the Queen? But she wasn't a witch, she was a *mganga*. The word was mistranslated in some languages. Witches specialize in messing with people. If lightning strikes in a village, as a rule it means a witch is on the move. Then a fortune-telling man would be called in to study mirrors and animal entrails and maybe have a peep into a crystal ball before reporting where the suspected witch lived, the one who had sent down the bolt in question. Then they would set fire to her *and* her house, to be on the safe side.

"Without proof?" said Sabine.

"No, no. *With* proof. The fortune-teller."

Although the witches were pretty crafty. Or, at least, they were if they felt they were in the danger zone for being identified as witches.

"The danger zone?"

"Yes. Well-off late-middle-aged ladies. Preferably widows. Someone for the rest of the village to envy."

"A successful woman," said Allan. "They've plagued men in every age, on every continent."

"You're awfully enlightened, these days," said Julius. He longed for the friend Allan had been before he'd got infected with whatever this was.

Allan nodded thoughtfully. "The downside of the black tablet," he said. "I wholeheartedly apologize."

Meitkini didn't know much about how things worked elsewhere, but in Africa it was strikingly often that widows with money turned up in the fortune-teller's crystal ball.

"Crafty, you said," said Sabine. "How do you mean?"

Meitkini enjoyed playing the role of teacher. Miss Sabine and the others knew shockingly little about what life was like in his corner of the world.

"Sales of lightning rods are higher on this continent than all other continents combined. It doesn't cost many shillings to install a lightning rod on a hill. And then the lightning will strike there instead. And the suspected witch can continue being suspected for a while longer."

"But the Queen in Nairobi doesn't need lightning rods?"

"That's right. Because, as I said, she's not a witch, she's a *mganga*. Let me guess, Miss Sabine, you would like me to explain what a *mganga* is?"

He didn't wait for the obvious answer.

Well, for one thing, a *mganga* believed in God— nothing else would do. But that faith in God was mixed up with a little bit of everything else. Like herbs, rituals, and roots with magical powers. A true *mganga* understands that every affliction humans face has physical or divine causes. An infected appendix is pointless to operate on if the underlying cause is beyond our understanding. The same goes for HIV and AIDS. In those cases, intangible power is much more effective.

"Intangible power?"

"Magic. Exorcism. Or why not a cup of Olekorinko's blessed miracle medicine? Always with the purpose of doing good, otherwise . . . warning, witchcraft."

Julius had listened to this conversation without getting involved. But now he was curious about something. "Listen, Meitkini. Green asparagus. Could there be something magical in it?" He was picturing a business opportunity beyond anything he'd ever come up with before. Gustav Svensson's miracle asparagus! Cures all! Buy some today!

"It's possible," said Meitkini. "But when it comes to my appendix, I'd prefer the operation."

Sabine needed time to think. Had all her mother's stories been based on a linguistic misunderstanding? Was it time to relegate her mother's principles and accept that it wasn't possible to make use of them? Or was there a third way?

_____

It took three hours to get to the border between Tanzania and Kenya. It was marked with a largish rock at the edge of the road, and none of the Swedes would have noticed it if their driver hadn't slowed down to point.

"Welcome to my homeland," he said, as they passed the rock.

"Look, that rental car has been behind us ever since we left Olekorinko and his bodyguards," said Sabine, who was still bewildered and shaken by what they had experienced.

She had no desire to be set on fire, with or without the gasoline.

Allan turned around to glance backward. He asked to borrow Meitkini's binoculars.

It was a bit far off, but it looked like there was only a driver. A woman. In a blazer. On the African savannah? The same blazer, even, as . . .

"If you stop over there, Meitkini, I'll talk to the woman behind us. I think she may be an old acquaintance."

Dusk was starting to fall and the Maasai scanned their surroundings. A calm herd of zebras were walking on a rise to their right. Calm! To the left, a group of baboons were preparing for the night. They were calm too. And there was no bird activity in the air. Thus there were no lions or buffalo nearby. Meitkini said it was safe to stop, but whatever Karlsson was planning to do must not take long. It would be dark within fifteen minutes, and then none of them would be allowed to set foot outside the car.

Stop? Here? What did he mean, "acquaintance?" Who could have any acquaintances in the middle of nowhere? Julius had been infected by Sabine's anxiety. Trusting the 101-year-old's uneven good sense out in the wildest wilds had little to recommend it. Why not just keep going?

"Take a deep breath, dear asparagus farmer. And back out again. It's going to be okay, you'll see," said Allan.

When Meitkini parked alongside the road, the rental car did the same, 160 yards away. Allan crawled out of the Land Cruiser and down to the ground. He took a few steps toward the car behind them, raised the binoculars again, and realized he had been right. He lowered them and called to the blazer-clad woman, "Come here, Madame Real Estate Broker! Don't be shy!"

Tanzania, Kenya

Agent B had finally managed a few hours' sleep, shivering in her back seat. And a few more in the morning, once the sun had warmed the air. After that, she'd got absolutely nothing out of the day. It was easy not to run into Karlsson among the ten thousand other people. On the other hand, it would have been impossible to find him. All B could do was stake out the Swedes' car and follow them at a safe distance when they left. Or half safe, as it turned out, because they didn't take the same way back. Instead they turned north onto even worse roads than the ones that had brought them to Olekorinko.

Any agent understood the imprudence of tailing someone by car unless you had at least two helpers. One was supposed to be ahead, the other behind. Keeping in constant contact via walkie-talkie.

But the agent was, once and for all, alone on this pointless assignment. And the road was not a road: it was more of a livestock path. The risk of being discovered was considerable.

B kept as great a distance as possible. She drove with the headlights off to avoid beaming them into the rear-view mirror of the target car. But she couldn't let the Swedes and their driver out of her sight. At any moment they might make a turn and she would lose them forever.

It was a tough balancing act. B was also plagued by thoughts from the previous night. How had it all turned out like this? She was alone on a rocky, unpaved road heading through the African savannah. Alone in every imaginable way. Undercover. Feeling she was working full-time on ruining her already sufficiently ruined life.

At that moment, things went from bad to worse: the target was now sitting in the middle of the road calling to her as if they were old friends.

Agent B considered putting the car into reverse and disappearing. But the situation was too complicated. The 101-year-old enemy might just as easily be a friend. And, anyway, now that B had been discovered, she would never know which it was unless she changed tack.

And what did she have to lose? When she got home, she would give her notice. Become a beat cop in Rödelheim? That might be nice. But what would happen if she got a toothache and had to visit the local clinic?

The agent rolled up to the old man and his car. She stepped out and walked over to Allan without a word.

"Good day, good day," said Allan. "Find any exciting properties to broker since we last spoke?"

They were in the one place on Earth a professional real-estate broker was least likely to visit on the job.

Agent B had spent the last seven years of her life being beyond secret. She was suffering from exhaustion. She was hungry. And thirsty. And tired of herself and her life. And she was standing across from a man who might be the enemy but might be a friend.

Enough was enough. Agent B made up her mind.

"No, I haven't. My name is Fredrika Langer and I am employed by the Federal Republic of Germany to try to prevent the spread of enriched uranium from Africa to—as one example—North Korea."

"I was starting to suspect something along those lines," said Allan. "You were behind us in the line at the airport in Dar es Salaam. Then we ended up next to each other on the plane and it turned out you had no idea where you were going. When I surmised there wasn't any real estate to broker in Musoma you agreed. We were so ridiculously mistaken. A little while ago I recognized you—you haven't changed your blazer since yesterday. And out here on the savannah, you couldn't be after anything other than me and my friends, could you?"

"That's correct," said the agent. She had never felt so unprofessional in all her life.

"What's going on?" asked Meitkini.

"Quite a bit," said Allan. "May I introduce you to one another?"

Up to this point, Meitkini had had club and knife at the ready, but he understood from Allan's tone that he wouldn't need them. The miserable agent had already acknowledged that she had approached four potential enemies on the savannah with no weapon whatsoever. Look, another failure to stack up with the rest.

When the formalities had been dealt with, Allan suggested that the new addition to their group could also be invited to Meitkini's camp. They had a lot to talk about. "Don't you agree, Mrs. Langer?"

Yes, she did.

"And we certainly can't stand around here. Don't you agree with that as well, Mrs. Langer?"

Yes, she did.

"Then let's go," said Meitkini. "Follow me, Mrs. Langer."

Allan chose to ride in the German agent's car, so they could begin chatting at once. This put Agent Langer in a better mood. If Karlsson was playing with her, he would soon talk himself into a corner. In which case it would still be true that she was in the wrong place—unarmed and having said too much—but at least she would know it.

During the rest of their journey, as it grew dark around them, Allan gave her the short version of events from the hot-air balloon onward, with some choice flashbacks to earlier points in his life. Agent Langer believed every word. There were too many verifiable items to Karlsson's advantage. If he were a major uranium smuggler, running errands for North Korea, why would they have fled the country instead of staying put? And how could any uranium smuggler in his right mind come up with the bright idea to bring nine pounds to the United States, only to have it dumped at the German embassy in Washington with a love letter to Angela Merkel?

"The director of the laboratory in Pyongyang mentioned a shipment many times larger than the first one," said Allan. "Does the uranium in question come from around here, given your presence and interest?"

Yes, that was what the agents suspected. There wasn't much reason to deny it. From Congo, to be more precise. And the same ship that had picked up Karlsson and Jonsson a few months earlier was out at sea again. "We're reasonably sure that the handover will take place just south of Madagascar."

"Then what are you doing here?"

Agent Langer became annoyed. "If it weren't for you, Mr. Karlsson, I would have been somewhere else."

"Oh, I see," said Allan.

With each passing moment, the road seemed to get worse. At some points it had been rerouted, thanks to African downpours that created torrents of water that ate up parts or the entirety of the road that once had been.

Here and there, stretches went straight through a stream. Sometimes the road was divided in the middle by a boulder or log that wasn't where it should have been. This made it too narrow to pass oncoming traffic on one of the sides so there were certain brief single-lane stretches. Traffic signs of any sort are a rare sight on the Kenyan savannah. In instances where the road splits, common sense must rule when it comes to choosing right or left. Meitkini chose left, born and raised as he was in a country with left-hand traffic.

But Agent Langer was only on an involuntary visit. What was more, she had spent the first thirty-three years of her life a stone's throw from Autobahn 5 outside Frankfurt am Main. The crucial difference between the A5 and Kenya's county highway C12 was not that the former functioned at 120 miles per hour and the latter at six, max, but that in Kenya you don't drive on the same side of the road as they do in Germany.

The long and the short of it was that the agent, unlike Meitkini, rounded a large boulder on the wrong side. The waiting stream had two separate fords, with eleven yards between them. The western one functioned as it should, while the latest cloudburst had washed away great masses of earth from the eastern. An observant and conscientious Maasai had put up a warning sign to say that the upcoming ford was no longer a foot deep but more like a yard and a half. But since the Maasai, like Meitkini, always kept left, he hadn't expended any effort on warning the other side, too—the side Agent Langer was coming from.

The agent drove cautiously down the slope as the depth went from one inch to five times that in just one second. The vehicle tipped violently forward and got

stuck with both its front tires in the deep hole lurk-
ing beneath the surface. Parts of the engine ended up
under water and, in a matter of seconds, it had stopped.

"Oops," said Allan, who had to hold on to keep from
falling in. "If I were to guess, I would guess that Madame Agent has got us into a mess."

Agent Langer thought things just kept getting worse,
and at an insane rate. It had become clear a few hours
ago that she was in the wrong part of Africa. Now it
appeared that, in addition, there was no way she would
get out of there until someone managed to fish out and
repair the car for her.

It turned out to be an adventure, getting Allan and
the agent across to the other side. Meitkini used a
branch to determine how far out in the water he could
dare to drive his own car, and got close enough for the
German and the Swede to climb from hood to hood,
then on to safety, in the company of Julius and Sabine.

"Your car will have to stay put," said Meitkini. "It
will have to be pulled out from the other side, with a
towrope, and that's not the sort of thing you should do
in the middle of the night, around all the animals. Also,
I can't imagine that the engine is in good enough shape
to start, now that you've chosen to put it under water."

"I did not *choose* to put it under water," said Agent
Langer.

Kenya

The disillusioned agent sat on the porch of the tent she had been assigned at the camp where Meitkini was a guide. She was experiencing some inner turmoil, and she still couldn't sleep. Instead she greeted the dawn in solitude. The tents were scattered across the hillsides of the verdant valley of savannah and bush that belonged to the camp. Just 220 yards farther down there was an expansive watering hole. After sunrise, a pair of dik-diks came to slake their thirst, but had to slink away to make room for a herd of elephants. The silence in the valley was magnificent. Like in Germany, thought Agent Langer, and yet so different.

The peace was broken by Allan and Julius, who came plodding along the path from the camp lounge.

With dawn, the wild animals stopped hunting for prey, so it was safe to go for a walk.

"Good morning, Madame Agent. Sleep well?" Allan inquired.

"We brought breakfast, if you'd like some," Julius said, holding up the tray he was carrying.

Madame Agent? Well, okay, she had revealed herself. And Karlsson hadn't been discreet about what he knew.

"Yes, thanks," Agent Langer lied. "I slept well. And I wouldn't mind some breakfast. Please, sit down."

The woman and the two men shared coffee, fried eggs, and papaya from the camp's own garden as they sat down to talk about the future. All while the cool dawn turned into a decently warm day, there at an altitude of about sixty-six hundred feet, just south of the equator.

Allan had brought his black tablet and said he would be happy to share whatever he might discover on it. In which case he would skip how many people had drowned in the Mediterranean since last time because Julius was tired of hearing about that.

Julius asked Allan not to torment the agent as he had tormented Julius and Sabine for far too long already, but the agent nodded politely. It might be pleasant to hear what was going on beyond the savannah and bush. Had the Supreme Leader in the East come up with any new nonsense?

Surely he had, Allan imagined, but nothing that had reached the tablet. He would like to offer something a little different, if it was of interest.

"No!" said Julius, as Allan continued.

At home in old Sweden, the Transport Agency had purposely sent its entire database to a company in Eastern Europe, contrary to the recommendation of the Security Service. They had outsourced the handling of secure information about fighter pilots and government agents. Now the newspapers were revealing that the director of the agency faced being fired and receiving seventy thousand kronor in fines and at least four million in severance pay.

"Let me guess, Agent Langer, you have no colleagues stationed in Sweden. I can't imagine that would be necessary," said Allan. "Up there, we have no secrets from each other or anyone else."

Allan noticed that Julius was sulking in his corner. Because of a piece of news? Surely he could tolerate a little bit.

Trump was still Trump, it seemed, while Saudi Arabia seemed to be in free fall toward Western decadence. Not only would women be given the right to drive, but now both men *and* women would be allowed to go to the movies for the first time since 1983. Maybe before the dust settled they would also be able to have a drink and feel normal.

When Allan received no response to his ponderings, even as Julius remained sulky, he changed the subject. "Maybe this will cheer you up, Julle." And he told them about the Ghanaian soccer referee who had just been banned for life after giving South Africa a penalty in a match when a poor Senegalese player happened to be hit with a ball in the *knee.*

Julius still hadn't reacted (aside from a comment about how his name wasn't Julle), in contrast to the German agent.

"Isn't hitting the ball with your knee allowed?" wondered the woman who had spent her whole life avoiding sports as entertainment. Or entertainment in general, now that she thought about it.

"Right, that's the point. But FIFA—which is famous for its corruption, by the way—felt that the referee was corrupt. So now the match is to be replayed."

Ongoing sour face from his friend on the sofa. There was only one thing left to try. In sports talk, it was called putting the ball in Julius's court.

"From one thing to the next: Might you have any relationship with asparagus, Madame Agent?"

This was a question Agent Langer had not seen coming.

"Asparagus?" she said. "I have a long-standing, rather close, and very good relationship with asparagus. My grandfather was born and raised in Schwetzingen."

"Schwetzingen," said Allan. "Sounds like some sort of mixer."

Agent Langer said that those in Schwetzingen might certainly have a drink or two, and even a third before the night was over, yet the name of the city had nothing to do with alcohol but rather with asparagus.

"Tell me more!" said Julius, sitting up straight.

"Welcome back," said Allan.

It turned out that Fredrika Langer had a lifelong love of asparagus—the white kind, but still. Her grandfather, Günther, had been one of the premier asparagus farmers in Schwetzingen in his day. He had crawled around in the sandy earth and seemed to be in close personal contact with each individual plant. And at home, with her grandmother, Matilda, he had created fabulous meals out of that white gold. Starters, main courses, and even desserts!

"White?" said Julius. "Isn't real asparagus green?"

This was the only thing he and Gustav Svensson had argued about in Bali. The Swedish-Indian had insisted they should diversify their operations, that 20 percent of the plants should produce a white harvest rather than a green one.

Agent Langer smiled for what had to be the first time in a year. "With all due respect, Mr. Jonsson, I don't think you know what you're talking about."

Meitkini's safari customers arrived as planned and were given a proper welcome by their guide. The Swedes and the German would have to manage as best they could for a few days.

Allan spent these days on the big veranda by the lounge, with a view of the verdant valley and the watering hole, where there was fresh drama to watch just about constantly. After the dik-diks came the elephants, and when they had finished, the lion woke. A lone rhinoceros also made regular visits. And the giraffes, which were so poorly constructed that they had to do the splits in order to take a drink.

The 101-year-old felt content with just about everything. The view, of course. The drinks young John at the bar delivered without even being asked. And John's technical abilities! Just think: if you linked the tablet to something called a "network," news from all corners of the world popped up five times faster. The same news, to be sure, but still.

Sabine preferred to sit farther inside the lounge, so that her concentration was not continually disturbed by Allan's many stories. She was devising various plans for bringing clairvoyance into a mass-meeting project, according to the principle "Better to cheat ten thousand participants out of a few dollars each than to get three hundred dollars out of one." And with a strong preference for leaving God out of it.

"Mass clairvoyance," she mumbled to herself. "On Wednesday at eleven o'clock we'll link ourselves up with Elvis. Ten-dollar admission fee. Twenty for a personal question."

No, that was no good. What if she added a tea that would open up the participants' minds? Secret tea? Maybe a little LSD in it to give their reputation a real boost . . .

"How's it going?" Allan wondered, from a short distance.

"Don't bother me!" Sabine responded.

Not too well, she thought.

Julius and Agent Langer mostly stuck to the other side of the lounge, with a view of the camp's organic garden. They were in agreement that the climate there, at an altitude of sixty-six hundred feet, certainly seemed suitable for asparagus. But the same wasn't true of the iron-rich red earth. Julius said that *white* crap-sparagus could probably be grown in just about anything, but the green kind required a fine, sandy soil. Agent Langer countered, saying that the white kind required the same, but it hardly mattered what sort of soil one grew the green stuff in: it would still be inedible.

The two asparagus-lovers generally got on well, aside from the part about green versus white.

Arrogant Agent A called, interfering. He reported that, in cooperation with the BND-payrolled chief of border patrol and eighty of his men, an invisible wall had been constructed between Tanzania and Mozambique. It was only a question of time before the smugglers drove into it. "Pity you're not here. I'll get all the praise."

The formerly so meek Agent B had been energized by her new asparagus relations. Enough, anyway, to wish all bad things upon her boss. "So lovely for you," she said. "If the uranium slips through anyway, I'm sure it will be possible to make it all my fault, don't you think?"

Lead Agent A wasn't used to B arguing with him. "Now, don't be upset just because you didn't have the sense to be in the right place. How's it going with Karlsson? Have you found him yet?"

"No," Agent B lied. "But I did get stuck on the savannah in the car I rented. In a few days I can get help to tow it out of a stream."

Lead Agent A chuckled. "Funniest thing I've heard in a long time. So you'll be staying up there." He told her that *Honor and Strength* was, according to reports, still heading for the Cape of Good Hope, Cape Agulhas, and—in all certainty—the southern tip of Madagascar. That meant the smuggled uranium would be crossing the border between Tanzania and Mozambique any day now. "And then I suppose I'll have no choice but to call the chancellor myself and tell her the news," said A.

Communicating it via the vacationing director of the BND, as instructed, would not give the proper boost to his career.

Agent Langer returned to Julius in the lounge. She noted that, in his company, she experienced something similar to a zest for life.

"Hello, my misguided asparagus friend, may I join you?" She smiled as she said it. It was an affectionate battle, this clash between green and white.

Julius responded, "Hello yourself, color-blind one. Have a seat."

Kenya

The tourists left, satisfied after a few days in the area that's called the eighth wonder of the world. Meitkini once again had time for Allan, Julius, Sabine, and the German, who of course needed a hand with her car. Sabine had suggested that she and the old men stay a few more days at the camp, if that was all right. The lounge was conducive to thinking, but she still hadn't got as far with her future business plan as she had hoped.

Meitkini was delighted. He would be more than happy to spend a little more time with the Swedes, now that he didn't have work to get in the way. Except for the German and her car, of course.

"The German," thought Agent B. Or "Madame Agent." Wonder what it would be like to exist in a context where you had a name and an identity you were allowed to talk about.

"My name is Fredrika," she said. "Nice to meet you."

Meitkini looked ashamed.

Fredrika Langer's phone rang. What if the boss had captured . . .

No, he hadn't. He just wanted, for the fifteenth time, to know if she was on her way. Fredrika gloomily responded that she was in the process. The car would be out of the stream in an hour or so, and then they just had to get the engine working. She could be at Musoma for a flight the next morning.

"Fly straight to Madagascar and we'll meet up there. Those bastards must have slipped through somehow."

The call ended, and Meitkini went on: "Then should we just head out to the stream, all of us together, and tow out your car . . . Fredrika . . . make sure it works, and send you on your way? Then the rest of us can go on a real safari tour on our way home, before it gets dark."

Allan said it would be interesting to get an even closer look at the activity he'd experienced at the watering hole. He could always look up pictures of giraffes and leopards on his black tablet, but it wasn't the same.

The others agreed. Julius was sorry Fredrika had to leave, but he understood that duty called.

With a few safari detours on the way, it took an hour and a half to reach the stream where Agent Langer had so infelicitously parked the front half of her Land Cruiser a few days earlier. The stream was still there.

The same was not true of the car.

"It seems someone has already been along to help," said Meitkini.

"And taken the car as thanks," said Allan.

Fredrika Langer hid her face in her hands. Someone had stolen the vehicle that was meant to take her back to Tanzania so she could continue her southward journey. What on earth would she do now?

Meitkini urged her to buck up. He suggested that they return to camp after the promised safari tour. They would drop the Swedes off there, then drive to Musoma overnight. "You can report the car stolen, Fredrika, before you get a flight out. It could be worse, couldn't it?"

Yes, that was true. Okay, that was the plan.

But things didn't go as planned.

The safari tour was truly something special. Even Allan, who never allowed himself to be impressed, was impressed by what he saw. Meitkini had the right vehicle and the right status to be authorized to search for the animals where they lived, not where they just happened to be on a road. Or whatever one should call those rocky paths.

It was cheetah cubs play-fighting while their mother kept watch for lions. It was herds of zebras, Thomson's gazelles, and wildebeest. It was a humongous female elephant with a week-old baby tripping along between her back legs. It was the snouts and eyes of four hippopotamuses waiting for night to fall so they could leave the water and find food. It was, in short, fantastic.

No one in the group noticed, but it was suddenly about to get dark.

"Oops," said Meitkini. "Time to track down the road again."

He found what he was looking for and they began their journey back to camp.

Near the equator, the shift from dark to pitch black happens fast. Wild animals' eyes glittered along both sides of the road: many were beginning their work.

After just over half an hour through the savannah, they saw something glowing red in the distance. The taillights of a car? Yes, indeed.

"Gracious me, it's a traffic jam," said Allan.

They came closer. The vehicle was standing still. It seemed to be having problems. Meitkini gave the group their orders.

"Stay in the car! Not one foot outside! That goes for you too, Allan."

"Don't you worry about me, Meitkini. I never move unless it's necessary."

Meitkini could tell from the wrench on the ground next to the left rear wheel that the tire had a puncture. It was a blue Hilux with a large wooden box in the bed. A lone man sat in the front, cautiously peering out of the rolled-down side window. Meitkini drove the Land Cruiser up alongside it. Allan was in the front passenger seat, decently worked up. It was always exciting to meet new people.

"Good day, sir," he said. "My name is Karlsson. Allan Karlsson. Might you have a name as well?"

The man in the Hilux was black, middle-aged, and short of stature. He gave Allan a cautious look before responding. "Smith," he said. "Stan Smith."

"Imagine that," said Allan. "Do you play tennis?"

"No, I have a flat tire," said Stan Smith, unaware that he had a tennis-playing namesake who was white and almost six and a half feet tall—not a fellow with whom he was likely to be confused.

Meitkini said he had noticed a wrench near the flat tire and wondered if Mr. Smith had left the car in the dark to change it. If so, this was absolutely not recommended.

Stan Smith seemed to hesitate before replying. "I didn't leave the car. But my traveling partner did. He was taken by the lions twenty minutes ago."

What horrible news. Yet Mr. Smith appeared calm and collected.

"I'm very sorry to hear that," said Meitkini. "Would you like to climb across into our car, and spend the night at our camp nearby? I can make sure someone drives you back to help you change the tire first thing tomorrow morning."

Stan Smith shook his head. "Thanks, but no thanks. I can't leave my cargo."

Allan looked at the large wooden box in back. "What's in it, if I may ask?"

Stan Smith hesitated once more. "Necessities," he said.

"Necessities," Allan repeated. "Yes, such items are good to have. Though it rather depends on what sort, of course."

Imagine—

Stan Smith hesitated yet again. Allan was good at registering that kind of thing.

"It's for the poor," Stan Smith said, and it didn't look as if he wished to expound any further on the matter. "Just go on. I can make it through the night."

Meitkini shrugged and made a move to leave. Stan

Smith was perfectly correct that he would survive the night if he just stayed in the car until dawn. And if he didn't want any help, he didn't have to have any.

With that, the matter would have been settled if it hadn't been for Allan, who had a little more on his mind.

"That's a very nice briefcase, Mr. Smith," he said.

The stranded man was startled.

"The fact is, I once carried one just like it," Allan went on. "North Korean design. I'm sure of it, for I'm very familiar with the entire range of North Korean briefcases. It's rather limited."

That was all it took for the situation to go in a new direction. Goodluck Wilson, a.k.a. Stan Smith, quickly opened his North Korean briefcase and took out a revolver. He opened the sunroof of the Hilux, stood on his seat, and aimed his weapon alternately at Allan and Meitkini in the front, at the women and the man in the back.

"Stay where you are!" he said.

For one instant, time stood still. In that moment, Goodluck Wilson had time to analyze his situation.

He found himself in the middle of the pitch-black Kenyan savannah, where there were more wild lions than anywhere else on Earth. He had perhaps four miles to go to the local airport, where the box containing 880 pounds of enriched uranium would be transferred that night, or the next night at the very latest. He had a flat tire, but here was an alternative vehicle. He might be able to take off in it, with the help of the revolver in his hand. Revolvers, after all, are known for getting people to do what their owners say. In this case, that might be to demand that the old man, his driver, and the three back-seat passengers exchange their car for his.

In which case, all that remained was the uranium issue. He couldn't leave it behind. If he opened the box, he could force his hostages to move the forty twenty-two-pound boxes into the Land Cruiser, one box at a time. But that would require one to work on the ground—under threat of his weapon, yes, but also exposed to the lions. Would the revolver even be enough to maintain discipline over the group under such circumstances?

And, also, this group. Who *were* they? How the hell had that old white man recognized his briefcase? It was unreal.

Just think how much the human brain can manage to do when time is standing still. Goodluck Wilson continued his pondering. Another option was to shoot everyone who currently posed a threat to this whole multimillion-dollar affair. But that wouldn't help him move forward. Not until the morning, when he could change cars or tires without aid. How many safari cars would have time to swing by before this?

And that was about where the instant ended. Time started moving again. As a Maasai, Meitkini had a throwing club on a loop on his trousers. With it he could strike a moving wild animal from a distance of forty yards. The blow would be hard enough to make the animal reconsider, to the extent that it could consider anything at all.

Animal or human, essentially there was no difference. From only three yards away, it would be easy enough to land a blow to the forehead of the man who called himself Stan Smith and was likely named something else. A buffalo struck in the side by the club would feel pain. A man who took it to the forehead would die on the spot.

Meitkini acted, quick as lightning.

"Nice throw," Allan said encouragingly.

"Thanks," said Meitkini.

Julius and Sabine said nothing: it had all happened too fast for them. The same went for Fredrika Langer. She was the one to break the silence.

"Exactly what just happened?" she asked.

Allan responded.

"What exactly happened was—I'm guessing—that Madame Agent, Fredrika, just found her eleven hundred pounds of uranium. Just think—it really is a small world."

Congo

A few months earlier, it had been quite an adventure to get the test cargo to Madagascar, where the North Koreans picked it up. But the rest of the trip to Pyongyang had gone well. A few days before Goodluck Wilson's ill-fated encounter with Allan and his friends, he had initiated "Operation Jackpot." The Supreme Leader far, far away wanted to buy the eleven hundred pounds that had accidentally become 880 pounds. And it would happen now. After all, they couldn't just keep the uranium in the hut in the middle of the village, halving itself every four-billionth year.

But nine pounds was one thing. Eight hundred eighty was another. It was easy to get the load into Tanzania via Burundi, by way of well-targeted bribes, but the next border, between Tanzania and Mozambique, was heavily guarded. The border patrol officers there took their jobs seriously. People like that were Goodluck Wilson's pet peeve.

What was more, he had likely left a number of traces behind, having managed that route once. Goodluck Wilson didn't believe in luck, despite his name. He believed in cleverness.

The leader of the watchdog force had needed to think up a new plan.

So he had.

Everyone who was on the lookout for enriched uranium, or other exciting items that were worth a lot of money on the international market, assumed that the cargo was on its way to the nearest coast, the Tanzanian one, or the next nearest, the one in Mozambique. So Goodluck Wilson settled on a different route. The load would go straight north, to the Serengeti, where the Maasai kingdom was. The Maasai herded cattle and raised goats and generally didn't get involved in the modern world. Above all, like the wild animals that migrated north each summer on the hunt for more fertile areas, they didn't pay attention to national borders. The border of Tanzania and Kenya ran straight through the Maasai land, with no patrols. Telling a

Maasai that he couldn't herd his two hundred cattle across a certain line on the ground just couldn't be done.

The plan was to transport the load of uranium in a Hilux from Congo, via Burundi, south of Lake Victoria, into the Serengeti, across the border into Kenya, and all the way to the insignificant Keekorok Airport. It consisted of one runway made of mineral-rich red earth, and a terminal building the size of a newspaper stand. Air Kenya came from Nairobi to drop off safari-hungry tourists and pick up others who had finished touristing. When the sun went down, the newspaper stand closed and the airport stopped functioning. Not a single person would be in the vicinity until the next morning.

A person who didn't have pure intentions but did have bright enough landing lights on his airplane, and a decent navigational system, could easily and freely land and take off again in the dark with no witnesses but the occasional giraffe or zebra. Goodluck Wilson needed only to ask the Russians to put him in touch with the right pilot and that would be that. The Russians because the North Koreans were unreachable: they were like ghosts in the night.

Once the load was delivered, the plane would fly to

the coast, and from there it would travel at an altitude of forty yards across the sea, all the way to a well-trampled field near the southern tip of Madagascar. There, the secretive North Koreans would take over. As long as they had eighty million dollars with them in exchange.

The last bit was slightly worrisome to Goodluck Wilson. But only slightly. The payment of a hundred thousand for the initial test delivery had gone as it should. That time it had been in advance. Suddenly, one day, a strange man who looked Asian was standing outside Goodluck Wilson's office. He had a briefcase in either hand, and said nothing but "Name?"

"Goodluck Wilson," said the head of the watchdog force, and refrained from asking the same question in return.

The Asian nodded, then said that one briefcase contained the agreed-upon amount of money, while the other indicated exactly how his employer wished to have the delivery packed. The lead lining was already in place.

And that was that. The Asian left as quickly as he had appeared and hadn't been seen since. Goodluck Wilson had no way of knowing, but he suspected the man had come from the North Korean embassy in Kampala. It was easy to get from Uganda to Congo.

And back again. Goodluck would have chosen a fishing boat across Lake Albert, but there were other ways.

Be that as it may. The important thing was that the North Koreans had proven they could deliver. Just as he had immediately afterward. Everything had gone fine that time; everything would go fine again.

Thought Goodluck Wilson.

Kenya

A frequently used Land Cruiser, designed for the tough terrain of the African savannah, will get a puncture about once a week. A Hilux, under the same circumstances, will be affected somewhat more often. A person who is only on a short visit, and is sufficiently cautious, has a good chance of avoiding the bother of changing tires.

But the rocks are many, and sharp. The risk is always present. After nightfall it is important to be even more watchful, for if the accident happens you are not as alone on the edge of the road as you might wish. The lion slinks through the dark on the hunt for food. So does the leopard, which the Maasai call the "murder machine." Even the hyena can be pretty unpleasant. The angriest animal of them all, the Cape buffalo, has probably called it a night, given that your puncture hasn't occurred in just the wrong spot. And which spot that is is impossible to know.

In short, in the event of a flat tire at night, you should:

Stay. In. The. Car. Until. It. Gets. Light.

But what if you don't have time? What if you have 880 pounds of enriched uranium in your truck bed and an airplane has just landed under cover of darkness at a poor excuse for an airport forty minutes away, impatiently waiting for its delivery? And with eighty million dollars at stake?

Perhaps not everyone would do the same, but Good-luck Wilson did believe in luck after all. Not for himself but for his favorite cousin Samuel. His cousin was sent out with a flashlight to change the wrecked tire. He defied almost all statistics by getting so far as to have mounted the spare and was about to replace the nuts when two lionesses came out of nowhere from two different directions.

Lions think logically, and always in the same way. They don't have the ability to tell a living being from its engine-driven vehicle so long as the being has the good sense to remain inside said vehicle. If, for example, an open-cab car full of safari-loving humans arrives, the lion sees the totality, not each individual potential meal. And it thinks three things: (1) Can I eat this? (No, it's too big.); (2) Can it eat me? (No, a long life has taught me that utility vehicles and trucks never attack.) (3) Can I mate with it? (No, I don't think I'll ever be that kinky.)

But when someone leaves the safety of their elephant-sized vehicle, the lion gets very different answers to its questions. (1) Can I eat this? (Yes, and it will be delicious!) (2) Can it eat me? (No, how would that work?) (3) Can I mate with it? (No, I don't think I'll ever be that kinky.)

A lion's speciality is to aim its initial blow at the victim's nose and mouth so at first Goodluck Wilson heard nothing of the attack but a muffled rustling sound, and the wrench striking the hard slope as it fell from his cousin's hand. Then he saw two pairs of glowing eyes in the darkness and the sound of crunching bone reached him.

And then he understood.

He understood that he was left alone. His first thought was not for his cousin or his cousin's family: instead he wondered how the four million dollars that had just been freed up should be divided. He arrived at the conclusion that he would do best to keep it for himself, so as to avoid strife within the group.

Just after the lionesses dragged the remains of his dead cousin into the bush, so that first the males and then the cubs had something to feast on, a vehicle appeared on the road. Here? In the middle of nothing and nowhere? And almost in the middle of the night? Dammit!

Kenya

Meitkini had learned how to handle a spear, knife, and club when he was three years old. At the age of four, he had the misfortune, as a cowherd, to come face-to-face with a buffalo. The greatest misfortune belonged to the buffalo, however, for the four-year-old's spear landed almost where it was meant to and he managed to stay hidden under a bush as the life slowly drained from the beast. Eleven years later, the fifteen-year-old boy was sent out on the savannah, with only the clothes on his back and his spear, knife, and club. Nothing more. That was how it worked. The boys who came back to the village a year later were accepted into the adult world: they were Maasai warriors for real. If they didn't come back, the question was no longer of interest.

Yes, Meitkini came back, as did all his friends. Those

who have been taught to survive from the age of three tend to do just that.

Now, at thirty-two, he asked his fellow travelers to take off all the clothing they didn't absolutely need and gather up all the blankets that were in the car. Meanwhile, Meitkini himself climbed into the back and grabbed the extra can of gasoline.

He tossed strategically placed piles of gasoline-drenched clothing and blankets around both cars, then handed out flashlights to all his companions and instructed them in which direction to aim the beams. He then dropped a match on top of each pile of fabric, which immediately began blazing wildly.

"There we go," he said. "Now I'll climb down and lift the boxes out while those of you who can manage it receive them. That should work."

As a final safety measure, he handed a crowbar to Fredrika: he had found it next to the gasoline can.

"Throw this if you see anything approaching."

She nodded seriously. For the moment, she felt like a field agent again.

Ten minutes later, Meitkini was done. The piles were still burning. Fredrika Langer was still standing at the ready with the crowbar. The last thing Meitkini did was lift the dead Stan Smith out of the car and lay him in the ditch.

"Are you leaving him there for the lions?" Sabine asked.

"No," said Meitkini, who had recognized four pairs of glowing eyes not far off in the bush. "For the hyenas."

Back at camp, things had changed. Fredrika Langer didn't go into the details with Meitkini: she just said it was no longer urgently necessary for them to rush off to Musoma together.

"Lovely," said Meitkini. "In that case, are you ladies and gentlemen content for me to ask John to pour us something pleasant in the lounge before we sit down for a late supper?"

"Something pleasant in the lounge sounds pleasant to me," said Allan.

The others nodded in agreement.

Fredrika Langer appeared to have a more pleasant time in the lounge than any of the others, including Allan. She needed it. Partly because of Allan Karlsson she was now sitting on 880 pounds of enriched uranium, all weighed out and ready—that is, a hundred times more than Karlsson had already managed to present to Chancellor Merkel.

Agent Langer's boss had long stood watch along the 370-mile border between Tanzania and Mozambique, looking for the uranium that was currently in Kenya. Now he was probably doing the same thing in Madagascar. Fredrika felt she needed more time to think before she called her boss with the news.

What should she do? Not even taking into account how tired she was of everything.

"You look worn out, Madame Agent," said Allan. "Fredrika, I mean. Have things perhaps been a little much lately?"

And then there was Karlsson. Who saw right through you.

As everyone gathered around the table to enjoy a late three-course meal on the veranda, with a view of the pitch-black valley, two headlights popped up in the distance. At first they were just a faint flicker in the darkness: obviously someone, or several someones, was slowly approaching the camp.

Julius began to worry.

Sabine began to worry.

Fredrika Langer began to worry.

Meitkini checked to make sure he had his club.

"A visitor?" said Allan. "Exciting!"

The starter arrived, but it remained untouched. The car was getting close. Oh, dear God, it was an ordinary old car! A taxi! That had made it the entire way?

"Could it be someone who's missing Stan Smith?" wondered Fredrika, who had gone to fetch the crowbar to be on the safe side.

"Hmm," Meitkini mused. "But how would missing him lead to us?"

The taxi stopped just below the veranda. A man thanked the driver, handed over some money, and stepped out. His eyes searched the people standing in a row and landed on Julius, second from the left.

"Hello, my friend," said Gustav Svensson. "Nice to see you!"

Indonesia

It had been difficult there on Bali, in his solitude, to be Gustav Svensson. And it wouldn't have made anything easier if he'd gone back to being Simran Aryabhat Chakrabarty Gopaldas.

Gustav's mentor in the export of vegetables of uncertain origins had vanished. Gustav himself had, by way of faulty decision-making, caused the wholesaler in Sweden to be locked up for an indeterminate length of time. The asparagus was flourishing, but Gustav had nowhere to send it. He had both asparagus and expenses. What he needed was Julius and money.

Still, there was some of the latter left. Gustav racked his brains for every last rackable idea. And he could come up with no better plan than to invest the remainder of his assets in finding his partner.

But where was he? The last sign of life had come from America. And Pyongyang before that. Julius could be in Argentina by now. Or New Zealand. Or anywhere in between.

Gustav fervently wished he could just call his partner. But that wouldn't work, because the last thing Julius had done before he disappeared was give away his phone. To Gustav.

Send a message, then? An email? No, Julius wasn't wired that way. Nor was Gustav, to be fair. The only option left was his friend Allan's tablet. It had been on constantly every day on Bali, and it probably still was, but what help was that?

Unless . . .

A wild idea took shape.

He'd received the phone from Julius, who in turn had got it from Allan, who in turn had got it from the hotel manager at the same time as he received his tablet. Everything had been set up before the manager had handed the package to the hundred-year-old who had since had time to turn 101.

Gustav had hated himself for not having the phone switched on when Julius had tried to call. As punishment he forced himself to learn how to use the new technology properly. The first thing he discovered was that batteries discharge unless they get recharged.

The second thing was something called "Bluetooth." And then there were oddities like "roaming" and "tethering" and . . . exactly! "Find my iPhone." Gustav had thought this was the strangest function of all, considering he was holding it. But if you dug deeper it turned out that the service also covered Allan's black tablet.

What if . . .

But surely it couldn't be that easy, could it?

Then again, why not? Just about everything had gone to hell so far, but his luck had to change sometime, right?

Kenya, Germany

Gustav Svensson had "found 'his' iPad" and was given a proper welcome into the group. Now they had to get rid of the uranium. Allan was beside the office phone. It rang four times at the other end, then someone picked up.

"Hello?"

That was how Chancellor Merkel always initiated calls on her private phone. She didn't announce who she was.

"Hello yourself," said Allan. "Might I be speaking to the very chancellor herself? In which case, will my English be understood, or is Russian to be preferred? We could also get by with Mandarin."

"Who is calling?" Angela Merkel asked in Russian.

"Didn't I say? This is Allan Karlsson. I've found an

awful lot of enriched uranium for you, in addition to what I've already delivered, so to speak."

Angela Merkel had not yet begun to eat her breakfast. She was sitting at the small desk outside her bedroom in her dressing gown and had been browsing through documents regarding the day ahead when the phone rang. *That* phone. The one ten people, tops, knew about.

"I don't feel comfortable about this conversation," she said guardedly. "How did you get my number?"

"I understand you may wonder about that, Madame Chancellor. I could be anyone. An admirable level of suspicion! And important, frankly, in your position."

"Thank you, but you didn't answer my question."

"Didn't I? That's probably because I've become so forgetful in the last forty years. But I imagine you'll venture to believe that I am who I am when I say that I wrote you a letter, in a great hurry, on a couple of napkins, not long ago. Although that note was in English, now that I think about it."

Chancellor Merkel lowered her guard a few millimeters. "Go on."

"Well, that was a tremendously pleasant dinner with your UN ambassador. What was his name again? Konrad! That's it. A good man. Picked up the tab and everything. Including drinks. He wasn't stingy in the least. Although can you believe the Germans put an apple flavor in their vodka? Why?"

Angela Merkel lowered her guard another millimeter. "Well, it's not as if the apple in vodka is a constitutional law," she said. "But what I meant, Mr. Karlsson, was that perhaps you could instead tell me more about . . . the napkins you mentioned."

In the event that the man at the other end of the line could reproduce their message, it would be possible at least to consider believing that he was who he claimed to be. He had already told her which language the note had been written in.

"Oh, yes, right. Well, the thing was, Konrad visited the lavatory. I suppose he was . . . that is . . . it took some time for him to return."

"The napkins," said Chancellor Merkel.

"Well, they were in one of those racks in the center of the table, so I grabbed one and started writing. And then another, and another. Perhaps we don't need to delve into their contents. Haven't you already read them? And, after all, I'm the one who wrote them."

Either he isn't who he says he is, or he's very dense, thought Angela Merkel. But then she recalled that he was said to be a little over a hundred years old, so she supposed she could give him another chance.

And with that she had lowered her guard another millimeter without even noticing.

"If this conversation is to go on for any longer, I want to ascertain that Mr. Karlsson is who he says he is. So would you please do me a kindness and tell me what you—if you are you—wrote to me. If I'm even me."

She added the last bit in the event that she was dealing with a blackmailer. In doing so, she had refrained from acknowledging that she had any part in this bizarre conversation.

"Now I understand," said Allan. "If you are you—and I'm assuming you are because I placed this call to you—you received a report from me about how my asparagus-farming friend Julius and I came across nine pounds of enriched uranium in a North Korean briefcase. Did you know, incidentally, that all briefcases in North Korea look the same?"

"Please go on," said Angela Merkel.

"Right. Well, first, I suppose we were thinking we would hand the briefcase over to what's-his-name, Trump, the President of the USA. But then it turned out he wasn't really *right*—a far too common trait among world leaders, I've noticed. If you'll forgive the observation."

"Go on."

"So then I was over him, as the kids say. But you, Madame Chancellor, I have faith in, thanks to my black tablet. I imagine you're certain to have dealt with those nine pounds in the best way possible already, and perhaps you have space for eight hundred eighty more."

Karlsson definitely was the person he claimed to be. The proof wasn't that he had reproduced enough of the details from the message on the napkins, but that he was sticking to the exact half-muddled tone of the letter. The chancellor let down her guard completely. "*Eight* hundred eighty?" she said. "Wasn't it supposed to be eleven?"

She was right about that, the chancellor, thought Allan. He and Julius had counted the boxes, weighed and reweighed them, and two hundred pounds were missing. But surely the smugglers hadn't sent 880 pounds one way and the last two hundred twenty another. If it was about minimizing the risk, shouldn't the load have been divided down the middle?

"A perfectly correct observation, Madame Chancellor," said Allan, when he had finished thinking. "But perhaps it's partly that my sources weren't completely trustworthy, and partly that there may have been delivery issues. In all likelihood, it's both."

Allan reflected upon this for a few seconds more.

"Still there?" the chancellor asked, when the silence at the other end seemed a bit too lengthy.

"Yes, I'm here. And I've completed my analysis. I say: delivery issues."

Angela Merkel realized what a fix she was in. The election was three days away, and she was about to be saddled with eight hundred eighty pounds of enriched uranium. It had to be dealt with tidily and discreetly.

"Still there?" Allan wondered.

Yes, she was.

"I would have liked to send over the eight hundred eighty pounds, but it was a bit easier last time—what I've got here won't fit into a briefcase, North Korean or otherwise. I need an airplane. From Africa—that's where I am. And a runway in Germany, if only you would be willing to pull a few strings, Madame Chancellor, so we aren't shot down on approach. Just think how that would look. Eight hundred eighty pounds of uranium raining down on Berlin."

The chancellor buried her forehead in her hand. And thought: eight hundred eighty pounds of uranium raining down over Berlin days before the election.

She pulled herself together and formulated a few questions that were still hanging over her. Could Mr. Karlsson tell her where, more precisely, he and the uranium were currently located? And was he perhaps working in cooperation with another representative of the Federal Republic? After all, a few of them were stationed in Africa on the matter in question.

Allan told her that he was in Kenya, that he had first considered contacting the Kenyan government, but there had just been an election—in that sense, they were a bit ahead of Germany—and it had ended so poorly that the man who had just won had immediately lost what he had just won in the Supreme Court, so now the election had to be done all over again. Either the opposition had been tricked out of winning the election, or they had tricked others so it would look like they'd been tricked. Allan would feel more secure with the uranium in the arms of the chancellor.

In her arms or on her shoulders—it was bad either way, but she understood his reasoning. Then again, it would never end well if human trouble-magnet Karlsson was allowed to fly into Germany, with or without his current cargo.

"And how was any contact with German representatives in this matter?" she said.

"Good, thanks," said Allan.

Angela Merkel found that he was uniquely gifted at not answering questions.

"I think it would be best if the Federal Republic

picks up the cargo in question," she said. "Kindly provide the exact geographical information and I will see what I can do."

Exact geographical information? How did you give that? And when breakfast was on the table.

"I will absolutely provide that, Madame Chancellor. But exact geographical information isn't exactly my speciality. I'm better at ending up wherever I end up. May I call again tomorrow morning, at the same time, and we can work out the details?"

The chancellor began to answer, but Allan was hungry and had no time. He hung up.

"Breakfast is ready, Allan," said Julius.

"I see that. I'm coming," said Allan.

Kenya

The group's money would soon run out, and Gustav Svensson's arrival meant yet another mouth to feed. Sabine had known since her days as a businesswoman in Sweden that she could do calculations. First she'd had to learn about deficit, then credit, after the coffin sales had taken off, and now they were back to deficits.

And it seemed that no profitable clairvoyance plans were going to turn up. She almost had the urge to try an LSD trip to get unstuck, but the drug market was non-existent in Maasai Mara. She wouldn't have taken that step anyway. If her mother, in that state, had hunted for ghosts in front of trains, there was a good risk she would do the same in front of the lions.

Now it wasn't only Julius and Fredrika sitting in the

lounge and talking asparagus: Gustav Svensson had joined them. Although "talking" asparagus was an understatement. They were "worshipping" asparagus.

The mutual understanding seemed to be that the climate at sixty-six-hundred feet above sea level at the equator was perfect! Green, it would be. Or white. Or both, depending on whom you were listening to.

But also, everything was beyond tragic because the soil was all wrong. And had been for a long time. Remains left by humans from two million years ago had been found in the adjacent valley. In the same hard red soil that the asparagus lovers were now cursing.

"Then buy new soil," Allan said, from nearby on the veranda, with his nose in his tablet. "Then again, don't, because I just did it for you."

What had Sabine and the asparagus lovers just heard?

"You bought soil? For here? With what money?" Sabine said.

"You bought soil? For here? What kind?" said Julius.

"What kind?" said Gustav.

"What kind?" said Fredrika Langer.

Allan had been surfing around, got tired of all the moaning and groaning, and decided to do something about it. There was plenty of sandy soil in Nairobi, and with a few clicks it had been ordered. Four hundred tons, to start. That ought to go pretty far, right?

"Let me ask you again. With what money did you just buy four hundred tons of soil?" said Sabine.

"None at all," said Allan. "Things aren't so advanced here in Africa. They'll send an invoice."

"And who were you thinking would pay for it?"

"Oh, that's what you meant. Don't we have some money left from the coffin business?"

"No."

"Then I will ask you to let me think about it."

Sabine's financial objections were drowned by the topic at hand. Fredrika Langer had grown most eager of all. "Hell's bells!" she said. "Four hundred tons would be enough for almost the entire field beyond the organic garden. We'll have to make sure to keep watch at night, so the baboons don't ruin our fun."

Gustav Svensson's entire face lit up. "Four hundred tons!" he said, without truly comprehending how much this actually was.

Meanwhile, Julius had already entered the next phase. "Let's see, how can we best guide the trucks? The slope begins almost immediately on the other side of the garden, so maybe it'll be best to squeeze them between the souvenir shop and the office. What do you all think?"

No one but Sabine considered the fact that there were not sufficient assets in place to pay for the soil. Nor did anyone manage to recall that they didn't live where they were staying, and that at least one of them, Fredrika, had another life, far away.

"What kind of mess have you made this time?" Sabine said, once she had left the enthusiastic group and strolled over to the old man on the veranda.

"Mess?" said Allan. "They're happy as clams."

"But we don't have any money."

"We haven't had it before. Relax, Sabine! We only live once. That's the only certainty in life. How long, though—that varies."

Kenya, Madagascar

Fredrika Langer was sitting on a win. That is to say, the uranium. And the phone number to the chancellor, the one that wasn't to be used except in an emergency.

"Emergency this, emergency that," Allan had said. "Shall I handle the phone call?"

So he did. He would call again the next morning. This was all as surreal as it was uplifting.

Her boss had sent her into the savannah hundreds of miles from where one might reasonably expect any action, even as he had placed himself in the perfect position. And then everything had gone topsy-turvy. At any moment, he would be calling from Madagascar to reassure himself that she was on her way. Not that he cared about her, but without her around he had no one upon whom to dump all the small matters and the even tinier ones.

Fredrika asked John at the bar for a glass of water; he poured it and she managed to take her first sip before her phone rang.

"Fredrika Langer, how may I be of service?" she said, with the aim of annoying her boss from the start.

"It's me, you idiot. Have you reached Musoma yet? You were supposed to—"

She interrupted him. "No. I'm skipping Musoma. Sticking around here instead. Me and the uranium."

Agent A wondered if he'd misheard. Had Langer found the uranium? Up there?

"Yes. These things happen, you know."

"Don't touch it! I'm coming right away. Where are you?"

"In Kenya."

"But where in Kenya, for Chrissake?"

Agent Langer looked around. "On the savannah, I think."

"Answer me properly, Langer, or I'll bash in your head when I get there."

"You'll have to find me first."

What was going on? Was she obstructing her boss?

"If you don't want to be fired, you will give me your exact position *this minute!*"

That threat didn't land where it was intended to.

"Fired? If anything, Chancellor Merkel was hinting at a promotion last time we spoke."

Agent A was struck by a sudden breathlessness. Had that dunce Langer spoken to the chancellor behind his back? Where had she got the phone number?

"Yes, of course, you should have been the one to have it, not me. After all, you're the boss, for heaven's sake, but you didn't think it befitted the boss to carry around our operations folder. And I certainly understand—it must weigh nearly three and a half ounces."

This was pure catastrophe.

"Give it to me this instant!" he said. "That is an order."

"No, I can't. This line isn't secure. It's such a shame you were forced to send me in the wrong direction. Should I call her for you? No, silly me, I've already done that."

She could hear her boss breathing heavily.

"The chancellor mentioned something about a medal. For me, that is, not for you."

"Listen here," Agent A tried.

"But what would I do with a medal? I should resign instead. I probably have about a year's worth of overtime to use up, so I think I'll start right away. You won't have to see me ever again. And, better still, I won't have to see you."

Fredrika Langer's description of events wasn't quite accurate: Allan had been the one to make the phone call to Berlin. But anything that would torment Agent A was fair game. The part about resigning had felt extra good to say. Might as well make it true as soon as possible.

"But, please, Langer," said Agent A. "Just . . . tell . . . me . . . where . . . you . . . are . . ."

Her boss took it one word at a time, doing his best to breathe.

"I told you. Kenya. I think. But I'm busy now. Angela's calling on the other line, you know. Awfully nice woman. Bye."

She hung up and threw her phone into the stream that meandered prettily from the camp to the watering hole.

"Is all well?" wondered Allan, who had seen what she'd just done.

"Very well, thank you," said Former Agent Langer. "Very well."

Kenya, Germany

Exactly twenty-four hours after his first call to the chancellor, Allan called again. Merkel answered after the first ring.

"Good morning, Chancellor. I suppose it's best I call the chancellor 'Chancellor' as often as possible while I still can—you never know what may happen on Sunday."

"Good morning, Mr. Karlsson," said Chancellor Merkel.

"I'm calling to inform you, Madame Chancellor, of where your people can fetch the package. Or the box, rather. The boxes. The uranium, in short."

"Good. Let's hope you manage to do so this time, before you slam down the receiver in my ear again. Tell me," she said, gripping her pen at the desk outside her bedroom, wearing the same dressing gown as she had worn the previous morning.

He recommended that the Federal Republic sneak in at low altitude and land in the dark at the Keekorok Airport in Maasai Mara.

"If you come straight down from Berlin, then hang a slight left over Kampala, Keekorok is not far into the countryside, just after Lake Victoria. Alternatively you can come in an arc from the other direction. In that case, it's directly to the right from Lamu, along the coast of Kenya. After an hour or so, Keekorok will show up beneath you."

Was Karlsson out of his mind?

"Perhaps a slightly more legal arrangement would be to explain the situation to the Kenyan government in Nairobi. But there's the chance it might be overthrown between the informing and the fetching."

Chancellor Merkel had no intention of confirming over the telephone their prospective plans to trespass illegally on the territory of another nation, especially not two days before the election. Instead she responded: "I hear what you're saying. Please give me the coordinates."

Coordinates? This was beyond Allan's capacity. But Meitkini was standing next to him, listening in, and jotted down what the chancellor had asked for.

"I've just received a note. Oh, I see, this is what coordinates are. It actually reminds me of atomic fission, at first glance."

Allan recited; Angela Merkel took notes.

"When do you estimate the goods can be ready, Mr. Karlsson?"

Madame Chancellor could decide that for herself. That very night, or the next one, perhaps.

Without directly confirming the arrangement, Angela Merkel informed him that the night after next might be worth aiming at. For example, at 1 A.M. "Anything else we need to discuss in the meantime?" she asked.

Allan had a sudden flash of inspiration. "Yes, there may be, since the chancellor was kind enough to ask."

"Well?"

"We happened to incur some expenses related to ensuring that the uranium didn't end up in North Korea."

Chancellor Merkel smelled a rat. Thus far, Karlsson had given no indication that he wanted remuneration. "Expenses?" she said.

"Among other things, it became necessary for us to purchase four hundred tons of soil for the good of our cause."

Soil? What had that to do with the enriched uranium? No, she didn't want to know. "And what is the current market price for four hundred tons of soil?" she asked, in a chilly tone.

It was rich in sand and of the highest quality. And it required extensive arrangements to transport it from Nairobi.

"Ten million, more or less," said Allan.

"Ten million euros for four hundred tons of soil?" said Chancellor Merkel.

So Karlsson was a gangster, after all. One who was attempting extortion.

"Heavens, no," said Allan. "Ten million Kenyan shillings."

Angela Merkel quickly brought up the current exchange rate on her laptop. What a relief! The Kenyan shilling was worth 0.008 euros. Karlsson was demanding what corresponded to the amount the well-off nation made in surplus in two minutes at the current rate. Their conversation had already lasted twice that long.

"Naturally you will be compensated for your soil, Karlsson," she said, still without wishing to know what or whom he might be intending to bury in it. "If you give me an account number, I'll take care of it at once."

"One moment, Madame Chancellor," said Allan, and asked for Meitkini's help.

Receiving payments from abroad was an everyday

occurrence at the camp. Meitkini wrote down a series of letters and numbers for Allan.

"Thanks," said the chancellor. "Now, if you'll excuse me, I'm going to hang up. I have a few matters to take care of."

Quite a lot of things, actually. She had to organize the transport to Keekorok before she rushed right back to saying and doing nothing. The polling stations would open in forty-eight hours.

Germany

The Bundestag voting had been going on for several hours when a Transall C-160 landed at the German Navy base in Landkreis Cochem-Zell, after completing its mission to Africa.

Forty boxes of unknown contents were transferred to one of the airport's cargo vehicles for its 330-yard journey to the armored bus that would take over. The next leg was also the last. Six miles away waited a bunker in which was stored, among many other items, nine pounds of enriched uranium. It was about to receive a refill.

The bus was strategically parked at the outermost gate on the eastern side of the military airfield, partially hidden behind two large election posters. It was as if the chancellor herself were watching over the transport. She gazed down from the posters, smiling her Mona Lisa smile at the soldiers who carried enriched uranium between the vehicles. She said, "For a Germany where we live well and happily."

She had good reason to smile. The election forecasts said she would win, although complicated government negotiations awaited her. Furthermore, her envoys had flown into and out of Kenya without incident. The Kenyans, happily, were too busy worrying about themselves.

An hour or so later, the bunker was sealed. The chancellor and her professor had been to vote, and were now eating a quiet dinner, just the two of them.

"It seems that Mr. Karlsson won't influence the German democratic process after all," said the professor.

"Well, the polling stations don't close for another hour. He still has time," said Chancellor Merkel.

Kenya

"No one is perfect, especially not me," Allan apologized.

Meitkini and Sabine had called him into the camp office and asked him to explain a deposit of eighty thousand euros from Germany into the camp's account. Allan explained that he had kindly asked Chancellor Merkel for aid equaling the cost of the soil he had purchased. And that in her genuine benevolence she had granted it.

"But isn't eighty thousand ten times more than the soil cost?" Sabine asked.

"Yes, so I've understood. There are so terribly many zeros in the Kenyan currency that I must have been completely flummoxed."

"Are you telling the truth now, Allan?" Sabine asked sternly. "You can't just go around cheating the Chancellor of Germany out of money."

At that moment, Julius entered the room. He heard the last bit. "Why not?" he said. "What's going on?"

Sweden

Margot Wallström had not yet lost her job, and much suggested that things would stay that way. But that didn't stop her being in a state of inner turmoil.

The Nazi in Rosengård, whom Allan Karlsson had promised to keep alive, had indirectly taken his own life during a confrontation with the police near Copenhagen's international airport a few hours later. One couldn't blame Karlsson for that. Or could one? After all, the entire airport circus had started when he (or whoever was driving) had parked his hearse on the pavement outside the main entrance to the departures hall. Anyone should understand what that could lead to.

The minister for foreign affairs had made sure to stay abreast of the police's supplementary work. And now the investigation was complete. With the help of security cameras and general piecing together, it was clear that Sabine Jonsson was the main suspect in the crime. Karlsson and Jonsson might potentially be defined as accessories, but since the somewhat lazy prosecutor had been satisfied with the criminal charge of "parking in a no-parking zone," there was nothing to slap the two men with. Sabine Jonsson, however, could expect to receive a fine of seven thousand Danish kroner.

In any case, it felt like a good thing that the trio had left the country. How it felt that the Nazi had departed this Earth was something the minister tried not to think about. In her position, you didn't wish death upon others.

She was on her way to see the prime minister for an analysis of the result of the previous day's parliamentary election in Germany. This meant that Karlsson wouldn't haunt her for at least a few hours, and that, if anything, felt good.

"Hi, Margot, have a seat," said Prime Minister Löfven.

Both agreed that the German election results were not as positive as one might have hoped. At the last second, the ultra-right had won increased support even as the Social Democrats didn't deliver at all—both facts were worrying.

Margot Wallström's analysis of why the outcome was worse for the sensible powers than one might have expected and hoped was very down-to-earth: Hurricane Irma's advance in the days leading up to the election. It had laid waste to Puerto Rico and appeared for quite some time to pose a deadly threat to Florida. During this week of drama, Donald Trump hadn't uttered a single new stupid remark. What was more, the media had other things to focus on than his previous and typically ongoing idiocy. For a limited time—but a crucial one, for the German election—he didn't appear to be the clear opposite to Angela Merkel he *de facto* was. The general public had a good, but short, memory. When Trump temporarily wasn't seen as a guarantee of a less secure world, Merkel lost important percentage points that were then plucked up by the president's cousins on the far right.

The prime minister was surprised at the minister for foreign affairs' candor. Her analysis was unusual but perfectly reasonable.

Thus he decided to call Chancellor Merkel to congratulate her, although her parliamentary situation would be troublesome. "Do stay, Margot. The chancellor and I have no secrets from you."

Ten minutes later, the call was put through. Prime Minister Löfven congratulated both the chancellor and Europe in general. The stability represented by Madame Chancellor was good for all.

The chancellor thanked him. She had already accepted a dozen or so calls of congratulation from leaders all over the world. This was one of many—and yet it wasn't. Allan Karlsson, who had played such a major role in her life of late, was, of course, Swedish.

The prime minister had the speakerphone on. As a result, the minister for foreign affairs could hear. What she heard was sensational.

"Thanks again, Prime Minister," said Chancellor Merkel. "Let me take this opportunity to send a greeting to the Swedish citizen Allan Karlsson, who did such an exemplary job at avoiding giving help to Kim Jong-un in what he shouldn't have help with."

The prime minister was surprised by this turn in the conversation, but no more than that. Margot Wallström still hadn't found the right time to tell him about her further adventures with Karlsson, post New York.

"I'll do that," said the prime minister. "Is there any particular message you'd like me to pass on?"

Angela Merkel was in a good mood after her victory. The enormous issues she would confront in building a government hadn't completely dawned on her yet. "Oh, tell him he's welcome to visit me if he ever happens to be in Berlin. I'd be happy to share some cabbage soup."

Minister for Foreign Affairs Wallström couldn't believe her ears. Was Allan "What-the-Hell-Has-He-Done-This-Time" Karlsson friends with the Chancellor of Germany?

When the conversation was over, she turned to her prime minister. "I think I'll go home. It's been a long day."

Madagascar, North Korea, Australia, USA, Russia

The North Korean courier in Madagascar stood there with eighty million dollars, waiting for a large quantity of enriched uranium that never arrived. *Honor and Strength* hadn't been able to wait any longer: it risked attracting the attention of American satellites. The courier realized all the blame would be laid on him, at which point he decided to shoulder the burden on his own. Thus he allowed himself and the eighty million dollars to go up in smoke.

Kim Jong-un was furious. Not so much about the uranium—after all, he had the plutonium centrifuge now. But the money! The captain of *Honor and Strength* was obviously involved. Upon his return he would receive the exact welcome he deserved.

The captain had already figured this out. Perhaps

that was why his ship was suddenly struck by distress off the western coast of Australia, at which point the captain took the opportunity to seek political asylum at the immigration authority in Perth. In the interrogations that followed, he gave up everything he knew and had been involved in, including the meeting with the 101-year-old Swiss man he'd found floating in a basket in the middle of the Indian Ocean. The Australians in turn forwarded this information to the CIA, who found reason to inform President Trump.

Everything about Allan Karlsson's doings in the Indian Ocean were already available to read in the UN report Margot Wallström had submitted, but with its seventy-two pages it was seventy-two pages too long for Donald Trump to deal with. So the president drew his own conclusions.

"How stupid can people get?" he said. "A Swedish Communist is floating around in a basket in the ocean and gets picked up by a North Korean one? Coincidence, my ass!"

So he ordered the CIA to apprehend Karlsson and put him on trial.

"For what, Mr. President?" wondered the new director of the CIA (new, because the previous one had been fired by the same president).

"That's not fucking up to me to figure out," said the president.

With that, the director of the CIA excused himself and put the matter aside, certain that the president would forget the whole thing within two weeks.

Gennady Aksakov was more confused than angry, and he was already pretty angry.

"What's going on, Gena?" President Putin asked his friend.

"Well, where should I start?" said Gena.

"Start by telling me what's weighing on you," said Volodya.

So he did.

His contact in Congo, Goodluck Wilson, had failed in his uranium mission. The first indication of this was the report from the Russian-controlled pilot of the transport flight that had landed under cover of night at a tiny airport in Maasai Mara. Wilson and the uranium had never turned up. Not at the appointed time and not the next night, which was the previously arranged backup time in case of unforeseen complications.

"Did he get cold feet?" the president wondered.

More than that, Gena could tell him. Not only his feet, but every other part of Goodluck Wilson had been eaten by an unknown number of hyenas about four miles from the airport. The car was still at the edge of the road, but the cargo was missing. Apparently he'd had a puncture.

"Bad luck," said Putin. "So where is the uranium now?"

That part, Gena did not know. The pilot's contacts on the ground had given testimony of an unidentified airplane that had landed and taken off at Keekorok Airport a few nights later. Based on that information, it would seem pointless to search for the uranium in Kenya, or even in Africa.

"Maybe it's just as well," said Putin. "Kim Jong-un already has what he needs—that is to say, more than he ought to have."

Gena had to agree on that point. But that wasn't the end of the story.

"No?"

No, there was also this part about Allan Karlsson.

"The one who killed your Nazis in Sweden?"

"Yes, and in Denmark."

"What has he done now?"

"He's farming asparagus."

President Putin loved asparagus.

"Great," he said. "Where?"

"In a valley in Kenya. In Maasai Mara. Between the airport and the bushes where the hyenas ate Wilson."

The president laughed. "And how do you know that?"

"The bastard is tweeting about it!"

Putin laughed even louder.

"Shall we send someone down to kill him?" Gena wondered.

But President Putin was a good sport through and through. "We've been outsmarted by a 101-year-old, Gena. Let the old man be. We've got a World Cup to worry about. May the best-doped team win!"

Sweden, USA, Russia

Sweden's first year on the Security Council was wearing toward its end.

Wearing is right, thought Margot Wallström.

She had accomplished quite a bit, but not when it came to a détente between North Korea and the United States. One monumental ego on either side of the Pacific Ocean was two too many.

She really wanted to blame her failure on Allan Karlsson, who had managed to muck things up on four continents in just a few months. Nothing had been heard from him for some time now. Was he busy getting ready for a fifth continent?

But, deep down, she knew Karlsson wasn't to blame for anything. He just seemed to have a knack for being in the wrong place at the wrong time.

For 101 years in a row.

"Democracy Dies in Darkness," said the *Washington Post*, and proceeded to go through all of President Trump's lies and misrepresentations during his first year in the White House. Freely interpreted, this headline meant something along the lines of "May Truth Prevail."

But it didn't. Toward the end of the year, the president averaged five and a half false statements each day. In his defense, it should be pointed out that he kept the average up by repeating the same falsehood many times over. The *Washington Post* was rude enough to count each untruth as an untruth, even though it had also been put forward the day before and the day before that.

Thus counted, the president had lied, made things up, or twisted the truth about the former president's health-care reform at least sixty times. And when he expressed himself about the tax burden in the United States it had gone wrong 140 times, even though he was corrected on each occasion. Fake media were, once and for all, evil personified.

Gena and Volodya celebrated the New Year together, as always. Tradition dictated that they toast with a cup of tea at midnight. Their common goal of giving Russia the world position it deserved (and preferably a little more) was too important to booze away.

Exactly twelve months earlier, their toast had been to the developments in the United States, and the approaching inauguration of Donald J. Trump. Ever since election night, a whole division of Gena's internet-based army of young men and women had been devoted to covering all their tracks, while three other divisions constantly took up new positions to make sure the collapse of the United States wouldn't get derailed.

Another twelve months previously, the friends had celebrated Brexit. Two enormous victories in as many years.

The year 2017 had not been as successful. The chaos in the USA was, of course, fantastic in many respects, but it was also frightening. It prompted humility in facing the future. High up on the agenda was the question of whether it was time to get rid of Trump. And, if so, then preferably Kim Jong-un as well. There was an alternative solution, but Volodya and Gena had to sleep on it.

Beyond this, they had to admit that they had missed their chance, over the past year, to sink Europe as well. The developments in France were what bothered them most. The stage had been set for a duel between François Fillon and Marine Le Pen. Right against super-right. Gena was sitting on information about Fillon that could have given Le Pen an edge. And then some jerk at *Le Canard Enchainé* figured out the same thing and published it—too damn early! Paying his wife five hundred thousand euros of taxpayers' money to do nothing did not, of course, turn out to be popular. Fillon was done for, and with him went Russia's chances of sinking Europe by way of Paris.

Berlin went better, later on. But it seemed that the cat with nine lives, fucking Merkel, would succeed at forming a coalition government despite the odds.

Oh, well, you couldn't have it all. The relative calm in the Middle East remained. The fools in the EU and NATO refused to comprehend that Bashar al-Assad would be taken away in the long run, and in an orderly fashion. To *bomb* him away would be tantamount to bombing Russia out of having influence, not to mention the monumental chaos that would arise in Syria's place. Given the circumstances, you had to take the occasional bad chemical weapons attack with the good. The quasi-democracy in the West had not learned a thing from Libya: that much was clear. What was more, the constant stream of refugees into Europe served Russia's purpose. Each poor wretch who managed to get a residency permit in any of the continent's stupidest countries only fed the xenophobia in the neighboring country. The unwillingness to help was greatest in those places that had never helped yet. That was how human resentment worked.

"Cheers to you, my dear friend," said Vladimir Putin, raising his teacup.

"Happy new year," said Gennady Aksakov.

At which they exchanged *novogodnye podarki*— New Year's gifts—and looked to the future.

"Where in the world is our next project, do you think?" asked Gena. "Italy?"

"No, they're doing fine on their own."

The advantage to toasting with tea on New Year's Eve is that you are alert and clear-headed the next morning. Vladimir Putin didn't know how things were on that front with Kim Jong-un when he lifted his presidential phone for a direct call between leaders.

The context of the call was the off-the-rails developments between the fools in Pyongyang and Washington. This had to end now! Grotesque amounts of necessities were packed up each day in Vladivostok and smuggled over the border to North Korea so that the little big man and his people wouldn't have to starve while they battled the world on Russian orders.

Kim Jong-un picked up after two rings.

"Good morning," said President Putin. "Or afternoon, if you will."

"Good afternoon, Vladimir Vladimirovitch," said Kim Jong-un. "What a nice surpr—"

"Shut up," said Putin. "From now on you will do exactly as I say. First you will announce that your shitty country will attend the Olympic Winter Games in Pyeongchang. Then you will—"

He didn't have time to order the mounting of a charm offensive on the United States before it was Kim Jong-un's turn to interrupt.

"With all due respect, Vladimir Vladimirovitch, you can't tell—"

"Of course I can," said Putin. "And that is what I have just begun to do."

Kenya

"Fredrika Langer's locally grown asparagus" was sold across half of Germany, in lovely bunches with black, red, and yellow ribbons around their middles. Her price was 20 percent lower than that of all her competition, each of whom was at the economic disadvantage of actually growing their German asparagus in Germany. Fredrika's local product, incidentally, was not as locally grown as she would have liked: it would take time for the Kenyan plants to deliver. In the meantime the Indonesian ones would have to do—they were, after all, equally German.

Gustav Svensson was no longer a valid brand in Sweden, but that was fine with Julius Jonsson. Gustav was much needed at the Kenyan operations anyway.

He was the one who knew how much distance there had to be between each furrow; he knew how deep they should be, and how wide at the bottom. He was the one who patiently spoke to every single plant, in Hindi. And he was the one who, just as patiently, experimented his way to the optimal blend of fertilizers: two parts elephant dung and one part buffalo for the white asparagus; two parts buffalo and one part wildebeest for the green.

Sabine spent her days at the office just beyond the lounge. It turned out she really was useless as an entrepreneur, but she was a superstar at calculating and administrating what other entrepreneurs accomplished. She reinvested 80 percent of the overage in fresh soil. With the last 20 percent she bought the camp from the man who had inherited it from his father and was never around anyway. He needed the money to continue living his deeply destructive life in Kinshasa, with wine, women, and Congolese song.

Meitkini sent Fredrika Kenyan red roses every day for three months before her heart finally melted. Five months after that it turned out she was pregnant. If it was a boy, Meitkini wanted to name him Uvuvwevwevwe.

Fredrika said she would hope for a girl.

All this happened while Allan spent his days on the veranda with a view of the watering hole. His new hobby was Twitter. Not only had he discovered what it was, he had also ventured onto it himself. He did not, however, understand that in doing so he was telling the whole world where he was.

He was glad to see how satisfied the kids were with life. But there was something gnawing at him. He had started to see a pattern in the flow of news on his black tablet.

On the whole, the world was a better place than it had been a hundred years earlier, even if progress didn't seem to happen in a straight line. It went up and down in cycles.

As far as Allan could tell, it was currently on the way down. The risk was that it wouldn't turn up again before a sufficient number of people, for a sufficient amount of time, did sufficiently awful things to each other. After that people would start thinking again.

It had always been this way. But was it so very certain that it would be this way again? Researchers had just announced that the average level of intelligence was in a downturn. Allan read that people who spent too much time with their black tablets lost the ability to have a conversation. The thing about the tablet was that it tended to talk *at* its owner more than *with* them. As a result, people were going all over the internet and letting others think for them to the extent that they were on their way to becoming stupid.

Allan was concerned when he realized that *truth* was losing ground along with intelligence. It used to be easy to know what was true and what wasn't. Vodka was good. Two plus two was not five.

But since people weren't talking to each other anymore, it ended up that whoever said the same thing the most times won. Some had refined this talent to the point of repeating themselves several times in the course of a few seconds. In the course of a few seconds.

What concerned Allan most of all, however, was that he realized he was concerned. Everything was the way it was. Couldn't it just turn out the way it turned out, without a whole lot of hassle along the way?

Sabine happened along and noticed that the old man had put down his black tablet. He was sitting with his arms crossed and gazing across the savannah with an empty expression. "What are you thinking about, Allan?" she asked.

"Too much," said Allan. "Far too much."

Extra thanks to:

Senior Editor Sofia Brattselius Thunfors for being smart as a whip.

Editor Anna Hirvi Sigurdsson for being the same.

Colleague Mattias Boström for doing research like no one else.

Agent Carina Brandt for spreading my work all over the world.

Good friend Lars Rixon for reading, hmming, and liking.

Uncle Hans Isaksson for reading, hmming, and liking in secret.

Asparagus expert Margareta Hoas at Lilla Bjers for valuable knowledge, decently misrepresented by the author.

Cultural genius Felix Herngren for being the person he is and for inspiration for the story.

Thanks also to:

The princess, Jonatan, and Mom. Just like that.

Jonas Jonasson

THE NEW LUXURY IN READING

We hope you enjoyed reading
our new, comfortable print size and found it
an experience you would like to repeat.

Well – you're in luck!

HarperLuxe offers the finest in fiction and
nonfiction books in this same larger print size and
paperback format. Light and easy to read, HarperLuxe
paperbacks are for book lovers who want to see
what they are reading without the strain.

For a full listing of titles and
new releases to come, please visit our website:

www.HarperLuxe.com

SEEING IS BELIEVING!